D0034874

JANET TRONSTAD
A Bride for Dry Creek

Shepherds Abiding in Dry Creek

Love Inspired

Recycling programs
for this product may
not exist in your area.

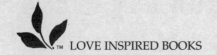 LOVE INSPIRED BOOKS

ISBN-13: 978-0-373-65158-0

A BRIDE FOR DRY CREEK AND
SHEPHERDS ABIDING IN DRY CREEK
Copyright © 2012 by Harlequin Books S.A.

The publisher acknowledges the copyright holder
of the individual works as follows:

A BRIDE FOR DRY CREEK
Copyright © 2001 by Janet Tronstad

SHEPHERDS ABIDING IN DRY CREEK
Copyright © 2007 by Janet Tronstad

www.LoveInspiredBooks.com

Printed in U.S.A.

CONTENTS

Books by Janet Tronstad

Love Inspired

*A Bride for Dry Creek
*Shepherds Abiding in
  Dry Creek
*An Angel for Dry Creek
*A Gentleman for Dry Creek
*A Rich Man for Dry Creek
*A Hero for Dry Creek
*A Baby for Dry Creek
*A Dry Creek Christmas
*Sugar Plums for Dry Creek
*At Home in Dry Creek
†The Sisterhood of the
  Dropped Stitches
*A Match Made in Dry Creek
†A Dropped Stitches Christmas
*Dry Creek Sweethearts
†A Heart for the
  Dropped Stitches
*A Dry Creek Courtship
*Snowbound in Dry Creek
†A Dropped Stitches Wedding
*Small-Town Brides
  "A Dry Creek Wedding"
*Silent Night in Dry Creek
*Wife Wanted in Dry Creek
  Doctor Right
*Small-Town Moms
  "A Dry Creek Family"

**Sleigh Bells for Dry Creek
**Lilac Wedding in Dry Creek
**Wildflower Bride in Dry Creek
**Second Chance in Dry Creek

Love Inspired Historical

*Calico Christmas at Dry Creek
*Mistletoe Courtship
  "Christmas Bells for Dry Creek"
Mail-Order Christmas Brides
  "Christmas Stars for
  Dry Creek"

*Dry Creek
†Dropped Stitches
**Return to Dry Creek

JANET TRONSTAD

grew up on her family's farm in central Montana and now lives in Pasadena, California, where she is always at work on her next book. She has written more than thirty books, many of them set in the fictitious town of Dry Creek, Montana, where the men spend the winters gathered around the potbellied stove in the hardware store and the women make jelly in the fall.

A BRIDE FOR DRY CREEK

Set me as a seal upon thine heart,
as a seal upon thine arm: for love is strong as
death… Many waters cannot quench love,
neither can the floods drown it.

—*Song of Solomon* 8:6–7

Dedicated with love
to my two brothers and their wives:
Ralph and Karen Tronstad,
Russell and Heidi Tronstad.
May God be with all of you
now and forevermore.

Chapter One

A single fly buzzed past Francis Elkton and swooped up to the bare lights that hung from the rafters of the old barn. Francis didn't notice the fly, but on most nights she would have even though her eyes were now half-closed as she slow danced to an old fifties tune.

Francis was an immaculate housekeeper. And a first-class manager. She often said, in her job with the City of Denver, that the two went hand in hand. You only needed to look in someone's top desk drawer, she'd say, to predict what kind of a city manager they would be. Whether it was paper clips or people or drainage pipes, everything needed an order.

She would never have tolerated an out-of-place fly if she hadn't been so distracted.

But tonight, the fly was only one more guest at the wedding reception, and Francis was too busy trying to keep her unwanted memories in their place to give any attention to the proper place of a mere insect. Every time she opened her eyes she realized that things were not turning out the way she had planned.

She'd taken a three-month leave from her job and come back to Dry Creek, Montana, because she thought she'd be able to stand up to her past—to look her memories of Flint L. Harris square in the eye— and be free of him once and for all. She was mentally cleaning out her files, she told herself. Throwing away outdated papers. Putting her life back in order even if it had taken her twenty years to face the task.

The only reason she'd decided to do it now was that Sam Goodman, her neighbor in Denver, had said he would not wait forever to marry her. She'd realized suddenly that she could not give her heart to Sam, or any other man, until she got it completely back from Flint.

It had been a sentimental decision to come back to Dry Creek to purge herself. She reasoned that the memories had started here in this ranching community, in the shadows of the Big Sheep Mountains. And they would surely end here if she just screwed up her mind and willed them to be gone. It was like reaching deep inside herself to pull out the roots of an unwanted weed that had refused to die over the years.

But, for the first time since she'd come back, she realized her heart wasn't bending to her will. The past had not grown dimmer because she'd stood up to it. No, the past was right here before her in living color whether she wanted to see it or not.

The pink crepe paper streamers coming down from the rafters were the same color her high school class had used twenty years ago for their prom. Back then her classmates had gone to Miles City to school and had decorated the gym there with their streamers.

Tonight, the dance was being held in the large old barn her brother Garth had built for loading cattle. He had not used the barn for his cattle for several years now, and the community of Dry Creek had scrubbed it clean for their annual Christmas pageant some months ago. On a cold winter night like tonight, the inside of the barn shone bright and the windows were covered with frost.

Dry Creek was fast making the barn into an informal center for all kinds of occasions. Like tonight's dance to celebrate the wedding of Glory Becker and Matthew Curtis. The dance wasn't a prom, but the music was the same. The same swaying music. The same soft laughter of other couples in the background.

Francis could close her eyes and almost imagine it was Flint who held her in his arms. Flint with his shy halting gladness to see her and the tall wiry length of his twenty-year-old body. Even back then, she should have known that dancing with him would come to no good

"Francis?" A slightly alarmed man's voice growled in her right ear.

Francis blinked and then blushed. Jess, one of her brother's older ranch hands, had invited her to dance, and it was his face that now looked at her suspiciously. She hadn't realized until he spoke that her arms had crept up his back until she had him in an embrace that was more than friendly. She shook the memories from her eyes, cleared her throat and loosened her arms. "Sorry."

"That's okay." Jess ducked his head, apparently reassured once the sensible Francis was back. Then he added teasingly, "After all, your brother did tell me to stick close to you tonight."

"He's not still worried about that phone call?" Francis gladly diverted the conversation to her brother's needless caution. "Just because some guy calls up and says someone might be out to kidnap me—it's all nonsense anyway. Even if Garth did know something about the rustlers who have been hitting this area—which he doesn't—well, it doesn't make sense. Before they start making any threats, these rustlers should find out if Garth knows anything that's a danger to them. Any manager would tell them that's the first step. They might be criminals, but that's no excuse for sloppy planning. You need to identify your problem and then verify how big it is before you can even hope to solve it."

"Way I hear it, it wasn't just some guy that called."

Apparently Jess only heard the first part of what she'd said. Francis had noticed that the ranch hands who worked for her brother tended to let their eyes glaze over when she tried to teach them management techniques.

"The man never gave his name," Francis corrected stiffly.

"Didn't need to from the way I heard it," Jess mumbled. "Begging your pardon for mentioning him. Still—can't be too careful."

No wonder she was having so much trouble getting rid of her memories of Flint, Francis thought. He seemed to have more lives than a stray alley cat. She'd bury him one day and he'd be resurrected the next. Did everyone in Dry Creek know about that phone call?

"I don't believe it was Flint Harris on the other end of that phone call. For pity's sake—he probably doesn't even remember Dry Creek." *Lord knows he doesn't remember me,* Francis added silently. "He never had roots in Dry Creek. He only came here that one spring because his grandmother was ill. He hasn't been back since she died."

"Hasn't sold her place yet, though," Jess argued. "Even pays taxes on it. That's got to mean something."

"It means that it isn't worth selling. Who would buy it? The windows are all broken out and it's only got five acres with it. The only thing you could raise there is chickens and with the low price of eggs these days—"

Francis stopped herself. She didn't need to be her own worst enemy. She needed to forget chickens. That had been their adolescent dream—that they would live with his grandmother and make their living by selling eggs. A fool's dream. Even back then, it wouldn't have kept them in jeans and tennis shoes. She cleared her throat. "The point is that Flint Harris is nowhere near here."

"Like I said, I'm sorry to bring the louse up. If I'd have been here back then and met the boy, I'd have given him a good speaking to—treating a nice girl like you that way."

Francis stopped dancing and looked at Jess. He seemed to expect a response. "Well, thank you, but that wouldn't have been necessary. I could take care of myself even back then."

"If you say so."

Francis looked at him carefully. There it was. A steady gleam of pity in his eyes.

"Those rumors are not true." Francis bristled. The one thing she didn't miss in Denver was the gossip that flowed freely in a small community. "While it is true that he and I drove to Las Vegas after the prom and looked for a justice of the peace, it is not true that we were actually married."

"Mrs. Hargrove says—"

"Mrs. Hargrove wasn't there. I was. The man was not a justice of the peace. My father called down there and asked. They had no justice of the peace by that name. It doesn't matter what words we said, those papers we signed were worthless."

"You signed some papers?" The pity left his eyes. It was replaced by astonishment. "You still have them?"

"I didn't say I have papers," Francis said patiently. The last time she'd seen those papers, Flint had had them. She remembered the way he had carefully folded them and put them in his coat pocket. She hadn't realized at the time that any young bride with any sense asks to keep the papers herself—especially when the wedding takes place in Las Vegas. That should have been her first clue.

"Besides, that is long ago and done with," Francis said briskly. "As Mrs. Hargrove probably told you, even if it had been a marriage, it would have been the shortest marriage ever on record in Dry Creek—probably the shortest in all of Montana. I don't even think it lasted forty hours. We had the trip back from Vegas and then he dropped me off at my dad's to pack. Said he was going to Miles City to buy me some roses—every bride needed roses, he said—those were the last words I ever heard from him. He never came back."

Francis believed in slicing through her pain quickly and efficiently with a minimum of fuss. She'd held her breath when she recited the facts of those two days with Flint and now she let it out slowly. "I'm sure it was one of the smoothest exit lines in the book and I fell for it. Five weeks later I made arrangements to graduate early from high school and I left for Denver. That's all there was to it."

"But no one knew," Jess reproached her softly.

"That's the only reason the folks here still remember it. No one but your father knew and then you just left so suddenly. These were your neighbors and friends. They cared about you, they just didn't know what was happening. Even now Mrs. Hargrove keeps trying to think back to something she could have said to make it better in those days for you—blames herself for not taking a more motherly role in your life—what with just you and your dad out there alone when Garth was in the service—keeps having this notion that Flint did come back in around that time and stopped at her place to ask for you."

"She's confused," Francis said flatly. People meant well, but it didn't help to sugarcoat the truth. "If he'd tried to find me, he'd have tried my father's place. He knew where it was. He'd been there enough times."

"I suppose you're right."

The dance ended and suddenly Francis felt foolish to be standing there arguing about whether or not a man had stopped to see her neighbor twenty years ago. "I think I'll sit the next one out if it's all the same to you. You can tell my brother I'll be fine. I'll just be taking a rest."

Jess looked relieved. "I could use a break myself. My arthritis is acting up some."

"Well, why didn't you say so? We could have sat the last two dances out—no need to be up and moving around on a cold night like this."

"It is a blistering one out tonight, isn't it?"

"All the more reason to forget about the kidnapping threat," Francis agreed. "No one but a fool would be out setting a trap tonight. It's too cold. No, I think the kids are right when they said it was that rival gang they have in Seattle calling to make mischief."

Francis's brother, Garth, had offered the use of his ranch to a woman who ran a youth center for gang kids in Seattle. At the moment, thirty of the kids were learning to be better citizens by spending a few weeks in Dry Creek, Montana. Garth had been in charge of teaching the boys how to be gentlemen, and Francis had been astonished at his patience. He'd had them out in the barn practicing how to dip and twirl their dance partners, and the boys had loved it.

A rich society woman from Seattle, Mrs. Buckwalter, was underwriting the cost of the trip to Montana, and Francis couldn't help but notice how excited the older woman was tonight. Mrs. Buckwalter couldn't have been prouder of the teens if she'd given birth to every one of them.

And Francis couldn't blame her. The teenagers sparkled at this dance, the boys in their rented tuxedos and the girls in the old fifties prom dresses they'd borrowed from the women of Dry Creek. It was hard to believe that they were members of various gangs in Seattle. A few dance lessons and a sprinkling of ties and taffeta had transformed them.

"That's really the logical explanation," Francis concluded. If the other gang could only see the youth center kids now. She couldn't help but think they'd be a little jealous of the good time these kids were having.

"Maybe." Jess didn't look convinced. "Just don't take any unnecessary risks—your brother will have my hide. He's worried, you know—"

"Even if Flint did kidnap me, he'd never hurt me— no matter what Garth worries about." As Francis listened to herself saying the words, she realized how naive she sounded. She didn't know what kind of a man Flint might be today. She'd often wondered.

Jess looked at her. "Still, things happen."

"What could happen?" Francis waved her arms around. She might not know about Flint, but she did know about the people of Dry Creek. At least a hundred people were in the barn, some sitting on folding chairs along the two sides, a few standing by the refreshment table and dozens of them on the floor poised ready to dance to the next tune. A lot of muscle rested beneath the suits that had been unearthed for this party. "One little scream and fifty men would come to my rescue. I'm surrounded by Dry Creek. There isn't a safer place in all the world for me."

Jess grunted. "I guess you're right. Maybe you should go visit with Mrs. Hargrove a bit. Talk to those two little boys that belong to Matthew Curtis. Find out how they like the idea of having a new mama."

Francis smiled. She was fond of the four-year-old twins and liked to see them so happy. "Everyone knows how they feel about that. She's their angel. If their dad wasn't going to marry Glory, I think they'd wait and marry her themselves."

Meanwhile, outside in the dark...

Flint watched a fly buzz up to the headlight of the old cattle truck. Now, what was a fly doing in the middle of a Montana winter night so cold a man's nose hairs were likely to freeze?

Flint slid into the niche between two cars and hunched down in his black leather jacket. The worthless jacket was nearly stiff. That fly didn't belong here any more than Flint and his jacket did. He would bet the fly had made the mistake of crawling into that cattle truck when it'd been parked someplace a lot warmer. Say Seattle. Or San Francisco.

Even a rookie FBI agent would make the connection that the truck didn't belong to anyone local. And Flint had been with the Bureau for twenty years. No, the truck had to belong to the three men he'd identified as cattle thieves. He'd call in their location just as soon as he had something more concrete to tell the inspector than that he'd listened to them talk enough to know they were brothers.

The last time he'd made his daily check-in call, one of the guys had said the inspector was grumbling about him being out here on this assignment without a partner. Flint told him he had a partner—an ornery horse named Honey.

The fly made another pass close to Flint's face, seeking the warmth of his breath.

Flint half cursed as he waved the fly away. He didn't need the fly to distract him from the mumbled conversation of the three men. They'd been standing in front of the cattle truck arguing for several minutes about some orders their boss had given to deliver a package.

Flint sure hoped they were talking about which cattle to steal next.

If not, that probably meant his tip was accurate and they were planning to kidnap Francis Elkton. He hoped Garth had taken the phone call he had made seriously and was keeping Francis inside, in some controlled area with no one but the good ladies of Dry Creek around her.

Flint envied all of the people of Dry Creek the heat inside the barn. The warmest he was likely to get anytime soon was when he went to feed Honey some oats.

It hadn't taken him more than a half hour on Honey's back to realize that her owner must have had a chuckle or two when he named her. She was more sour than sweet. Still, Flint rubbed his gloved hands over his arms and shivered. Honey might be a pain, but he missed her all the same. She was the only breathing thing he'd talked to since he came to Montana.

By now Honey would be wondering when they'd go home. When he'd ridden her to town tonight, he'd tied her reins to a metal clothesline pole in a vacant lot behind Mr. Gossett's house. The pole was out of the wind, but Honey would still be anxious for warmer quarters. Last night, he'd bedded her down in an abandoned chicken coop that still stood on the farm he'd inherited from his grandmother when she died fifteen years ago. As far as he knew, no one but gophers ever visited the place anymore.

He was half surprised the men hiding by that cattle truck didn't use horses. The terrain on the south slopes of the Big Sheep Mountain Range wasn't steep, but it also wasn't paved. There were more fences than roads. The long, winding strings of barbed wire and aging posts did little in winter except collect snowdrifts. Flint had followed a dozen of those fences to reacquaint himself with the area last night and didn't see anything more than a thick-coated coyote or two.

But then these men probably didn't know how to ride a horse. Which meant they weren't professionals. If they had been pros, they would have learned before heading out here on a job like this. A pro would realize a horse would be a good escape option if the roads were blocked. Yes, a pro would learn to ride. Even if he needed to learn on a bad-tempered horse like Honey.

Flint's observations of the men had already made him suspect that they were not career kidnappers. They were too careless and disorganized to have lived long if they made a habit of breaking the law. But Flint knew that the crime syndicates liked to use amateurs for some jobs—they made good fall guys when things went sour.

Granted, the Boss—and the Bureau didn't know who he was yet—had other reasons to use amateurs here. A pro would look so out of place in this rural community he might as well wear a red neon sticker that said Hired Killer—Arrest Me Now.

The fact that the men were too tender to ride horses made Flint hope that they would give it up for tonight and go home. The night was clear—there was enough moonlight so that Flint could see the low mountains that made up the Big Sheep Mountain Range. But it was ice-cracking cold and not getting any warmer.

The little town of Dry Creek stood a few miles off Interstate 94, which ran along the southern third of Montana from Billings on through Miles City. The town was nothing more than a few wood frame houses, an old square church, a café called Jazz and Pasta that was run by a young engaged couple, and a hardware store with a stovepipe sticking up through the roof. The pipe promised some kind of heat inside. Flint had not gone in to find out if the old Franklin stove he remembered was still being used. He hadn't even tried to find an opening in the frost so he could look in the window.

The memories Flint had of his days in Dry Creek were wrinkled by time, and he couldn't be sure if all the details like the Franklin stove were true or if he'd romanticized them over the years, mixing them up with some old-fashioned movie he'd seen or some nostalgic dream he'd had.

He realized he didn't want to know about the stove so he hadn't looked inside the hardware store.

Flint had only spent a few months in Dry Creek, but this little community—more than anywhere else on earth—was the place he thought of as home. His grandmother had lived her life here, and this is where he'd known Francis. The combination of the two would make this forever home to him.

None of the chrome-and-plastic-furnished apartments he'd rented over the years could even begin to compete. They were little more than closets to keep his clothes out of the rain. He couldn't remember the last time he'd cooked anything but coffee in any of them. No, none of them could compete with the homes around Dry Creek.

Even old man Gossett's place looked as though it had a garden of sorts—a few rhubarb stalks stuck up out of a snowdrift, and there was a crab apple tree just left of his back porch. There were no leaves on the tree, but Flint recognized the graceful swoop of the bare branches.

The trash barrel that the man kept in the vacant lot had a broken jelly jar inside. Flint suspected someone was making jelly from the apples that came off the tree. It might even be the old man.

Flint envied the old man his jelly and Flint didn't even like jelly. The jelly just symbolized home and community for him, and Flint felt more alone than he had for years. Maybe when he finished this business in Dry Creek, he should think about getting married.

That woman he'd started dating—Annette—he wondered if she could make apple jelly. He'd have to find out—maybe he should even send her a postcard. Women liked postcards. He hadn't seen any that featured Dry Creek, but maybe he'd stop in Billings when this was all over. Get her something with those mountains on it. In the daylight the Big Sheep Mountain Range was low and buff-colored with lots of dry sage in the foreground. Looked like a Zane Grey novel. Yes, a postcard was a good idea. That's what he'd do when this was all over.

From the sounds of the ruckus inside that old barn, the whole community of Dry Creek, Montana, was celebrating tonight. All eighty-five adults and the usual assortment of children.

Flint had checked the vital statistics before he headed down here. The place didn't have any more people now than it had had that spring he'd spent at his grandmother's place. The only new people that had come to the community were the busload of Seattle teenagers who were there for a month to see that all of life wasn't limited to the city streets. As long as Francis stayed with the people inside the barn, she would be safe.

That thought had no sooner crossed his mind than the side barn door opened. A woman stood silhouetted in the golden light from inside the barn. Flint felt all breath leave his body. It was Francis.

Francis let the winter air cool her. The ruby-red material of her dress was thin, but it had still suddenly gotten much too hot inside the barn. The rumor that Flint had been the one who made the phone call to Garth this afternoon had opened up all of the speculation about her and Flint. She saw it in the eyes of her neighbors. They were asking themselves why she'd never married, why she'd moved away so quickly all those years ago, why she'd never come back to live in Dry Creek until now—why, why, why. The questions would be endless until they'd worried her heart to a bone.

She only wished the asking of the questions would help her find an answer, she thought ruefully. Because, even if no one else had been asking those questions, she would be asking them.

But not tonight, she decided. Tonight she would just breathe the crisp night air and look at the stars that were scattered across the sky like pieces of glitter sprinkled over velvet. She used to love to go out on a winter's night like this and find the Big Dipper.

Now where is it, she asked herself as she stepped through the open door and outside. The barn was hiding the constellation from her. But if she went over by that old cattle truck she could see it.

She suddenly realized she hadn't gone looking for the Big Dipper in many years.

Flint swore. No wonder being a hero had gone out of style. His leg still stung where Francis had kicked him in her glittery high-heeled shoes, and one of his toes could well be broken where she had stomped on it.

Next time, he'd let the kidnappers have her. She was more than a match for most of the hired toughs he'd seen in his time. She'd certainly hold her own with the men in the cattle truck.

And thinking of his toes, what was she doing with shoes like that, anyway? Women only wore shoes like that to please a man. That meant she must have a boyfriend inside that old barn. That was one statistic he hadn't thought to check before heading out here.

Flint's only consolation was that his horse seemed to know he needed her and was behaving for once.

"Now I know why they call you Honey," Flint murmured encouragingly as he nudged his horse down the dark road.

"Hargh." An angry growl came from the bundle behind him, but Flint didn't even look back. Except for being temporarily gagged, Francis was doing better than he was. He'd even tied his jacket around her. Not that she had thanked him for it.

"Yes, sir, you're a sweetie, all right," Flint continued quietly guiding his horse. Honey knew the way home even if it was only a humble abandoned shed.

That horse could teach some people the meaning of gratitude.

Or, if not gratitude, at least cooperation, Flint fumed.

If it wasn't for his years of training as an agent, Flint would have turned around and told Francis a thing or two. What did she think?

There was no time for niceties when he knew those two hired thugs were waiting for Francis. He'd heard them repeat their instructions about kidnapping Garth's sister in her black jacket with the old high school emblem of a lion.

Early on in the evening, the two men made a decision to wait for her by the bus—parked right next to that old cattle truck they'd come in. They hoped Francis would tire of dancing and come to sit in the bus. Flint had winced when he heard the plan. The two men were clearly amateurs, unfamiliar with Montana. No one, no matter how tired, would come to rest in a cold bus when the engine wasn't running.

But he saw their dilemma. They couldn't face down the whole town of Dry Creek or even the busload of kids that would be going back to the Elkton ranch. That's why he wasn't surprised, after the men had waited a few hours and gotten thoroughly cold themselves, to hear them start talking about going home and waiting until the next day to kidnap Francis.

Flint was hoping they'd leave soon. And they would have, except who should come outside for a late night stroll but Francis. She wasn't wearing the black jacket, but Flint couldn't risk the thugs getting a close look at her and realizing who she was, even without the jacket.

There was no time for fancy plans. The only way to protect Francis was to grab her first and worry about the men later.

Flint knew the men might be a problem if they realized what he was doing, but he hadn't counted on Francis's resistance. He thought once she knew it was him she'd come quietly. Perhaps even gratefully. But the moment he saw recognition dawn, she fought him like he was her worst enemy. He hadn't planned on gagging her until she made it clear she was going to scream.

And all the while she was kicking and spitting, he'd been doing her a great service.

Yes, he sighed, he could see why being a hero had gone completely out of style. It wasn't easy being the knight on the shining white horse. Not with the women of today. Come to think of it, it wasn't even easy with the horses of today. Honey made it clear she'd rather be eating oats than rescuing a damsel in distress.

"Tired, that's what you are," Flint said softly as he leaned over the horse's neck. Honey sighed, and he gave the horse another encouraging nudge. "We're both tired, aren't we? But don't worry. We're almost there. Then I'll have something sweet for you."

The bundle behind him gave an indignant gasp and then another angry growl.

"I was talking to the horse." Flint smiled in spite of himself.

Chapter Two

Francis wished she had worn those ruby silk flowers in her hair like the teenagers had urged her to do. At least then, when the horse shook her, the petals would fall to the ground and leave a trail in the snow for someone to follow when they searched for her in the morning. Maybe if she were lucky, some of the sequins on her long evening dress would fall to the ground and leave a trail of reddish sparkles.

She still didn't understand what had happened.

One minute she'd been looking at the night sky, searching for the tail star of the Big Dipper. The next minute she'd felt someone put an arm around the small of her back. She hadn't even been able to turn around and see who it was before another arm went behind her knees and she was lifted up.

Suddenly, instead of seeing the night sky she was looking square into the face of Flint Harris. For a second, she couldn't breathe. Her mind went blank.

Surely, it could not be Flint. Not her Flint. She blinked. He was still there.

She was speechless. He was older, it was true. Instead of the smooth-skinned boy she remembered, she saw the face of a man. Weather had etched a few fine lines around his eyes. A tiny scar crossed the left side of his chin. His face was fuller, stronger.

Oh, my Lord, she suddenly realized. *It's true. He's kidnapping me!*

Francis opened her mouth to scream. Nothing came out. She took a good breath to try again when Flint swore and hurriedly stuffed an old bandanna into her mouth. The wretched piece of cloth smelled of horse. She understood why it smelled when Flint slung her over his back like she was nothing to him but a sack of potatoes in a fancy bag. He then hauled her off to a horse tied behind Mr. Gossett's house.

Once Flint got to the horse, he stopped to slip some wool mittens from his hands and onto her hands. The mittens were warm inside from his body heat, and the minute he slid them onto her hands, her fingers felt like they were being tucked under a quilt.

But she didn't have time to enjoy it.

There was a light on in old man Gossett's house, and Francis struggled to scream through her gag. She knew the man was home since he never went to community gatherings. He was a sour old man and she wasn't sure he'd help her even if he knew she was in trouble. Through the thin curtains on his window, she saw him slowly walking around inside his kitchen. Unless he'd grown deaf in these past years, he must have heard her. If he did, he didn't come outside to investigate.

Flint didn't give her a second chance to scream. He threw her over the back of the horse, slapped his jacket on her shoulders and mounted up.

Ever since then she'd been bouncing along, facedown, behind his saddle.

Finally, the horse stopped.

They had entered a grove of pine trees. The night was dark, but the moon was out. Inside the grove, the trees cut off the light of the moon, as well. Only a few patches of snow were visible. From the sounds beneath the horse's hoofs, the rest of the ground was covered with dried pine needles.

The saddle creaked as Flint stood to dismount.

Francis braced herself. She'd been trained to cope with hostage situations in her job and knew a person was supposed to cooperate with the kidnapper. But surely that didn't apply to criminals one knew. She and this particular criminal had slow danced together. He couldn't shoot her.

She'd already decided to wait her chance and escape. She had a plan. Flint had made a mistake in putting the mittens on her. The wool of the mittens kept the cord from gripping her wrists tightly. When Flint stepped down on the ground, she would loosen the tie on her wrists, swing her body around and nudge that horse of his into as much of a gallop as the poor thing could handle.

Flint stepped down.

The horse whinnied in protest.

"What the—" Flint turned and started to swear.

Francis had her leg caught around the horn of the saddle. She'd almost made the turn. But almost wasn't enough. She was hanging, with one leg behind the back of the saddle and one hooked around the horn. She'd ripped the skirt of her ruby sheath dress and all she'd accomplished was a change of view. Her face was no longer looking at the ground. Instead, she was looking straight into the astonished eyes of Flint L. Harris.

Francis groaned into her gag. She'd also twisted a muscle in her leg.

And she'd spooked the horse. The poor thing was prancing like a boxer. Each move of the beast's hooves sent a new pain through Francis's leg.

"Easy, Honey," Flint said soothingly as he reached out to touch the horse.

Francis saw his hands in the dark. His rhythm was steady, and he stroked the animal until she had quieted.

"Atta girl." Flint gave the horse one last long stroke.

Flint almost swore again. They should outlaw high heels. How was a man supposed to keep his mind on excitable horses and bad guys when right there— just a half arm's length away—was a dainty ankle in a strappy red high heel? Not to mention a leg that showed all the way up to the thigh because of the tear in that red dress. He was glad it was dark. He hoped Francis couldn't see in his eyes the thoughts that his mind was thinking.

"She'll be quiet now." Flint continued speaking slow and calm for the horse's benefit. "But she spooks easy. Try to stay still."

Even in the darkness inside the pine grove he could see the delicate lines of Francis's face behind the gag. Her jaw was clenched tight. He hadn't realized—

"I know it's not easy," he added softly. "I didn't mean to frighten you."

A muffled protest came from behind the gag.

Francis had worn her dark hair loose, and it spilled into his hands when he reached up to untie the gag. Flint's hands were cold, and her hair whispered across them like a warm summer breeze. He couldn't resist lingering a moment longer than necessary inside the warmth of her hair.

"It's not how I meant to say hello again," Flint said as he untied the bandanna. And it was true. What he'd say when he met Francis again had gone from being a torture to a favorite game with him over the years. None of his fantasies of the moment had involved her looking at him with eyes wide with fear.

"Don't pretend you ever meant to see me again." Francis spit the words out when the gag was finally gone. Her voice was rusty and bitter even to her own ears. "Not that it matters," she quickly lied. "I—"

Francis stopped. She almost wished she had the gag in her mouth.

"That was a long time ago," Francis finally managed.

"Yes, it was," Flint agreed as he finished unraveling the cord he'd used to tie Francis's hands behind her. It might seem like a long time ago to her. To him it was yesterday.

"Cold night out," Flint added conversationally as he stuffed the cord into his pocket. He needed to move their words to neutral territory. Her wrists had been as smooth as marble. "Is it always this cold around here in February?"

"It used to be," Francis answered. She'd felt Flint's fingertips on the skin of her wrists just at the top of her mittens. His fingers were ice cold. For the first time, she realized the mittens on her hands must have been the only ones he had. "Folks say, though, that the winters lately have been mild."

"That's right, you don't live here anymore, do you?" Flint asked as he put his hand on Francis's lower leg. He felt her stiffen. "Easy. Just going to try and unravel you here without scaring Honey."

Flint let his hand stay on Francis's leg until both his hand and that section of her leg were warm. He let his hand massage that little bit of leg ever so slightly so it wouldn't stiffen up. "Don't want to make you pull the muscle in that leg any more than it looks like you've already done."

Flint had to stop his hand before it betrayed him. Francis was wearing real nylon stockings. The ones like they used to make. A man's hands slid over them like they were cream. If Flint were a betting man, he would bet nylon like this didn't come from panty hose, either. No, she was wearing the old-fashioned kind of nylons with a garter belt.

This knowledge turned him first hot then cold. A woman only wore those kind of stockings for one reason.

"You won't be dancing any time soon," he offered with deceptive mildness as he pressed his hands against his thighs to warm them enough to continue. "So I suppose that boyfriend of yours will just have to be patient."

"He has been," Francis said confidently. "Thank you for reminding me."

Francis thought of Sam Goodman. He might not make her blood race, but he didn't make it turn to ice, either. He was a good, steady man. A man she'd be proud to call her boyfriend. Maybe even her husband. She almost wished she'd encouraged him more when he'd called last week and offered to come for a visit.

Flint pressed his lips together. He should have thought about the boyfriend before he took off with Francis like he had. It had already occurred to him that he could have simply returned her to the good people of Dry Creek. Instead of heading for the horse, he could have headed for the light streaming out the open barn door and simply placed her inside. If it had been anyone but Francis, he would have.

But Francis addled his brain. All he could think of was keeping her safe, and he didn't trust anyone else— not even some fancy boyfriend who made her want to dress in garters and sequins—to get her far enough away from the rustlers. He had to make sure she was safe or to take a bullet for her if something happened and those two kidnappers got spooked.

Still, a boyfriend could pose problems. "I suppose he'll be wondering where you are," Flint worried aloud as he slowly turned the saddle to allow Francis's leg to tip toward him.

Francis stared in dismay. Flint was helping her untangle herself, but he was obviously positioning her so that she would slide off the back of the horse and into his arms.

"I can walk," Francis said abruptly.

"You'd have better luck flying at the moment," Flint said as he put a hand on each of her hips and braced himself. "Put your arms around my neck and I'll swing you around."

"I don't think—" Francis began. Flint's hands swept past her hips and wrapped themselves around her waist. She took a quick, involuntary breath. Surely he could feel her heart pounding inside her body. The material on this wretched dress the girls had talked her into wearing was not at all good for this sort of thing. It was much too thin. She could feel the heat from Flint's hands as he cradled her waist.

"You don't need to think—just move with me," Flint directed. He couldn't take much more of this.

It must be the cold that made his hands even more sensitive than usual. He not only felt every ridge of beaded sequin on the dress, he felt every move of her muscles beneath the palm of his hands. He knew she was trying to pull herself away from him. That she was struggling to move her leg without his help. The knowledge didn't do much for a man's confidence. He remembered the days when she used to want him to hold her.

"You're going to scare the horse," Flint cautioned softly. Beneath the sequins, the dress felt like liquid silk. Flint had all he could do to stop his hands from caressing Francis instead of merely holding her firm so he could lift her off the horse.

"Where'd you get the horse, anyway?" Francis forced her mind to start working. *Everything has a place,* she reminded herself. If she could only find the place of everything, this whole nightmare would come aright. She could make sense and order out of this whole madness if she worked at solving one piece of the puzzle and then went on to the next piece. She'd start with the horse.

"A small farm outside of Billings," Flint answered.

His hands spanned Francis's rib cage. He could feel her heart pounding. "They rent horses."

"Why would you rent a horse?" Francis persisted. One question at a time. It helped her focus and forget about the hands around her. "You don't live around here. They must usually rent to ranchers."

Flint stopped. He could hardly say he needed a horse to rescue her. She'd never believe that. Then he remembered he didn't need an answer. "That's classified information. Government." Flint had her circled, and there was no reason to stall. "Move with me on the count of three."

All thought of the horse—and its order—fled Francis's mind.

"One. Two." Flint braced himself. "Three."

When Flint pulled, his hands slid from the middle of Francis's rib cage to the top. He almost stopped. But Honey was beginning to tap-dance around again, and he had to follow through.

Francis gasped. The man's hands were moving upward from her rib cage. There was nothing for it but to put her arms around his neck and swing forward.

"Atta girl," Flint murmured. Even he didn't know if he was talking to Francis or the horse. And it didn't matter. He had Francis once again in his arms. Well, maybe not in his arms, but she was swinging from his neck. That had to count for something.

Francis winced. Her leg was swinging off the horse

along with the rest of her body, and her leg was protesting. But she gritted her teeth. "Let me down."

Flint went from ice to fire in a heartbeat. He'd been
without a jacket after he gave it to Francis, and his
chest was cold. But the minute Francis swung against
him, his whole insides flamed. His jacket had only
been draped over her, and now it fell back to her shoulders. He felt the cool smoothness of her bare arms
wrapped around his neck and the swell of her breasts
pressed against his shirt.

"I can't let you down." Flint ground the words out.
"You can't walk through a snowdrift in those heels."

"I can walk barefoot."

"Not with that leg," Flint shifted Francis's weight
so his neck didn't carry her. Instead, he had his arms
around her properly this time. There were no bad guys
here. He could carry her like a gentleman. "Besides,
you'd get frostbite."

Francis didn't argue. She simply couldn't think of
anything to say. She had been swiveled, swept up in
his arms and now rested on Flint's shoulder with a
view of his chin. This was not the way anything was
supposed to go. She was supposed to be forgetting
him. "You nicked your chin the night of the prom,
too."

"Huh?"

"When you shaved—the night of the prom, you
nicked your chin. Almost in the same place."

"I was nervous."

"Me, too."

"You didn't look nervous," Flint said softly. He had tied Honey to a branch and was carrying Francis out of the pine grove. "You were cool as a cucumber."

"I hadn't been able to eat all day."

"You were perfect," Flint said simply. He was walking toward the small wood frame house. "Everybody is hungry at those things, anyway. You think there'll be food and it turns out to be pickled mushrooms or something with toothpicks in it."

Flint stopped. He was halfway to the house, and he knew someone had been here recently besides himself and Honey. A faint smell was coming from the house—the smell of cigars. He'd only known one man to ever smoke that particular brand.

"I'm going to set you down and check out the house," Flint whispered. It could be a trap. The cigars weren't a secret. "Be quiet."

Francis shivered, and not from the cold. Even in a whisper, Flint's voice sounded deadly serious. For the first time, she was truly afraid. And, for the first time, it occurred to her that if it were known by now that she was kidnapped—and it surely would be known once Jess checked around the barn—then someone would be out to rescue her. And if they intended to rescue her, they would also be out to hurt—maybe even kill—Flint.

The very thought of it turned her to ice. She could

cheerfully strangle Flint herself. But seeing him hurt—really hurt—was something else again.

Think, Francis, think, she told herself as Flint slid her out of his arms to a dry space near a pine tree. The shade of the tree made the night darker here than anywhere. Even the light of the moon did not reflect off her sequins when she was sitting here. She could no longer see his face. He was a black shadow who crouched beside her.

"Be careful," she whispered at his back as he turned to leave. The words sounded futile to her ears. And then she saw his black silhouette as he drew a gun from somewhere. He must have had a gun in the saddlebag. Or maybe he had a shoulder holster.

Francis didn't want to be responsible for Flint being hurt. But anyone who was here to rescue her would think nothing of shooting Flint. *Think, Francis, think.* There had to be a solution. She couldn't just sit here and wait for the gunfire to begin.

That's it, she thought victoriously. She knew she could think of a solution. It just needed an orderly mind. If there were no kidnapping, there would be no need for any shooting.

Francis forced herself to stand. Her one leg wobbled, but it would have to do. She took a step forward, praying whoever was inside that wooden house would have sense enough to recognize her voice.

"Flint, darling," she called in what she hoped was a gay and flirtatious voice. She was out of practice, but even if her voice wasn't seductive she knew it was loud enough to be heard through the thickest walls. "I thought you said there was a bed inside this old house for us to use."

There, she thought in satisfaction, *that should quell any questions about a kidnapping.* It would, of course, raise all sorts of other questions, but she could deal with that later. She wondered who of the many Dry Creek men had come to her rescue.

Flint froze. Only years of training stopped him from turning around to stare at Francis. The deep easy chuckle that rumbled through the walls of the house confirmed his suspicions about who had smoked the cigars. The cigars could be duplicated. The chuckle never. It was safe to turn around.

Flint could only see the silhouette of Francis, but it was enough. He walked toward her and said the only thing he could think to say. "I told you to keep quiet. That could have been anyone inside."

"I didn't want you to be shot on my account," Francis whispered airily as she limped toward him. "If you just let me go now, there'll be no kidnapping."

"There never was a kidnapping. This was a rescue."

"A rescue?" Francis turned the word over in her mouth and spoke low enough so that whoever was inside the house could not hear. "Don't you think that's going a bit far? I don't think anyone would believe it's a rescue— I think we better stick with the seduction story."

Flint shook his head. No wonder being a hero was so difficult these days.

"Not that they'll believe the seduction story, either." Francis continued to whisper. Her leg was painful, but she found it easier to limp than to stand. "I must look a sight by now."

The deep darkness of the night that had gathered around the pine trees lifted as Francis moved toward him. "I wonder which of the men from Dry Creek knew enough to drive out here and wait for us. Pretty quick thinking."

Flint held his breath. In the night, he could look at Francis and not worry about the naked desire she would see in his eyes any other time. His jacket had fallen off her shoulders under the tree, and her arms and neck gleamed white even in the midnight darkness. The sequins of that red dress glittered as she moved, showing every curve in her slender body. She was beautiful.

"It's not one of the men from Dry Creek," Flint said softly. "It's my boss."

Francis stopped. She'd never thought—never even considered. And she should have—there's an order to everything, she reminded herself blindly. One needed to know the place of everything. And a kidnapping, she noted dully, required a motive and, in this case, a boss.

Francis stared unmoving at the weatherbeaten deserted house that used to belong to Flint's grandmother. The white paint had peeled off the frame years ago, leaving a chipped grayness that blended into the darkness. Gaping black holes marked where the glass had broken out of the windows.

"He must think I'm a fool," Francis whispered stiffly.

Francis looked so fragile, Flint moved slowly toward her. She looked like a bird, perched for flight even with her sprained leg muscle.

"No, I'm sure he doesn't think that at all," he said softly.

When he reached Francis, Flint picked her up again. This time he cradled her in his arms properly, as he had wanted to each time he'd picked her up tonight. For the first time, she didn't resist him. That should thrill his heart, Flint thought. But it didn't. He knew Francis wasn't warming toward him. She'd just given up.

"And that bit about the bed." Francis continued to fret. "I'm a middle-aged woman. He must think I'm a featherbrain—especially because he knows why you have me out here."

"He does, does he?" Flint asked quietly. It came as somewhat of a surprise to him that he'd rather have Francis kicking his shin with her pointed high heels than to have her lying still in his arms feeling foolish after having done something so brave.

The angle wasn't perfect for what he needed to do, but Flint found that if he bent his knee and slowly

lowered Francis until she was securely perched on
the knee, he could crane his neck and do what he
needed to do.

He bent his head down and kissed her. He knew
his lips were cold and chapped by now. He knew that
the quick indrawn breath he heard from Francis was
shock rather than passion. But he also knew that they
both needed this kiss more than they needed the air
they were breathing.

Flint took his time. He'd waited twenty years for
this kiss and, planned or not, he needed to take his
time. He felt the stiffness leave Francis's lips and he
felt them move against him like they used to. He and
his Francis were home again.

"Thank you." Francis was the first one to breathe
after the kiss ended. Her pulse was beating fast, but
she willed it to slow. "At least now your boss won't
think I'm delusional—he'll think you at least tried
to seduce me. Middle-aged or not." Francis stopped
speaking to peer into the darkness of the broken windows. "He is watching, isn't he?"

For the first time since he'd bent down on one knee,
Flint felt the bone-chilling cold of the snow beneath
him. He might be home again, but Francis wasn't.
"You think the kiss was for my boss's benefit?"

"Of course. And I appreciate it. I really do."

Flint only grunted. He must be losing his touch.
He went back and picked up his jacket to wrap around
Francis.

Chapter Three

"There's trouble in Dry Creek." The words came out of the other man's mouth the moment Flint kicked open the door to the abandoned house and, still holding Francis, stepped inside. "Kidnapping."

"I know," Francis said stiffly. She was glad she'd have the chance to show she wasn't a ninny. "That's me."

"Not unless you got here in the back of a cattle truck, it's not," the other man said mildly, a lit cigar in his mouth and a cell phone in his hand. The only light in the room was a small flashlight the man must have laid on the table recently. The flashlight gave a glow to the rather large room and showed some bookcases and a few wooden chairs scattered around the table.

"Well, surely there's no point in kidnapping more than me."

"It appears they have some woman named Sylvia Bannister and then Garth Elkton."

"Oh, no." Francis half twisted herself out of Flint's arms. "I'll need to go help them."

"You can't go." Flint finished carrying her over to one of the chairs and gently sat her down.

"That's right. I'm a prisoner."

"You're not a prisoner," Flint said impatiently and then turned to the older man. "It better be me that goes. I've gotten a little acquainted with the guys responsible for this. Might have picked up a tip or two."

While Flint was talking, he was rummaging through a backpack resting on another chair. He pulled out an ammunitions cartridge and put it in the pocket of a dry jacket that was wrapped around the back of the chair. Then he pulled out a pair of leather gloves.

"Mrs. B called it in." The older man gestured to his cell phone. "Said to hurry. Some kids are chasing the truck in a bus as we speak. You can use my Jeep. Parked it behind the trees over there." The older man jerked his head in the opposite direction they had ridden in from. "It'll get you there faster."

"Not faster than Honey," Flint said with a smile as he walked toward the door. "She can beat a Jeep any day. She makes her own roads."

Flint opened the door and was gone in a little less than five seconds. Francis knew it was five seconds because she was counting to ten and had only reached five when the door creaked shut. Her teeth were chattering and she didn't know if it was because she was near frozen or because she was scared to death. She hoped counting would force her to focus and make it all better. It didn't.

"I've got one of those emergency blankets in here someplace," the older man said as he turned to a back-pack of his own leaning in the corner of the room. "Prevents heat loss, that sort of thing."

"I'm okay." Francis shivered through the words. She felt helpless to be sitting here when someone had kidnapped Sylvia and Garth.

"Not much to that dress," the older man said as he walked over to her and wrapped what looked like a huge foil paper around her. "Especially in ten-below weather."

The paper crinkled when she moved, but Francis noticed a pocket of warmth was forming around her legs. It would spread. "I didn't plan to be out in it for so long without my coat."

"I expect you didn't." The man went back to his pack and pulled out a small hand-cranked lantern. He twisted the handle a few times and set the lantern on the table. A soft glow lit up the whole room. "Something must have gone wrong."

"Flint kidnapped me."

That fact seemed to amuse the older man. "Yes, I forgot. You mentioned that earlier. Sorry to spoil your plans."

"They were hardly my plans. You're the boss. They were your plans." Francis knew it wasn't always wise to confront criminals. But the old man seemed fairly harmless, and she did like to keep things clear.

"Sounded more like a lover's tryst to me." The man sat on one of the chairs.

"Humph." Francis didn't want to go into that.

"Not that it's any of my business," the man continued and looked around the room. "Although I can assure you that if Flint told you there was a bed, he lied."

"Humph." Francis was feeling the warmth steel up her whole body. She could almost feel cozy. "We don't really need a bed."

"Good."

The man sat for a few minutes in silence and then got up and went to his pack and drew out a can. "Peaches?"

"I'd like that."

The man opened the peaches with the can-opening edge of a Swiss knife.

"Handy thing," he said as he flipped the blades into the knife and put it in his pocket. "Flint gave me this one almost fifteen years ago now."

"You've known him for that long?"

The man nodded. "Almost as long as you have if you're who I think you are."

Francis wondered if this were a trick to find out who she was. But then, she reasoned, it hardly mattered. Flint certainly knew who she was, and he would be back soon to tell his boss anyway.

"I'm Francis Elkton."

The man nodded again. "Thought you must be. But I guess I'll share my peaches with you anyway. Figure you must have had your reasons for what you did."

"Reasons for what?"

The man shrugged. "It's old history. Flint went on and so did you. I wouldn't even have remembered your full name if I hadn't seen that."

There it was. The man was pointing to a faded family Bible. One of those with the black leather cover stamped, Our Family With God.

"I'm in there?" Francis moved outside the warmth of the foil blanket to stand up and walk to the bookcase. The Bible was closed, but she saw that a ribbon marker had been left through the center of the book. Curious, she opened it.

The man was right. There was her name. Francis Elkton.

The words read, "United in Holy Matrimony Flint L. Harris and Francis Elkton on the day of our Lord, April 17—"

"Who wrote that there?" Even the temperature outside could not match the ice inside her. She'd never seen the words like that, so black and white.

The man shrugged. "It was either Flint or his grandmother."

"His grandmother didn't know we—" Francis gulped. She could hardly say they had gotten married when the most they had done was perform a mock ceremony.

"Then it must have been Flint."

"He must have stopped here before he left that day."

The man nodded. "I expect so. A man like Flint takes his marriage vows serious. He'd want to at least write them down in a family Bible."

"There were no marriage vows," Francis corrected the man bitterly. "We said them before a fake justice of the peace."

The man looked startled. "There was nothing fake about your vows."

Francis felt a headache start in the back of her neck. "I'm afraid there was. The justice of the peace was a phony."

"I checked him out. He was pure gold."

"You can't have checked him out. He didn't even exist. Phony name and everything."

Francis still remembered the smug look on her father's face when he got off the phone with a city official in Las Vegas and informed her there was no such justice of the peace.

The peaches were forgotten. The older man looked cautiously at Francis and said softly, "I did a thorough check on Flint myself before he came into the Bureau. I knew he had potential and would go far. I wanted to be sure we did a complete check. I talked to the justice of the peace personally. And the county sheriff who arrested Flint on that speeding ticket."

Francis felt her headache worsen. "What speeding ticket?"

The old man looked at Francis silently for a moment. "The day after you were married, Flint was arrested on a speeding ticket just inside the Miles City limits. Thirty-eight in a thirty-five-mile-an-hour zone."

"No one gets a ticket for that."

"Flint did. And because he didn't have the hundred thousand dollars cash to post bail, he did ninety days in jail."

Francis put her hand to her head. "That can't be. No one does that kind of time on a traffic ticket—and they certainly don't have that kind of bail."

The man kept looking at Francis like he was measuring her. Then he continued slowly. "I talked to the sheriff who made the arrest. He was doing a favor for someone. The arrest. The high bail. The ninety days. It was all a personal favor."

"Flint never hurt anyone. Who would do that?"

The silence was longer this time. Finally, the man spoke. "The sheriff said it was you. Said you'd changed your mind about the marriage and didn't have the nerve to tell Flint to his face."

"Me?" The squeak that came out of Francis's throat was one she scarcely recognized as her own.

The man looked away to give her privacy. "Not that it's really any of my business."

Francis needed to breathe. *Reason this out,* she said to herself. *Reason it out. Put the pieces in their places.*

It will make sense. There's an order to it all. You just need to find it.

"But I hadn't changed my mind." Francis grabbed hold of that one fact and hung on to it. The whole story revolved around that one piece, and that one piece was false. That must make the whole story false. "I wanted to be married to Flint."

The man lifted his eyes to look at her. With the soft light of the lantern on the table, Francis could see the pity in the man's eyes. "I'm beginning to think that might possibly be true."

Francis was numb. She'd fallen into a gaping hole and she didn't know how to get out of it. She couldn't talk. She could barely think. "But who would do such a thing?"

Francis knew it was her father. Knew it in her heart before she had reasoned it out with her head. He was the only one who could have done it.

Her father had been upset when she and Flint had driven up and announced their marriage. She hadn't expected her father to be glad about the marriage, but she thought he'd adjust in time. She'd been relieved when Flint had suggested he drive into Miles City to buy roses for her. If she had some time alone with her father, Francis had thought, she could change his mind.

She and her father had talked for a while and then she went in to pack. There wasn't much she needed to take. Some tea towels she'd made years ago when her mother was alive to help her. The clothes she'd been wearing to school. A few pieces of costume jewelry. The letters Garth had written her when he was overseas.

She'd filled up two suitcases when her father came in to say he'd called Las Vegas and found out that the justice of the peace was a fake.

At that moment, Francis had not worried about her father's words. If the justice of the peace was a fake, she'd calmly reasoned, she and Flint would only find someone else to marry them again. Flint had made a mistake in locating the proper official, but they would take care of it. They'd marry again. That's what people in love did. She started to fold the aprons her mother had given her.

When she finished packing, Francis went down to the kitchen to prepare supper for her father. It was the last meal she'd make for him for a while, and she was happy to do it. She decided to make beef stew because it could simmer for hours with little tending after she left.

Four hours later her father invited her to sit down and eat the stew with him. She knew Flint could have driven into Miles City and back several times in the hours that had passed. Francis refused the stew and went to her room. He must have had car trouble, she thought. That was it. He'd call any minute. She stayed awake all night waiting for the phone to ring. It was a week before she even made any attempt to sleep at nights.

"It was my father," Francis said calmly as she looked Flint's boss in the eyes. "He must have arranged it all."

"I'm sorry." The man said his words quickly.

The inside of the cold house was silent. Francis sat with the open Bible on her lap, staring at the page where her marriage vows had been recorded and a scripture reference from Solomon had been added. As she looked at it closely, she could see that the faded handwriting was Flint's. She wished she could have stood with him when he recorded the date in this Bible. It must have had meaning for him or he wouldn't have stopped on his way into Miles City to write it down.

"Surely Flint—" She looked at the man.

He was twisting the handle that gave energy to the emergency lantern on the table. He didn't look up from the lantern. "He didn't want to tell me about you. Didn't even mention your name. But he had to tell me the basics. I was only checking out his story. Part of the job. We needed to find out about the arrest. It was on his record."

"So he thinks it was me who got him arrested."

The temperature of the night seemed to go even lower.

The man nodded.

Francis felt numb. She had never imagined anything like this. She had assumed Flint had been the one to have second thoughts. Or that he had never intended to really marry her anyway. He wasn't from around here. She never should have trusted him as much as she did. She repeated all the words she had said to herself over the years. None of them gave her any comfort.

"He should have come back to talk to me."

"Maybe he tried," the man said. He'd stopped cranking the lantern and sat at the table.

The silence stretched between them.

"Mind if I smoke?" the man finally asked.

"Go ahead," Francis said automatically. She felt like her whole life was shifting gears and the gears were rusty. She'd spent too much of the past twenty years resenting Flint. Letting her anger burn toward him in the hopes that someday her memories would be light, airy ashes that could be blown away. But instead of producing ashes that were light, her anger had produced a heavy, molten chunk of resentment that wouldn't budge in a whirlwind.

There had been no blowing away of old, forgotten memories. These past weeks in Dry Creek had already proven that to her. She was beginning to believe she would be forever shackled by her memories. But now it turned out that the whole basis for her anger was untrue. Flint had not left her. She had, apparently, somehow left him.

A rumbling growl came from the man's coat pocket.

"Excuse me," he said as he reached into his pocket and pulled out a cell phone. "That'll be Mrs. B."

The conversation was short, and all Francis heard were several satisfied grunts.

"Flint's got them in custody," the man said when he put his phone back in his pocket. "He's holding them in something he called the dance barn in Dry Creek. Said you'd know where it was. Told me to bring you with me and come over."

"So I'm free to go?" Francis asked blankly as she looked up. She'd been so distressed about everything the man had told her she hadn't realized her first impressions of him must not be true.

"Of course," the man said as he stood and put his backpack on his shoulders.

"But who are you?"

"Inspector Kahn—FBI," the man said as he fumbled through another pocket in his coat and pulled out an identification badge.

"But—"

"The cattle business," the man explained as he showed the badge to Francis. "It's interstate. Makes it a federal crime."

"So the FBI sent someone in." Francis took a moment to look at the badge so she could scramble to get on track. She had heard the FBI was working on the case. They had asked Garth to help. "So you really didn't need Garth, after all."

Inspector Kahn grunted. "Not when I have a hot-head like Flint working for me."

"Flint works for you?"

Inspector Kahn grunted again and started walking toward the door. "Sometimes I think it's me working for him. I'd place money that the reason he's so keen for me to get there is because he wants me to do the paperwork. Flint always hated the paper side of things." He looked over his shoulder at her. "You coming?"

"Yes." Francis certainly didn't want to stay in this cold house any longer than she needed to. She pulled the jacket Flint had given her earlier over her shoulders and picked up the Bible.

The inspector looked at the Bible. "I expect you'll need to talk to Flint about this marriage business."

"I intend to try."

The inspector smiled at that. "Flint isn't always an easy man to reason with. Stubborn as he is brave. But you know that—you're married to him."

"I guess I am, at that." The ashes inside of Francis might not be blowing away, but she could feel them shifting all over the place. It appeared she, Francis K. Elkton, had actually been married to Flint L. Harris some twenty years ago.

For the umpteenth time that night, Flint wondered at the value of being a hero. He had saved Garth Elkton's hide—not to mention the even more tender hide of the attractive woman with him, Sylvia Bannister—

and they were both giving him a shoulder colder than the storm front that was fast moving into town.

In his jeans and wool jacket, Flint was out of place inside the barn. Not that any of the men there hadn't quickly helped him hog-tie the three men who had kidnapped Garth and Sylvia and attempted to take them away in the back of an old cattle truck.

But the music was still playing a slow tune and the pink crepe paper still hung from the rafters of that old barn. And Flint felt about as welcome as a stray wet dog at a fancy church picnic.

"There, that should do it." Flint checked the knots in the rope for the third time. He'd asked someone to call the local sheriff and was told the man was picking up something in Billings but would be back at the dance soon. He hoped the sheriff would get there before the inspector. Maybe then some of the paperwork would be local.

"Who'd you say you were again?" Garth Elkton asked the question, quiet-like, as he squatted to check the ropes with Flint.

"Flint Harris."

"The guy who called me the other night about the kidnapping?" Garth sounded suspicious.

"Yes."

"Still don't know how you knew about it."

"Because I've been freezing my toes off the past few nights following these guys around." Flint jerked his head at the men on the floor. Flint could see the direction Garth was going with his questions and he didn't appreciate it. "If I was one of them, don't you think they'd at least recognize me?"

Flint looked at the three men on the floor. They looked quarrelsome and pathetic. He didn't appreciate being lumped in with them. But at least it was clear that none of them claimed to have ever seen him before now.

"They didn't seem too clear about who their boss was," Garth continued mildly. "Could be they wouldn't recognize the man."

"I can't tell you who their boss is, but he's using a local informant," Flint said in exasperation. "We've got that much figured out. And I'm not local."

"You were local enough for my sister."

Ah, so it's come to that, Flint thought. It seemed he'd never get a square break from an Elkton. "Let's leave your sister out of it."

The mention of his sister made Garth scan the room. "Where is she, anyway? Thought she'd be back inside by now. I heard Jess was looking for her."

"She was with me." Flint resigned himself to his fate.

"With you? What was she doing with you?"

"Don't worry. She'll be back here any minute now."

"She better be or—" Garth seemed unaware that his voice was rising.

"Now, now, boys."

Flint looked up. He'd recognize that voice anywhere. He grinned as he looked at the woman who had been his grandmother's staunch friend in her final days. "Mrs. Hargrove! How are you?"

Mrs. Hargrove had aged a little in the years since he'd seen her last. And she was wearing a long velvet maroon dress tonight instead of her usual cotton gingham housedress. But she held herself with the same innate dignity he always expected from her. "Doing just fine, thank you."

"You know him?" Garth asked Mrs. Hargrove skeptically.

"Of course," the woman replied warmly. "He was in my Sunday school class for six months when he was here, and if he doesn't get up off that floor and give me a hug pretty soon, I'm going to be mighty disappointed."

Flint felt less like an unwelcome dog just looking at the woman. He stood up and enfolded her in his arms.

"I still miss that grandmother of yours," Mrs. Hargrove whispered as she held him.

"So do I," he whispered back.

"It comforts me to know she's with our Lord," she added and then leaned back to look Flint in the eye. "And I'm still working on her final request of me."

"Oh?" This was something Flint had not heard about.

"I pray for you every day, son," Mrs. Hargrove said with satisfaction. "Just like she would be doing if she were alive."

Flint had faced bullets. But nothing had made him feel as vulnerable as those words did. In his astonishment, he mumbled the only thing he could think of. "Well, thank you." To his further amazement, he meant it.

"And here you've come back to us a hero." Mrs. Hargrove stepped out of his arms and spoke loudly so that everyone could hear. "This is Essie Harris's grandson, folks. Let's give him a good welcome home."

With those words, Flint was transformed from the unwelcome stray into the prize guest. A murmur of approval ran through the folks of Dry Creek, and he heard more than one person mutter that it was about time.

"Here, let me introduce you around," Mrs. Hargrove said as she took Flint's arm. "You probably don't remember everyone. Here, this is Doris June—you might have met her, she went to school with Francis."

Flint found himself shaking hands with an attractive blond woman about his age. "You were a cheerleader, weren't you?"

The woman nodded. "The coach was always hoping to find a way to get you to try out for the basketball team."

"I was busy helping my grandmother."

"I know." The blonde smiled.

"And this is Margaret Ann." Mrs. Hargrove moved him on to another pleasant woman.

Flint noticed Mrs. Hargrove introduced him to the women first. The men hung back. They didn't seem as willing to shake his hand as the women were. In fact, some of them still looked at him with suspicion thick on their faces.

"Francis should be here soon," he said to no one in particular. He knew why the men didn't trust him. "She really is fine."

Flint had no sooner finished his words of reassurance than the barn door opened and his words came true. Francis was back.

The men of Dry Creek looked at Francis in disbelief and then looked at Flint, the suspicion hardening on their faces.

Flint would have cursed if Mrs. Hargrove wasn't standing, speechless, at his elbow.

Francis stood inside the doorway. She must have had dropped the jacket on her way inside, because she wasn't wearing it, and her neck and arms were pearl white. Her hair tumbled around her head in a mass of black silk that was sprinkled with dry pine needles. She had a bruise on her arm that was deepening into a ripe purple.

Flint could have tried to explain away the bruise and the needles. But he knew he'd have a more difficult time talking his way past the ragged tear in Francis's dress that went from her ankles to a few inches short of her waist. Even now Francis had to hold her dress shut around her with one hand while she carried something behind her back in the other hand.

"It was the horse," Flint stammered into the silence. He'd been called to testify in federal drug investigations, but he'd never felt the pressure of his testimony like now.

"She was with you." The quiet steel in Garth's voice came from behind him and prodded. "What happened?"

"Now, boys." Mrs. Hargrove found her breath and interrupted again. "Can't you see Francis is frozen to the bone? There'll be time for sorting this all out later."

Flint met the metal in Garth's eyes and smiled inside. He might not like the steel at his back, but he was warmed to know that Francis had such a loyal protector.

"Nothing," Flint assured the other man quietly. "Francis is fine."

Chapter Four

Francis blinked. Her eyes had become accustomed to the black night, and when she stepped into the golden light inside the barn, she felt like a spotlight was on her. She blinked again before she realized that every single person in the barn, even those three men tied in a muddle at Garth's feet, were staring at her.

"What happened to the music?" Francis took an uncertain step forward. The audio system that someone had set up was attached to an old record player, and the scratchy music it had been playing was reminiscent of the fifties. Before she'd gone to look for the Big Dipper an hour or so ago, however, the record hadn't skipped like the one that was on in the background now. "Why isn't anyone dancing?"

"Are you all right, dear?" Mrs. Hargrove was the first to move, and she stepped toward Francis.

"I'm fine—fine," Francis stammered. She looked at her dress, and for the first time realized how she must look. The fabric on her ill-fated red dress was thin in the best of circumstances, but the section she held in her hand was nothing more than flyaway threads held together by sequins. "It was the horse."

"The horse did that to your dress?" Garth asked, disbelieving, as he, too, stepped forward.

"Well, no, I ripped the dress when I tried to get off the horse." Francis realized as she said the words that they didn't sound very plausible. The polite eyes of her neighbors told her they didn't believe her. She tried again, a little defensively. "Well, I wasn't just getting off—I was going to ride Honey so I needed to swing my leg around."

"It doesn't matter, dear," Mrs. Hargrove said soothingly as she patted Francis on the shoulder, and then exclaimed, "Why, you're ice-cold! Come over by the heaters."

Tall electric heaters stood at the far side of the barn. Garth had them installed when the barn was used several months ago for the Christmas pageant. Francis let Mrs. Hargrove start leading her over to them.

"Here, let me carry that for you," Mrs. Hargrove offered as she held out her hand.

"Oh, it's nothing," Francis said quickly. She let go of the threads of her dress so she could slip Flint's family Bible under her arm more securely. She didn't know how Flint would feel about her taking the Bible, even though he'd left it in his grandmother's deserted house years ago and any stranger traveling through could have picked it up and taken it. That fact had bothered her the whole ride in. How could he leave something like that—something that spoke of their wedding—for strangers to take? Or for the wind to blow away?

Sequins fell from her dress as she hobbled closer to the heat. She felt a long shaft of cold on her leg where her dress was torn and a small circle of even colder metal where her garter fastened to her nylons.

A ripple of slow, approving murmurs moved through the group of men—most of them single ranch hands—already standing near the heaters.

Flint felt every muscle in his body tense. He didn't know which of those men around the heaters was Francis's boyfriend, but Flint didn't think much of him. What kind of man would let other men see that much leg of his girlfriend? Especially when the girlfriend looked like Francis. He doubted there was an unmarried man here tonight who wouldn't go to bed with the image of those red threads trailing across Francis's leg.

"Doesn't anybody use tablecloths anymore?" Flint took a dozen long strides to get to the food table and looked around impatiently. The tables were wrapped in a pink bridal paper with pink streamers placed every few inches twisting from the table to the floor.

"You're hungry?" Francis stopped to stare at Flint.

Flint only grunted as he tore several of the streamers from the back of the table. "These will have to do."

The streamers were wide, and Flint had his hand full of them when he kneeled by Francis. "Hold still."

Flint began wrapping the streamers around Francis, starting at her waist and moving on to her hips. The crepe paper wasn't any heavier than the material in that red sequin dress, but it held the pieces of Francis's dress together. Flint knotted the first strip around her waist as an anchor and then began to wrap her like a mummy from her waist to her knees.

"I can do it," Francis said as she shifted awkwardly to keep the book behind her back.

If Francis hadn't acted so uncomfortable, Flint would have taken at least another minute before he focused on the book she was obviously trying to hide from him.

"That's Grandma's," Flint said, tight-lipped. He supposed Francis had read what he wrote that day. Well, there was nothing for it. He had been a fool, but he wouldn't apologize.

He remembered the day he'd arrived at his grandmother's house after leaving Francis at her father's to pack. His grandmother had been at a church meeting in Dry Creek and wasn't home. On impulse Flint had pulled his grandmother's family Bible off the shelf and recorded his marriage. Then he put the Bible back.

The book wasn't his grandmother's reading Bible, but it was important to her nonetheless. Her wedding and the wedding of Flint's parents had been recorded on its center pages. He'd planned to pull the Bible out and surprise his grandmother when he came back from Miles City that day.

But it was three months before he came back from Miles City, and by then the ink would have been fully dried on the divorce papers he'd signed in jail. He had no calm words to explain what had happened, so he left the Bible on the shelf. As angry as he was with Francis, he didn't want the good people of Dry Creek to force her into accepting a marriage she didn't want. He didn't even tell his grandmother what had happened. If she ever saw the words, she never asked about them in their weekly phone conversations.

Even after all these years, Flint still didn't want Francis to be publicly blamed. He doubted the good people of Dry Creek would think much of a woman who abandoned her marriage vows within hours of saying them. They might not be as forgiving as he had learned to be.

"Don't worry. Your secret's safe," Flint murmured as he impatiently knotted one of the crepe streamers just above Francis's knee. He wished there was more noise in this old barn, but it seemed like everyone would rather watch him wrap Francis in crepe paper than dance with each other. "You were just a kid. I'm the one who should have had sense enough to stop it before it went as far as it did."

"I was no more a kid than you were. I was certainly old enough to know my own mind," Francis snapped back in a low whisper. She hadn't counted on having this conversation in front of a hundred curious witnesses with Flint kneeling in front of her and angrily wrapping crepe paper around her legs. But if that was the only way to have it, she'd do it. "You should have realized that instead of—"

"Me?" Flint reared back when he finally heard the mild tone of reproof in Francis's voice. It was one thing to forgive her. But it was asking a bit much of him to let her take that tone with him. "I should have realized something? The only thing I should have realized was that you were too young for the responsibilities involved in getting mar—"

Flint suddenly heard the silence. The bride and groom who were celebrating their wedding tonight were standing still as statues. Even the men tied together into a pile at Garth's feet had stopped scraping their feet along the wood floor. A hundred people were watching, and no one was crumpling a paper cup or moving in their chair. Someone had shut off the record player, so even that empty scratching had stilled. This old barn had never been so quiet.

Flint willed his voice to a mild whisper. "You were a bit young, is all. That's not a crime."

"It would have been a crime if I hadn't been so caught up in my career," Francis replied as the reality of the situation became a little clearer. Bigamy. What if she had married, never knowing that she was already married? She wondered if the law forgave such silliness. "You at least knew we were married."

"Married?" The word was picked up by someone standing near them and passed around the barn quicker than a fake dollar bill at a carnival.

Flint looked up as a new group of men slowly gathered from around the barn and moved over by the heaters. These men had a look about them he'd seen in combat. He'd wager the lot of them worked for Francis's brother. They all had calluses on their hands and scuffed boots on their feet. He expected he could take any of them in a fair fight. By the hardening looks on their faces, he figured he'd have to do that very thing before the night was over.

"Maybe we better discuss this outside," Flint said calmly as he stood up, twisted the last piece of crepe paper into a tidy roll and set it on the corner of the refreshment table.

Flint didn't want to call Francis a liar in front of her family and friends, but if she thought he'd buy some story about her being drunk or confused that night in Vegas, she was going to be disappointed. He knew she hadn't had a drop of liquor to drink. They hadn't even opened the complimentary champagne that came with the wedding ceremony. And, while she had been wonderfully starry-eyed, she had not been confused.

Francis nodded. The warmth from the heaters was uneven, and she shivered. "Let me look for my jacket."

Francis ran her eyes over the people in the barn, looking for Sylvia Bannister. The last time she'd seen Sylvia she had been wearing Francis's black lion jacket, a remembrance from long-ago high school years. As Francis looked over the small clusters of her friends and neighbors, they began to shuffle in sudden embarrassment and start to move.

"You're welcome to borrow my jacket." Mrs. Hargrove stepped forward efficiently with a wool jacket in her hands. "I won't be needing it since I'll be dancing—if someone will put the music back on."

The crowd took the hint. Someone flipped a switch, and an old Beatles song started to play. A few of the women walked to the refreshment table and poured more punch in the bowl. The kidnappers, tied in a heap to one side of the barn, started to twist their rope-bound feet and complain that there wasn't even a local law official there to see to their comfort.

"We got our rights, too," the stocky brother started to protest. "Ain't right we're kept tied up like this just so he—" the man jerked his head at Flint "—can play Romeo in some snowdrift with his Juliet."

"Yeah." One of the other brothers took his lead. "We ain't even had supper."

"I'm not feeding you supper," Flint said in clipped exasperation, although he almost welcomed the excuse to turn from Francis and focus on business for a minute. "Give me a break, you've only been arrested for fifteen minutes. And it's almost midnight—you should have eaten supper hours ago."

"Well, we didn't get a chance to eat before." The brother whined.

"You should always take time for a proper meal," Francis said automatically as she slipped her arms into the jacket Mrs. Hargrove held out for her. "Good nutrition makes for a more productive worker."

Flint snorted as he nodded his head toward the kidnappers. "Trust me, they don't need to be more productive."

"I think there's some of those little quiche appetizers left," Mrs. Hargrove said as she headed for the refreshment table. "The Good Book says we need to look out for our enemies."

"The Good Book says a lot of things," Flint said as his eyes skimmed over Francis. Yes, she still had it in her hand. His grandmother's Bible. "Not all of the things written in its pages are true."

Flint heard Mrs. Hargrove gasp, and he hurried to explain. "I mean some of the things that are handwritten—by a person in their own Bible—aren't necessarily true."

"Essie stood by everything she wrote in that Bible of hers." Mrs. Hargrove defended her friend. "And I'd stand by them, too."

"It wasn't something Grandma wrote," Flint said softly. He suddenly had a picture of his grandmother sitting down in the evening at her old wooden table and reading her Bible. She'd have her apron on and the radio humming in the background as she'd mouth the words. She read silently, but occasionally—when the words seemed either too wonderful or too horrible to be held in—she'd speak them aloud to whomever stood by.

Flint had never seen anyone else read a book like it was a letter that had come in the morning mail. He had secretly envied her the faith she had even though he knew it wasn't for the likes of him. Even then he didn't feel like he'd ever clean up good enough to merit much faith. But his grandmother was a different story. He didn't want anyone to question his grandmother's faith. "It wasn't something she wrote down. It was something I wrote. By mistake."

Mrs. Hargrove looked Flint full in the eyes before she smiled. "I can't think of a better place to write something—whether it's a mistake or not, only God knows."

Flint snorted. "Well, God isn't the only one who knows on this one. Wish He was. At least He can keep a secret."

"I can keep a secret." Francis was stung.

"I'm not worried about you, sweetheart," Flint said wryly as he smiled at her. "It's my boss I'm worried about. I know you can keep this secret—you've kept it for the past twenty years."

"Sometimes a secret needs a good airing out," Mrs. Hargrove offered breezily as she finished stacking some petite quiches on a small paper plate and started toward the tangle of men on the floor. "Especially those old ones."

By now several couples were dancing, and those

who weren't dancing had politely turned their attention to other things.

"We do need to talk about it," Francis said firmly as she pulled the wool jacket closer around her. She searched in the pocket and found a hairpin. Just what she needed. She swept her hair up and gave it a couple of twists. Organizing her hair into a neat bun made her feel more in control. "There are things you don't know."

Flint stood by helplessly and watched the transformation of Francis. She'd gone from being a bewitching damsel in distress with handfuls of silken hair to a very competent-looking executive who wouldn't tolerate a hair out of place or a thought that wasn't useful.

"You don't need to make it right with me, if that's what you're thinking." Flint didn't want to have this final conversation with Francis. He was quite sure the executive Francis didn't approve of that long-ago Francis who had run off to be married. "Whatever happened on that day to make you change your mind, it is okay. I've made my peace with it."

"But that's not the way it was at all," Francis protested.

Francis buttoned the wool jacket around her. Mrs. Hargrove was several sizes larger than she was, and Francis liked the secure feeling the too-large jacket gave her. She must look a sight with the green plaid jacket on top of her skirt of pink crepe paper and red sequins.

"Speaking of the inspector, where is he?" Flint knelt to test the knots on the three men sitting patiently on the floor. He looked at Francis briefly. "Thought he was coming with you."

"He was. He got a call from the sheriff saying he had a flat tire down the road a piece. The inspector went to help him."

Flint grunted as he finished checking the knots. "He just wants to avoid the paperwork with these guys."

The door opened, and a square of cold midnight was visible for a moment before the inspector stepped inside the old barn and brushed a few stray snowflakes off his coat. "Did I hear you say paperwork? Don't worry about that. I'll do it."

Flint had never heard the inspector volunteer to do the paperwork.

"You'll maybe want to…" The inspector had walked over to where Flint knelt and inclined his head slightly in the direction of Francis.

So much for privacy, Flint thought. But if he talked to Francis here, the inspector wouldn't be the only one listening. "I'll talk to her later."

"That's too late." The inspector leaned down and whispered, "You better do it now before—"

The door to the barn opened again, and the inspector groaned. "Too late. He's here."

Flint looked at the open doorway but didn't see what the problem was. It was only the sheriff. The man looked decidedly uncomfortable, with patches of snow stuck to his jeans and his parka pulled close around his head. Tonight wasn't the best night for getting a flat tire.

Then the sheriff stepped all the way inside, and Flint noticed two other people crowding in the door behind him.

They both had big city stamped all over them. The woman was tall, lean and platinum. Her face was pinched with cold, but that didn't take away the look of expensive makeup. Definitely uptown.

The man was more downtown. Flint would peg him as a banker. Maybe vice president or loans officer. He had the look of a bean counter, but not the look of command. He was wearing a brown business suit and lined leather gloves. Expensive gloves, Flint thought a little jealously, wondering what snowdrift his own gloves had ended up in tonight.

"Robert!" the woman exclaimed loudly and started walking to the man Flint knew to be Robert Buckwalter.

So that was it, Flint thought as he stood up quickly. The inspector must be worried that the woman would interfere with Mrs. Buckwalter's secret cover.

No one knew that Mrs. Buckwalter was working with the FBI on this rustling business, not even her son. Until they found out the identity of the person serving as the informant for the rustling outfit, they couldn't be too careful about strangers. Especially strangers who wanted to cozy up to FBI operatives and their families.

Ordinarily Flint wouldn't seriously suspect the woman. Not because she looked flimsy, but because he was pretty sure the informant had to be someone local. Only a local would have a cover good enough to have escaped everyone's notice and still have access to the information the rustlers would need.

Flint intercepted the blonde's path just before she reached Robert. "I'll need to see some identification."

The woman momentarily flushed guiltily, and Flint looked at her more closely. She was up to something.

"Identification?" She stopped and schooled her face into blankness. "I don't need identification. I'm with him." She pointed to Robert.

Flint couldn't help noticing Robert flinching as the other man protested. "Now, Laurel, you know that's not—"

Flint almost felt sorry for the man. He'd seen Robert earlier, working as a kitchen helper to the young woman chef his mother had sent out here with a planeload of lobsters for the party tonight. Flint had seen Robert land his small plane near Garth's ranch a few days ago in the early morning hours. A man as rich as Robert—with the whole Buckwalter fortune at his feet—would have to be besotted to slice radishes for two hours. "She's with you?"

"I wouldn't say *with*." Robert stumbled. He glanced at the young woman standing next to him in apology.

"I know Laurel—of course I know her—our families are—well, my mother knows her better, so, no—I wouldn't say *with*."

"It was *with* enough for you on Christmas!" Laurel staged a pout that would do justice to a Hollywood starlet.

"Well." Flint backed away. He would have liked to help Robert out—he seemed like a decent man—but the FBI couldn't arrest a woman for flirting.

It wasn't until Flint turned that he realized his tactical mistake. The inspector wasn't worried about the woman. He was worried about that man who was walking to Francis with a determined look in his eyes that demanded she welcome him.

"You must be the boyfriend," Flint said as he walked to Francis. It was inevitable. The evening had been doomed from the start.

"I hope I'm more than a boyfriend," the man said, a little smugly, Flint thought, as he reached Francis and leaned over to peck her on her lips. "Now that she's had time away to think about things."

"Sam." Francis marveled that her voice sounded calm. She felt a growing urge to scream. "What are you doing here?"

"Well, I got to thinking. It's time you came back—how much thinking can a woman do?" The man laughed a little too heartily. "So I flew up to get you."

"Now's not a good time."

"Oh, I know. The inspector was telling me there's

been lots of excitement here tonight. Seemed to think I'd be better off going back to Billings for the night, but I told him it was nonsense. It would take more than a few bad guys to rattle my Francis. She's the most sensible woman I've ever known."

Flint thought the man must be blind to think "sensible" summed up a woman like Francis. Didn't he see the shy warmth in her eyes when she first met someone? Hadn't he felt the slight tremble of her lips when she was kissed?

"Known a lot of women, have you?" Flint asked the man. He refused to think of the man as Sam. As far as Flint was concerned, the man had no name. And no future.

"Huh?"

Flint admitted the man didn't look like he could have known many women, but that didn't stop Flint from resenting him. "Just checking up on your background."

"Flint's with the FBI," Francis said, tight-lipped with annoyance. "He checks up on everybody."

"Oh, well, that's okay then." The man smiled at Flint and held out his hand. "Always nice to meet one of our nation's security men. Men like you keep us all safe."

Flint grunted. The man made it sound like Flint was a school crossing guard. Important enough for someone who did that sort of thing. Flint wondered if

Francis actually loved the guy. He glared at the man until the man dropped his hand.

"You own a house?" Flint knew women loved big houses.

"A bedroom loft condo in downtown Denver," the man said with pride. "The Executive Manor complex."

Flint grunted. Close enough. The only house he could claim as his own was sitting just north of here on five desolate acres only chickens could love.

"Francis would want a tree or two."

The man looked startled. "I told her we could get a few ficus plants. They'd do."

Flint nodded. Francis just might settle for them, after all. Suddenly, Flint felt old. He had lived too hard and fast. At least the man standing before him looked stable. Maybe that was enough.

"You ever kill a man?"

"I beg your pardon?" The man was looking at Flint in alarm.

"It's a simple question—ever been in the military?"

The man shook his head. "Bad feet."

"Ever been arrested?"

"Of course not." The man was indignant. "And I certainly don't see the point of these questions—if I'm under suspicion for something I have a right to know. And if you're planning to arrest me, I demand a chance to call my attorney."

Flint smiled wryly. He almost wished he could arrest the man. "No, I'm just checking up on you."

"Well, I'll let it go this time," the man said pompously. "Mostly because the inspector here said you'd rescued Francis from those hoodlums. I should be thanking you for helping my fiancée, not sitting here arguing."

"Fiancée." Flint felt a cold draft down his neck. It appeared the ficus had won.

"I never agreed to marry you." Francis felt the need to sit down and start counting. Everything was unraveling. "Actually, I can't marry you."

"Nonsense. Of course you can. I've thought about it, too, you know. Granted, we don't have some fairy-tale romance, but a woman your age doesn't expect that. We have more important reasons to get married. Stability. Companionship. There's no good reason for either of us to stay single."

"There's him." Francis pointed at Flint. The air inside the barn had cooled until it had an icy edge to it, and someone had dimmed the lights for slow dancing. A song of love betrayed was filling the barn with a quiet sadness, and more than one couple moved closer together.

"Him?" Sam looked at Flint like he suspected him of being part of a police lineup. "What's the FBI got to do with anything?"

"It's not the FBI. It's him. He's my husband," Francis whispered.

"You're joking." Sam looked at Flint again and then dismissed him. "You don't even know him."

"I used to know him. We were married twenty years ago."

"Oh, well, then," The man visibly relaxed. "He's your ex-husband."

Flint didn't like the direction the conversation was taking. "If Francis doesn't want to marry you, she shouldn't. And there's no reason she should ever settle for companionship."

"If you're her ex, you have no say in this at all." Sam looked Flint over like he had been pulled out of that police lineup and pronounced guilty. "Besides, I'm sure she's realized by now that I'm the kind of husband that she should have. Solid. Steady. A man like you is okay for a woman when she's young— What we don't do when we're young." The man gave a bark of a laugh. "Why, I was in a protest march myself once— But that was then and surely by now Francis knows your kind doesn't hold up too well over the years."

"My kind? What do you know about my kind?" Flint forced the words out over his clenched teeth.

"I know you left her," Sam said calmly. The brown-suited man looked smug and confident. He glanced at Francis indulgently. "I know Francis and she'd stick by her word. So I know it's you who left."

"She was young. And scared. And me— I must have seemed like some wild guy back then. I can't blame her for having second thoughts." Flint gave a ragged laugh. "I would have left me if I'd had a choice. I was mad at the world for letting my parents die.

Mad at school. Mad at friends. Mad at God. The only good thing about me was Francis. I can't blame her for leaving me."

"But I didn't," Francis said softly. "I didn't leave."

Flint snorted. "That's not what the sheriff said."

"I wasn't the one who had you arrested." Francis said the words carefully. She felt like she was walking some very important, invisible line. She tried to take a deep breath, but failed. "It was my father."

"But the sheriff said—"

"My father may have lied to him." Francis was almost whispering. They seemed to burn their way up through her throat. "I waited for you to come back that day."

Flint heard the words and stared at Francis. He shook his head like he was clearing his ears. What was she saying?

"But—" Flint took one more stab at understanding. He could see in her eyes that she was telling him the truth. "But there were papers—divorce papers—"

"Had I signed them?"

Flint shook his head slowly. "I thought you'd sign them when they were given to you."

Flint still remembered the pain of seeing those papers. At first, he'd refused to sign them, pushing them away when the sheriff brought them to his cell. But on the third day, he'd decided to give in. The sheriff said Francis was pleading with her father to get the papers signed, that she was not eating she was so upset. He couldn't bear for her to be upset. He'd bruised his fist by hitting the wall of that cell after he'd finally shoved the signed papers through the bars to the sheriff.

"You were begging me to sign them."

Francis shook her head. "No."

Sometimes the world tips on its axis. Sometimes it rolls completely over. Flint's world rolled over so many times he didn't know which side was up. "I don't understand. Are you saying that you never signed those papers?"

"I never even knew they existed," Francis said softly. "I suppose my father meant to give them to me. But I left before long and—no, I never saw the papers."

"But then—"

Francis nodded. "We're still married."

Somehow the music had stopped again, and everyone was listening.

"Well," Mrs. Hargrove finally said softly. "Well, if that don't beat all."

At the edge of the crowd...

The old man slipped into the barn unnoticed. He knew he shouldn't be here. Knew one of those knuckleheads the boss had hired to do the job tonight might recognize his voice or the angle of his chin. The disguise he'd worn when the boss talked to them out at the deserted Redfern place might not hold.

But he'd tired of watching the horse, waiting for that FBI agent to return. The old man had spotted the agent snooping around Dry Creek several days ago, but he hadn't wanted to risk making himself known by trying to get rid of the man.

He hadn't even told the boss about the agent. He was scared of the boss and was afraid the boss would want him to do something to the agent. Something dangerous. When the boss had come to town a year or so ago, he'd been friendly. The boss had seemed to understand that the town of Dry Creek owed him. But now the old man wasn't so sure. The boss wasn't friendly anymore when he called. He kept asking the old man for more and more information.

And it was dangerous.

The old man hadn't figured on the FBI getting involved. The FBI made him nervous. The old man had always figured that the only lawman he'd have to outsmart was Sheriff Wall.

But this agent was a lot brighter than Sheriff Wall. The old man was afraid the agent already suspected something.

The old man couldn't afford to be caught. Couldn't afford to go to jail or have a trial. He didn't think he could bear to speak in front of that many strangers. Why, they put a dozen people on a jury. He didn't talk to a dozen people in a year. And he never gave anything like a speech. No one would ever understand that the town of Dry Creek owed him. No, he couldn't risk getting caught.

The old man knew he couldn't stay in this town.

But he didn't know how to leave, either. He didn't drive his old pickup anymore. The tires had long since flattened into pancakes, and he just let them sit. Sometimes, when the mood took him, he'd sit in the battered pickup and listen to the news on the radio. But he didn't drive.

Mrs. Hargrove did his weekly grocery shopping for him, and she'd always been willing to do an extra errand or two for him. But he could hardly ask her to drive him to Mexico.

Chapter Five

Flint sat on the edge of the steps going into the barn. The moon was still high in the night sky. A slight wind was blowing. He'd give odds that a blizzard would roll off the Big Sheep Mountains before dawn. He could hear the sounds of the townspeople inside cleaning up after the party. He'd just sent the three would-be kidnappers off with the sheriff. He wished he had a cigarette, even though he hadn't smoked in ten years.

The door opened, and Mrs. Hargrove stepped out. "There's a cup of coffee left." She had a jacket draped over her shoulders and a mug in her hand. "Thought you might want it. It's from the bottom of the pot so it'll be strong."

"Thanks." Flint smiled at the woman as he reached up for the cup. "The stronger the better. I don't expect to sleep tonight anyway."

"I wouldn't suppose so," Mrs. Hargrove agreed as she sat down beside him. "It isn't every day you discover you're married." She smiled at him kindly. "You should be sitting here with your wife, not me."

Flint snorted. "My wife took off in a puff of exhaust fumes. Back to her brother's place with her fancy fiancé."

"Well, I expect it will take some getting used to—the whole idea."

Flint looked at her in astonishment. "She's not getting used to the idea. Didn't you hear her? She's practically engaged to what's-his-name."

"Engaged isn't married," Mrs. Hargrove replied calmly. She pulled her jacket around her more firmly, and Flint was reminded of a general preparing for battle. "It's you she's married to in the eyes of the Lord."

Flint bit back his retort. Even a general didn't always know which battles could be won. "Can't imagine the eyes of the Lord will stop her from divorcing me quick as she can. He seems to have been content to look the other way for twenty years. Why break His record now?"

"Why, Flint Harris, what a thing to say—if your grandmother heard you, she'd—she'd…" Mrs. Hargrove appeared at a loss for what his grandmother would do.

Flint helped her out. He smiled. "She'd make me sit in that straight-back chair by the window while she prayed out loud asking the Lord to help me count my blessings and forgive my faults. I used to hate that more than anything. Used to ask her to just take away the keys to my pickup like normal kids."

"That would be Essie," Mrs. Hargrove said fondly. "She prayed over everything."

"She once prayed over a chicken that was sick—fool bird ate a marble." Flint could still picture his grandmother. She had unruly gray hair that she wore pushed back with an elastic headband and strong lines in her face that even wrinkles couldn't unsettle. "I'm glad she's not here to see me now."

"Oh, well, she would understand—you didn't know Francis's dad would set you up that way."

"It's not just that. It's who I am. She'd be broken-hearted if she saw me now."

"Essie was tougher than you think. Her heart didn't break easy. Besides, she always said it was never too late to repent. If you don't like who you've become or what you've done, it's not too late to ask God for forgiveness and start anew."

"She was wrong," Flint said as he took the last gulp of hot coffee and stood. "Sometimes it is definitely too late."

"Flint L. Harris, that's utter nonsense you're talking." Mrs. Hargrove stared up at Flint from her perch on the steps. "Just because you've had a few troubles in life—"

"Troubles?" Flint gave a wry laugh. "Troubles were the good times."

"Essie always worried so over you, child," Mrs.

Hargrove said softly as she stood. "Said you took all the bad times to heart. Like they were all your fault. Your parents dying. Even the weather—you used to fret if there wasn't enough rain to suit you."

"Grandma needed rain for that garden of hers."

"Your grandma got by just fine with what the Lord provided—she didn't need you to fret for her."

Flint remembered the lines on his grandmother's face. "I couldn't stand by helpless."

"Ah, child." Mrs. Hargrove reached out a hand and laid it on Flint's arm. "We're all helpless when it comes right down to it. We're dependent on Him for the air we breathe, the food we eat. So don't go thinking you need to do His job. The world is a mighty big weight for anyone to be carrying around—even a grown man like you."

The touch on his arm almost undid Flint until he wondered what Mrs. Hargrove would do if he confessed what troubles had crossed his path in life. He'd seen corruption. Hatred. Evil at its finest. A man couldn't see what he'd seen in life and remain untouched.

Flint winced inwardly. He sure didn't stack up pretty when you stood him next to a choirboy like Sam. He'd wager the man didn't even have a parking ticket to haunt his dreams.

Flint felt like an old man. He'd seen too much bad to truly believe in good anymore. He wasn't fit for a woman like Francis.

"Oh, don't let me forget to give you this." Mrs. Hargrove reached into the large pocket of the jacket and pulled out his grandmother's Bible. "She'd want you to have it."

Flint grimaced as he reached for the book. "I always regretted just leaving it there after she died. Seemed disrespectful somehow. I should have come back for it years ago."

"The important thing is that you came back now," Mrs. Hargrove said softly. "Even if it was just to do your job."

"Speaking of my job—" Flint had left the inspector inside with the last of the paperwork "—I better get back to it."

The barn was almost empty. The folding chairs were neatly stacked against the wall. The crepe paper streamers were being swept into a jumble in the middle of the floor by two aging cowboys. The refreshment table was stripped bare, and that was where the inspector was sitting and filling out the last of the forms.

"I always wonder if it's worth it to arrest them," Flint said softly as he walked over and sat down in a folding chair near the inspector.

The inspector looked up and chuckled. "The bean counters would just add another form asking us to explain why we let them go."

"I suppose so."

"Besides, I'm almost finished. I told the sheriff I'd

come by in the morning around six and we'd set up the interrogation. Should really do it tonight, but there's a storm moving in."

"Oh, I can meet with the sheriff—"

The inspector looked up from the papers and assessed him. "You haven't had a good night's sleep in days now—I can meet with the sheriff."

The heaters had been turned off in the barn an hour ago when the guests left. The air, both inside and outside, had gradually grown heavy with the promise of snow. The windows had another layer of frost gathering on them.

"Besides," the inspector continued softly. His breath clouded around his face. "You couldn't bring Francis to the interrogation."

Flint grimaced. "Trust me. I doubt she'd go anywhere with me."

The inspector nodded. "It'll be a challenge to guard her."

Flint wasn't surprised the inspector had followed his line of thinking. They'd worked together for so long they knew the routine. "She's not safe here. Not until we arrest the man who hired those goons to do the kidnapping."

The inspector nodded again. "She doesn't know she's still in danger?"

Flint snorted. "Francis? She didn't believe she was in danger the first time."

"Too bad. If she was scared, we could get her to

agree to spend some time in the jailhouse in Miles City. Protective custody. Or to at least have a twenty-four-hour guard on her. I don't like the thought of you having to guard her."

"Me? I've guarded hundreds of folks."

"But never your ex-wife," the inspector said as he laid down the pen and folded the last of the forms. "Besides, it's not her that I'm worried about. It's you. If we weren't out in the middle of nowhere I'd ask one of the other boys to come over and guard her."

"I can handle it."

The inspector grunted and looked square at Flint. The older man's eyes darkened with concern. "Just how come is it that you've never married?"

"Lots of guys in this business are single,"

The inspector grunted again. "That's because they marry and divorce and marry and divorce. Not many never marry." The older man paused a minute and then shrugged. "Well, it's your business, I guess."

"I won't even need to see Francis when I guard her," Flint said defensively. "I thought I'd just do a stakeout. Nobody needs to know I'm there."

The inspector looked up at this sharply. "There's a blizzard coming in. Folks around here say it might fall to ten below before morning. You can't play the lone ranger on that horse of yours tonight."

The inspector was right. Flint knew it. He just hadn't faced the truth yet. "I'm not sure Francis would let me stay in the house with them."

"That brother of hers won't be too happy, either, but he'd do anything to protect her."

Flint snorted. "Trouble is—it's me he's protecting her from."

"I'll call and give him the order," the inspector said as though that settled it. "If one of my men has to go out there on a night like this, the least Elkton can do is to let you inside the house."

The chair in the Elkton kitchen was comfortable enough for sitting, but not comfortable enough for sleeping. Flint wondered if that was why Garth had pulled it out of his den begrudgingly when Flint had shown up at one o'clock in the morning. The inspector had made the arrangements and Flint only had to tap lightly on the kitchen door to have it opened by Garth.

"Thanks for coming." Garth ground the words out reluctantly. "It wasn't necessary, though. The boys and I can keep Francis safe."

"Like you did tonight?"

Garth grunted. "If you hadn't taken off with her like a wild man, she would have been all right."

"She would have been kidnapped. Maybe worse, with those goons."

The two men measured each other for a moment with their eyes. Garth was the first to look away. "Like I said—thanks for coming."

"You're welcome."

Garth reached behind him and pulled a floor lamp

closer to the chair. He snapped the light on. "I've turned the heat down a little, but you should be warm enough. I've brought a few blankets down."

"Thanks."

Garth smiled. "If you get hungry, there's some cold lobster in the refrigerator."

"Thanks. I'll be fine."

Garth turned to leave the kitchen. "We've got a double lock on all the doors now, and the windows are frozen shut. I don't expect trouble."

"Good."

Garth looked at him and nodded before he started up the stairs.

Flint settled into the chair. He'd spent more hours lately than he wanted to count on Honey's round back, so a chair, even an uncomfortable one, was welcome. The sounds of the kitchen lulled him—the steady hum of the refrigerator, the soft meter of the clock, the low whistle of the blizzard as it started to blow into the area.

Only a fool would be out on a night like tonight, Flint thought as he relaxed. The boss of the rustling outfit wouldn't be able to get replacement men into Dry Creek until at least tomorrow. Tonight they were safe.

Flint half woke while the light was so new it was more black fog than anything. Sometime in the night, he'd left the discomfort of the chair and slept, wrapped in several wool blankets, on the kitchen floor. He'd unstrapped his holster gun and laid it beside his head. He'd used his boots for a pillow, even though, with his six-foot-three frame, that meant his toes were sticking out the end of the blankets. He wondered if he wouldn't have been better to have left the boots on his feet for the night. His dreams hadn't merited a pillow, anyway. He'd tossed and turned, chasing faceless phantoms across a barren landscape until, somehow, the face of Francis appeared and his whole body rested.

The air snapped with cold. Frost edged its way up the windowpane nearest him. But, cold and miserable as it was, Flint woke with one thought drumming through his head—he, Flint L. Harris, miserable man that he was, was married to Francis Elkton. Legally married to her. That had to count for something.

He had a sudden urge to get up and go pick her some flowers like he'd done in that long-ago time. Yellow roses were her favorite. He could almost picture her smelling a bouquet of roses. He decided to close his eyes and let his mind go back to dreaming for a few sweet minutes to see if the face of Francis would return.

Francis hadn't slept. The moonlight filtered in through the small frosted windows in her bedroom. She had lain in her bed and counted the stripes on the faded wallpaper of her old bedroom until she thought she'd go crazy. In the past, counting had always calmed her so she could sleep.

When the counting didn't work, she'd mentally made a list. List making was good. She made a list of the groceries they would need to buy to make lasagna for everyone some day this week. With Sylvia, the kids from her youth center and the ranch hands, they were feeding forty-some people at each meal. Planning ingredients required arithmetic and list making. Francis spent fifteen minutes figuring out how much mozzarella cheese they would need. It didn't help.

Thinking of cheese reminded her of Sam. She didn't question why. She grimaced just remembering him. She supposed he was peacefully sleeping downstairs on the living room sofa. What was she supposed to do with the man? He couldn't have shown up in her life at a worse moment. With luck, he'd see reason in the morning and catch a flight back to Denver.

And Flint—she was still reeling from the knowledge that she had actually been married to him for the past twenty years.

When they'd gotten back to the ranch last night, Garth had gone into the den and pulled out an old business envelope. Francis's name was handwritten on the outside of the sealed envelope, and Garth explained that before he died their father had given it to him to give to Francis when she became engaged. Garth had always assumed it was a sentimental father-to-daughter letter. It wasn't.

Francis had left the whole envelope on the kitchen

table. She'd opened it enough to know the contents were the old divorce papers.

No wonder she was unable to sleep, Francis finally decided around four o'clock. Her whole life had turned upside down in the past twelve hours. She'd seen Flint again. She'd found out he was her husband. She'd thoroughly embarrassed herself to the point that he felt he had to kiss her to save her pride. She'd felt both sixteen and sixty at the same time. It stung that the only reason he was even here in Dry Creek was that he had a job to do. At least she'd had the decency to come back here to mourn their lost love. He hadn't even come back to pick up his family's Bible.

Finally, the darkness of the night started to soften. The hands on her bedside clock told Francis it was almost five o'clock. She'd given up on sleep, and she got out of bed and wrapped a warm robe around her. She might as well set out some sausage to thaw for breakfast.

She had checked last night, and there was a case of sausages in the freezer downstairs. There were one hundred and sixty links in a case.

If Francis hadn't been dividing the number of sausages by the number of breakfast guests, she would have noticed there was something a little too lumpy about the pile of blankets that someone had left on the kitchen floor. But she hadn't wanted to turn on any lights in case they would wake Sam in the living room. She was used to the half-light of early Montana mornings.

Her first clue that something was peculiar about the pile of blankets was the whispered endearment, "Rose." She recognized the voice even as she was tripping on a blanket corner—or was it a boot?—and was falling square into the pile of—

Umph! Chest. Francis felt the breath slam out of her body and then felt her chin solidly resting on a man's chest. She groaned inside. Even if she didn't know the hoarse voice, she'd recognize that smell anywhere— half horse and half aftershave. She moved slightly, and then realized her dilemma. Her elbows were braced one on each side of Flint's chest, and her fuzzy chenille bathrobe was so loosely tied that, if she raised herself up more than an inch or two, any man from Flint's perspective, if he opened his eyes, would see her navel by way of her chin and all of the territory between the two.

Not that—she lifted her eyes slightly to confirm that his eyes were closed—not that he was looking.

Francis studied his eyelids for any betraying twitch that said he was really awake and just sparing them both the embarrassment of the situation. There was none.

Francis let out her breath in relief. A miracle had happened. He hadn't woken up when she fell on him, and if she moved lightly, she would be up and off of him without him even knowing she'd fallen.

The congratulatory thought had no sooner raced through Francis's mind than she had another one—only a dead man wouldn't feel someone falling right on top of him! Francis moved just slightly and cocked her head to the side. She laid her ear down where Flint's heart should be, and the solid pounding reassured her that he was alive.

Francis dismissed the suspicion that he was drunk—she would smell alcohol if that were the case. He must just be so worn out that he'd sleep through anything. She'd heard of that happening.

Flint lay very still. He was afraid if he opened his eyes Francis would stop the delightful wiggling she was doing on his chest. He'd felt the smooth warmth of her cheek as she laid it over his heart. It was sweet and arousing all at the same time. He almost couldn't keep his pulse normal. He sure couldn't keep his eyes completely closed. His eyelids shifted ever so slightly and his eyes opened a slit so that he could see the ivory warmth of Francis—he looked and almost sighed. She could pose for drawings of the goddess Venus rising from her bath.

And then everything changed. Flint could almost see the moment when the warmth of Francis turned to stone.

Francis had managed to locate the belt on her robe and cinch it tighter before she realized what she had interrupted. Flint was dreaming. A floating half-awake dream that kept him in bed even though the only pillows he had were his own boots and his mattress was nothing but hard-as-nails floorboards. A dream that sweet wasn't about some distant movie star or unknown woman. No, Flint was lying there with that silly dream smile on his face because of a woman named Rose. Rose! Suddenly, Francis didn't care if she did wake Flint up.

With the flat of her hands fully open on the floor on either side of Flint, Francis lifted herself up and none-too-carefully rolled off Flint.

"It's you." Flint finally opened his eyes and smiled.

Francis was sitting beside him, a peach-colored fuzzy robe tied around her tighter than a nun's belt. Her hair wasn't combed, and a frown had settled on her forehead.

Francis grunted. "Yeah, it's me. I suppose you were expecting this Rose woman."

"Huh?"

"Not that you aren't entitled to dream about whoever you want to dream about—"

Francis stood up.

Flint lay there. He'd never noticed Francis's toes before—never seen them from this angle before. But right across from him, sitting as they did at eye level to him since he was flat on the floor, he marveled at them. How had he never noticed what dainty little toes she had?

"What are you doing here, anyway?" Francis demanded in a low voice. She didn't want to wake the whole household. "Who let you in?"

"Garth."

Her brother was the densest man on the face of the earth. "I guess Garth would take in anyone on a night like last night."

Flint didn't answer. He suspected Garth might draw the line at letting him in under ordinary circumstances. But he didn't want Francis to know that. "Blistering cold last night."

"Well, now that you're here you might as well stay for breakfast—I just came down to get it started."

Flint deliberately winced as he lifted his head a few inches off the floor and then fell back into the pile of blankets.

Francis took the bait and knelt beside him. "You're hurt? I'm so sorry about falling on you. I tripped and, well—" Francis had reached out and was running her hands lightly over Flint's sides. "Do your ribs feel all right?"

His ribs felt like a hammer was pounding against them, but he knew it was only his heart. Francis was bending over him and her hair was trailing against his chest. It was like being brushed with feathers. Black, glossy feathers. "It's more the sides of my back."

Francis didn't hesitate. To reach his back without

him moving, she had to straddle him again and run both hands along his side.

Flint sighed. There'd been little luxury in his life. Francis's hands felt like silk—or satin—maybe even rose petals.

The sigh was a mistake. Flint knew it the moment Francis's hands stopped.

"You're not hurt at all," she announced abruptly.

Flint grinned. "Can't blame a man for trying."

"You're incorrigible," Francis scolded. She should move. She knew that. But she rather liked staring down at Flint like that. His grin made him look younger than he had since he was nineteen. Only he wasn't nineteen any longer. His early morning whiskers were brushed with gray toward his sideburns. He had a scar on his face that hadn't come from falling out of a tree. And his eyes—his eyes lived in shadows.

Francis didn't realize a tear had fallen from her eye until Flint reached up with a warm hand and wiped it away.

"It's okay," Flint said simply. He didn't move the hand that had found the tear. Instead, he lifted the other hand to cup Francis's face.

Francis heard a grumble behind her, slow and insistent. She didn't want to move. But someone else was up in the sleeping household.

"What's going on here?"

Francis's heart sank. Of all the people sleeping in

the house tonight, this was the last person she wanted to have to deal with right now. "Sam."

Francis turned her head slightly, and Flint dropped his hands from her face. She felt the morning cold keenly after their warmth. Sam had plaid flannel pajamas on, and still he had two blankets wrapped around his shoulders.

"There's no need for you to be up." Francis hoped he would take the hint. "Let the house warm up a little first."

Sam grunted. If he heard the hint, he didn't heed it. "What's going on?"

Francis sighed and moved so that she no longer straddled Flint. "I tripped and fell."

Only a blockhead would buy that explanation, Flint thought in bitter satisfaction. He and Francis had been seconds away from a kiss. Surely, it had been obvious.

"Oh." Sam seemed uncertain. He didn't sound convinced, but he apparently didn't want to challenge Francis. "Well, I need to talk to you."

"Can't it wait?" Francis asked as she adjusted all of the chenille in her robe until she looked more respectable than a grandmother. Once she was adjusted, she glanced at Flint again a little shyly.

Flint noticed the pink in her cheeks even if the blockhead Sam didn't.

"Francis is busy now," Flint offered. "You can talk to her later."

Flint had a problem in life—he didn't know when

to quit fighting a battle. Sometimes, like today, it cost him. He saw it right away in the way Francis's chin went up and her eyebrow raised.

"No one answers for me. I can talk now."

Flint knew he needed to backtrack. Francis wasn't a woman who liked being told what to do. He rolled his blankets around him closer like he was contemplating going back to sleep. "Yeah, I won't be in the way."

Sam started to puff up. "I want to speak to Francis alone. I am, after all, her fiancé."

"Well, that's a problem," Flint said lazily. "Because technically I'm still her husband."

Sam puffed up in earnest. "I doubt that marriage is even valid anymore."

"Don't count on it," Flint said as he stood.

"Please—" Francis started to scold the two men. She fully intended to. She just hadn't counted on Flint standing up right at that moment. Sam was wrapped in plaid flannel and gray wool blankets. He looked like an overgrown boy. But Flint—Flint looked every inch a man. His shirt was unbuttoned and half off his shoulder. Francis had seen his chest muscles when she'd fallen on top of him, but nothing prepared her for the majesty of him standing there. The sight of him made her mouth grow dry. It also made her cranky. "I can talk to whomever I want to talk to."

Flint nodded and smiled. He wasn't going to lose the war on this one just because he couldn't give in on a battle or two. "Of course you can."

Chapter Six

Flint took his time walking down the stairs. There were creaks in steps fourteen and nine. He'd have to remember that. He had taken Francis's hint and left her alone with Sam so that the two of them could talk. For precisely seven minutes. In his opinion, they'd had twenty years to do their talking, and seven minutes was long enough for whatever Sam had to say.

"Where's Francis?" Flint could see into the kitchen from the bottom of the stairs. Someone had finally turned a small light on over the sink, and it outlined the kitchen appliances. The clock over the refrigerator was illuminated, and the hands shone at half past five o'clock. Early morning still in most places, he thought.

"You and I need to talk." Sam ignored the question. He had wrapped the blankets around him more closely and smoothed back his hair. He cleared his throat like he was ready to give a speech, and Flint's heart sank. "We need to settle some things—"

"You and I don't have anything we need to settle," Flint said mildly as he turned so he could see into the living room. Maybe Francis had gone in there. She certainly hadn't gone up the stairs.

"Francis and I think—" Sam persisted.

"Francis asked you to talk to me?" Flint turned.

The words sliced through the air one syllable at a time. Flint didn't raise his voice. In fact Sam had to lean forward to hear the words clearly. But even in their quietness, the words made Sam Goodman stumble and step back.

"Well, we—"

"You didn't answer my question. Did Francis ask you to talk to me?"

"Well, we—"

"And just where is Francis, anyway?" Flint had finally looked completely around.

"She went out to gather the eggs for breakfast."

"Outside! You let her go outside alone!"

Flint didn't breathe again until he stood in the open door of the chicken coop beside Garth's working barn. There was Francis. She was all right. Well, as all right as one could be in a chenille bathrobe and men's boots in the freezing morning after a blizzard.

"Don't do that again." Flint strapped on the gun holster he'd grabbed on his way out the door. He'd run to the chicken coop, following the footprints in the snow. He'd known the footprints could be a decoy— that a clever kidnapper could have set up an ambush for him. But he ran anyway. The air was so cold his breath puffed out white smoke.

Francis looked up. This wasn't her morning. Every time she turned around there was a man looking at her like she was doing something wrong. "I'm only getting the eggs."

Francis slipped her hand under another laying hen and found a warm egg. The chickens weren't used to being visited this early, but they'd behaved with remarkable poise. Maybe it was so cold they weren't interested in protesting. "Sixteen so far."

She wished she'd stopped to do more than comb her hair this morning. The cold would have added pink to her cheeks, but it was an uneven redness and she wished she'd put on some foundation. Or some eyeliner. Her eyes tended to disappear without eyeliner.

She knew she didn't look as good when she first woke up as Flint did. His rough whiskers and tousled brown hair made him look rugged, especially with the morning light starting to shine behind him.

"You are not to go out by yourself." Flint leaned against the doorjamb and said the words clearly. "If you want to go get eggs, I'll take you."

Francis slid her hand under another warm hen. There were several dozen laying boxes in the chicken coop, each stacked on top of another. Every hen had her own nest lined with straw. Francis had looked around earlier to see where the rooster was, but she hadn't seen him. He had been unusually aggressive lately, and she always tried to check on him when she entered the coop.

"You're not still worried about me! You caught the kidnappers."

"We caught the goon guys," Flint explained patiently. Why would the sight of a woman plucking eggs from beneath those sleeping chickens affect him like this? "We still don't know who the local contact person is—and we're a long way from catching the boss of the whole operation."

"Well, certainly they won't want me. I'd think by now they'd give up."

"We're not dealing with juvenile delinquents here. They aren't likely to be distracted just because some little guys in the operation get taken in. No, they'll stay with it. They're in this deep already."

"But what am I supposed to do?" Francis laid the basket of eggs on a shelf and turned to face Flint completely. "I can't live my life in a bubble and you can't guard me forever."

Want to bet? Flint thought. "You can take reasonable precautions."

"I do take reasonable precautions. I've been trained by the city of Denver in hostage survival. And how to deal with a terrorist. I'm as prepared as any average citizen could be."

Flint didn't want to tell her how many average citizens were dead today. "Humor me. Until we find the local informant, I intend to guard you."

"But—"

"No argument. That's the way it's going to be."

"But what about—"

"Don't even ask about Lover Boy inside there. He can wait to be alone with you."

"He's not—"

Flint held up his hand. "And another thing. You're going to have to tell me you want that divorce. If you're so set on getting divorced from me, I'd at least like the courtesy of hearing it from your own lips this time."

"Who said—"

"The envelope's on the kitchen table. Still has the coffee stain from twenty years ago—"

In the shadows of the chicken coop Flint could see that Francis looked tired and worried. All of the vinegar went out of his anger.

"I just think you should ask me this time. Tell it to me straight."

Francis watched Flint turn polite. The brief hope that she'd felt when Flint stormed into the coop died. He didn't intend to fight their fate. "I see."

"It was mostly my fault anyway. I had no business asking you to marry me. I figure your dad knew that."

Francis felt every one of her thirty-eight years.

"You'd be better off with someone like Sam anyway," Flint rambled on. *You can stop me anytime.*

"He'll give you a stable home and—and—ficus. He seems like a decent enough person. Steady."

"Yes, he's steady all right." Francis didn't like the direction this conversation was going. Flint might be totally indifferent to her, but she didn't want him to encourage her to marry another man. She didn't know why he even needed to pretend to care about who she married. And then it hit her. He had his Rose. He probably wanted that divorce. "You don't need to worry about me. I don't intend to press you on anything. You're completely free."

Completely free. The words echoed in Flint's ears. Why did they have to sound like a prison sentence? "I'm not worried."

"Well, you don't need to be," Francis repeated as she gathered herself together. It had been twenty years, for pity's sake. She searched in the pocket of her robe for a hair clip and found one. She was a middle-aged woman and needed to start acting her age.

Francis reached up, twisted her hair into a tidy bun and then clipped it into place. "I'll finish getting these eggs in and fix you some breakfast."

Flint's throat was dry. "Don't bother just for me, unless the others are getting up."

Francis picked up her basket again and returned to her task. "They'll be up soon enough. I may as well get all the eggs."

Francis knew her eyes were blurry. She told herself firmly it was because of the dust in the chicken coop. All that grain and straw made for dust. Dust led to allergies and red eyes. It certainly wasn't tears that made it hard for her to see.

Francis slipped her hand under another feathery body.

Flint had turned to look outside the coop door. A white expanse of smooth snow covered the area around the ranch outbuildings. The only footprints were the ones he and Francis had made. The thick snow made the silence even more pronounced, and it blanketed the low foothills that led up to the Big Sheep Mountains.

Flint was too relaxed. That's what he told himself later.

The indignant screech of the rooster awakened his instincts. Animals were often the first to notice danger. He turned as the feathered black bird half flew out of the box it had been occupying.

Francis screamed.

After looking at the snow, it was hard for Flint to see clearly when he turned to look inside the coop. White dots swam in front of dark shadows. He couldn't swear there wasn't something in some corner. Something that black rooster had just noticed. He didn't have time to even look closely.

Years of training kicked in, and Flint took four giant steps toward Francis and wrapped his arms around her before rolling with her to the floor of the coop. Once they hit bottom, he turned so that his bulk would take any bullet that might come from any corner.

Francis couldn't breathe. She forgot all about being a middle-aged woman in a fuzzy bathrobe. Her heart was beating so fast she could be inside the pages of a French spy novel. She could only see the bottom half of Flint's face, but any doubts she had about the danger she was in faded. Flint was stone-faced serious. Deadly, almost. He truly believed someone might still be after her. He'd pulled the gun out of his shoulder holster.

Dear Lord, someone could really be after me! The realization rose like a prayer to a God she rarely thought of anymore. She wished she had stayed closer to Him. Maybe then this panic wouldn't send her emotions skittering around.

Francis wasn't prepared for the panic she felt. The training sessions she'd had about hostage situations didn't come close to preparing her. "They can have my money."

Flint looked down. Francis was lying on her back beneath him. The clip had fallen out, and her hair spread around her face like black silk. He hadn't realized he'd scared her. "Where's that fool rooster going to spend your money?"

"It's just the rooster?" Francis started to breathe again.

"Looks like." Flint choked back the rest of the reassuring words. He'd spoken too soon. He heard a sound.

Outside. The soft crunch of a foot on snow. Very soft. But there. Definitely there. He shouldn't have given in to the urge to reassure Francis. Unless that rooster wore boots, they were not alone out here.

"Shh." Flint mouthed the warning silently.

Francis felt the coil of Flint's body. Every muscle was alert even though he hadn't moved. Francis willed her body to shrink. She'd heard the footstep, too. It didn't seem fair that Flint was obviously using himself as a shield between her and whoever was outside the chicken coop.

There was no other footstep. Someone outside was listening.

Flint almost swore. That meant whoever was on the other side of that knotted wood wall was military trained. Not that that was necessarily a bad thing, he reminded himself. Amateurs were always more dangerous to deal with than professionals, because amateurs sometimes missed and got the wrong target.

Flint slowly moved so that he was no longer sprawled across Francis.

"Move to the corner," he mouthed silently as he jerked his head in the direction of the right corner.

If Francis went to the right, he'd stay in the middle. That way, just in case there were any bullets, she wouldn't be close enough to him to draw fire. He hoped.

Francis mutely shook her head. She didn't want to

cower in some corner while Flint faced the danger alone. She mouthed, "I can help."

Flint didn't have any more time to argue with her. He knew whoever was outside would be making a move soon.

"Francis?" The low whisper came from outside the chicken coop, and Francis recognized it immediately.

"Garth?"

Flint didn't move his hand from his gun holster until he saw the dark silhouette of Garth Elkton in the open doorway of the chicken coop.

"What in blazes is going on in here?" Garth demanded.

The ground beneath her back was ice-cold, but Francis didn't want to move. Her older brother had always scolded her when she'd misbehaved as a child, and she recognized the same sound in his voice today. "Nothing."

"Nothing?" Garth asked incredulously.

"I was guarding Francis," Flint explained, in his best government-business, don't-bother-me voice. It usually backed people off. It didn't even faze Garth.

"I can see what you are doing," Garth snorted. Francis's brother had obviously rushed out here in a hurry. He'd pulled on a pair of jeans, but he wore nothing over the thermal underwear that covered his chest. "There's not a square inch of light between the two of you. I don't even want to know what you are doing out here rolling around on the ground."

"You think I'd pick a place like this to seduce a woman? At five in the morning? In freezing weather?"

"I think you'd pick any place you could, Romeo. Anyplace. Anytime. It's just that when it's my sister, you go through me first."

Francis looked at the two men and sighed. That's all she needed. A few macho games. "Garth, I'm not a child. I can take care of myself."

Garth looked at her and shook his head. "But the chicken coop?"

"I was gathering the eggs."

"At this hour of the morning?" Garth finally looked around and saw both the basket of eggs and the rooster, strutting aggressively in the corner. Garth seemed to visibly relax. "Well, no wonder you're flat on the ground. Big Ben here doesn't like to get up before the sun. I'm surprised he didn't chase you out of here."

"I think you interrupted him," Flint said. The black rooster was watching the three humans with a growing annoyance in its beady eyes. "He doesn't want to take on all three of us—at least not yet."

"Don't worry, big fella," Garth cooed to the rooster. "We can take a hint. We'll leave you to your beauty sleep."

It took Francis fifteen minutes to pick all of the straw out of her hair. She sat on a straight-backed chair in the kitchen and willed the full light of morning to arrive.

"Well, I didn't know everything was all right," Sam

protested for the tenth time. "I thought I should call the sheriff. What am I to think when I hear a scream and Garth tears out of here like the place is on fire?"

Francis tried to be fair. The fact that Flint had wrapped his body around hers when he thought she was in danger and Sam had merely put a call in to the sheriff did not make Sam a coward. Cautious maybe, but not a coward.

"I can't reach either one of them. That means they're both coming." Flint paced the kitchen with his cellular phone in his hand. "I hate to have the sheriff and Inspector Kahn drive all the way out here when we've got it under control."

"But I didn't know," Sam repeated. "I would never have raised the alarm if I hadn't thought you were both in trouble."

Flint grunted. They were in trouble, all right. Not that Lover Boy had to know about it. "The rooster did make enough noise to raise the dead."

Sam nodded and pulled his blankets closer around his shoulders. "I did what I thought best."

"Of course you did," Francis reassured him. Each time she ran a comb through her hair more straw appeared. She knew what she was doing wrong. She'd given in to vanity and was using a tiny silver comb instead of the working woman's brush she would normally use. And all because Flint insisted on watching her. Well, he wasn't so much watching as guarding. But she wanted him to know she was classy. That she didn't ordinarily lounge around in a fuzzy old robe and pick straw from her hair. She hoped he noticed that the comb was real silver—it was one of her few truly elegant, feminine possessions.

"Well, I expect they'll be here any minute now." Flint nodded toward the basket of eggs on the table. "I think it's only fair that they get some breakfast when they do arrive." He looked at Sam. "You want to scramble the eggs or tackle the pancake batter?"

"Me?" The man looked like Flint had asked him to skin a snake.

"You cook, don't you?" Flint said as he looked around the kitchen. He opened a drawer and pulled out a spatula. Then he reached down and got a glass bowl off a bottom shelf.

"Well, I guess…" Sam stuttered.

"Good," Flint said as he put the bowl on the kitchen table. He hadn't cooked an egg in over a decade, but Lover Boy didn't need to know that. "The inspector likes a little cheese in his scrambled eggs. It's not good for him, but it'll put him in a better mood." Flint opened a canister of flour on the counter. "On second thought, put a lot of cheese in those eggs. It's a long trip out here and the roads are probably packed with snow. He might have had to use a shovel."

"Okay," Sam agreed and then looked at Francis sheepishly. "You'll help me?"

"She can't," Flint said emphatically. He walked toward the refrigerator to get the carton of milk. He hadn't cooked recently, but how hard could it be? He'd read the recipe on the flour sack already. "She needs to go get dressed."

That robe that Francis wore could cover a monk, and Flint would still find it attractive just because he could remember what the soft ridges of the chenille felt like under his hands. And he didn't like her to wear the robe in front of Lover Boy. Sam was slow, but he just might figure out how soft and cuddly Francis was in that robe. Then they'd really have trouble. Flint didn't think he could endure guarding Francis if Lover Boy started hugging her.

"I can put the coffee on first," Francis offered.

"Just show me where the can is and I'll get it going," Flint said.

Flint already knew where the coffee was, but he didn't mind having Francis come over and stand next to him while she reached up on tiptoes to bring the can down from its tall shelf. He could smell her perfume. It was fainter than last night and it was unmistakably mixed with the smell of chicken, but he found that he thoroughly liked it.

"Two scoops," Francis instructed as she handed the gold can over to Flint. "It says three in the directions, but it's too much."

Flint nodded. "Don't worry. We'll have breakfast ready in no time."

* * *

The smell of coffee was rich when there was a knock on the kitchen door fifteen minutes later.

"That'll be them," Flint said as he wiped his hands on the towel he'd wrapped around his waist. "Put the eggs in the skillet."

The inspector liked the extra cheese in his eggs and he didn't fuss too much about being called out on a cold winter morning. Sheriff Wall didn't complain at all.

"Glad to be away from them," the sheriff muttered when Flint apologized for the false alarm. Sheriff Wall had left his snow boots by the door and his parka on a nearby chair.

"I suppose they're rattled by the arrest." Flint sympathized. He'd grown to know the three men better than he wanted when he had them staked out. "First time for them, I'd bet."

Sheriff Wall snorted. "They ain't rattled. They keep going on about their rights."

"We read them their rights."

"Oh, those rights they have down pat. It's the other rights they're adding to the list. Some legal mumbo jumbo about humane treatment of prisoners. To them, that means a right to clean sheets. And softer pillows. And doughnuts!" Sheriff Wall stopped as though he still couldn't believe it. "Doughnuts! I asked them if they saw any all-night doughnut shop in these parts. I'd be out getting doughnuts for myself if there were any to be had within thirty miles. Told them they could have their bowl of oatmeal and be grateful for it. We don't run no four-star restaurant here."

"Doughnuts would be nice," Sam said a little wistfully. His banker look had worn off, and he looked disheveled now that he had a little flour on his pajamas and his hair was uncombed. "Don't even have to cook them."

"You're doing fine, Lover Boy. Just grate a little more cheese." Flint turned his attention to the pancake he was frying. He had poured a perfect circle of dough on the hottest place on the griddle. He'd even slipped a pat of butter underneath it. He'd done everything he could to make this pancake melt-in-the-mouth perfect. He'd timed it to the opening of the door upstairs. He smiled. He was right on target.

"Something smells good," Francis said as she walked into the kitchen.

"Good morning." Inspector Kahn smiled at Francis.

Francis had showered and washed her hair in a peach shampoo Sylvia had given her. The smell lingered, and she put on some peach hand lotion, as well. She'd scrubbed her face until her cheeks were pink and then put on a light lip gloss. She thought about putting eyeliner and eye shadow on but she didn't want anyone to think she was making a fuss. It was enough that she pulled out the ivory cashmere sweater she'd gotten for Christmas last year and put on her gold earrings.

"Sorry about the mix-up," Francis said to the inspector as she sat down at the kitchen table. She studiously avoided looking at Flint over by the stove. "I should have considered the consequences before I went out to get the eggs. I usually do, you know. I'm in planning—for cities. I know that one thing leads to another and to another."

"I know your job history."

"You do?"

"Of course," the inspector said as he raised his coffee cup to his lips. "We made brief profiles on everyone in Dry Creek when this rustling started."

"You mean I was a *suspect?*"

"Not really." The inspector gave a quick smile and looked toward Flint. "We—even Flint—figured you weren't too likely."

"Well, I certainly wouldn't steal cattle from my own brother."

"Oh, no, that wasn't the reason we ruled you out. Actually, Garth being your brother made you more likely. Maybe you had a grudge. Maybe you figure you should have inherited more when your father passed away."

"I never gave it a thought."

The inspector shrugged. "People do. In the best of families. Whether it's cattle or stocks and bonds."

"Well, Flint would know that I'd never—" Francis started to protest again and stopped. She had no idea what Flint thought of her or had thought of her for the past twenty years.

"Pancake?" Flint interrupted as he set a plate on the table that held a perfectly round, perfectly browned pancake.

"Thank you."

"Would you like some coffee, too?"

"I can get her coffee if she wants it," Sam said. The other man had left his assigned duties of chopping onions for the next breakfast shift and walked over to the table.

Flint noticed Francis wince as she got a whiff of Sam's hands. Flint hadn't spent twenty years fighting crime for nothing. He could set someone up with the best of them.

"I've already got the pot," Flint said as he reached back and pulled the pot off the stove. "I'll take care of Francis."

"You don't need to—I've known her longer than you have," Sam said, tight-lipped. He didn't move back to the counter where he had been chopping onions. "You can't just waltz in here and take over."

"I'm not taking over," Flint said mildly. "Just doing my job. Pouring her some coffee, that's all."

"She's wearing my sweater," Sam said triumphantly as he finally turned.

"You bought her that cashmere?"

Sam nodded. "For Christmas."

Flint didn't like that. A man didn't buy a woman something as soft as cashmere without running his hands all over it, usually with the woman inside it.

Flint found he didn't like the thought of Sam touching Francis. He didn't like the idea of Francis wearing that sweater, either.

"We're going to have to be going," the inspector said as he pushed his chair away from the table.

"Yeah," Sheriff Wall agreed. "Roads have been closed to everything but four-wheel drives. I should get back to the office unless anyone needs me."

"I didn't know the snow was that bad." Flint cheered up. "You think it's high enough to keep the bad guys out for a while?"

The sheriff shrugged. "The Billings airport has been closed since last night. Even if they could fly anyone in from the West Coast, they'd be stuck in Helena. And most of the rental cars would never make it to Dry Creek."

"That means I'm not in danger?" Francis asked in relief. "Flint doesn't need to keep guarding me?"

The thought of Flint leaving didn't please Francis. But she would like to know if he would stay with her even if he didn't need to guard her because it was his job.

"Now, I wouldn't say you're out of danger," the inspector said slowly as he looked at the scowl on Flint's face and then at Francis. "The odds of trouble have gone down, but they haven't disappeared. I'd say you're in danger until we figure out who the informant around here is. Until then, you'll need to be guarded."

"You mean someone who's already here is the informant?"

The inspector nodded. "Someone who has been here all along. The rustlers are getting a local tip-off."

"I don't suppose you could be wrong?"

"Not much chance."

Francis squared her shoulders and looked at the inspector. "Then we have work to do. I'm happy to help figure out who the informant is—and see if it is someone local. I'm pretty good at setting up a cross-tabbed table—if you want to look at who has been around at different times."

"You'd be working with Flint," the inspector said. "Might be good for you both."

"Oh."

Flint grunted. It didn't escape his notice that Francis was in a mighty hurry to get away from him. You'd think a woman would like a man who was spending so much effort working to keep her alive.

"Why don't you set up shop at the hardware store in Dry Creek?" the inspector suggested. "I think it might be good for people around here to see that the FBI is doing something—their taxes at work, that sort of thing."

"That'd be a good place." Francis ate the last piece of her pancake. "It's more businesslike there. We won't be distracted."

And I won't be distracted, Francis vowed. There was a step-by-step path in every relationship, and she fully realized that she and Flint could not take the next step in getting to know each other again until this rustling business was settled.

"We could try the café instead," Flint offered.

"You're hungry?" Francis stood up from the table. "Of course, you probably don't like eggs and pancakes—I can fix—"

"I like pancakes just fine," Flint protested as he waved her back to her chair. "I just made batter for another dozen more."

"Well, then, why go to the café?"

"A café has candles," Flint explained wearily. "I thought we'd like a candle on the table."

Now she understood, Francis thought. Flint wanted to burn any paper they wrote on right at the table. Her face blanched. He was right, of course. There could be an informant around any corner. A dangerous informant.

Flint sighed. He hadn't made that many romantic suggestions to women in the past few years, but he couldn't believe it was a promising sign when the woman's face went ten shades whiter. Times couldn't have changed so much that a candlelit dinner—or lunch—wasn't considered romantic.

Chapter Seven

The café wasn't open yet so Flint had to content himself with taking Francis to the hardware store. It was nearly impossible to date someone in a place like Dry Creek. Especially when the woman you were dating didn't know you were courting her. All this talk of crime didn't set a very romantic mood. And a hardware store! There wasn't even a dim light anywhere. At least not one that wasn't attached to a fire alarm.

Flint was tempted to ask the clerk behind the counter if he could borrow the small radio he had plugged in by his stool. They might get lucky and hear a country-and-western love song. But the clerk was Matthew Curtis, a minister who had recently gotten married and was probably in some romantic haze of his own.

Matthew had married Glory Becker, the woman who had become famous locally as the flying angel in Dry Creek's Christmas pageant. Flint hadn't been in Dry Creek then, but he'd read reports. He'd even heard the gossip about how the angel had brought the minister back to God. A man like Matthew wasn't likely to let folks listen to anything but hymns, and that sure wouldn't help a man's courting.

But that wasn't the only reason Flint hesitated. Flint was reluctant to ask a minister for anything, even a minister who was now a clerk in a hardware store. Flint half expected the man to question him about the Bible Flint still carried with him. Flint knew he could have left the book in the pickup he had borrowed from the inspector, but he didn't. He liked having his grandmother close by—wished she were here now with her brusque no-nonsense approach to life.

"It couldn't be number twenty-six," Francis announced as she consulted the notebook she'd been writing in all morning. She'd given each person in Dry Creek over the age of sixteen a number so that she could be more objective about them. Flint had cautioned her that children under the age of sixteen were also capable of crime, but she wouldn't listen. She insisted no child in Dry Creek could be involved. "Number twenty-four is sweet. And he wouldn't know a Hereford from a Guernsey. I can't see how he'd ever set up an operation like that. I think maybe I should delete people who don't know the cattle business, too."

Francis wished she could delete all the suspects in Dry Creek. It made her feel old to realize that someone she had known all her life could be stealing from the ranchers around here. Anyone from Dry Creek would know the thin line that separated some of the ranchers from success and failure. A rustling hit could mean some of them would need to sell out. Who would do that?

They were both sitting on the hard-back chairs that formed a half circle around the Franklin stove that was the centerpiece of the store. Flint was relieved to find out that this part of Dry Creek at least was the way he remembered it. Usually, an assortment of men would be sitting around this stove sharing worries about the weather or information about crop prices. But the snow had kept them home today.

"I remember you raised a Hereford calf for 4-H that year," Flint mused leisurely. The snow outside would keep even the most determined villians away. The FBI had already analyzed all the people in Dry Creek. Flint knew Francis wouldn't come up with anything new. The inspector had assigned her the task so she'd have something to worry about while she was with Flint. It wouldn't have taken a tenth of the inspector's powers of observation to see that Francis was all nerves around him, Flint thought. It'd take more than a fancy flowchart to make her happy with him guarding her. "You even named him—what was it?"

"Cat."

Flint chuckled. "Yeah, I remember now. You had wanted to have a kitten instead, but your dad said you were in cattle country and—if you were that set on having a pet—it was a calf or nothing."

"It could be number sixteen." Francis looked up from her list and frowned slightly. "I hope not, though. He has two little kids and his wife has been sick a lot. He needs the money, I'm sure, but—"

"You loved that Cat of yours," Flint continued staunchly. It was real hard to strike a light note when Francis insisted on worrying over the guilt of her neighbors. "Bet there never was a calf like him."

"Her." Francis finally looked up from her list. "I picked a her so that she could go on to be a mother and have calves of her own."

Something about the tightness of Francis's voice warned him. Francis had always wanted children. Should have had children. That was the one dream she'd shared with him back then. "I hadn't thought about that—"

"It's not important."

"Of course, it's important," Flint protested. Until now, he'd just thought of those wasted twenty years as a trick being played on him. He hadn't had time to adjust and realize what they had meant for Francis. "You were meant to be a mother. That's all you ever wanted to be."

Francis blinked and looked at her list. "We don't always get what we want in life."

"I know, but—" Flint had a sudden flash of a little girl who would have looked like Francis. He'd never realized the sum total of his own loss until that minute. He could have had a daughter. Or a son. His life could have meant something to someone besides the FBI. "How could this all have happened?"

Francis looked at Flint. She'd been nervous all morning around him—wondering what he thought of her hair, of her clothes, of the words she spoke. All of those things suddenly didn't seem so important now as she looked at him, the defeat plain on his face.

"It certainly wasn't your fault," Francis comforted him softly.

"Well, it wasn't yours, either."

"I could have had more faith in you."

Flint snorted. "You were a kid. What did we know?"

"It was just one of those things."

"Like fate?" Flint challenged. He had fought many enemies in his life, but he'd never tackled fate before. It was like boxing with a shadow. There was no way to win. "You're saying it was our fate?"

"Well, maybe not fate, but—" Francis glanced over at Matthew and lowered her voice. She'd given this a lot of thought in the hours she'd lain awake last night. She'd remembered snatches of what she had learned in Sunday school as a child when her mother used to take her. "But it must have been God's will."

"Well, I don't think much of God then if He's got nothing better to do than mess up the lives of two young kids so crazy in love they couldn't see straight."

Flint knew he was speaking too loudly for Francis's comfort. She kept looking at Matthew. "And I don't care who hears me on that one. It wasn't fair."

Francis looked at Matthew. She remembered pictures of God in his long white robes. She had never considered the possibility that God was unkind until last night. He had always seemed distant, like her father. But never unkind. "I'm sorry."

Matthew stopped polishing the old lantern that was sitting on the counter. "Don't be. I happen to agree with Flint there."

"You do?" Flint was as surprised as Francis.

Matthew nodded. "It's what drove me out of the ministry."

"So you agree with me?" Flint asked for clarification. He thought ministers always defended God. That was their job. "You're not taking God's side in this?"

Matthew laughed. "I don't know about there being sides to this issue. I know it's not fair—" he assessed Flint "—and you—you're probably sitting there wishing there was some guy you could arrest and make pay for all of this."

Flint gave a short, clipped laugh. "There's something about an arrest that levels the field again."

"Only there's no one to arrest," Matthew continued. He walked around the counter and stepped over to the small table that had been set up next to the window. A coffeepot sat on the table, and the flavor of good coffee had been drifting through the air for some time now. Matthew turned to Flint and Francis. "Coffee?"

"Yes, thanks," Flint said as Francis nodded.

"The most frustrating thing about injustice is that usually we can't do anything about it," Matthew said as he poured coffee into three thick, white mugs.

"You're saying there's nothing we can do about bad things?" Francis asked.

"Now, I didn't say that." Matthew turned to look at them again. "Sugar or cream? Or maybe a flavor? I've got some orange flavor. Or raspberry."

"Plain for me," Francis said.

"Me, too." Flint watched as Matthew balanced the three cups on a small tray and brought them over to where he and Francis were sitting.

"We need to get some TV trays around here," Matthew apologized as he pulled up a wooden box with his foot. "The regular clientele never was one for fussing, but lately—"

"Since Glory's been around," Francis finished for him in a teasing tone.

"Well, you have to admit she does bring a whole new brand of people into the store here." Matthew laughed and then sobered. "I'm blessed to have her in my life."

Matthew carefully set the coffee cups on the box within easy reach of both of them. "And it's a blessing I almost let get away just because I was stuck on the same problem that is plaguing you two."

"And that would be?" Flint prodded. He didn't know the ex-minister well, but he'd watched him at the wedding reception the other night. Matthew had had kind words for everyone present.

"Being so preoccupied with my anger toward God for what had happened in the past that I was totally unable to accept any blessings in the here and now."

"But you still hold God responsible?" The conversation was getting under his skin, and Flint realized he really wanted to know what the minister thought.

"Of course," Matthew agreed as he pulled up another straight-back chair and joined them in front of the Franklin stove. "But it's not always that easy. Like for you two—you can sit there and be mad at God for letting you be pulled apart twenty years ago or you can sit there and thank Him for bringing you back together now."

"But we lost so much," Flint said.

"Maybe," Matthew said as he took a sip of hot coffee. "But I'd guess there's things you gained along the way, too. Who would you be today if you hadn't parted back them?"

"We'd be chicken farmers," Flint said, and smiled. "Living on my grandmother's old place. But at least the windows would be fixed."

"And I would have had a child," Francis added shyly and cupped her hands around her mug as though she had a sudden chill.

"Maybe," Matthew said. "But then maybe something would have happened and that child would be nothing but a heartache to you—maybe there'd be a sickness or who knows what. The point I'm making is that when God takes us down a path all He asks is that we're willing to go. He doesn't guarantee that there won't be troubles on that path. All He guarantees is that He'll walk it with us."

"That sounds so easy," Flint said.

"Doesn't it?" Matthew agreed as he set his coffee cup down. He grinned at Flint. "Trust me, it's not as easy as it sounds."

Flint reached down beside his chair and picked up the Bible he'd lain there earlier. "My grandmother tried to pray that kind of faith into me when I was here with her."

"Well, she must have succeeded," Francis said.

Flint looked at her in surprise.

"You wrote a verse next to our marriage lines," Francis explained softly. "It must have meant something to you at the time."

"I didn't write any verse," Flint said as he flipped the Bible open to the center pages where the family record was kept. He looked down and saw the writing. "It must have been my grandmother. She must have written something down. And here I thought I'd covered my tracks and that she didn't know—"

"Song of Solomon," Francis said as she stood and looked over Flint's shoulder. "Verses six and seven— chapter eight. Let's read it."

"Now?" Flint looked at the Bible.

"Why not? If your grandmother had something to say about our marriage, I'd like to hear it."

Flint shrugged and started to page through the early part of the Bible. "I guess you're right."

Flint skimmed the verses his grandmother had selected before he cleared his throat and read them aloud. "Set me as a seal upon thine heart, as a seal upon thine arm: for love is strong as death… Many waters cannot quench love, neither can the floods drown it—" Flint's voice broke and he couldn't continue.

"Those are sweet words," Francis said softly. "I thought she might have picked something about the folly of youth or trusting strange women."

Flint smiled. "My grandmother liked you."

"She must have thought I left you, as well."

Flint looked at Francis. "We were all a-tangle, weren't we? So many if onlys—"

"It just wasn't right."

"No, no, it wasn't." Flint looked at Matthew. "You know, you seem like a good person. But I just don't see how God could let this happen."

Matthew nodded, rather cheerfully, Flint thought. "So you think He could have stopped you?"

"Stopped me?"

"Yeah, when you decided to run off to Vegas that night—you must think God could have stopped you."

"Not unless He sent in a tornado."

The door to the hardware store opened, and a blast

of snowy wind blew in with the well-wrapped figure of an older woman. She had to remove two head
scarves before Flint recognized Mrs. Hargrove.

"A tornado," she gasped when she could speak.
"Don't tell me we're getting a tornado on top of this?"

"Of course not," Matthew assured her. "This is
Montana, not Kansas."

"Well, nothing would surprise me anymore," Mrs.
Hargrove muttered as she removed her gloves and set
them on the counter. "Everything in Dry Creek has
gone topsy-turvy these days."

"Something must be happening to bring you out in
this kind of weather," Matthew agreed calmly as he
walked over and helped Mrs. Hargrove struggle out of
her coat. Flecks of snow still clung to the plaid wool.
"Why don't you sit by the fire and tell us all about it
while I get you a cup of that cocoa you like."

"Oh, it's just old man Gossett." Mrs. Hargrove
started to mutter as she walked to an empty chair
and sat down with a sigh. "I swear I don't know what
that man is thinking."

"Mr. Gossett?" Matthew said in surprise as he
turned from the coat hook behind the counter. "I've
never heard anyone complain about him before—I
mean except for the usual—his drinking and his cats."

"That man—I swear he's stretched my Christian
patience until there's only a thin thread left," Mrs.
Hargrove continued and then looked at Flint. "Oh,

I'm sorry—you probably don't know him. I wouldn't want you to think he's typical of the folks hereabouts."

Flint had never seen Mrs. Hargrove so flustered. He turned to Francis. "What number is he?"

"Old man Gossett?"

"Yes."

"Why, I—" Francis was scanning her paper. "I think I forgot to put him on the list."

"Forget anyone else?"

Francis was running her finger down the column. "Let me do a quick count—no, I'm only one short."

"He's an easy one to forget," Mrs. Hargrove said with irritation still fresh in her voice. "Forgets himself often enough—as long as he has a bottle he's never seemed to care about anything or anyone."

"What's his name?"

Mrs. Hargrove looked at him blankly. "Why, Gossett. Mr. Gossett."

"His first name."

"Well, I don't know." Mrs. Hargrove frowned in thought. "He's always called old man Gossett. I try to call him Mr. Gossett myself because it reminds me he's one of God's creatures, but I don't think I've ever heard him called anything else. Just old man Gossett or sometimes Mr. Gossett."

"Didn't his father settle Dry Creek?"

"Back in the big drought in the twenties," Mrs. Hargrove said as she nodded. "Folks here talk about it sometimes—our parents and grandparents all pretty much had settled around these parts after the Homestead Act of 1902. But they wouldn't have stayed if it hadn't have been for the Gossett who was alive then. He started this town and named it Dry Creek to remind folks that they could survive hard times. Made us a community."

"So Dry Creek owes the Gossett family a lot?"

Mrs. Hargrove shrugged. "In a way. Of course, it would be different if it was the first Gossett. I was a little girl way back then, but I remember him still. Quite an impressive man. Never could figure out why his son didn't measure up."

"You must remember," Francis interrupted. She was chewing on the tip of a pencil. "If you knew old man Gossett when he was a boy, you must have known his name."

"Why, you're right," Mrs. Hargrove said. "It's just he's been old man Gossett for so many years—but you're right, back then he wouldn't have been—" She closed her eyes and then smiled. "Harold. It's Harold. Little Harry, they called him. Little Harry Gossett."

Mrs. Hargrove was clearly pleased with herself as Francis added the man's full name to her list.

"Now he's eighty-three," Francis declared.

"Eighty-three in what, dear?" Mrs. Hargrove leaned over to see Francis's list more clearly.

"You didn't tell us your news." Flint interrupted the older woman quickly before she could ask any more questions. He didn't relish telling her that all

her friends and neighbors were suspects in aiding the
rustlers. So far, most of the people in Dry Creek all
believed the rustlers were outsiders, from the west
coast, they figured. They would never look at their
own ranks.

"Why, bless me, you're right," Mrs. Hargrove said
as she straightened in her chair. "And after I hurried
all the way over here."

"It's not the boys, is it?" Matthew asked in alarm.

Mrs. Hargrove smiled. "Your boys are fine. They're
with Glory. It's just that Mr. Gossett—Harold—has
been trying to talk Glory into driving him into Miles
City, and I was afraid she'd weaken and say yes." Mrs.
Hargrove looked around sternly. "I told them both no
one had any business driving anywhere in weather like
this and that if all he wanted was a bottle of something
to keep him warm until the roads cleared he'd be welcome to my vanilla."

"I don't think a bottle of vanilla would keep him
happy enough." Flint almost smiled.

"I read in the newspaper that vanilla is ninety-nine
percent alcohol and alcoholics sometimes tip back the
bottle," Mrs. Hargrove announced.

"Unless you have a gallon of it, though, it's not
going to be enough."

"Well, Glory might give him hers, too."

Flint had a mental picture of all the ladies of Dry
Creek emptying their cupboards to keep Mr. Gos-

sett happy during the blizzard. It was neighborliness at work.

"Do you think we should be giving him anything?" Francis worried. "Maybe now's a good time for him to quit."

"He doesn't want to quit." Mrs. Hargrove grunted in disapproval. "He wants to talk someone into braving this weather just to take him to a store. Or a bar, more like it."

"I could go talk to him," Flint offered. He would like to get reacquainted with the man Dry Creek had forgotten even while he lived in their midst. "I'll tell him there's a fine for endangering lives or something like that."

"Scare him?" Mrs. Hargrove asked, but Flint couldn't tell whether or not she liked the idea.

Flint shrugged. "Just slow him down. If he can wait until tomorrow, the roads will be better."

"The wind might stop, too," Matthew offered. "The forecast says this storm will blow through tonight."

"It really is too bad he can't quit," Mrs. Hargrove said softly. "That little boy wasn't so bad, now that I remember him from all those years ago. Wonder whatever happened?"

Flint kept his hands in his gloves while he knocked on Harold Gossett's front door. Flint had convinced Francis to wait outside in the pickup for him while he spoke with Mr. Gossett. It was probably nothing, but Flint had a feeling about this man. If anyone had a grudge against Dry Creek, he'd bet it was this Gossett fellow. He knocked again.

A shadow crossed the peephole in Gossett's front door. Funny, Flint thought, no one else in Dry Creek felt the need for a peephole. Even if they locked their doors, they just called out and asked who was outside. But you couldn't arrest someone for having a peephole in their door. If you could, all of California would be in jail. Maybe Gossett just wanted to avoid his neighbors as much as they wanted to avoid him.

The door opened a crack. The inside of the house was dark. A subdued light came in through the blinds that were drawn at each of the windows. There wasn't much furniture. An old vinyl recliner. A television that was blinking. A wooden table pushed against one wall with rows of beer bottles stacked up underneath it. The house smelled of cats, although it wasn't an unpleasant smell.

"Hi," Flint said as he took his glove off and offered his hand to the man inside the house. "My name's Flint Harris."

"Essie's grandson." The older man nodded. The man was heavyset with a looseness to his face that came from drinking too much. He was wearing a pair of farmer overalls over thermal underwear that had holes in both of the elbows. If the man was planning to go to Miles City today, he certainly wasn't worried about making a good impression once he got there.

"I wanted to introduce myself," Flint said. He was beginning to doubt his suspicions about the man. He certainly didn't look like he'd come into any money lately. Not with the way he lived. "I've tied my horse out back on the other side of your yard a few times of late."

"Ain't my property."

"I know," Flint continued. "I checked it out first. Still, I thought you might have been curious."

"Nope."

The older man started to close the door. Flint moved his foot to block it.

"Just wanted to talk to you about your conversation with Glory Becker—I mean, Glory Curtis."

Gossett's eyes jumped slightly in guilt. "I wasn't talking to her."

"That's good, because it would be foolish to try to drive into Miles City today. I was worried when I heard that's what you were planning."

The older man swallowed. "I wasn't going no-where."

"That's good," Flint repeated. He was beginning to see why Mrs. Hargrove found the man exasperating. "See that you don't. At least not until the blizzard breaks. Nothing's that important."

The old man nodded vacantly. Flint had seen that kiss-off-to-the-feds face enough times to know that it didn't mean the man was agreeing to anything. Still, there wasn't much else Flint could do. He moved his foot so the door could close.

Francis opened the door on the driver's side so Flint could slip into the pickup.

"What do you know of Gossett's drinking style?" he asked as he turned the key to start the motor.

"He drinks lots."

"But lots of what? He's got enough beer in there to keep an army happy, but he might be out of something else. Maybe he uses beer as a chaser for hard liquor and he's out of hard liquor?"

Francis shrugged. "Must be. Why else would he be so set on going into Miles City?"

"Maybe he's out of cat food. I understand he's got lots of cats."

"Yes, but he could borrow cat food from anyone in Dry Creek. Folks often borrow back and forth in the winter months instead of making a special trip to Billings or Miles City."

"Maybe he's got a lady friend he visits?"

"Old man Gossett?" Francis asked in genuine surprise.

"Well, you never know," Flint said as he backed away from the Gossett house. At least he had Francis thinking about romance again.

"Old man Gossett," she repeated.

Well, maybe not romance, Flint thought wryly as he started driving down the short road that was Dry

Creek. She sounded more like she was thinking of a circus act.

"Oh, look," Flint said as he drove level with the café. "It's open"

A black Open sign was hanging in the window of the café under another more permanent sign that read Jazz and Pasta.

"We could stop for coffee," Flint offered.

The interior of the café smelled of baking bread and spicy tomato sauce. Black-and-white linoleum covered the floor, and several square tables were set up for dining.

Ah, here we go, Flint thought as he saw a small candle in the middle of each table.

"Allow me." Flint held the chair for Francis.

Now they were getting somewhere, Flint thought.

His heart sank when Francis pulled out her checklist.

"I think we need to consider thirty-four, too," she said. "He got his hair cut."

"His hair cut?"

"Yeah, and it wasn't anyone around here who did it," Francis said. "You can't get a cut like that in Miles City even—I'd say he's been to Spokane or Boise."

Flint sighed. Francis would have been a terror on the force. "You want to talk about some guy's haircut?"

"It could be important," Francis persisted. *Besides,*

I don't know what to say to you. I'm afraid of saying anything that's going to rock this boat we're on.

Our lives could be important, too, Flint felt like saying. But he didn't. Maybe Francis was right. Maybe it was too late for them to go back to what they once were.

The minister, Matthew, had seemed hopeful, saying they should thank God for bringing them together now instead of being angry for being separated earlier. But even if God was bringing them together now, why was He bothering? It seemed more like a cosmic joke than anything—bring the two young lovers back together so they could realize what they had missed during all those years.

Flint let his hand drop to the Bible that sat on the seat next to him. He felt comforted just touching the thing—maybe more of his grandmother's faith had gotten under his skin than he ever realized. He had a sudden urge to pray and wished he knew how. Wished that words would form on his lips to express the confusion inside his heart. But his lips were silent.

Chapter Eight

A teenager walked out of the back of the restaurant. She was wearing a white chef's apron over faded jeans, and her shaggy hair was dyed a bright copper red. As she walked she pulled an ordering pad out of the apron pocket. She snapped her chewing gum. "Can I get something for you folks?"

"Hi, Linda," Francis greeted the teen. "How's business?"

"Not bad," Linda said and smiled. "We've decided to open for the breakfast crowd now—so far so good— we got seven breakfast orders from Sheriff Wall already this morning. We didn't have doughnuts, but Jazz makes a mean biscuit served with honey. The sheriff bought a dozen extra biscuits. Asked me to cut little holes in them so they looked like doughnuts," Linda shrugged and smiled again. "And folks around here think I'm weird because I got my nose pierced."

The teenager tilted her face so Flint and Francis could see the sparkling stud in the side of her nose.

"Nice," Flint said with a smile. Linda's face was scrubbed clean and fresh-looking.

"Just the right touch," Francis agreed. She was glad Linda had forgotten about the black lipstick she sometimes wore.

The teen took their order for coffee and biscuits and called out, "Two for a combo—make it sticky!" to someone in the back before walking over to the coffee urn that rested on the counter at the side of the large room.

"What number is she?" Flint whispered to Francis.

"Linda?" Francis seemed surprised. "Well, she's number twenty-seven, but I don't really think—"

"She's in a public place," Flint reminded her. He enjoyed watching Francis's eyes. Their gray depths had lost all semblance of calm. "Good place to get information. Overhear talk about cattle. Maybe know when a rancher is sick and not making his usual rounds."

"But the ranchers don't hang out here," Francis protested firmly. "Besides, their café has only been open since Christmas Eve. Most of the rustling happened before that."

"True." Flint liked the way Francis's eyes got passionate in their defense of the young woman. He tried a different tactic. "How old do you think she is?"

"Eighteen, I think."

"And this Jazz guy that works the restaurant with her?"

"Duane? A year or two older."

"Just like us," Flint said softly. "That was the age we were when we got married."

The old man looked in the back window of the café. He knew that this window beside the black cookstove wouldn't be frosted up and would still be hidden from the people inside the café. He had to stand in a snowbank to get a good view through the window, but that didn't bother him. He'd be a lot colder if he didn't find a way to get to that bus in Miles City.

What were they talking about? The FBI man and Francis. She was a smart one, she was. He'd known her mother. She had been the same way. Never did understand why she had married Elkton when she could have married him. He'd been somebody back then before the drinking.

The FBI man thought he was so clever, coming to his door with some nonsense about the roads. But the old man wasn't fooled. Since when did the federal government care about cars driving in snow?

Besides, he had seen the agent look in his trash barrel the other day and take out an empty jelly jar that had broken. The jelly was crab apple, left over from a summer when Mrs. Hargrove had canned some jelly for him from his tree. The agent put the jar back, but the old man wasn't sure if he'd taken a fingerprint off of it somehow. The agent must have. What did the government care about empty jelly jars?

It all made the old man nervous. He had to get out of town. That Glory Becker wasn't much of an angel as far as he was concerned. Wouldn't even drive him to Miles City in that Jeep of hers. And she had good tires. He'd checked them out. He'd half considered stealing them to put on his pickup, but he couldn't use a tire iron anymore. Couldn't drive his pickup even if it had tires on it, when it came right down to it. He hadn't driven anything for a good twenty years now— he'd be surprised if he'd know how, especially if he was behind the wheel of a newfangled car.

He was an old man, plain and simple. He was surprised the Becker woman hadn't agreed to help him. What kind of Christian charity was she showing—she just said no and kept talking about the twins. You'd think she was their real mother the way the woman went on about them. Little Joshua and little Joey. It made the old man want to gag. He knew it wouldn't hurt the little creatures to stay home alone for a day. Might even do them some good. Take some of the happy shine off their infernal faces.

Disgusting. And no help at all.

He'd have to try something else. And soon. Before any more snow got dumped on the roads and the bus got canceled.

Francis felt her nerves stretch tighter than a new drum. The day had stiffened her like a board. She was grateful Garth had convinced Sam to spend the day with some of the ranch hands in the bunkhouse. She suspected they were teaching him to play poker. If they were, he'd be there until supper trying to win his money back.

She wished she had something like that to worry over. She'd tried to keep her mind organized, but she hadn't succeeded. Her thoughts kept straying—kept going back to the wistful look on Flint's face when he realized that Linda and her fiancé, the Jazz Man, were the same age she and Flint had been when they eloped to Las Vegas.

Linda and the Jazz Man were working toward their dream. The two teenagers had sat with her and Flint after they had their biscuits and talked about the farm they planned to buy when they'd saved enough money. Their faces shone with their dream. They were halfway to their goal already. Every dollar helped. They had looked happy when Flint offered to pay them fifty dollars if they would go out to his grandmother's old place and bring Honey back to the small building behind the café so they could feed and water her for a day or two.

Francis sighed. She wished her own dreams were as simple to fulfill.

"You okay? Flint asked me to check."

Francis glanced up and saw her brother standing in the doorway and looking at her in concern. She had told Flint she was going into the den and didn't want to be disturbed. It was taxing to be guarded—especially by Flint. They'd spent the whole day together. It was almost time for supper, and Francis needed some time alone before she offered to help the others prepare the meal.

"Yeah, sure," Francis answered. "Tell Flint I'm fine."

She was sitting in the old rocker in the den. The room was growing darker as the last of the day's light seeped in through the frost-covered windows. The furniture in Garth's house had been replaced in the past few years, but the rocker was one thing that would never leave. This was the chair their mother used to sit in when she read to them when they were each small. Garth kept it in the corner of the den that couldn't be seen from the door. Francis suspected he used it as an escape place, too.

"Want to talk about it?" Garth offered as he pulled over a straight-backed office chair and sat down. "I suppose you're still mad at Dad."

Francis grimaced. "He could have told me. I spent so much time being angry with Flint. Even if Flint had gone on with his life by then, Dad should have told me."

"Probably meant to," Garth mused. "Dad was never much good at talking, and I'd guess it got harder to tell you as the years went on."

Francis hesitated and then took the plunge. "And I've been thinking about Mom, too."

Garth sat still. "Oh."

"Do you remember her taking us to church? I always remember her getting you and me ready and taking us to Sunday school and then church."

"Yeah." Garth was noncommittal.

"Why did she?"

Garth seemed surprised. "Why? I never thought about it. She just did. That was part of her being Mom."

"Do you think it meant something to her? You were older than me when she died, and I can't remember." Francis could tell it was painful for Garth to talk about their mother, but she pressed on. "I can remember her sitting in this chair about this time late every afternoon—just before she started getting supper ready and before Dad came in from the fields. She'd sit a bit and read her Bible and then pray. I know she prayed with us later, when we went to bed, but this was just her time. I haven't thought about that for years. I wonder—did she really believe it all?"

"Yeah," Garth said softly. "I think she did."

They were both silent for a minute.

"I wish she were with us now," Francis whispered. Maybe her mother would know how to untangle the feelings Francis was feeling. Maybe she'd even know how to help Francis pray to the God she herself had known so well.

"So do I, Sis. So do I."

Francis looked at her brother. She hadn't noticed how weary he was looking, either. "Troubles?"

Garth shrugged.

Francis took a shot. She'd noticed how her brother looked at the woman from Seattle. "How's Sylvia doing?"

Garth grunted.

"She likes you, you know," Francis offered softly.

Garth's wince told her she had hit the sore spot.

"She's got better things to do with her life than liking me," Garth said harshly as he stood up and pushed his chair to the desk. "She deserves someone better."

"Maybe you should let her decide that," Francis said as Garth walked toward the door.

"It's already decided. If you need me, I'll be out back chopping some more wood for winter," Garth said as he opened the door.

Francis had seen the huge stack of wood Garth had already chopped in the last two days. "Don't we have enough wood?"

"Not enough to suit me."

Francis nodded. It looked like she wasn't the only one in the family with troubles in love.

Flint was in the kitchen pacing. The hands on the clock over the refrigerator seemed to crawl. What was Francis doing, locked in the den like that? He knew she had looked more and more strained as the day wore on, but he wished she would talk to him. The fact was, if she didn't come out soon, he was going to go right in and demand that she talk to him. Yes, he said to himself, that's what he'd do. It was his duty, after all. He was guarding her. On official government business. He had a right to know how she was.

Flint looked at the clock in exasperation. Two minutes down. He was beginning to understand why the inspector didn't want him to serve as guard to Francis. Being around her all day was doing things to him that he wasn't able to control. Before he knew it, he was going to make ten kinds of fool of himself doing something like demanding she talk to him. He'd never demanded that someone in protective custody talk to him before—at least not about their feelings. The FBI didn't care about feelings. It worried about the who, where and when questions.

Flint looked at the clock. One more minute. Ah, there she comes. Flint heard the faint click of the doorknob and turned to face the small hall that led to the den.

"Relax. It's just me," Garth said as he walked through the open door.

"Oh."

"She'll come out soon," Garth offered gruffly as he walked over to the rack of coats that hung near the kitchen door and pulled a jacket off a peg. He turned back and looked at Flint squarely. "Don't leave her this time."

"I never left her the first time," Flint protested and

then smiled. This was as close to a blessing as someone like Garth would give him. "You don't have to worry. Francis isn't that interested in me these days. I'm only her guard."

Garth grunted as he pulled on the jacket. "I've officially turned down the FBI's request, you know. There's no reason to kidnap her."

"The bid has already been put out," Flint explained. He'd gone over that in his mind, too. "If it's put out with a crime syndicate, it's probably too late to pull back the orders. There might have been a backup in place before we even arrested those other goons."

"I'll tell the boys to keep their eyes open."

"I'd appreciate that."

A rush of cold air entered the kitchen as Garth opened and then quickly closed the outside door. The clock crawled two more minutes before Francis opened the door from the den. Flint tried to pretend he wasn't waiting for her and turned to face the wall. Ah, good, there was a calendar tacked to the kitchen wall about level with his eyes.

"Tomorrow's Sunday, isn't it?" Francis asked as she walked down the hall.

Flint scrambled to look at the calendar more clearly. "Yes, I guess it is, at that. Why?"

"No reason," Francis said as she walked over to the kitchen sink and turned the water on. "I just thought if it was Sunday tomorrow I might go to church."

"Church?"

"I mean, if that's all right with the FBI." Francis reached into a cupboard and pulled out a teakettle. "I know I'm being guarded, but it's only church. The FBI couldn't object to that."

Flint groaned. He knew the FBI would object. He'd be placing the person he was protecting square in the middle of every suspect in Dry Creek. Everyone would be rounded up under one roof with no weapons check and predictable times when everyone from the minister on down would stand for long minutes with their eyes closed. A lot could happen with all those closed eyes. A smart kidnapper could nab their victim and hustle them out the door before the prayer finished.

"I'd really like to go," Francis continued as she put the kettle under the faucet and began to fill it with water. "And you'll be there, so there's really no danger."

The easy confidence with which Francis said the latter was Flint's undoing. She trusted him. "We'd have to sit in the back row."

"That'd be fine." Francis looked at him and smiled. "I'm sort of a back row kind of person anyway—I haven't been in church for years."

"And I won't be closing my eyes when I pray," Flint assured her.

"Oh, well, surely, there's nothing to worry about at church," Francis said indignantly.

Flint didn't remind her that the hit man that had come after Glory Beckett had chosen the Christmas pageant as the place to make his attempt on her life. The way Flint heard it, it was only the quick thinking of Matthew that had saved the woman's life.

"I'll call Mrs. Hargrove and tell her to be on the lookout tomorrow for someone who is in church but doesn't usually attend," Flint said as he walked toward the telephone. That should pinpoint any problems. "I wonder if it's too late to get some kind of metal detector set up in the entrance hall."

"I don't remember that the church has an entrance hall," Francis offered. She hadn't been in the church for years, but her memories were of a large square room that opened directly onto the street. Concrete steps led up to the double doors that opened into the main room of the church. Two rows of old, well-polished pews faced the front of the church, and tall narrow windows lined the walls. A dark linoleum covered the floor, and a strip of carpet was laid over that to cover the aisle between the pews.

"I should alert Matthew, too," Flint muttered as he picked up the telephone to dial. "Maybe he could shake everyone's hands before the service instead of after. He can do a visual check for weapons that way. Of course, we're probably okay as long as the roads stay closed." He turned to Francis. "Don't suppose you've heard the weather lately?"

"I heard Robert Buckwalter ask Garth earlier. I think that he was hoping to fly his plane out of Dry Creek." Francis grimaced at Flint. "Either that or I hear he's thinking of having more supplies flown in somehow. Tricky business. Garth said the latest forecast was for wind and continuing cold. Unless the county snowplow can get through on the roads, I don't think cars will make it through."

"And none of the rental places rent anything but cars?"

"No, Sheriff Wall checked on that—also told the places at the Billings airport to let him know if any strange men were making a fuss about not being able to rent a four-wheel drive."

"What about women?"

Francis looked at him blankly.

"They might hire a woman," Flint said softly. "In a place that doesn't expect a woman, that could be a key element of surprise. And my guess is that they'll go for a professional this time—someone who is supposed to get in and take the hostage out without attracting any attention."

"But a woman would stick out more than a man," Francis protested. "More men travel through these parts, looking for ranch jobs or following the rodeo circuit."

"Like Sam," Flint offered.

"Sam would never," Francis protested. "I can't believe you'd even think he'd be a kidnapper."

Flint shrugged. "It's probably not him. But it could be the woman that came looking for Robert Buckwalter."

Flint had already had the bureau run a check on the woman, and she sounded like she was little threat to anyone but Robert. The report he had gotten back suggested the woman was there to try and convince Robert to marry her.

Any man who could fly in a load of lobsters on his private plane to feed a bunch of inner city kids, as Robert had done, had money to spare. That meant the woman's motive was simple. She had sighted her prey.

The blonde was having problems paying back some gambling debts and she needed to raise lots of cash fast. She'd already slipped the information to her creditors that she was on the verge of getting engaged to Robert. Flint had taken a close look at that plane Robert landed several nights ago on the snowy pasture by Garth's barn. The plane was so new it still held the smell of the mocha leather seats that turned the cockpit into a relaxation center. No doubt about it. That plane belonged to a rich man.

Marriage to Robert would certainly get the blonde out of hock. But then so would doing a little favor like kidnapping someone for a crime syndicate.

"We can't be too careful," Flint said.

"Well, I can't live in a bubble," Francis said as she sat down at the kitchen table. "We can take reasonable precautions, but that's all we can do."

Flint started to dial the number for Matthew Curtis. He wondered if the minister would be willing to rope off the last two rows on one side of the church. That way Flint could keep a neutral empty zone around Francis. She probably wouldn't like it, but he would rest easier with that arrangement.

"Besides—" Francis gave a little smile "—if another kidnapper is around here they will have noticed that the woman to kidnap, if they really want to rattle Garth, is Sylvia Bannister."

Flint looked at her in question.

"I think my brother's in love," she said softly.

"Garth?"

Francis nodded. "He might not know it yet, but, yes, Garth."

Francis was even more convinced that her brother was in love when he ate supper in the bunkhouse with a few of the men instead of joining the rest of them in the house. She wondered if all men got as grumpy as Garth when they fell in love. If that was the case, she didn't have to worry about Flint. He'd been smooth and polite to her ever since he'd agreed to attend church with her in the morning. He didn't look like he had a care in the world. He certainly didn't look like a man in love.

"Pass the salt?" she asked Flint as they sat in the middle of the table, surrounded by boisterous teenagers. The beef stew she had helped make for supper didn't really need more salt, but it was the only conversational opener that came to her mind.

"Sure," Flint said as he lifted the little glass bottle and passed it to her. "Want pepper?"

"No, thank you." Francis smiled stiffly. Well, that wasn't much of a conversation starter. At this rate, they'd never get the important conversations going. Not that the supper table was a good place to have such a conversation, anyway. Maybe they should wait until they drove to church tomorrow. Flint had already made it clear the two of them were going alone in the four-wheel-drive pickup he was driving.

Chapter Nine

The supper dishes were done, the cows were fed and the house was dark. But Francis couldn't sleep. She lay in the single bed in the small bedroom that had been hers for her entire girlhood. When she lay there, the years evaporated and she felt just as young and insecure as she had thirty years ago. She missed her mother.

Strange, she thought, she hadn't missed her mother for years. She thought about her on holidays and sometimes when she saw a woman who had that same shiny black hair, but she never really missed her deeply. Francis had been ten when her mother died, and it seemed like such a long time ago. She had long ago firmly closed the door on those young memories of her mother.

But tonight, Francis missed her. She wished she could ask her mother what she felt about love and happiness. And faith. Had her mother found comfort in her faith or had it been a mere duty to her?

Francis remembered their home had known laughter as long as her mother was alive. After her mother died, no one laughed anymore.

Francis felt a moment's envy of Flint because he had his grandmother's Bible and had something to hold that had been precious to her. Then she remembered that her own mother's Bible was on a shelf in the den. Like the rocking chair, Garth had never moved it even after all those years.

Francis pulled her chenille robe off the peg behind the door and slipped her arms into its sleeves. The night air inside the house was chilled, so she moved fast. She tucked her feet into fuzzy peach slippers and tightened the belt on her robe.

Once covered, she turned on the small lamp beside her bed. If she left her door open, the lamp should give enough light so that she could sneak down the stairs and pull the Bible off the shelf without waking anyone.

Sam was sleeping on the living room sofa again tonight, and she supposed Flint was in the kitchen. She had no desire to wake either one of them.

Shadows filled all the corners of the house as Francis stepped into the upstairs hallway. She always liked the house at night. Everything was peaceful and stone quiet. When she was in Denver, she missed the absolute still of a Montana night.

Francis stepped lightly down the wooden hallway. The light from her room filtered softly into the darkness of the stairway.

Creak! Flint woke from a restless sleep and stiffened. Someone was slowly walking on the stairs. He'd tested the stairs already and found creaks on steps fourteen and nine. With only one creak, he couldn't tell if the person on the stairs was going up or down. Either way, he needed to check it out.

Flint stood silently and shrugged the blankets off his shoulders. He quickly moved along the wall that led to the stairs. He heard another creak, this one closer. Good, that meant someone was coming down the stairs instead of going up. It was less likely to be an intruder.

Flint stood beside the stairs as a shape came into view. He recognized Francis as much by the smell of the peach lotion she wore as by the shape she made in her bathrobe.

He wouldn't have guessed that the sight of Francis in her bathrobe would affect him so deeply. It wasn't even that he'd like to cuddle her up to bed—and he would like to do that—it was more that he was suddenly aware of the nights of lying together in front of the fireplace and talking he had missed.

That bathrobe got to him. It certainly wasn't the sexiest robe in the world. He'd seen his share of see-through black robes and sleek silk numbers. They were

all sexier than that old robe. But the robe reminded
him of the comfortable love he'd missed. The kind of
love one saw on the faces of couples who were celebrating their fiftieth anniversaries. The kind of love
that was for better and for worse. He'd missed it all.

"It's me," he whispered. He didn't want to frighten
Francis, and she was sure to see him before she came
much closer. He thought a whisper would be soft
enough.

Francis yelped all the same as she turned around.
"What are you doing there?"

"I heard someone on the stairs," Flint explained
softly. "I didn't know if they were going up or going
down."

Francis nodded. "I'm just going into the den to get
a book."

"Anything I can get for you?" Flint realized he'd
never spent an evening with Francis reading. He didn't
even know what kind of books she liked. "A mystery?
No, not for this time of night. Maybe a romance."

Francis shook her head. "The only reading books
my brother keeps around are his collection of Zane
Grey novels."

"We could sit a bit and read them."

Flint liked that idea. It was comfortable—the kind
of thing old married couples did.

Francis shook her head. "I don't want to wake anyone." She rolled her eyes in the direction of the living
room where Sam was sleeping.

"Oh." Old married couples certainly didn't have to worry about unwanted fiancés sleeping in the living room, Flint thought.

"I'll just be a minute."

Flint walked with her into the den and stood by the door while Francis reached up and pulled a large book off the shelf.

"Thanks," Francis said as she left the den. "I remembered this belonged to my mother."

"I don't remember you talking about your mother."

"I didn't."

Francis still couldn't sleep a half hour later. She lay in her bed with her mother's Bible propped up before her. She wished she'd taken the time to look at her mother's Bible earlier. Her mother had written notes throughout the book.

Next to Psalm 100, verse five—"For the Lord is good; His mercy is everlasting, and His truth endures to all generations"—her mother had written a note. "Yesterday my baby girl was born! I'm so very happy!"

Next to Matthew 5:4—"Blessed are those who mourn, For they shall be comforted"—her mother had written in a slower hand, "What will my babies do without me?"

Her mother's life was bound up in the pages of the Bible Francis had pulled off the shelf. Her worries were all there in black-and-white. Her dreams were noted. Her joys. Francis hugged the Bible to her after reading it for a time. She'd never expected to know her mother like this.

The sun strained to rise, and the old man sat in his kitchen and urged it on. He'd been impatiently waiting for morning as he sat next to his west window and polished his old hunting rifle. He'd found a box of ammunition in a dresser drawer last night, and it was sitting on the table ready to be loaded.

If the sun rose hot enough, maybe some of this blasted snow would melt and someone would be willing to drive him to Miles City today, the old man thought. But then he remembered—it was Sunday. The only folks in Dry Creek he could count on to do him a favor all insisted on attending church on Sunday mornings.

He looked around his house. It was like he'd never really seen it for years. When had the walls gotten so stained? And those curtains. They were little more than threads hanging from curtain rods. He should pack some things for his trip, but he couldn't settle on what. Finally, he pulled out the old photo album that had belonged to his parents and put it in a plastic grocery bag. That and the rifle were really the only things he needed to take.

He was halfway to the door when he remembered the cats. What would he do about the cats? He put down the rifle and bag and opened the cupboard door.

He pulled all the tins of cat food out of the cupboard and stacked them on the counter. They were all gourmet tins—chopped chicken livers and tuna. He always bought expensive cat food. Then, one by one, he ran his manual can opener around their lids. As soon as a can was opened, he sat it on the floor.

By the time he finished, he had twenty-nine open cans on the floor. He didn't pet any of the cats that gathered at his feet, and they didn't expect it. He never petted the cats. He'd been content to simply feed them.

The old man comforted himself about the cats. When people realized he was gone, they'd come and take care of the cats, he told himself. The cats would all find good homes. Surely, the people of Dry Creek would take them in.

The old man fretted until finally the sun had softened the darkness enough so that he could put on his coat, pick up his bag and gun and walk across the street to the pay phone beside the café. He'd never put a telephone in his house—couldn't abide the demanding ringing of one. But today he needed to call the bus depot in Miles City and find out if the Greyhound bus was able to get through on the roads.

The bus wasn't coming. The short phone call let him know that the bus service was canceled for Sunday because the interstate was closed until the snowplows could get through. The next bus was scheduled for Monday.

The old man swore. Monday could be too late. The

more he had thought about that cocky FBI agent—coming right to his door and forcing the old man to talk to him—the more nervous he became.

He couldn't stay in Dry Creek until Monday.

The old man had a brief vision of himself driving his old pickup in the other direction, to North Dakota, without tires. The roads were covered with snow. Maybe the tire rims would get him there. He knew it was hopeless as he thought about it. Even if he got to the North Dakota border, he'd still be stranded.

He saw a cream-colored business card slipped into the door of the café, and he pulled it out of the crack. That hotshot Robert guy and someone—the man hadn't written the name clearly—had gone out to the plane. The additional supplies had been parachuted down last night, as ordered. They would be back as soon as possible.

The old man wished he was the one with the plane. That would sure solve his problems. A plane didn't need to wait for any snowplows.

It wasn't fair, the old man decided, when some folks like Robert Buckwalter had fancy planes and a senior citizen like himself didn't have anything but his two aching feet to get himself around in good weather or bad.

And then the old man heard it—the soft whinny of a horse coming from nearby. He listened. It was coming from behind the café. Something about the mournful whinny of the horse told him that she was alone and missing her master.

He rubbed his hands together in triumph. The horse was back! That's what he needed. A horse didn't need tires, and even if the old man couldn't quite remember how to drive, the horse wouldn't care.

Francis let the sunshine filter through the thick frost on her bedroom window. She didn't need full sunshine to feel like this was going to be a good day. She felt more hopeful than she had in years. She'd connected with her mother last night, reading her mother's Bible. Something in her had softened while she read. She was looking forward to going to church this morning more than she had expected when she first announced her desire to Flint. She felt like she'd never really paid attention in church before, and now she wanted to observe everything—to see it through her mother's eyes.

Francis smelled coffee before she started down the stairs later in the morning.

Flint was dressed in slacks and a gray turtleneck and was standing by the sink sipping a cup of coffee. If he'd noticed the creaks she made walking down the stairs, he didn't comment on them.

"You're up early," Francis said as she walked to the cupboard and pulled out a cup.

Flint grinned. "I wanted to be ready in case you wanted to go get eggs again this morning."

Francis groaned. "I think I'll wait until that rooster is awake."

"Suits me." Flint set down his coffee cup and reached over to pick up the leather shoulder holster that was on the counter. The holster was snapped shut, but the butt end of a gun was clearly visible. He hooked it over his shoulder.

Francis heard the hard footsteps on the hallway floor before she saw the outline of Sam entering the kitchen.

"You're wearing a gun to church?" Sam gave a pointed, reproving look in Flint's direction.

Flint felt the joy of the morning harden. Sam looked all starched and pressed. Since when was Sam planning to come to church with them? "I'm on duty."

"Flint's been kind enough to agree to let me attend the services," Francis said stiffly. She had never noticed before just how much of a pain Sam was. Had he always been this self-righteous? "It's been a lot of extra work, especially since he still has his responsibilities."

Sam grunted and adjusted his silk tie. "I doubt there will be many people at the service anyway, the way the snow has covered the roads."

"I've checked with the sheriff," Flint said. "The roads are passable with a four-wheel drive."

Flint had made arrangements for the sheriff and the inspector to both attend the services. One man would sit on each end of the pew where he and Francis sat.

Sheriff Wall had said he didn't usually attend, but he'd wanted to go and check the furnace in the old church, anyway. He was somewhat of a self-taught electrician, and the folks of Dry Creek often called on him for an odd piece of electrical work. He'd told Flint he'd check out the furnace early Sunday morning. That way he'd be there to see if anyone was snooping around the church building before the regular members got there.

"Anyone want some toast?" Flint said as he slipped two slices of bread into the toaster.

"I thought I'd take Francis to breakfast in Dry Creek before church," Sam said smugly as he adjusted his suit jacket. "Give her a break from all of this business."

Flint pushed in the button on the toaster. He studied Sam out of the corner of his eye. The man's face was innocent as a lamb's. But that didn't mean he wasn't capable of betraying someone. Flint wondered if someone could have gotten to Sam. The man certainly seemed intent on getting Francis away from anyone's protection. "You can take her to breakfast when we've caught all the rustlers. Until then, you'll just need to be patient."

"Of course," Sam said smoothly. "I wouldn't want to do anything that would put Francis in danger. Although—" Sam paused "—she wouldn't be defenseless with me around. I have my cell phone. I could call the sheriff in a heartbeat."

Flint grunted and bit back his words.

"Anyone like jelly on their toast?" Francis asked from the corner of the kitchen where she was bending to examine the shelves in a lower cupboard. "The kids have used all of the jelly Garth had, so Mrs. Hargrove brought us some she had canned." Francis pulled up a jar. "I think this is apple jelly."

"Does everyone around here make their own apple jelly?"

"Well, maybe not everyone." Francis opened the jar with a pop to the lid. "Some folks make chokecherry jelly instead—or rhubarb jam."

Flint let himself imagine what it would be like to live in a place where everyone had the time to make jelly. It certainly wasn't anything like the cities he'd lived in over the past ten years, where people didn't even take the time to smear jelly on their toast let alone make the stuff.

"I'll have my toast dry," Sam said as he sat down at the breakfast table. "I wouldn't want to get jam on my suit."

For once Flint was glad he could claim official business. He wouldn't have to offer Sam a ride into church with him and Francis, and in ordinary circumstances there would be little he could do to avoid it.

It was an hour later before it was time to leave for the church service. Garth and all of the kids had had a pancake breakfast while Francis was upstairs taking a shower and getting ready.

Francis lingered in the hot spray of the shower. The air inside the house was cold even though the steam from countless showers upstairs and the cooking downstairs were warming it up. When Francis stepped out of the shower, she wrapped a thick towel around her head and quickly slipped into her robe for the dash to her room.

She might as well not have dashed, Francis thought. Ten minutes later, she was still shivering, standing in front of her closet, wondering what to wear.

Her problem was one of image. She wanted to look competent—to show Flint that he didn't need to worry about her safety—but she also wanted to look appealing. A man like Flint must have dated many women in the years since she'd known him. Probably sophisticated women, too. The kind of woman who finds it exciting to date someone who wears a gun. The kind of woman who, if she wore a robe at all, wore a silk and lace one instead of a fuzzy one.

Francis sighed. Her navy striped suit was the obvious choice for competency, but it seemed a little needlessly drab. Not feminine enough. It was, however, the kind of suit that made up the endless parade of suits she'd worn for years in her job. And it was the kind of suit that filled her closets in Denver, and here, as well.

The only truly feminine dress she owned was the long ruby evening gown she had worn to the dance the other night.

Francis wondered when the last time had been that

she cared what a man thought about what she wore. She'd never asked Sam, and she couldn't remember him ever remarking on anything she wore. Except for her old bathrobe, and that was only because it annoyed him.

Thinking of her evening gown reminded her that she did have pieces of that outfit left. If she put on the ivory lingerie she'd gotten to wear with that sequined ruby dress, she'd at least feel desirable. The ruby dress was little more than threads in her closet now, but the accessories were still good.

Finally, she settled on wearing the navy suit skirt and a light blue silk blouse with a pearl necklace.

By the time Francis slipped her feet into the strappy high heels she'd also purchased to wear with the sequined dress and ran a mauve lipstick over her lips, she decided she could at least compete with women like this Rose person who apparently visited Flint in his dreams.

"Coat?" Flint held up a parka jacket for Francis almost as soon as she came into the kitchen.

Something about Francis was different, and Flint didn't like the hungry look he'd surprised in Sam's eyes. The other man might look like he was all starch and collar, but Flint guessed he wasn't as comfortable with Francis as he looked. And who could blame him? Francis had a softness about her face that would make any man want to explore her further.

"So soon?"

Flint nodded. "I want us to be all set in the church before the regulars start to come in."

"I'll see you after the service," Sam said a little grimly to Francis as he looked at Flint.

Flint nodded. Sam hadn't been too happy about the arrangements, but Flint had insisted. There was only a remote possibility of trouble, but he didn't want to have to worry about Sam if anything did happen.

Everything looked white and gray when Francis stepped out of the house. She had accepted the parka from Flint and had wrapped a wool scarf around her neck, as well. It was hard to be a fashion plate in the middle of a Montana winter. The air was so cold her breath made short white puffs, and she pulled her scarf up so that it covered her chin. White snow lay softly over the yard outside the house. A few dog prints and the prints Flint had made when he went out earlier to warm up the pickup were all that disturbed the soft white blanket.

"Garth said we got another four inches last night," Flint noted as he opened Francis's door on the four-wheel-drive pickup. At the same time, he looked in the back of the pickup to check that the usual winter shovel hadn't been taken out to be used on some farm chore. It hadn't. "The roads will be rough."

"Maybe some of it will melt off by the time we come home from church," Francis said as she climbed into the pickup cab. She'd needed to take her high heels off and put snow boots on, but she carried the shoes in her hands. She's slip them on when she got to church just like most of the other women would do. "Might all melt."

"Not likely." Flint had already become accustomed to the Montana cold. When it snowed, the air was heavy. But the rest of the time, the air was light and brittle.

Flint opened and closed his own door quickly. The heater was working, and the air inside the pickup cab was slightly warmer than that outside.

Flint removed his gloves and turned the heater to defrost. The windows were fogged over, but the defroster was already clearing small circles on them. He breathed in deeply. He could smell the fragrance of peaches coming from Francis. "Nice perfume."

"It's just lotion."

Sylvia had lent her the lotion when she had heard Francis and Flint were going to attend church together.

Francis smiled to remember the other woman standing with the bottle of lotion in her hand.

"But it's not a date," Francis had protested half-heartedly as the other woman flipped open the cap to the lotion and tipped it toward Francis's hands. "It's just church."

Sylvia had smiled and squeezed some lotion into Francis's outstretched hands. "You're going to a church, not a convent. Lots of romances start there."

Francis had smoothed the lotion into her hands and

arms and now, talking to Flint, she was glad she had. "Winter is always hard on the skin."

Flint shifted from Park into Reverse and looked in the rearview mirror.

"It's the cold moisture in the air," Francis muttered as she watched Flint back the pickup away from the ranch house. He'd shaved since last night. His skin was smooth, and the lines of his face were more pronounced than when he had a little stubble. He'd put a suit jacket over his shoulder holster, and his gun blended into the contours of his chest so that it wasn't noticeable. His head was turned so that he could look back while he steered the pickup past a snowdrift. Francis had never noticed what a strong neck he had. Of course, when she'd known him, he'd been a young man of twenty. His neck had had plenty of years to change since then. They'd both changed in those years.

"And the wind," Francis continued. "It's been windy for the past few months. Must be El Niño or the drought or something,"

Flint had turned the pickup around, and he was heading down the gravel road that ran down Garth's property to the main county road. The road was bumpy. The November rains had filled the road with ruts. Those ruts had frozen solid in December and stayed that way. .

"The drought makes it hard for the ranchers around here," Flint said. He had listened to the ranch hands at Garth's place. The men talked about the weather first thing in the morning and the last thing at night. Last summer had been dry, and although the winter had been cold, the snowfall in the mountains had been below normal.

"Some of them are on the verge of selling out," Francis said. "One more dry summer could do them in. The cost of feed gets too high, and they can't afford to run as many cattle."

Flint grunted in sympathy. "They need to diversify. Ranch part time and then do something else."

"Don't think they haven't tried to do that," Francis said. "But there's no business around here. Only three or four jobs—the post office, the job Matthew does at the hardware store, and then the café—but Linda and Duane run that."

"It'd be a pity for anyone to leave," Flint said. The morning sun was fading from red to pink as it inched its way up the sky. When he looked to his right, he saw the foothills of the Big Sheep Mountain Range covered in a thick collar of snow. Snow hadn't collected on the sides of the mountains, and they were a gray-brown. "It's a beautiful, restful place to be."

Flint was surprised at the sentiment he felt. He thought he'd grown more callused than that over the years. A home was only a place to hang one's hat. He would have bet he'd learned that lesson. Any land was the same as any other. Each plot of dirt the same as any other plot.

"Everyone has been thinking of business ideas,"

Francis said. "From dude ranches to quilting factories. Even jelly making—Mrs. Hargrove said folks might pay for some of the homemade jelly folks around here make."

"I still can't believe everyone around here makes jelly," Flint said incredulously. "What century is this, anyway?"

Francis only smiled. "We've lived through long, hard winters in Dry Creek. Makes us appreciate home-canned jellies and fruit. Nothing tastes better when the snow is deep than something you've grown yourself. Brings back the smell of summer."

For the first time, Flint began to think about those five acres his grandmother had left him in her will. He hadn't given them any attention for years. Maybe now, before he left, he should plant something. He didn't need to plant fruits or vegetables on them, but some kind of plant would be nice. Maybe some rose-bushes would do well down by the trickle of a creek that ran through his grandmother's land during the spring months when the snow ran off the mountains. Wild roses might grow without extra water. Or a tree. A tree would surely grow. He suddenly realized he'd never planted anything anywhere before.

The sun had lost its pink and was a thin bright yellow that hovered over the day.

The pickup cab was warm enough, and Flint turned the defroster off. The steering on the four-wheel drive was stiff and required all of Flint's attention. Still, it was cozy inside the cab as he and Francis bumped along the county road. On each side of the narrow country road were wide ditches that caught the snow. Beside each ditch was a fence running along the road, dividing the grassland. The road rose and then dipped along with the low, rolling countryside.

"Robert moved his plane," Flint noticed. The small plane had been parked beside that far fence for the past three days. Now a thin path made by the plane wheels ran through the snow. "Must be desperate if he's thinking of taking off in this kind of snow."

"I hear the café needed supplies and he was having some airlifted in. I think they're just dropping the supplies by the old plane. That's why he moved it—so the drop would go smooth."

"Must be nice to be rich."

Francis smiled. "I hear he's bringing in crates of frozen asparagus and caviar. His mother is determined to bring the finer foods to Dry Creek for the kids. It's almost a cross-cultural experience for most of them to tackle something like caviar."

"They can live full lives without caviar," Flint said.

Francis shrugged. "It doesn't hurt them to try new things."

Garth's ranch buildings were behind them as they drove, and Flint saw another ranch off to the left in the distance. The house and outbuildings were sheltered by a small grove of trees, their branches leafless and stark on a winter day. Someone had planted those trees in some past hopeful time.

Flint was looking for the low-lying outline of a small plane, but instead he saw something else low on the horizon. He could see a horse and rider from a distance coming down the road.

Now what is some fool doing out with a horse on a morning like this? Flint thought, forgetting that it had not been that many mornings ago when that rider would have been him.

Chapter Ten

The horse grew more familiar as Flint drove closer to it. Finally, he even recognized the man riding the horse.

What had possessed that old man to strike out on horseback with the snow from last night's blizzard still fresh on the ground? If the old man didn't care what happened to himself, he should at least be more considerate of Honey.

The last time Flint had seen Honey she'd been cozy in the old chicken coop on his grandmother's place. He'd made arrangements for Duane Edison to bring her back to the café and keep her in the shed behind the place. Flint planned to visit Honey there after church and take her a few of the apples he'd gotten from Mrs. Hargrove. He'd discovered the horse had a fondness for them.

The ruts in the road were deeper, and Flint needed to slow down as he came closer to the old man. The pickup wasn't going more than five miles an hour. The old man crossed the road so that he would be riding past the passenger side of the pickup.

"What's he up to?" Flint asked.

Francis started to roll down her window. "Must be rabbit hunting. He's got his rifle with him. Mr. Gossett," Francis called cheerfully. "Good morning."

The old man was still in front of the pickup when he stopped riding.

A warning prickle ran down Flint's spine. Something about the determined set of the old man's shoulders made him uneasy. "Don't open the door. And roll that window back up."

Francis turned to him in disbelief. "You're going to leave him here?"

"Yes."

"But he's an old man and it's freezing out there," Francis protested. "Look at him. He might even be senile. Wandering around without a scarf on his head. He'll catch pneumonia."

Flint hesitated. He didn't want Francis to think he was heartless. The old man did look almost senile. Maybe Flint's spine had known too many bad men over the years so that he couldn't tell the bad from the simpleminded. Still. "I didn't tell him to saddle up and play cowboy on a morning like this."

"But he's on Honey," Francis added as though she and the horse were now fast friends. "You know she isn't enjoying this romp through the snow. Look at her. She looks hungry."

"She's had plenty of oats. She just wants one of those apples I have in the back of the pickup."

Francis looked through the cab window to the bed of the pickup. There they were—a dozen apples tied in a red mesh bag.

"Tell him I'll send someone back for him," Flint said to Francis as he pulled closer to the old man. "But then roll up that window. We can't be too careful."

"You suspect Mr. Gossett?" Francis asked in surprise as she eyed the old man through the windshield dubiously. "Surely he's harmless. I wouldn't think he'd be—you know—"

"Bright enough?"

Francis nodded. "And he doesn't know anyone but a few people in Dry Creek. Never has any visitors or anything. No friends. No family."

"A man doesn't need friends to commit a crime. Nor does he need to be particularly intelligent."

Francis began rolling down the pickup window again. The crank was stiff and she bent her head as she moved it. She stopped when the window was a third of the way down and called to the old man who was just a little ahead of the slow-moving pickup. "Don't worry. We'll send someone back for you. And you should have a scarf in weather like this. Is there one in your pockets?"

The old man scowled. The woman in the pickup

sounded like his mother. Scolding him for forgetting something like he was a little kid.

He'd show her who was a little kid, the old man thought in satisfaction.

"I don't need a scarf," the old man said as he took the barrel of his rifle and slapped it against the rump of the horse so that she nervously jumped into the middle of the road and reared up.

Flint swore as he pushed his foot hard into the brake pedal. Honey was practically on top of the pickup hood when she reared up like that. "What in blazes?"

The pickup stopped, and Flint instinctively put his right hand out to push Francis down in the seat.

"What—" Francis resisted the shove, more out of bewilderment than anything else.

But it was enough. The time he'd taken to try to shield her behind the metal of the pickup cost him. He should have gone for his gun first, he told himself later. By the time he brought his hand to his holster the harmless old man had swung his rabbit-hunting rifle around and had drawn a bead on Francis.

"Easy now," Flint murmured. Francis was staring at the rifle. "Don't move."

"Throw the gun out of there." The old man sat on the horse and yelled.

Flint put his hands up in plain view. Next time, he'd trust his spine. "Let me step out first."

The first thing Flint needed to do was to put some distance between himself and Francis. Guns went with guns, and he'd bet the old man would swing the barrel of that old rifle around to follow him if he stepped outside the pickup. At least then, if there were any bullets fired, Francis would have a chance. An old rifle like that probably wouldn't hold more than one bullet. If Flint could get the man to fire at him, Francis would be safe.

The old man snorted and steadied his gun. "I ain't that stupid. You've got to the count of three."

Francis was frozen. She told herself she should know what to do. She'd taken a hostage negotiation class at work. She was supposed to know what to do. But her mind was blank.

"One." The old man called out the number with a certain amount of satisfaction.

"I'm putting it out now," Flint said as he slowly moved his hand toward the holster. The defroster had been off long enough that the windshield on the pickup had a thin film coating it. In another five minutes, the view would be fuzzy from where the old man sat on the horse. But Flint didn't have five minutes. "I'll need to open the door to throw it."

"Stick it through the window," the old man ordered.

So much for that idea, Flint thought. He'd considered opening the door and swinging down to shoot at the old man from there. He'd be far enough away from Francis that the bullet from the man's rifle wouldn't be coming in her direction.

Francis was cold. She could feel her teeth start to chatter.

Flint could hear her teeth start to chatter. He didn't dare look at Francis, though. He kept his eyes on the old man.

"Two." The old man counted loudly.

Flint touched the butt of his gun as he unsnapped his shoulder holster smoothly. "Take it easy. It's coming."

"Handle first," the old man instructed.

Flint drew the gun out with the fingertips of one hand. "No problem."

Flint squeezed the barrel of his gun as he swung it around to the side of the pickup. The cold made the gun slippery, and he had to hold it tight.

"I need to roll my window down."

The old man shook his head slightly. "Push it through the other window by Francis."

Flint didn't like reaching across Francis with his gun. It would keep the eyes of the old man focused on her. But Flint didn't hesitate. He reached over to the few inches of open space in Francis's window.

The gun slipped over the side and clanked against the side of the pickup on the way down.

The old man lowered his rifle a little. Not much, but enough so that Flint began to breathe again.

"It's not too late to let us go, you know," Flint called out the window to the old man. "Whatever it is that's bothering you—we can talk about it."

"Ain't nothing bothering me," the old man said. "I just need to get out of here."

"Well, why didn't you say so?" Flint forced his voice to relax. The safe period in any hostage situation was the setting of the terms. "I'd be happy to take you someplace. Just put the gun down and we'll see that you get where you need to go."

The old man slid off the back of the horse right next to the pickup. The barrel of his rifle wavered, but Flint didn't make any sudden moves. A gun in the hands of an amateur was always a potentially deadly thing. It was too easy to underestimate someone.

"I'm sure the boys in the bunkhouse have something to drink, as well," Francis offered quietly. "Whiskey, for sure. Maybe some Scotch. I'm sure you'd like a little drink for the road."

"Don't have time for a drink," the old man said as he reached out and opened the door beside Francis. "Move over. I'm coming in."

The old man grabbed the inside back of the cab and started to pull himself in. He must have remembered Flint's gun, and bent down to pick it up from the ground.

"If you want me to drive you somewhere—maybe Miles City—I'd be happy to," Flint said calmly, not commenting on the other gun. He was afraid of this. His own gun made the man's rabbit rifle look as harmless as a water pistol. "But we don't need Francis to come along. Why don't you let her get out and ride the horse back to her brother's ranch."

"I'm not stupid," Mr. Gossett snapped as he shoved himself into the cab and slammed the door behind him.

"No one ever said you were," Flint murmured soothingly.

The heat inside the cab was beginning to warm the old man's clothes, and they were starting to smell.

The old man eyed Flint and Francis. "Nobody's leaving here, and you'll drive me where I tell you—but it won't be Miles City. The road past Dry Creek is closed. I heard Highway 89 is blocked off until the snowplows get through. Don't think a pickup will get through."

"Maybe your best bet is the horse, then," Flint said. *Sorry, Honey,* he thought ruefully. *You take him away, and I'll come get you both—and I'll bring you some of those apples you like. And not just the small bunch I have in the back of the pickup. I'll shake down a whole tree for you.*

The old man snorted. "Couldn't pay me to get back on that animal—she's practically worthless. Stubborn as a mule. Almost had me setting out on foot a time or two."

Flint smiled inside. He could always count on Honey.

"If no one can drive you and the horse won't take you," Francis said, "then you need to decide whether it is really important that you go. If it's groceries you need—or something more substantial to drink than tea—or anything else—"

"What I need is to get out of the state!"

"Then you'll need to wait," Francis said calmly. She had hoped he was just a fool in search of alcohol. The alternatives were not as pleasant. "There's no way to go today."

"There's the plane—the plane that flew in to bring the lobsters for the party," the old man said with satisfaction in his voice. "The plane that that millionaire fellow owns. That's where I want you to take me."

"I don't know where the plane is." Flint stalled. "He might have even flown it out of here."

"Just follow them tracks," the old man said as though that settled the matter. "I was starting to follow them when I spotted you. Decided no point in riding on that old horse. Especially when you've got a warm pickup that'll get us there just as good."

Flint looked over to see the wide tracks of the plane that ran on the other side of the fence. Why couldn't Robert Buckwalter have driven his plane deeper into the pasture instead of along the fence?

The old man nodded. "You can go now."

The roads were frozen, bumpy, and Flint needed both hands to control the steering on the pickup. But he still curved his shoulder slightly away from the seat so that Francis could nestle close to him. Francis sat with her legs on the driver's side of the stick shift.

Flint knew her decision to be so close to him was made because she wanted to be as far away as possible from the old man, but he welcomed her presence anyway. It felt right to have her sandwiched in next to him.

Francis watched Flint's hands on the steering wheel. He'd taken off his gloves so that he could grip the wheel more securely, and the cold made the skin on his hands whiter than usual. They were strong hands, the fingers big and agile.

She had a sudden recollection of the last time they'd sat this close in a pickup.

"Whatever happened to that old pickup of yours?" Francis asked softly.

The old man hadn't said anything since he climbed into the pickup. He'd just sat there with one hand holding Flint's gun and the other steadying the rifle against his leg closest to the door. Francis tried to pretend he wasn't there.

"My grandmother finally sold it to some other kid." Flint smiled. Until he'd met Francis, he'd poured his heart into that old pickup. "Wonder if he ever got our initials off the door."

Francis smiled. She had forgotten about the initials Flint had painted on the door. Two swirling black *F*s with lots of extra curlicues.

"He did." The old man surprised them both by speaking. "Jim Jett bought it—painted it black all over. That took care of the initials."

"I don't suppose there's much in Dry Creek you don't know," Flint began tentatively. He wondered how the man would respond to flattery. "You being a pillar of the community and all."

The old man snorted. "You know I ain't no pillar of nothing."

"Well, your father was." Flint continued the conversation and prayed the old man had liked his father. "I heard what he did in the big drought—getting people to stay and make a town. He was a real hero in these parts."

"He was a fool. He should have left Dry Creek when he had a chance. The whole town never amounted to anything. And my father—all he ever had to his name was his few acres in Dry Creek, Montana."

"He had friends," Francis added softly. "And the respect of his neighbors."

"It took me two years to save up enough money to buy a decent headstone for his grave," the old man muttered bitterly. "After that, I figured why bother."

"But you never left the area?" Flint asked softly.

"Where would I go?"

For a blinding moment Flint envied the old man his certainty about where he belonged in his life. Love it or hate it, Dry Creek was the old man's home. Flint had bounced around for years, never feeling connected to any place.

The old man pointed out the window. "There's the plane."

Flint could just make out the dark shape against the white snow ahead. No, wait. There was more than one black shape.

"There's another pickup there," Francis said, her voice neutral. Her mind was busy calculating the odds. Another pickup could be a problem or it could be a solution. She wondered which Flint thought it would be.

There was a time when she would have known what he thought. Would have comfortably finished his sentences for him when he talked. At the time, she had thought it was because they were so much in love. Now she wondered. They had been young and foolish. The fact that they had run off to Las Vegas without planning enough to even have luggage with them showed just how foolish.

"You'll stay in the pickup when we get there," Flint ordered Francis as he drove closer. He didn't like the fact that the old man was holding Flint's gun closer now. That gun had altogether too many bullets in it waiting to be fired.

"I'll say who stays where," the old man protested heatedly.

"She stays in the pickup." Flint ignored his words. The old man grunted.

"Maybe we should all stay—just turn around and go where we need to go in the pickup," Francis offered. She didn't like the thought of Flint being alone with the crazy old man. "The roads might be open. You know those weather people—they're always behind the times. Maybe the roads have been cleared by now. We could drive to the main road and find out."

Francis's leg had pressed itself against Flint. And her scent—she smelled of summer peaches. He didn't dare turn and look fully at her because he didn't want the old man to get nervous.

Besides, Flint didn't really need to see her to know what she looked like. He had memorized her face over twenty years ago and he could still pull the picture out of his mind. Her eyes were the color of the earth after the first fall frost, full of brown shadows and dark green highlights with shimmer that promised depths unknown. Her eyes were usually somber. He had loved to tease her just to watch that moment when her eyes would turn from serious to playful indignation.

Flint moved his hand to the knob of the gearshift even though he had no further gears left and wouldn't be shifting down. He just wanted to rest his hand closer to her.

Francis had never been more aware of Flint than she was at that moment. Maybe it was because of the danger around them. Maybe it was because of the long years she'd spent missing him.

Whatever it was, she had to slip her hand under her leg so that it wouldn't reach out and caress Flint's wrist. His arm was covered with the sleeve of a bulky winter jacket. His hands had been without gloves long enough now that they would be cold. But his wrist was the meeting place between cold and warm.

The pickup was bumping along closer to the plane. Without the four-wheel drive, the vehicle would have been stuck in at least a dozen different snowdrifts since they'd started following the plane tracks.

Flint had considered letting the pickup accidentally get stuck, but he didn't want to annoy the old man. Especially since staging a delay wasn't the best way to stop Mr. Gossett. Fifty years of progress would take care of that. Flint was confident the old man would take one look at the sophisticated instrument panel on the plane and give up any hope of flying it out of here. Even if the old man had flown a plane once in his youth, he would be bewildered today.

The fact that someone else was at the plane complicated things. Flint suspected it was Robert Buckwalter who had come out to the plane. If it was, the old man had a pilot. That would change the odds on everything.

Francis sensed Flint's worry. Nothing in his face had changed since they spotted that pickup, but she gradually sensed the tension in him. *We're really in danger,* she realized numbly. *Dear God.* The thought came to her almost unbidden. *We need help.*

Francis was tired of worrying about the problems between her and Flint. Just like she instinctively turned to God when she needed help, she also wanted to turn to Flint. They were in trouble, and she didn't want to face it alone. She slipped her hand from under her leg and brought it up to lightly touch Flint's wrist.

Flint's hand responded immediately. It moved off the gearshift and enclosed her hand.

I am home, Francis thought. His hand was cold. Ice cold. But it didn't matter. His hand could rival the temperature of the Arctic Circle and she'd want to hold it. She could face anything if they were together hand in hand.

Chapter Eleven

If a person didn't know better, this could be a view on a postcard, Francis mused.

The morning sun was bright on the snow-covered hills leading up to the Big Sheep Mountain Range. The mountains themselves were low and didn't have any of the peaks that were found in other mountain ranges in Montana.

There were no houses on the horizon and no trees. Usually there were no signs of civilization up here except the thin lines of barbed-wire fence that divided the various sections of land that had belonged to her father and now belonged to her brother, Garth. Some of the land would be planted in wheat this coming spring. Some of it would be left for free-range grazing. Right now, it was empty. All of the cattle had been brought closer to the main house because of the storm.

The only mar in the otherwise peaceful picture was the tracks in the snow. There were now two sets of tracks. One set was partially filled in with drifting snow. The other set of tracks was newer. Both led to the small twin-engine plane that was parked next to one of the barbed-wire fences that followed the country road. Past the plane was a piece of land that had been scraped clean of snow. Either a snowplow had done it or it had been shoveled clean by hand.

"It must be Robert," Flint said softly. There was no one standing outside in the area between the plane and the Jeep, but it must be Robert. Who else would care enough about an airstrip to make one on a day like this?

Flint felt a twist in his stomach. With an airstrip and a pilot, there would be no stopping the old man from flying.

That's what Flint had been afraid of— He didn't want the old man airborne. Not that he knew for sure they would all be safer if old man Gossett had no hope of getting that plane in the air. But gunfire was much more likely if the old man even thought he could get them in the air.

"I'll do the talking," Mr. Gossett announced suddenly. "Don't want you two scaring them off."

Flint stopped the pickup as far away from the plane as he felt he could. Whoever had driven the Jeep in here must be inside the plane. "They haven't got any place to go, anyway."

The old man renewed his grip on the two guns he held. "This won't take long."

"You'll want to be careful with that gun of mine," Flint said softly. "It's federal property. Use it to commit a crime and they'll lock you up and throw away the key."

The old man looked confused.

"You've seen the notices in the post office." Flint kept talking. The old man was of the era that could be intimidated by the government—maybe. "You'd do best to just leave it on the ground. Besides," Flint added for good measure, "that rifle of yours looks like it has seen some action. Don't think you'd need any more persuasion than she can give you."

The old man looked proud as he gripped the gun tighter. "She's a good shooter, all right."

There was a large tarp—no, it was a parachute, Francis realized—as well as ten, maybe twelve boxes sitting next to the plane. The parachute was white, and a dozen ropes swirled around it on the ground. On the other side of the parachute the four-wheel-drive Jeep was parked. Deep boot prints were all around the boxes and led up to the plane.

"That's the Edisons' Jeep," the old man said thoughtfully as he peered out the windshield. "Wonder if it's their boy, Duane, out there."

Flint prayed it would be. He thought the old man might have a harder time hurting someone from Dry Creek than he would a stranger. Sort of a you-never-hurt-the-ones-you-know theory.

"I heard Robert Buckwalter was having some

more supplies flown in for the café—with all the kids around these days they are running low on everything." Francis spoke nervously.

Mr. Gossett shook his head in disgust. "In my day, you wouldn't find anyone flying in supplies. We'd eat bread and beans if that's all that was available. Kids today are too soft."

Flint believed in diversionary tactics. He agreed heartily. "You can say that again. Most of them aren't worth their salt."

Francis felt the faint squeeze Flint gave her fingers. She understood his message.

"They should all be sent to reform school," Francis agreed. "Teach them some manners."

The old man nodded thoughtfully. "They wouldn't like it—locked in with everyone else. I know I wouldn't."

"We could meet with the authorities about this," Flint offered. He had his fingers crossed that the old man would take the bait. "They'll understand how you feel about being locked up. I'll drive you back to the café and we can make a call. If you turn state's evidence on this rustling business, you might get off with probation. I'll see to it that you meet with the right people—maybe even the state governor—or a congressman."

The old man snorted. "Worthless politicians. I'd rather deal with them kids any day."

"The press, then." Flint continued the bribe. "Say

you don't confess to anything. We could get the press out here and do an article for the Billings paper. You'd be famous."

The old man paled. Then he raised Flint's gun and jerked it at him. "Who in blazes wants to be famous? I just want to be left alone."

Well, that eliminated most of the mental-illness categories, Flint thought in resignation. He didn't know whether it would be easier to deal with someone who was crazy or someone who was stone-cold sane and just mean.

"You call out and let them know we're here." The old man jerked his head toward the plane. "They'll come out at the sound of your voice. Be friendly-like."

Flint hoped Mr. Gossett was wrong and that whoever was inside the plane would stay right there.

"Anybody home?" Flint rolled down his window and called out. "You've got company. Company and trouble—they come together—"

"Hush," the old man hissed.

Francis felt the sweep of frigid air coming in the open window. She wanted to snuggle closer to Flint, but she felt the tension in his body and did not want to be in the way if he needed to move fast.

Flint's heart sank. He saw a figure standing in the open door to the small plane. His hint had gone unheard.

"It's the chef," Flint murmured. Another figure joined the first. "And Robert."

"Let's go meet them," Mr. Gossett ordered Flint as he grabbed the door handle. "I've got plans."

Flint hoped he never heard the words "I've got plans" again. Mr. Gossett kept waving the guns around, and his plans were soon implemented. Robert Buckwalter was able to assess the situation quickly. Flint would wager the other man had had his own share of training in how to deal with hostage situations. Since Robert traveled internationally, he might even have some training on terrorist activities.

It only took a minute for Robert Buckwalter to assure the old man that he would fly him anywhere he could.

"The plane's only got enough fuel to fly to someplace like Fargo, North Dakota—or we could head for Billings if you want to stay in Montana," Robert explained to the older man just like he was a pilot planning a routine flight.

"I'll take Fargo. Let's all get in."

Robert nodded toward the old man and eyed him speculatively. "The fuel will last longer if the plane is lighter. I'd say you're about one hundred seventy pounds?"

The old man nodded.

"I'll go with you to fly this thing, but you don't want to take the others—it's unnecessary weight."

"I'll need a hostage."

Flint stepped forward. "That would be me."

The old man snorted. "I don't think so. I'll take

her." He jerked his head at the young woman who was standing by Buckwalter's side. "She's a skinny little thing. Can't weigh much."

"It's not just about weight," Flint said. He kept moving around, hoping to find a moment when the old man was off guard. But Mr. Gossett kept his gun trained on one of the women at all times. "I can talk to the authorities for you."

"You speak English?" He barked the words at the chef.

She nodded.

"She can talk for me," the old man insisted. "Now, you two men get all the boxes out of that plane. I don't want any unnecessary weight holding us back."

Francis shivered. She and Jenny, the chef who worked for Mrs. Buckwalter, were standing together near the door to the plane. Mr. Gossett stood nearby and held Flint's gun loosely in his hand.

"You'll be all right," Francis whispered to the young woman. "Flint will get help."

The young woman nodded mutely.

Francis prayed she was right. Once the plane was airborne she and Flint could drive one of the pickups the ten or so miles back to Dry Creek and get help sent ahead. If they could alert the airports in Fargo and Billings, they should be able to stop the old man without anyone getting hurt.

"Now, everyone out of the plane," the old man ordered.

All the boxes had been thrown to the ground. Flint and Robert jumped to the ground from the open door of the plane.

Flint had his plan. The floor of the plane was about four feet up from the ground. There would be no way the old man could climb into the plane and hold onto both guns at the same time. That would be when Flint would tackle him.

"Now—you two—get down on the ground." The old man jerked his gun at Francis and Flint.

"What?" Flint bit back a further protest. This was a twist he hadn't counted on.

"But it's cold." Robert stepped in. "Let them at least go sit in the pickup—or even the Jeep."

"The ground. Now," the old man ordered, his voice rising in agitation. "I don't have all day, I gotta get out of here."

Francis lowered herself to the ground. The snow was not yet packed, and it was like sinking into a down pillow. An icy-cold down pillow. She sat down with her legs crossed in front of her.

"You, too," the old man said curtly as he glanced over at Flint. "I want you with your back to her—" the old man shifted his gaze to Jenny "—and you get some rope from those boxes to tie them up."

"You're not going to leave them like that?" Jenny protested. "It's freezing out here. They'll—" Jenny swallowed and didn't finish her sentence.

Francis could finish it for her. If she and Flint were tied and left in a snowdrift like this, they could die.

"What does it matter to me if they get cold?" the old man demanded. "That'll teach them to come snooping around, asking questions. Butting into a man's private life."

Flint watched the old man and didn't like what he saw. Maybe it wasn't a choice of whether the old man was crazy or a criminal—maybe he was both.

"It's a federal offense to kill an FBI agent," Flint said softly as he moved to step between Francis and the old man.

"Not if it's an act of God," the old man said with a humorless chuckle as he shifted to adjust for Flint's move.

Unless Flint wanted to anger the old man, he knew he shouldn't move again right away. One step could be casual. Two would be a threat.

"But surely you're not planning—" Robert Buckwalter protested in disbelief from where he stood beside the plane.

"I'm not debating this," the old man said firmly, still keeping his gun bead steady on Francis at all times. "I suggest everyone just do what they're told."

Francis had kept her head down for this entire conversation. Flint wondered if she were praying and then decided he hoped she was. Maybe God would listen to someone like Francis. She sure didn't deserve to be out here in the middle of a snowdrift with a crazy man threatening to shoot her.

"Why should we do anything you say?" Francis looked up, and her chin came up defiantly. "You're going to leave us tied up here no matter what we do. You can't bring yourself to shoot us. But you'll let us freeze to death. From where I sit, there's not much else you can do to us."

Flint cringed when he heard what Francis said. The old man was unstable at best. Defiance wasn't a good choice.

For the next ten minutes, Francis tried to take her words back. She kept saying "I'm sorry" like it was a mantra. It hadn't mattered. The old man hadn't been listening.

She kept apologizing until the small plane moved down the makeshift airstrip and took off.

"It's okay, it'll be okay," Flint said behind her back, and Francis realized he had been saying the words softly for some time now.

Francis stopped apologizing to the old man who wasn't even there any longer. She was so numb she no longer shivered. The old man had shown what else he could do. First he'd taken Flint's jacket, then hers. He'd thrown the coats in the back of the plane. Then he'd forced her to remove her dress and Flint to remove his suit. Those, too, had gone into the back of the plane.

"Just to show you what a good guy I am, I'm leaving you your underwear." Mr. Gossett grinned. "Wouldn't want the proper ladies of Dry Creek to get in a tizzy when someone finds the bodies."

The old man laughed then instructed Jenny, "Tie 'em tight. Don't want either of them wandering around out here and getting lost."

Flint wanted to shout at the old man, to call him names. The strength of the desire shook him. He was losing his edge. It was unprofessional. He knew that. It wasn't by the book. It wasn't smart. *But it's Francis,* his mind screamed.

Flint forced himself to focus. He needed all of his energy just to keep himself and Francis alive.

Before the old man climbed into the plane, he took Jenny with him and walked to both vehicles. The Jeep's hood was stiff, but he had made Jenny open it and then he had reached in and pulled out a handful of spark plugs and stuffed them in his pocket. He had done the same with the pickup that Flint and Francis had driven.

It was at that point that Francis had broken down and started apologizing more loudly. She was still whimpering, the words coming softly from her lips.

Flint tried to move his arms so that he could turn around and hold Francis. He was terrified. The freezing cold was a worse enemy than any he had faced. At least with a kidnapper or a terrorist, you had the chance of talking them out of their plans. But the cold? What did the weather care for either threats or emotions?

Finally, Flint moved so that his hands could grip Francis's. The plane was growing smaller in the mid-morning sky. It had started east and then slowly turned to head west. The old man must have changed his mind and settled on Billings, after all.

Flint murmured again, "It'll be okay."

Francis hiccuped and then quieted. Her throat was beginning to hurt from the gulps of cold air that she had breathed. Every exposed inch of skin on her body was tingling. She felt like she was being pricked with a thousand daggers. She forced herself to focus. She was facing her death, and only a few things were still important.

"I should say I'm sorry," Francis said calmly. The only warm place on her body was her hand, and that was because Flint held it in his. "I should have waited for you twenty years ago instead of thinking you had deserted me. I should have trusted you."

"I should have trusted you, too," Flint said as he strained against the ropes tying them together so he could move his back closer to hers. Finally, their bare shoulder blades met. Francis leaned into him, and he could feel the elastic ridge of her bra strap. Their skins gradually warmed.

Flint continued to strain at the ropes. The old man had watched Jenny carefully as she knotted the ropes, but Flint believed she would have left them room to escape if there was any way she could.

"I wish we'd gotten to church this morning," Francis continued pensively. "I was thinking of going back, you know—not that I guess I was ever there much as an adult. But still, there's a sense of going back. Looking for the hope I'd lost."

"I know what you mean."

"It would be a comfort to know how to pray to God."

"My grandmother always said you just open your mouth and talk to Him."

"Still, it would have been nice to pray in a church," Francis continued, her voice drifting. "Do you suppose they'll come looking for us when we don't show up this morning?"

"Sure," Flint lied. He'd already thought of that. He and Francis had left early. No one would miss them for a half hour. By then the service would just be starting, and they would think that Francis was taking longer to get dressed or that they had gotten stuck in a snowdrift or changed their minds altogether. It would be a good hour before they would even start to worry.

Flint knew it would be several hours more before anyone would find them. And that would be too long for people left in a snowbank in ten-below-zero weather without even a shirt between them.

"But if they don't come right away we could make some kind of shelter from those boxes," Flint said brightly. He had no idea if a box house would keep them alive long enough. What he did know is that Francis needed hope. He needed it himself.

"And there might be something to start a fire with in those boxes," Francis agreed willingly. "Some cooking utensil or something. Chefs are always flambéing something or another."

Flint felt the ropes at his wrist start to give.

"Twist your hand away from me," Flint instructed. "I think I've got it."

One of Flint's hands scraped through the knot. He pulled his hand up and flexed his fingers. The cold was stiffening them more quickly than he had thought. He needed to act fast.

"If we had a fire, we might be able to find something to burn that would make enough black smoke to make someone curious," Flint said as he twisted his other hand to free it as well.

Finally, both of Flint's hands were free.

He turned and saw Francis's back. Her shoulders were hunched, and the thin line of her spine stood out whiter than the rest of her skin. She had curled her hair for church, and the curls still bounced. Her hands were still behind her back, and with the extra room in the knots since Flint had removed his hands, she was twisting her hands to free them.

The threat of death does strange things to a man, Flint reflected. It certainly made him dare things he wouldn't otherwise.

"Come." Flint turned Francis and drew her to him.

Francis knew that their only victory might be untying their hands. She knew they might not have a way to burn the boxes for heat and that they might freeze to death after all. But she would still be glad that they had freed their hands and could hug one another.

Flint's chest had changed since they used to embrace. He'd been a lanky young man, and his chest used to be wiry. Now his chest was solid. Muscles rippled as his arms tightened around her.

Flint almost couldn't breathe, and he wasn't so sure it was because of the biting cold in his lungs. He had Francis in his arms once again. He wanted to let his words of love spill out and cover them, but he didn't.

"I'll get us out of here," he said gruffly as he pulled away from her. "If it's the last thing I do, I'll get us out of here."

Francis nodded. She was too cold to think.

Dear Lord, she thought, *we might actually die out here.* This time the thought did not terrify her.

"But if not, you'll hold me some more, won't you?" Francis asked quietly. "I mean, if it turns out that there's no hope? I don't want to die alone."

"You're not going to die," Flint promised fiercely as he forced himself to stand. The cold was beginning to slow him, too. "I'm going to look through those boxes that just came in. Then I'm going to see if the cigarette lighter in the Jeep works."

Flint stood and eyed the boxes. It was so cold the snow wasn't melting, and the boxes were not damp at all. He slowly counted ten large boxes. Quite a parachute drop. Nine of them had the red stamped logo of a supermarket on them. Howard's Gourmet Foods.

Flint was walking toward the first of those boxes when he noticed the tenth box in more detail. It was a rectangular box with the imprint of some clothing store on it.

"Bingo!" Flint shouted, and turned to Francis.

She was huddled in the snow where they'd been tied. Her skin was too white, and her eyes were half-closed. That was a bad sign.

"You need to move around," Flint urged her as he quickly walked to her and held out his hand. "Come over here and let's open the boxes."

"I'm not sure I can," Francis said. But she took Flint's outstretched hand, and he slowly pulled her to her feet. Her body almost creaked as she moved.

"There's a clothing box." Flint led Francis over to where the boxes had been dumped. "Robert must have had them drop off some winter clothing along with the food."

"Maybe a—wool jacket—or thermal long johns," Francis whispered as Flint tore through the tape on the box. Her teeth were chattering in slow motion, and she needed to pause between words. "I do—hope—it's long johns."

"Well, it's—" Flint held up the first piece of clothing he pulled out and announced in disappointment "—a tuxedo."

The black jacket was made of silk. Even packed

away as it had been, it was obviously expensive. Expensive and light enough for a summer evening.

Francis hugged herself and rubbed her arms slowly. She couldn't even feel her fingers.

"They must have come late," Francis said hoarsely. "The dance is already over."

Flint noticed that a small receipt was tucked into the box under the tuxedo jacket. He pulled it out. "I don't think it was meant for the dance—these are addressed to Laurel Blackstone."

"The woman who came in—the one who knew Robert Buckwalter?"

Flint nodded as he pulled out a pair of men's slacks. The black slacks had a shiny, dark gray stripe down the leg. At least the slacks looked like they'd keep some of the cold away.

"My guess is she knew him rather well," Flint said as he pulled out the final garment in the box—a frothy wedding gown.

"My word," Francis breathed and then realized the implications of the dress. "Poor Jenny."

Francis had seen that the young chef was smitten with Robert Buckwalter. But it looked like Laurel Blackstone had expectations of her own.

The gown was beautiful. Francis reached out to touch the beaded flounces in the full skirt. Even in the bitter cold, she had to appreciate that gown. The bodice was made of soft ivory satin. A square-cut neckline was lined with satin trim and embedded pearls.

Yards of sheer net fell from the waist and formed a train. "I've never seen anything so exquisite."

"Well, it's yours," Flint said as he handed the dress to her.

"But, I can't—"

"I suppose we could reverse them—but I don't think the dress would do nearly as much for me as it would for you," Flint joked.

"But it's Laurel's wedding dress," Francis protested. She might be in an extreme situation, but good manners should still mean something. "I can't just put on someone's dress and then—lie down and die in it."

Flint's heart gladdened at the pink consternation on Francis's face. She always was one to be concerned about the proper time and place of things. It was good to have her back. He'd been worried when she seemed so listless.

"Well, I guess that means I have to get into it then," Flint teased as he lifted the cloud of net over his head.

"Oh, don't be silly," Francis protested like he'd known she would. "Give me that thing."

"Gladly."

Flint couldn't restrain himself. He lifted the cloud of white net high and then, stepping forward, settled it over both Francis and himself. Inside the tangle, his lips found hers.

Francis felt Flint's warm breath seconds before she felt his lips on hers. She didn't bother to hide the purr that vibrated deep within her. A kiss, she decided, was a very nice thing.

Flint was adjusting his violet silk cummerbund and muttering about the fact that only a woman would buy a fancy cummerbund and no shirt when he heard a sound that made him turn and scan the horizon.

"Well, hallelujah! Look at that!"

Francis turned to look in the direction Flint was pointing. The dress was strangely warm for being so frothy. "What is that?"

Flint didn't need to see more of the distant figure to know in his gut that it was who he thought it was. "Honey!"

The horse neighed in response to Flint's call and started to trot toward them.

"Well, well," Flint said to himself. He was right about that horse. She made a fine partner.

"She came to get us?" Francis asked in gratitude.

"Close enough." Flint grinned as Honey did as he suspected she might and stopped at the back of his pickup to sniff the bag of apples he'd tossed there earlier. "Close enough."

Flint was careful to give Honey only half of the apples before handing the red mesh bag, half-empty, to Francis. "Hold these."

Flint put his foot in the stirrup and swung himself into the saddle before reaching down and helping Francis climb up behind him.

Honey fidgeted for a moment, uncertain about the two adults on her back.

"Easy, girl." Flint soothed the horse as he smiled. The fidgeting made Francis lean in closer to him and clutch him fearfully around the middle.

Now this is how a hero is supposed to feel, Flint said to himself in satisfaction as he recalled the last time he and Francis had been riding Honey.

"Let's go to town," Flint said softly to the horse. "We've got a bride to warm up."

Chapter Twelve

Heading down the country road into Dry Creek, Flint held Honey to a fast walk, at least most of the time. Now that he and Francis had some clothes on their backs, their heat loss was much less. He didn't want to risk Honey overexerting and becoming so cold she couldn't go on.

"What time is it?" Francis asked behind Flint's back. She'd recently lain her cheek against his tuxedo jacket for warmth, and he liked her nestling against his shoulder blades.

Flint lifted the back of his jacket so that Francis's arms would be covered as she clutched him. It left a draft on the middle of his back where the cummerbund ended, but it kept her arms warm, and she snuggled even closer to him.

"Ten to eleven," Flint said after looking down at his sports watch. Mr. Gossett had apparently considered watches in the same necessary category as underwear and hadn't demanded that Flint take it off.

"Everyone will be at the church," Francis mumbled.

"That's what we want," Flint said. "We'll be able to mobilize everyone right away. The sheriff should be there still, and he can get in touch with the Billings police and any security they have at the airport."

"Do you think Jenny and Robert are all right?"

"Robert knows what he's doing." Flint comforted her as well as himself. "He won't take any unnecessary chances."

Flint didn't add that he was more worried about Jenny. He searched the skyline as though he might see the small plane. The young woman was high-spirited. High-spirited people tended to make themselves targets in hostage situations.

The morning seemed to warm a few degrees as the sun rose higher in the sky. It still wasn't warm enough to disturb the snow, however, and soft banks lined both sides of the country road they were riding down.

Honey seemed to sense they were close to Dry Creek and started to move faster as they took the last turn in the road before coming into the small cluster of buildings that made up Dry Creek.

Flint steered the horse toward the church. The white frame building with its steep roof and empty belfry had never looked so good to him. The double doors at the top of the cement steps were closed, so that must mean the service had started. If he remembered rightly, they kept the doors open in the summer during the services, and the hymns spilled out into the area around the church. He had sometimes sat on the last step and listened as a teenager. But in winter, the cold didn't allow open doors so the thick, stained pine doors were closed.

"Let's get you inside," Flint said to Francis as Honey stopped at the bottom of the church steps. The sky had grown overcast and dark. There'd be snow soon.

Flint swung his leg around awkwardly so he could dismount before Francis and help her. Once on the ground, Flint lifted his arms. "Just slide down. I've got you."

"My leg's like wood," Francis whispered as she leaned over.

Flint's heart would have stopped if it hadn't already been frozen. Thick rich waves of black hair tumbled from her porcelain face, and the wedding dress was cut to show off her curves.

How much torture can a man stand? Flint asked himself as he clenched his jaw and did his duty. He reached up, grabbed Francis by the waist and pulled her off Honey. Flint almost welcomed the prickles of icy pain that ran along his chest as Francis slid down him.

They were both freezing. Inside the church, the piano had begun to play an introduction to a hymn that sounded vaguely familiar. But outside, where they stood, snowflakes were beginning to fall.

"You just need to get your circulation back," Flint said soothingly, careful not to reveal either the tension that stretched inside him or his ever-increasing worry. At least they'd had snow boots and socks, so with luck they wouldn't have frostbite on their toes. "You'll be fine once we get you inside. Does that retired vet still go to church here?"

Voices inside, some off-key and some too loud, began to sing "Amazing Grace."

"Dr. Norris?" Francis tried to steady herself. A snowflake landed on her cheek. "I think so."

Flint hoped the vet was sitting inside right now. Francis relaxed her grip on his shoulders, and Flint could see she was trying to stand. She winced, and her face got even whiter than he'd thought possible. He needed to get her inside.

"Lean on me," Flint commanded. "Don't try to walk yourself."

"No," Francis protested. "I'll do it." She drew a breath of the frigid air to steady herself. "I take care of myself."

"Not while I'm around."

Flint didn't know where he got the strength. His arms shot daggers of icy pain through him every time he moved them. His feet had gone numb long ago. But he could not bear to see Francis struggle. Flint bent his knees slightly and scooped Francis up in his arms.

"Oh," she breathed in surprise.

Flint shifted Francis so one hand was free to grab the railing that divided the cement steps. Francis hung around his neck as he pulled them both up the five stairs. He could as well have been climbing Mount Everest for the effort those five steps took. His legs were like frozen sausages, and that lace—Flint thought he'd never seen a wedding dress so full of lace. Layers of ivory froth were everywhere. They trailed between Flint's legs. They covered his arm. The bag of apples that Francis still clutched in her hand beat a gentle tap-tap on his back. Snow was falling everywhere.

Flint reached for the doorknob and tried to turn it. It was no good. His hand couldn't grasp it. He couldn't bend his fingers. He tried again. Finally, he gave the bottom of the door a thudding kick.

Please, God, let someone hear me.

The words to the second verse of "Amazing Grace" were filtering through the door. Someone was trilling a soprano harmony.

Flint kicked again.

The door slowly opened, and a young girl looked around it. She must be about seven, Flint thought. She had serious eyes and short blond hair. Her eyes grew wide as she saw Flint and Francis.

"I thought it was Johnnie," she whispered. "He's the kind that'd kick at doors. You're not supposed to kick at doors," she added virtuously.

"I know. Can we come in?" Flint asked softly.

The girl nodded. "It's church. That's where brides are supposed to go."

The girl turned and opened the door wide.

Francis looked inside the church she'd visited often as a child. The walls were painted a light yellow, and thin sunshine streamed into the main room from tall rectangular windows of clear glass. The pews, made of solid oak over a hundred years ago, had an uneven patina because of the years of use. The church should look shabby, but it was too clean for that.

Today, the church was half-full. Obviously the snow had kept some people away. But Francis looked and saw Mrs. Hargrove and the Edison family. Glory Beckett Curtis was there with the twin boys. Doris June was sharing a hymnal with a handsome man Francis didn't recognize.

The air inside the church was warm, and the faint hum of the heater could be heard from the doorway. Someone had fashioned a bouquet from pine boughs and holly branches and put it in front of the solid pulpit.

Everyone in the small church was looking at their hymnals, singing in unison.

We'll just slip into a back pew and whisper with the sheriff, Francis thought. *No need to disturb everyone.*

But Francis hadn't reckoned on the little girl.

"It's a wedding," the girl announced loudly as she opened both doors wide for Francis and Flint. "They need to get married."

Everything in the church stopped. Francis swore she heard a gasp, but maybe it was just the last note sung. The pianist stopped with her hands half-raised off the keyboard. Matthew Curtis, the minister who had been leading the singing, lifted his head and looked straight down the aisle at them. Every other head in the church slowly turned and looked at the open doorway.

Flint almost swore. Then he looked at Francis and saw what the citizens of Dry Creek saw at that very minute. Francis was all ivory and pink, with wet snow-flakes like dewy sequins scattered over her face and arms. Ivory lace and netting spread out from her in luxuriant waves. The curls in her black hair had soft-ened, and strands of her hair hung down, covering his hands. Flint had never believed in fairy-tale prin-cesses until now. Francis was so beautiful he ached just looking at her. She was a bride.

Francis almost fainted. Then she looked at Flint's face and saw what the citizens of Dry Creek saw. He was fierce and elegant all at the same time. The black silk of his tuxedo jacket fit his broad shoulders like it had been tailored for him. But his bare chest where his shirt had been—ah, Francis thought, she could see why the women looking their way were speechless. He looked more pirate than groom, but he looked every inch a man to be reckoned with.

"We're not—" she whispered.

"We don't—" he murmured.

But no one listened. There was a long, indrawn breath of silence, maybe even of awe, and then an eruption of joy.

"Congratulations!" someone yelled from the front pew.

"Hallelujah!" someone else shouted. "It's about time!"

And then everyone moved at once.

"Oh, your grandmother," Mrs. Hargrove said as she stepped out of her pew and started toward them, dabbing a handkerchief at her eyes. "If she could have only lived to see—" She looked at the ceiling. "Or are you watching, Essie?"

The pianist's hands went to the keyboard, only now they were playing "Here Comes the Bride."

Francis felt the gentle hands of two young girls touching her dress reverently.

"We're not," Flint tried again.

"We don't," Francis tried, joining him.

"Why doesn't anyone tell me anything?" Sheriff Wall complained as he slipped out of the last pew and walked toward them. "If I'd know you were planning this, I'd have brought my marrying book."

"I've got my book," Matthew Curtis said, smiling widely from the front of the aisle. "What a great way to start a Sunday morning! A surprise wedding!"

Flint felt the twinge in his stomach grow into a knot. He'd been scared when old man Gossett pointed that gun at him. He'd thought he was a goner when the old man left him and Francis to freeze to death. But nothing—absolutely none of it—terrified him like this moment.

He knew now why he'd asked Francis to elope twenty years ago. That was all he had the courage for. Some quick marriage in Vegas had none of the glow that standing in this church in wedding clothes had. The good people of Dry Creek stood around him, and he was almost undone by the expectation he saw on their faces. They expected something from him—something good, something important, something lasting.

He, Flint Harris, did not have the grit to face that kind of responsibility. It was beyond him. He couldn't bear to disappoint everyone, and he was sure to fail.

Francis felt the joy leave her. For a moment, she'd been caught up in the dream. Maybe, just maybe she and Flint would go along with the enthusiasm of those around them. They'd be married—truly, gloriously married—finally.

Then Francis had looked up and seen the change in Flint's face. If she hadn't known him so well, she wouldn't have seen it at all. His jaw had tightened—not much, it was true, but enough. His eyes got a hunted look in them and grew hooded, like he wanted to hide his feelings. He was smiling, but it was only a motion of his lips.

He doesn't want to marry me, Francis thought dully. *He doesn't want to be impolite—to embarrass me in front of all of these people—but he clearly doesn't want to marry me.*

"There's been a misunderstanding," Francis said calmly. Strange how the cold that had nearly frozen her earlier hadn't touched her heart the way the cold in Flint's eyes did now. She nudged Flint, and he opened his arms so that she could slide to the floor and stand alone. She was, after all, alone. No sense pretending otherwise. "The clothes—they're not ours—"

The church went silent once again.

"Old man Gossett has kidnapped Robert and Jenny and is making them fly him into Billings."

"Why, the old coot," Mrs. Hargrove said indignantly. "Doesn't he know that's dangerous? It's already starting to snow again."

"I don't think he cares," Francis continued. "He has two guns and he wanted to meet some bus in Billings."

"Where's he got to go that's so all-fired important?" someone muttered.

Flint met the inspector's eyes. The inspector had been in the last pew, as they had agreed earlier, and the pew had been roped off with a gold cord, waiting for Francis to arrive.

"He's our man?" the inspector asked Flint quietly. "The informant?"

Flint nodded. "We'd better alert the police in Billings to pick him up at the airport. He's running."

"Armed and dangerous?" Sheriff Wall stepped closer to Flint. "I'll put out an APB."

Francis felt soft hands tugging at her dress. She looked into the face of the young girl.

"You're still a bride, aren't you?" the little girl asked, worried. "You're wearing a bride's dress."

"A dress doesn't make a bride," Francis answered softly.

"But the dress is the best part of the wedding," the little girl said, confident in her knowledge. "Except for the cake, maybe. Does this mean there's no cake, either?"

The girl's mother appeared at her side, "Hush, now, don't bother Francis with your questions."

"It's no bother," Francis said woodenly as she made an effort to smile at the girl. "And I wish there was a cake— I love wedding cake, too."

When Francis looked up from the girl, she noticed that Flint had gone to talk with the inspector and the sheriff. They were standing in the back pew muttering, and the inspector had his cell phone in his hand.

Flint had already borrowed a parka from the inspector and had replaced the tuxedo jacket with it. He hadn't wasted any time getting back to normal, Francis thought, as she let Mrs. Hargrove lead her to a pew so she could sit.

"Such a pity," Mrs. Hargrove muttered as she settled Francis in a pew and tucked her coat around Francis's shoulders.

Francis didn't know whether the older woman was talking about Mr. Gossett or the wedding that didn't happen, but she didn't ask.

Chapter Thirteen

Flint spit, then drove another nail into the side boards on his grandmother's house. The air was cold, and he felt a bitter satisfaction with the way the frigid air caught in his throat. The board didn't need that nail. It hadn't needed the other ten he drove in before it, either. But it was hammer or go crazy, and so he kept his hand curled around the tool and his mind focused on the nail. The solid blows of iron on iron suited him.

He sank that nail deep and pulled another one out of his shirt pocket. He had it positioned ready for striking when he heard the sound of a Jeep pulling itself up the slight incline that led to his grandmother's old house.

House, nothing, he said to himself as he looked at the weathered boards. The old thing could hardly be called a house anymore. It was more shack than house at the moment. When the windows had broken out, the snow and rain of twenty-some years had broken down the interior.

It would need to be gutted, he thought. A new roof and gutted.

The driver of the Jeep honked the horn as the vehicle slowed to a stop in front of the house.

Flint didn't want company. He'd already had a dozen congratulatory calls on his cell phone, telling him he was brilliant for figuring out that Mr. Gossett had changed his mind a second time and asked Robert to fly him to Fargo, after all. Flint had cut all the calls short.

Flint knew he wasn't brilliant. It didn't take brilliance to know what a cornered animal would do when you felt like you were one yourself.

Flint hit the nail square and grunted. He wondered how many nails he'd have to hit before he felt human again.

"There you are." Mrs. Hargrove's cheery voice came from behind him.

If it had been anyone else, Flint would have asked them to leave. Since it was his grandmother's dearest friend, he only grunted and hit the nail again. He hoped she'd take the hint. She didn't.

"I brought you some oatmeal cookies," she continued. "I remember how you used to like them."

Flint had no choice but to turn and smile at the woman. "Thanks. I appreciate that."

"I thought you might be out here," she mused as she set a small box down and wiped the snow off the top porch step. Then she eased herself down and unwound the wool scarf she wore around her head. "Never can hear with that scarf on."

Flint had a sinking feeling that meant she was going to expect conversation. "I'm fixing the side wall here."

Mrs. Hargrove nodded and was silent.

"Thought I'd put some windows in, too." Flint went on. Her sitting there silent made him nervous. "Maybe fix that leak in the roof."

"Essie would like that," Mrs. Hargrove finally said. "You living here."

"Me? Live here? No, I'm just fixing it up."

Mrs. Hargrove nodded. "You're going to sell it then?"

"Sell it? I couldn't do that—it's Grandmother's house."

Mrs. Hargrove was silent so long that Flint positioned another nail and hit it.

"Essie doesn't need the house anymore, you know," Mrs. Hargrove finally said gently. "You don't have to take care of it for her."

"She wouldn't like it if it was run down."

"She wouldn't blame you for it if it was."

"I wouldn't want to disappoint her," Flint said softly as he gripped the hammer and hit the nail again. "I've disappointed enough folks as it is."

"Essie was never disappointed in you."

"She should have been— I messed up enough times."

"Everybody messes up sometimes," Mrs. Hargrove

said softly. "Your grandmother knew that—she was a big believer in grace and forgiveness."

Flint grunted. "My grandmother was a saint."

Mrs. Hargrove chuckled. "Not to hear her tell it. She used to say the vein of guilt that ran through your family was thick enough to make somebody rich if they could only mine it."

Flint looked up for the first time. "But she never failed anyone. She was as close to perfect as anyone could be. What did she ever need forgiveness for?"

"We all need forgiveness," Mrs. Hargrove said softly as she placed a motherly hand on Flint's arm. "We all fall short somewhere or other. But we can't let it stop us or we'd never—" Mrs. Hargrove stopped abruptly. "Why, that's it! That's why you're out here pounding away at those rusty old nails instead of sweet-talking Francis! You're afraid."

Flint winced. "I wouldn't say that."

"And just what would you say, then?"

Flint grimaced. "I'm cautious—based on my knowledge of myself, I'm cautious about promising something and then disappointing someone."

"You don't love her, then?"

Flint squirmed. "No, that's not the problem."

"You intend to marry her and then leave her some-day and break her heart?"

"Why, no, of course not, I wouldn't do that."

Flint wondered if it would be too impolite to climb on the roof and take care of those loose shingles while he was thinking about them. Mrs. Hargrove had the tenacity of a bulldog.

"Well, son, what is it that's eating away at you. then?"

"I need to fix the roof."

"And that's why you can't get married?" she asked incredulously.

Flint sighed. There was no way out of this one but to go through the scorching fire. "I'm just not good enough, all right? Somewhere, sometime, I'd let her down. I'd forget her birthday. I don't make jelly, you know. Never learned how."

Mrs. Hargrove looked at him blankly.

"Even old man Gossett has a cellar full of crabapple jelly. He must be able to make it. Me, I can't even make a company cup of coffee—what kind of a husband would I make?"

Mrs. Hargrove didn't say anything.

"Besides, I've noticed some thinning in my hair. I could go bald someday."

"Your hair looks fine to me," Mrs. Hargrove interrupted skeptically.

"That's not the point," Flint said in exasperation. "It's just an example of what could happen, and anything could happen."

Mrs. Hargrove eyed him thoughtfully. "You don't have a clue about grace and forgiveness, do you? And after all those Bible verses I taught you in Sunday school, I would have thought one or two would stick."

"They did stick," Flint said softly. "It's just that being forgiven by God isn't quite the same as being forgiven by a flesh-and-blood wife you've disappointed."

Mrs. Hargrove snorted. "You can't fool me. You don't remember them, after all, do you? Recite me one."

"Now?"

Mrs. Hargrove nodded.

Flint's mind scrambled. "I remember one about four times forty—or was it eight times eighty?"

"Seven times seventy." Mrs. Hargrove shook her head. "That's how many times we're to forgive someone." She fixed him with a challenging eye. "Do you figure you'll mess up more times than that? That's almost five hundred times. Francis isn't likely to have nearly that many birthdays."

"Well, there'd be anniversaries, too. Every year April 17 will roll around—"

"Surely you're not planning to forget them all?" Mrs. Hargrove demanded. "Give yourself some credit."

Flint stopped in the middle of a swing with the hammer. He knew he wouldn't forget the anniversaries. He hadn't forgotten one of them yet. "I might not need to worry about the anniversaries."

Mrs. Hargrove nodded complacently. "They've been a sore spot, have they?"

Flint looked at her indignantly. How did she know these things?

The older woman laughed. "You're a Harris. None of the folks in your family ever took lightly to love. Essie used to say it gave everyone another reason to suffer."

Flint grunted and then admitted slowly, "I've hated April for years. The first five anniversaries I went out and got stinking drunk on April 17, and then sat down and wrote a scathing letter to Francis." He smiled. "I wrote down all my disappointments for the whole year like they were all her fault. Finally, I was able to tell her the good things, too—and how I missed her."

Flint concentrated on steadying another nail.

"Well, if you remembered your anniversary for years, what makes you think you'd forget it if Francis were with you?"

Flint didn't know. That was what had been gnawing at him for the past two days. He didn't know why he was so nervous about taking a flying leap into matrimony, he just knew that he was.

"You need to sit down with Essie's Bible," Mrs. Hargrove declared. "Maybe then you can make some sense out of yourself."

"Yes, ma'am."

The older woman eased herself off the porch and stood. "Remember, this is lightning country." She nodded at the nails in the piece of board. "Much more of that and this place will catch the next bolt that comes flying through."

Flint smiled. He wasn't so sure the bolt wasn't already here. "Thanks for stopping by."

"Just see to your reading."

Flint had no intention of reading the Bible, but he felt almost like he'd promised. And so he opened it after Mrs. Hargrove had left and began to read the verses his grandmother had highlighted. The afternoon slipped into dusk and the sun was going down before he realized he'd spent the afternoon looking for the answers to the gnawing inside himself.

When he realized what time it was, he pulled out his cell phone and made a call to the manager of his apartment building.

"Yes, I'd like you to send them overnight express." He finished his instructions. "I'll go into Miles City tomorrow and get them."

Francis was standing in the small bedroom she used at Garth's house. She was packing. Her old-fashioned suitcase was open on the bed. It was a good-quality suitcase, but it had none of the modern pockets and compartments. Francis always maintained that a neat person didn't need to fear packing and certainly didn't need compartments.

Francis's socks were neatly paired and folded with the toes under. Her bras were folded and laid conveniently close to her panty hose. She had loose tissue to pack around her slacks and two dresses. Organizing her clothes made her feel like there was something in her life she could control just the way she wanted it. She might not be good with men, but she was good with avoiding creases.

Francis had waited around for Flint Harris once before, and she couldn't bear to do it again. Flint's face had been cold when she'd last seen him three days ago, and it had nothing to do with the weather. Sam was getting restless and wanted her to fly back to Denver with him. She'd told him she'd be ready tomorrow. He might be a little dull, but Sam was a good man.

"You're leaving?"

The deep voice came from the doorway to the small bedroom, and Francis whirled.

"Who let you in?" Francis swore she'd fry the culprit in hot oil.

"Garth," Flint said simply. "He told me I have five minutes."

"That's five more than I would have given you."

Flint had his outdoor parka on, and there were flecks of snow melting on his shoulders. He might have had a hat on his head, because his hair was slightly rumpled. He was fresh-shaven, and his hands held a small plastic bag with the name of a Miles City drugstore stamped on it.

Flint nodded seriously. "I figured as much, and you don't even know the half of it." He hesitated and took a deep breath. "I have a drawer full of mismatched socks in my apartment, and baldness runs in my family."

Francis looked at him in astonishment.

Flint nodded glumly. "It's true. One of my mother's brothers. That's the worst odds, they say. And I don't know how to make jelly—or really good coffee—I guess I could maybe manage a cup of tea and dry toast—"

"What in the world are you talking about?"

"I've had to kill two men. They were evil men and I had to do it, but it's there all the same—plus I work too much." Flint staunchly continued his list. "Although I have been thinking about chickens for the last day or so, and maybe it's time to quit my job and take them on. I've made good investments over the years so money's not a problem. It'd work out."

Francis was becoming worried. "Did Dr. Norris check you out when we got back to Dry Creek? I've heard of sunstroke doing this to people, but maybe extreme cold acts in the same way—"

"Of course, if you don't still want to do chickens, we could try our hand at something else." Flint cleared his throat and continued his speech. He didn't want to get derailed. If he did, he might not get back on the track again. "I've decided I like Dry Creek. I like the church here and I think that's going to be important to me. And the air is good. Hard to get good air anymore."

Francis looked at Flint. His eyes looked clear

enough to swim in, and he didn't have any strange twitches happening with his mouth. Then she remembered the drugstore bag he carried.

"Is that medicine you have with you?" she asked gently. Maybe that's why she hadn't heard from him for three days. "You poor man."

Francis stepped to Flint and placed her hand on his forehead. "Did Dr. Norris give you something to take?"

Flint's mouth went dry. His voice croaked. "I'm not sick." Flint swore no man in the history of the world had bungled a job like he was doing.

"Of course you are," Francis said softly. "What else could this be?"

Flint took a deep breath and plunged. "It could be a marriage proposal."

Francis stared at him, her hand frozen on his cheek.

"Not a good proposal, I'll admit," Flint continued shakily. "But I thought you should know the problems up front. I've always believed in saying the truth straight out."

"Marriage?" Francis's voice squeaked. "But the medicine?"

"It's not medicine," Flint said softly. "It's cards— for you."

Francis looked around for support and sat on the bed.

Flint opened the bag and held up twenty envelopes. Some of the envelopes were white. Some pink. A few ivory. One even had pale green stripes on it. Each one had the number of a year written on it in black ink.

"They're anniversary cards," Flint said softly as he fanned them out on the bed next to her. "Bought the whole store out. One for each year—and inside is the letter I wrote you in that year."

"You wrote me?" Francis whispered.

Flint nodded. "I had to."

"Oh." Francis brushed a tear from her eye. She tried to focus, to think this new information through, but for once in her life she didn't care about the order of anything. "I thought you'd forgotten me."

"How could I forget the only woman I've ever loved?" Flint said softly. The tears gave him hope. He would carry this through in any event, but the tears did give him hope.

Flint pulled a long-stemmed yellow rose out of an inner pocket in his parka. It was the only yellow rose to be had in Miles City, and it was a little peaked. Then he dropped to one knee and offered the rose to Francis. "Will you marry me again? This time for good?"

"Oh." Francis swallowed.

"Is that an 'oh, yes' or an 'oh, no'?" Flint asked quietly.

"Yes," she stammered. "My, yes. It's an 'oh, yes.'"

Flint reached up and brushed the tears from her eyes before he leaned forward and kissed her. The pure sweetness of it sang inside of him. He didn't deserve someone like Francis.

"I could maybe do something about those socks."

Francis laughed and touched his cheek. Yes, he was real. "I don't care about the socks."

"This time let's get married in the church here in front of everyone in Dry Creek," Flint said. "I want to see my bride walk down that aisle."

Francis smiled dreamily. "Dry Creek does love a bride."

"Not half as much as I do," Flint said, smiling as he bent his head to kiss Francis again. "Not half as much as I do."

* * * * *

Dear Reader,

I should have my mother write you this note. She, having raised five usually wonderful children (of which I am blessed to be one), knows far more of the hope that goes into love than I do. Actually, most mothers know that kind of hope—the hope that their love will bear fruit, that their love will ease someone's pain and that it will even give that person an anchor in life. Love laced with hope is a useful kind of love. It sees beyond the romantic parts of love and looks to the future.

That's why, when I chose to tell the story of Francis, I knew it had to be a story of hope. We never know when we love someone what our hopes will bring. Francis did not know. Flint did not know. Only God knew.

May this story of Francis and Flint encourage you to love with hope and to trust God for a happy ending.

Janet Tronstad

SHEPHERDS ABIDING
IN DRY CREEK

And there were in the same country
shepherds abiding in the field, keeping watch
over their flock by night.
—*Luke* 2:8

Dedicated to my grandfather, Harold Norris.
I remember him for his small kindnesses
and his big heart. He was a good man.

Chapter One

"I am the good shepherd; the good shepherd giveth his life for the sheep."

John 10:11

Marla Gossett sat in her bare apartment on the one wooden chair she had left to her name. The apartment building faced a busy street in south central Los Angeles, with the constant hum of cars going by. Marla didn't even hear the noise any longer. She'd sold her sofa yesterday and the kids' beds the day before that. She wished she could at least take the beds with them, but they wouldn't fit in the car when they moved. Besides, they all had sleeping bags.

Right now she was in the middle of selling her lamp to the African-American woman who had moved in down the hall a week ago.

Marla had given up on selling the chair she was

sitting on. No one was willing to buy it with "XIX" carved into the arm. Not that she blamed them. She felt uneasy just sitting on the thing herself. She had put a notice in the hallway a week ago and several people had asked about the chair until they saw the numbers.

"You'll have a new life away from here," her African-American neighbor—Susan was her name—said softly. Susan was looking at the numbers on the chair. "Your son?"

Marla nodded. She wasn't proud that her eleven-year-old son, Sammy, had carved the sign of the 19th Street gang into her furniture. She told herself it was only natural for young boys to be impressed with the tough guys that ruled their neighborhood. The 19th Street gang was the largest Hispanic gang in Los Angeles. She knew her son was just an onlooker at this point. Other people didn't know that, though, and they were scared to buy the chair even if it was solid oak and had been the finest piece of furniture she owned.

The chair had been a wedding gift, and there was a matching wooden cross that came to hang behind it.

Susan looked up from the chair. "Well, I guess they have gangs everywhere. Where are you going, anyway?"

"A place called Dry Creek, Montana. My husband had an uncle who left us a house there before he died."

"Did your husband get a chance to show it to you?"

Marla shook her head. She had already shared her

vital statistics, so the woman knew her husband had died from lung cancer last year.

"Well, at least he left you with something," Susan said in a tone that implied she didn't expect much from men. "Of course, it would have been better if he'd gotten you some life insurance."

"We always thought there was plenty of time."

The woman nodded, and Marla wondered how it was that death had become so commonplace. Some days she wanted to scream at the injustice of it, but more often it just weighed her down with its ordinariness.

She had been a widow for over a year, and it still felt like yesterday. She'd married Jorge when she was nineteen, and it hadn't taken long for the blaze of romance between them to settle into a steady flame of affection. At least, she had assumed the flame was steady. That was the way it had been on her side.

The cancer came hard and swiftly. It wasn't until Jorge was gone that she had had time to think about her marriage. Near the end, when he could barely speak, Jorge confessed he'd been unfaithful several times and pleaded with her to forgive him. He said he didn't want to die with those sins on his conscience.

After his diagnosis, Jorge had started praying often and had asked her to move their wooden cross into the bedroom. It seemed to comfort him, and Marla was glad for that. She believed her husband did repent his sins. So what could she do? There was no time to work through her feelings. She forgave him because she had to, and then he lost consciousness, dying later that same night.

When he was gone, all Marla could think about was their marriage. She kept wondering if something was lacking in her, and if that was why Jorge had not loved her enough to be faithful or to even talk to her about his problems. Maybe she didn't inspire love the way other women did.

Even when he'd proposed, Jorge had not made any grand gestures of love toward her. Marla had not thought anything was wrong with that, though; she thought it was just the way he was. Marriage wasn't all about roses and valentines. She'd accepted that. But had she missed some clue? Or were there many little clues she had ignored? Was a woman supposed to keep a tally of things that would tell her if her husband still loved her? How could she not even have known he was unfaithful?

As her feelings for Jorge changed, Marla wondered if she'd ever really known her husband. Still, especially in the past few weeks, she'd wished he were still alive so they could share the problems about Sammy. Jorge might have been unfaithful to her, but he had loved Sammy. What would Sammy do without his dad?

Worrying about Sammy had made her take the cross out of the box, where she'd put it after Jorge died, and hang it on the wall again. Sometimes she'd look at it, searching for the solace her husband had found in it. She wished she could find an answer for Sammy there. The cross didn't speak to her the way it had to Jorge.

"Did you say Montana?" Susan was frowning for the first time.

Marla nodded. She wondered why the mention of Montana was disturbing her neighbor more than their earlier discussion about death had.

"They don't have much color there."

"You mean trees?"

Susan pursed her lips as she turned to study Marla. "No, I mean people."

Marla had combed her hair this morning, as she did every morning. It was freshly washed and fell smoothly to her shoulders. At thirty-five, she knew she was no great beauty, but her skin was light olive, and she'd been told her eyes were nice. Her brown hair didn't sparkle with highlights, but she looked all right. She wondered why Susan was looking at her with such an intense expression.

Her neighbor finally nodded. "You'll do fine, though. I'd guess you're—what—half Hispanic?"

"On my mother's side."

Susan kept nodding. "And your son and daughter. I've seen them. They could be white."

Jorge had been half-and-half—Hispanic-Anglo— as well. That had been one of the things they had in common. "They pride themselves on being Hispanic, especially my son."

Susan grunted. "That's just gang talk. He'll get over it quick enough when he's away from here."

"I'm not sure I want him to get over it," Marla said stiffly. "He should be proud of his roots."

So much had been taken from them. She had to draw the line somewhere.

"Take my advice and blend in," Susan said as she picked up the lamp. "You've got a better chance of getting a new husband that way. Especially in a place like that."

"But—" Marla protested. She wasn't sure if she was protesting hiding her roots to find a husband or looking for a husband in the first place. She supposed she would have to marry if she wanted a new father for her children. But she wasn't ready for that yet. What if a second marriage proved only how lacking she was as a woman? There was no reason to believe she'd do any better the second time around than she had the first.

"Trust me. No one wants to have a Hispanic gang member in their neighborhood, no matter where they live. If they don't know you're Hispanic, there's no reason for them to make the 19th Street connection."

"But Sammy's not in the gang. Not really."

Susan held up her hands. "I'm just saying these people will be nervous. There was an article in *Time* magazine last month—or was it *Newsweek?* Anyway, it was about gangs sending scouts out to small towns to see about setting up safe houses there. They want to have a place to send their guys so they can hide out from the police if things get bad. I wouldn't blame a small town for being careful."

"Well, of course they should be careful, but…"

Susan looked at the carving on the armchair again and then just shrugged. "I had a cousin drive through Montana a few years ago. If I remember right, he said the population is only about two percent Hispanic for the whole state. How big is this Dry Creek place you're moving to?"

"Two hundred people."

Susan nodded as she pulled the agreed-upon five-dollar bill from her pocket. "Then you and your kids will probably be the token two percent."

Marla frowned as she stood up. She was ready for the woman to leave. "We're probably not that far from a large city. Maybe Billings. There'll be all kinds of people there."

Susan snorted as she finished handing the bill to Marla. "All I can say is that you'll want to take your chili peppers with you. I doubt you'll find more than salt and pepper around there. It's beef and potato country in more ways than one."

Marla slipped the bill into her pocket. "We don't have a choice about going."

She didn't want to tell her neighbor that the police had come to her door a little over a week ago and warned her that Sammy was on the verge of becoming a real member of that 19th Street gang. She figured they were exaggerating, but she couldn't take a chance. She had given notice at her cashier job and started to make plans. She had to get Sammy out of here, even if it made every soul in Dry Creek nervous. At least she would own the house where they would live, so no one could force them to leave. Sammy and her four-year-old daughter, Becky, would be safe. That was all Marla cared about for now.

The neighbor took one more look at the scarred chair. "I guess we all do what we need to do in life. It's too bad. It was a nice chair."

Marla nodded.

"I wish you well," Susan said as she started walking to the door. "And, who knows, it might not be so bad. My cousin said they have rodeos in the summer and snow for Christmas. He liked the state."

Marla mumbled goodbye as the neighbor left her apartment. She'd been anxious about the move before talking to Susan. Now she could barely face the thought of going to Dry Creek. But looking down at the arm of that wooden chair, she knew she had to go. She'd lost her husband; she refused to lose her son, too.

She wouldn't hide their ethnic roots from the people in Montana, but she saw no reason to advertise them, either. And, of course, she'd keep quiet about Sammy's brush with gang life, especially because it would all be in the past once she got him out of Los Angeles. She was sure of that. She had to be. Dry Creek was her last hope.

Chapter Two

A few weeks later

Les Wilkerson knew something was wrong when his phone rang at six o'clock in the morning. He'd just come in from doing the chores in the barn and was starting to pull his boots off so he wouldn't get the kitchen floor dirty while he cooked his breakfast. It was the timing of the call that had him worried. He'd given the people of Dry Creek permission to call him on sheriff business after six and it sounded as if someone had been waiting until that exact moment to make a call.

Les finished pulling off his boots and walked in his stocking feet to the phone. By that time, enough unanswered rings had gone by to discourage the most persistent telemarketers.

"I think we've had a theft," Linda, the young woman who owned the Dry Creek café, said almost before Les got the phone to his ear. She was out of breath. "Or maybe it's one of those ecology protests. You know, the green people."

"Someone's protesting in Dry Creek?"

Dry Creek had more than its share of independent-minded people. Still, Les had never known any of them to do something like climb an endangered tree and refuse to come down, especially not in the dead of winter when there was fresh snow on the ground.

"I don't know. It's either that or a theft. You know the Nativity set the church women's group just got?"

"Of course."

Everyone knew the Nativity set. The women had collected soup-can labels for months and traded them like green stamps to get a life-size plastic Nativity set that lit up at night. Les was sure he'd eaten more tomato soup recently than he had in his entire life.

"Well, the shepherd's not there. We don't know what happened to him, but we can't see him. Charley says that Elmer has been upset about all of the electricity the church is using to light everything up. He says someone either took the shepherd or Elmer unplugged it to protest the whole thing."

Les had known there would be problems with people eating all that soup. It made old ranchers like Elmer and Charley irritable. It was probably bad for their blood pressure, too.

"Unplugging something is not much of a protest. It could even be a mistake." Now, that was a whole lot more likely than some high-minded protest, Les thought, and then he remembered promising the regular sheriff that he would be patient with everyone. "But I'll talk to Elmer, anyway, and explain how important the Nativity set is and what a sacrifice everyone made so we could have it."

Les was sure Elmer would agree about the sacrifice part. He'd said he was eating so much soup he might as well have false teeth.

There were some muffled voices in the background that Les couldn't make out over the phone.

"That's Elmer now. He just came in and he claims he didn't unplug anything. He says if we can't see the shepherd, it's because it's not there and Charley's right that somebody stole it."

"The light could be burned out." Patience went only so far, Les thought. He wasn't going to go chasing phantom criminals just because someone *thought* something was stolen. There hadn't been an attempted theft in Dry Creek since that woman had broken into the café two years ago. And she had not even taken anything. After all that time, it wasn't likely someone would suddenly decide to steal a plastic shepherd.

"Maybe it is a defective light," Linda agreed. "But I'm going to tell Charley and Elmer not to go over and check. It's still pitch-black outside. Charley's been looking out the café window for a good fifteen minutes, and it's still too dark to see if the shepherd is there. And if it's not there, then it could be a crime scene and we'd need the professionals." Linda's voice dipped so low that only Les could hear it. "Besides, the two of them could fall and break half their bones going over there in the dark. You know how that patch of street in front of the church is always so slippery when we've had snow. So I'll tell them you're going to handle it. Okay?"

"Sounds good," Les said. He'd rather safeguard old bones than chase after imaginary thieves any day. "I'll be right there."

Les usually made a morning trip into town, anyway, before he drove a load of hay out to the cattle he was wintering in the far pasture. The little town of Dry Creek wasn't much—a hardware store, a church, a café and a dozen or so houses—but the regular sheriff guarded the place as if it was Fort Knox, and Les, who was the town's only volunteer reserve deputy, had promised he'd do the same in the sheriff's absence.

Just thinking of the sheriff made Les shake his head. Who would figure that a man as shy as Sheriff Carl Wall would ever have a wedding, let alone a belated honeymoon to celebrate with a trip to Maui?

It was all Les could do not to be jealous. After all, he was as good-looking as Carl, or at least no worse looking. Les even owned his own ranch, as sweet a piece of earth as God ever created, and it was all paid for. Not every man could say that. He should be content. But for the past week every time he thought of

Carl and that honeymoon trip of his, Les started to frown.

If Sheriff Carl Wall could get married, Les figured he should be married, too. He was almost forty years old and, although he enjoyed being single, a man could spend only so much time in his own company before, well, he got a little tired of it. Besides, it would be nice to have a woman's touch around the place. Les knew he could hire someone to do most of the cooking and cleaning. But it wouldn't be the same. A woman just naturally made a home around her, like a mother bird making her nest. A man's house wasn't a home without some nesting going on.

Of course, Les told himself as he pulled his pickup to a stop beside the café, the sheriff had gone a little overboard with it all. He had completely lost his dignity, the way he had moped around until Barbara Strong agreed to marry him. Les would never do that. He had already seen too many tortured love scenes in his life; he had no desire to play the lead in one himself.

His parents were the reason for his reluctance to marry. They had had many very public partings and equally dramatic reconciliations. Les never knew whether they were breaking up or getting back together. The two of them should have sold tickets to their lives. They certainly could have used some help with finances, given the salary his father earned in that shoe store in Miles City. Half their arguments were about money. The other half were about who didn't love whom enough.

His parents were both dead now, but Les had never understood how they could be the way they were. They were so very public about how they felt about everything, from love to taxes. As a child Les had vowed to stay away from that kind of circus. It was embarrassing. Growing up, he never even made a fuss over his dog, because he didn't want anyone to think he was becoming like his parents.

No, Les thought as he stepped up on the café porch, if he was going to get married there would be no emotional public scenes. It would all be a nice sensible arrangement with a nice quiet woman. There was no reason for two people to make fools of themselves just because they wanted to get married, anyway.

"Oh, good. You're here." Linda's voice greeted Les as he opened the door.

The café floor was covered with alternating black and white squares of linoleum. Formica-topped tables sat in the middle of the large room, and a counter ran along one of its sides. The air smelled of freshly made coffee and fried bacon.

Elmer and Charley were sitting at the table closest to the door and they both looked up from their plates as Les stepped inside. They had flushed faces and excitement in their eyes.

"They already went over to the church," Linda whispered as she closed the door behind Les. "They snuck out when I was in the kitchen making their pancakes."

Les could tell the two men were primed to tell him something. It hadn't stopped them from eating their pancakes and bacon, though. All that was left on their plates was syrup. Les walked closer to them. Fortunately, no one had ever suggested people should have soup for breakfast, so that meal had always been safe.

"It's a crime," Elmer announced from where he sat. He had his elbows on the table and his cap sitting on the straight-backed chair next to him.

"We thought maybe you were right about the light just burning out," Charley explained as he pushed his chair back a little from the table. "We didn't want to bother anyone if that was all that happened, so we went over to take a look."

"Looks like a kidnapping to me," Elmer declared confidently, then paused to glance up at Les. "Is it a kidnapping if the kidnapee in question is plastic?"

"No," Les said. He didn't need to call upon his reserve deputy sheriff training to answer that question. "It's not even a theft if someone just moved the figure. That's probably what happened. Maybe the pastor decided the Nativity had too many figures on the left side and put the shepherd inside the church until he could set it up on the other side."

Les reminded himself to get these two men a new checkerboard for Christmas. A dog had chewed up their old cardboard one a month ago, and now, instead of sitting in the hardware store playing checkers, they just sat, either in the hardware store or in the café, and talked. Too much talking was giving them some pretty wild ideas. He couldn't think of one good reason anyone would steal a plastic shepherd, not even one that lit up like a big neon sign at night.

Charley shook his head. "Nah, that can't be it. All of the wise men are on the other side. The pastor wouldn't think there are too many figures on the left. Not even with the angel on the left—and she's a good-sized angel."

"Besides, we know it's not the pastor moving things around, because we found this," Elmer said as he thrust a piece of paper toward Les. "Wait until you see this."

Les's heart sank when he saw the sheet of paper. He had a feeling he knew what kind of note it was. It had a ragged edge where it had been torn from what was probably a school tablet. There must be a dozen school tablets in Dry Creek. The note was written in pencil, and he didn't even want to think about how many pencils there were around. Anyone could have written a note like this.

Les bent to read it.

Dear Church People,
I took your dumb shepherd.
If you want to see him again, leave a Suzy bake
set on the back steps of your church. It needs to

be the deluxe kind—the one with the cupcakes
on the box.

P.S. Don't call the cops.

P.P.S. The angel wire is loose. She's going to fall
if somebody doesn't do something.

XIX

Well, there was one good thing, Les told himself
as he looked up from the paper. There weren't that
many people in Dry Creek who would want a Suzy
bake set. That narrowed down the field of suspects
considerably. He assumed the XIX at the bottom was
some reference to a biblical text on charity. Or maybe a
promise to heap burning coals on someone who didn't
do what they were told.

"So it looks like the shepherd is really gone," Les
said, more to give himself time to think than because
there seemed to be any question about that fact, at
least.

Elmer nodded. "The angel is just standing there
with her wings unfurled looking a little lost now that
she's proclaiming all that good news to a couple of
sheep. You don't see anything standing where that
shepherd should be."

The door to the café opened briskly and an older
woman stepped inside. She had a wool jacket wrapped
around her shoulders and boots on her feet. Les
thought she still had to be cold, though, in that ging-

ham dress she was wearing. Cotton didn't do much to protect a person from a Montana winter chill.

"Mrs. Hargrove, you shouldn't be walking around these streets. They're slippery," Les said to the woman. The older people in Dry Creek just didn't seem to realize how hazardous it was outside after it snowed. And they'd lived here their whole lives, so if anyone should know, they should.

"Charley told me some little girl was in trouble." Mrs. Hargrove glared at Les as she unwound the scarf from around her neck and set down the bag she was carrying. "Something about kidnapping and theft. I hope you're not planning to arrest a little girl."

Les stepped over to help Mrs. Hargrove out of her jacket. "Someone stole the shepherd from the Nativity set. I don't even know who did it yet. But if it is a little girl, she'll have to be dealt with just like anyone else."

Les turned to hang Mrs. Hargrove's jacket on the coatrack by the door.

"Well, a little girl wouldn't have done that," Mrs. Hargrove said as she smoothed down the long sleeves on her dress. "Mark my words."

"Little girls can get into just as much mischief as boys."

One thing Les had learned in his reserve deputy sheriff training was that a lawman shouldn't make assumptions based on stereotypes about people. There were all kinds of stories about mob men who loved their cats and sweet-looking grandmothers who robbed banks in their spare time.

"Still, I say no little girl took that shepherd," Mrs. Hargrove said as she walked over to a chair next to Charley and sat down. "If she couldn't get the angel unhooked, she'd take the baby Jesus. What would she want with a smelly old shepherd?"

Les frowned. "Just because a man works with animals and lives alone, it doesn't mean he smells bad."

Les had a few sheep on his ranch, but the only full-time shepherd he knew was Mr. Morales, who lived in the foothills of the Big Sheep Mountains north of Dry Creek. Les figured bachelor ranchers needed to stick together. Once in a while he invited Mr. Morales down for breakfast. Les decided he needed to do that again soon. Smelly, indeed!

"Well, no, of course not," Mrs. Hargrove agreed and had the grace to blush slightly. "But still, I can't see that a little girl would—"

"Whoever took the shepherd wants to trade him for a Suzy bake set—the deluxe edition." Les walked over and gave the note to Mrs. Hargrove. "That sounds like a little girl to me. You recognize the writing?"

Mrs. Hargrove taught Sunday school and she knew all the kids in and around Dry Creek. When she finished reading the note, she looked up and shook her head. "I don't recognize it, but whoever wrote the note probably tried to disguise their writing, anyway."

Everyone was quiet for a minute.

"Are any of the classes in Sunday school memorizing the nineteenth verse of some book?"

Mrs. Hargrove shook her head. "Not that I know of. They wouldn't write it that way, anyway, would they? XIX? That's Roman numerals."

"I wonder about the Curtis twins," Elmer said as he reached for his cup of coffee. "I don't think they'd mess around with numbers, but they like cupcakes."

"They like to *eat* cupcakes. Those boys don't want to *bake* cupcakes," Linda said. "Besides, they're too busy with their new sleds to think up a scheme like this."

Les shrugged. "I don't know. Those boys live close to the church. I can't see any of the ranch kids coming into Dry Creek on a night like last night. For one thing, we would have seen tire tracks over by the church."

Les lifted his eyebrow in a question to Elmer and the man shook his head.

"Since there were no tracks, it means it had to be someone who was already in town last night." Les let his words sink in for everyone. Somebody in the center of Dry Creek had taken that shepherd. If there were no tracks, they couldn't blame it on a stranger passing through.

"Pastor Matthew won't like it if his sons stole the shepherd," Charley finally said, and then glanced over at Mrs. Hargrove. He must have seen the frown on her face. "Of course, I don't believe it was the Curtis twins. Not for a minute. They don't even know about Roman numerals. They can barely add up regular numbers."

"Nobody added the numbers," Les muttered before Charley could get himself in a spin. "They just put them out there."

"Well, the only other kids in town are those two new kids." Elmer stared down at his cup. "And what would they want with a shepherd? They've never even been to church."

There was another moment's silence.

"They've never been anywhere," Charley finally said. "We've heard there are two new kids, but has anyone ever seen either of them?"

Everyone just looked at each other.

"Just because no one's seen them doesn't mean they're thieves," Mrs. Hargrove protested. "We need to have open minds here."

"Still, you have to admit it's peculiar," Elmer said after a moment's thought. "We've all seen the mother, but she must keep those kids inside. The only reason we know about the kids is because there are three names on their mailbox and we know the woman is a widow, so it has to be a woman and her two kids."

The mailbox had sprung up next to the driveway of the old house when the woman and her children moved into town. Les figured they had not realized that everyone in Dry Creek collected their mail at the counter in the hardware store, so no one had any need for an individual mailbox by their house. The mailman made just one stop for the whole town, even though he'd started going out to some of the ranches this past year.

Les frowned. Now that he thought about it, he would have expected the woman to have taken her mailbox down by now. Surely she must know how useless it was. And another thing was coming to his mind. The woman hadn't seemed all that familiar with the hardware store the day he'd seen her there, either. Which all added up to only one possibility. "Somebody must be taking the woman's mail to her."

Les looked around. He'd bet it was one of the people sitting right in front of him.

"Well, I don't see what's wrong with that," Elmer finally said defiantly. "I figure it's only neighborly. Besides, it's no trouble to drop their letters in that box. They don't get many of them, anyway. The boy got a letter from Los Angeles, but it wasn't heavy. No two-stamper. And they don't get catalogs to speak of, either. Just the J. C. Penney Christmas catalog."

"The mail is protected by federal law. You shouldn't be touching anyone's mail without their permission." Les wondered if the sheriff's department should put out a book of rules for people. He wondered if anyone in Dry Creek would read it if they did issue one.

Elmer jutted his chin out. "All I'm saying is that there are the two kids, and if we haven't seen them, maybe it's because neither of them needs to go farther than their driveway for the mail. That's all."

"They could even be sick," Linda added softly. "It's flu season. They'd stay inside for sure if they were sick. Maybe they have colds."

"And I can't see sick kids stealing a shepherd," Mrs. Hargrove said. "Especially not in this weather. Their mother probably wouldn't let them go outside if they were sick, and they wouldn't be able to see the Nativity set from the windows in their house, so they wouldn't even know the shepherd was there. They can't steal what they don't even know about, now, can they?"

Les wondered how long the people of Dry Creek would protect a real criminal if one showed up. He hoped he never had to find out. "Forget the shepherd. Nobody said anybody wanted that shepherd. It's the bake set that seems to be the goal. If I remember right, one of those names on the mailbox is Becky. Sounds like a little girl to me. Especially since we know the mother's name is Marla something-or-other."

"It's Marla Gossett. Remember, I told you about her? Said it would be a good idea for you to get acquainted with that new woman," Elmer said as he looked up at Les. "Didn't I say that just the other day?"

Les grunted. "You didn't *say* anything. What you did was break the law by calling in a false fire alarm. That was a crazy stunt. And just to get me over to the hardware store while Mrs. Gossett was there."

"Well, it would have worked if you'd stayed around to talk. She's a nice lady. Charley and I both knew you wouldn't come over if we just said there was an eligible woman we wanted you to meet. When have you ever agreed to do something like that?"

"I have a ranch to run. I can't be running around meeting people all the time."

"Wouldn't hurt you to stop work for a night or two and actually go out on a date," Elmer muttered. "It's not like you're busy with harvest season."

Les had never known the two old men could be so manipulative. They definitely needed a new checkerboard. And a steak or two to get their blood going.

Les looked directly at Charley and Elmer. "The two of you didn't take that shepherd, did you? Just to give me a reason to talk some more with this Mrs. Gossett?"

The stunned expressions on the faces of the two men were almost comical.

"What would give you that idea?" Elmer demanded.

Les just grunted. He wondered if XIX was part of the telephone number for a dating service.

Charley grinned a little. "Well, this isn't like that. We don't have anything to do with the shepherd being gone."

Les felt a headache coming on. "Maybe it *is* the new people, then. I'll have to go and talk to them."

"Oh, no, you don't. You can't go over there and accuse the Gossetts of taking something," Mrs. Hargrove protested with an indrawn breath. "They're new here. We're supposed to make newcomers feel welcome."

"They're not welcome if they're going to break the law."

"But it's only a plastic shepherd," Linda said as she looked up from the chair she was sitting in. "You said yourself, it's not like it's a kidnapping."

"It's only a small crime," Charley added with a glance at Mrs. Hargrove. "The women's group didn't even pay real money for it. Just all those soup labels. Hardly counts as a crime, now that I think on it."

That was easily the third time Charley had looked to Mrs. Hargrove for approval in the past ten minutes, and Les knew what that meant. Not only was the sheriff married and off to Maui, but it looked as if Charley was sweet on Mrs. Hargrove. What else would make a man stop speaking his mind until he made sure a particular woman held the same opinion? No, Charley had either turned in his independence or he owed Mrs. Hargrove more money than he could repay.

Les sighed. He didn't know which would be worse. A debt beyond a man's means or one-sided love. Both of them turned a man's spine to mush. It had certainly done that to Charley. One look from Mrs. Hargrove and Charley would probably vote to send that plastic shepherd to the moon on taxpayer money. And Charley was a Republican who didn't believe in spending a dime on anything. Nothing should change a man like that. It just wasn't right. Besides, Mrs. Hargrove looked as if she didn't even know Charley was twisting himself in knots trying to win her approval.

Elmer was the only one who looked as if he was holding on to his common sense.

That was another thing Sheriff Carl Wall had warned Les about. The people of Dry Creek couldn't always be relied upon to see things in an objective manner. For one thing, many of them couldn't bear to see anyone punished. That's why it was so important that the law stood firm. It was for everyone's protection.

"Today it's a plastic shepherd. Tomorrow who knows what it will be?" Les said. "We have to stop crime where it starts."

Elmer nodded. "That's right. The law needs to have teeth to it. If the women's group hadn't collected all those soup labels, that Nativity set would have cost five hundred dollars. Who around here has five hundred dollars to throw away?"

There was a moment's silence. Five hundred dollars went a long way in a place like Dry Creek.

"Well, at least take some doughnuts with you if you're going to go over to that house this early in the morning," Linda said as she stepped over to the counter and took the lid off the glass-domed tray that held the doughnuts.

"And be sure and invite the children to Sunday school," Mrs. Hargrove added. She seemed resigned to the fact that someone needed to ask the hard questions. "I've been meaning to go over there with an invitation myself. It just always seems to be snowing every time I think of it, and you know how slippery the streets are when that happens."

"This is a criminal investigation. I'm not going to invite anyone to Sunday school."

Mrs. Hargrove looked at him. "It's the best place for someone to be if they've been stealing. I noticed you weren't in church yourself last Sunday."

"One of my horses threw a shoe and I needed to fix it. You know I'm always there if I can be." Les had come to faith when he was a boy and he lived his commitment. Quietly, of course, but he figured God knew how he felt about public displays of emotion. And even if he didn't dance around and shout hallelujah from the rooftops, he was steady in his faith.

"We miss you in the choir."

"I haven't sung in the choir since I was sixteen."

Mrs. Hargrove nodded. "You still have that voice, though. It's deeper now, but it's just as good. It's a sin to waste a voice like that."

Les had quit the choir when people started to pay too much attention to his singing.

"The Bible doesn't say a man needs to be in the choir." *Or perform in any other public way,* Les added to himself. "It's okay to be a quiet man."

"I know. And you're a good man, Lester Wilkerson. Quiet or not."

He winced. "Make that Les. Lester sounds like my father."

The church had been a home for Les from the day

he decided to accept a neighbor's invitation to attend. It was the one place his parents never went, and Les felt he could be himself there.

"I don't know why you never liked the name Lester," Mrs. Hargrove continued. "It's a good old-fashioned name. It's not biblical, of course, but it's been the name of many good men over the years."

"I like Les better. Les Wilkerson."

How did he tell someone like Mrs. Hargrove that he had loved his parents, but he had never respected them? He had never wanted to be his father's son, so he saw no reason to take his first name as well as his last.

Les was a better name for a rancher than Lester, anyway, he thought. He'd changed his name shortly after he'd signed the deed for his place. He had been twenty years old, and that deed had marked his independence from his parents. The name Les helped him begin a new life.

Linda handed him a white bag filled with doughnuts. "I put in some extra jelly ones. Kids always like the jelly ones."

"I wonder if that XIX on the note is the edition number on that bake set," Charley said.

"Maybe it's a clue," Elmer offered. "Is there something that is ten, one and then ten?"

"An *X* sometimes stands for a kiss," Linda said. "You know, when people sign their letters XOXO—kisses and hugs."

"I doubt anyone was thinking of kisses." Les figured he didn't have all morning to guess what the numbers meant. Not when he had people to question.

"You might ask the woman to come have dinner with you some night here," Mrs. Hargrove said as Les started to walk to the door. "Just to be sociable. Sort of show her around town."

"Nobody needs a map to get around this town. There's only the one street."

Ever since Charley and Mrs. Hargrove had managed to match up their two children, they had been itching to try their new matchmaking skills on someone else. Well, it wasn't going to be him.

Les would find his own wife when he wanted one and he would do it when no one was watching. He might even have gotten around to asking the new woman out eventually if people had left him alone. She seemed quiet and he liked that. Her brown hair was a very ordinary color. No streaks of auburn. No beauty-parlor waves. It was just always plain and neatly combed when he saw her. She didn't even wear those dangling earrings that always made him feel a woman was prone to changing her opinions from one minute to the next. All in all, he believed, she would be predictable and that was good. Les didn't want an unpredictable wife.

Yes, Marla Gossett might very well have suited him.

Now, of course, he couldn't ask her out. It would be pointless; she'd never accept. Not when he was going to be knocking at her door in a couple of minutes to ask if her daughter was a thief. Only a fool would ask for a date after that, and one thing Les prided himself on was never being a fool.

It was a pity, though. These days Les didn't meet that many quiet women who looked as if they'd make sensible wives. He'd noticed when he saw her in the hardware store that she was a sensible dresser, right down to the shoes she wore. Because of his father, he paid particular attention to a woman's shoes. They told a man a great deal. Still, everything about Mrs. Gossett had seemed practical that day, from her washable cardigan to her well-worn knit pants.

Most men liked a lot of flash in their women. But Les figured the quieter the better. He never really trusted a woman with flash.

Les wondered, just for a moment, if it would be worthwhile to let Mrs. Gossett know he was single, just in case she ever started to wonder about him the way he was wondering about her.

Then he shook his head. He didn't want to chase after an impossible dream. He didn't even know Mrs. Gossett and she didn't know him. What he did know were the reasons he wasn't likely to get to know her. He had to just let the thought go.

Chapter Three

Marla moved the hanging blanket slightly so she could look out the window of her new living room. The sun would be coming up any minute, but the small town of Dry Creek was still dark and quiet. Snow had fallen during the night and there was just enough light in the small circle from the one streetlamp to see that there were no fresh tire tracks on the road going through town.

That didn't mean she could relax and remove the blankets, though. Down the street there was a glow in the window of the café and she could see several figures through the big window. People had obviously come into town from the other direction and any one of them could decide at any minute to drive down the road toward her. If they did, they would soon be able to see inside her front window if she moved the blanket, and she didn't want anyone to look into her place until she was ready.

The words of her neighbor back in Los Angeles were never far from her mind.

Marla had cleaned her windows with vinegar yesterday and she could still smell the cleaning solution as it mingled with the scent of the mothballs from the blanket. The panes in the windows rattled because the putty was all worn away, but at least they were finally clean.

Today Marla planned to wash the walls. The paint was peeling away and she'd feel better if she knew the walls were brushed down and ready to go when she could afford to buy paint.

In a strange way, she was grateful for the necessity of scrubbing this old house. If it had been less filthy when she arrived here with her children, she might still be brooding over the change she'd made. She'd been nervous the whole trip up here, but now the peeling paint and thick dust called her to action and she had no time to fret.

She had not given any thought to the house until she arrived. If she had not been desperate, she would have turned around and driven away after she first looked inside the door. The house was set back from the street a little and there was a nice white picket fence around it. That part was how her husband had described the house to her. Marla had been okay with the idea of that white picket fence, but nothing Jorge had said had prepared her for the inside of the house.

Of course, her husband's memories of the house

had been from thirty years ago. Jorge wouldn't have recognized the house today, either. Even in their cheap apartment in Los Angeles, the paint had managed to stay on the walls.

Marla didn't want anyone from this small town to look past the fence and into her windows until she was ready. There wasn't much inside her house and, what was there was shabby. On the long drive up, she'd promised herself she would make a proper life for her children in Dry Creek, and she didn't want her relationship with the town to start off with the people here pitying them.

Somewhere around Utah, she'd realized that the ethnic difference was only part of what she needed to worry about. After all, her parents had raised her to be more Anglo than Hispanic, anyway. They'd even given her an Anglo name. She and the children might be able to fit in that way eventually. The fact that they were also poor was another problem. She knew that from the welfare days of her childhood. A lack of money would be harder to hide than anything.

Marla planned to get the house in shape before she did more than say a quiet hello to anyone. She didn't want her children to feel shame for either their heritage or their lack of possessions. First impressions were important.

That's one reason she had hung the plain khaki-colored blankets over the windows and left the Mexican-striped blankets as coverings for the sleeping bags.

Maybe if Sammy had had neighbors who expected good things from him back in Los Angeles, he wouldn't have been drawn to the 19th Street gang. Of course, the neighbors were only part of it. She knew she hadn't given him what he needed, either. She had been so preoccupied with taking care of Jorge that she hadn't paid enough attention to Sammy.

It was Sammy who most needed a new start.

Marla took a deep breath of the cool winter air. Despite the fact that the air was tinged with the scent of vinegar and mothballs, it still smelled clean and fresh when she compared it to what she'd breathed down south.

Dry Creek promised a new life for all of them and Marla intended it to go well. Even though she'd had car problems on the way up and hadn't had much money left after she'd paid for the repairs, she was determined she and her children were not going to be charity cases. Charity was never free; one always paid the price by enduring the giver's pity. She didn't want that.

She wanted her children to feel proud of who they were.

Besides, they didn't need charity. Any day Marla expected to get a check in the mail refunding the deposit on their apartment. Her rental agreement gave the landlord twenty days to refund the money and he'd probably take all that time. Once she had that check, she would have enough money to buy paint for the walls and a good used sofa. And that was after she put aside enough money to support her family for a few months while she looked for a job. She knew she needed to spend some time with her children before she started a new job, though. Too much had happened too fast in the past year for all of them. They needed time to be together.

At first Marla had worried that she would not have enough money to support her and the children for those few months. It seemed as if the cost of heating the house would take what little money she had, but then she had discovered that the fireplace in the living room worked and that there was a seven-foot-high woodpile half-hidden in the trees behind the house.

At last, something was going her way.

It looked as if, during the years when the house had stood empty, the trees had grown up around the towering stack of log chunks back there. She hadn't paid any attention to the stack until the children told her about it one day and she had gone out to look it over. The pile had good-sized logs meant for long winter fires. If need be, on the coldest nights, she and the children could camp in front of the fireplace to sleep.

At least heat was one thing that wouldn't require money for now.

Which was a good thing, because the refund check was going to total only around a thousand dollars. There wouldn't be much money left for extras. Christmas this year would be lean. She'd explained the situation to Sammy and Becky and they seemed to understand. Wall paint and a used sofa might not look like exciting Christmas presents, but it would make their house more of a home. She was letting each child pick out the color of the paint for their bedrooms and she was hoping that would be enough of a Christmas present.

Besides, they could make some simple gifts for each other this year. That could be fun for all of them. And she'd make the sweet pork tamales that were the children's favorite. It was her mother's special recipe and that, along with the traditional lighted luminaries, always meant Christmas to Marla.

Marla had brought dozens of corn husks, dried peppers and bags of the cornmeal-like masa with her when she moved to Montana. She remembered the words of the neighbor who had bought her lamp and she didn't want to take any chances. Christmas without tamales was unthinkable, and not just because of the children.

By the time Christmas was here, she hoped to be able to take the blankets off the front windows of her house and welcome any visitors inside. By then, she might even be comfortable offering visitors a tamale and explaining that she and the children had a Hispanic heritage.

Marla saw movement and stopped daydreaming about the future. The door of the café had opened and a man had stepped out. She had recognized the pickup parked next to the café when she first looked out the window, and so she figured the man standing on the café porch was Reserve Deputy Sheriff Les Wilkerson. He was probably getting ready to patrol through Dry Creek and had stopped at the café for coffee. Marla had seen the deputy walk down the street of Dry Creek every morning since she'd moved here and it made her nervous.

She hadn't heard of any criminal activity around, but she kept the children close to the house just in case. She'd called the school when they'd first arrived in Dry Creek and they had agreed, since it had been almost time for the holiday break, that Sammy could start his classes after Christmas. Becky was even more flexible. When she'd first noticed the sheriff patrolling the town, Marla had been glad she'd arranged to have Sammy close by for a few weeks, but maybe if the children were in school she'd at least know more about what was going on.

There must be something happening if a lawman was doing foot patrol. In Los Angeles that happened only in high crime areas. She hadn't heard any gunshots at night, so she doubted robberies were the problem. The deputy must be worried about drugs.

Marla had briefly met the man last Friday when she was at the hardware store looking for paint, and she had wanted to ask him about any local drug problems. But he had stayed only long enough to scowl at everyone and do something with an ashtray.

The two older men sitting beside the woodstove

talked about Les after he left. They made it sound as if he was somebody special. She supposed the older men wanted to reassure her that her children were safe here in Dry Creek with a lawman around, but, truth be told, the reserve deputy didn't make her feel better about the isolation of the small town.

She was used to lawmen, even reserve volunteer lawmen, who had a certain amount of swagger to them. Les didn't strut around at all. He looked strong enough, but he wasn't exactly brawling material. Not only that, he didn't even carry a gun.

She doubted there were any lawmen in Los Angeles who didn't carry a gun. There were certainly none the few times she'd visited her aunts and uncles in Mexico. Marla supposed Les would have to talk a criminal down, but when she'd been introduced to him, he hadn't seemed to be much of a talker. He'd only nodded and mumbled hello to her that day. He was even quieter than she was, and she was perfectly able to carry on a conversation. She'd do fine with talking when she had her house ready for visiting.

Of course, no one else seemed to be worried about Les's lack of conversational skills, and they knew the town and him much better than she did. Maybe he was one of those people who shone in emergency situations, but who didn't appear to be of much use at other times.

Les wasn't even wearing a uniform that day. He'd had cowboy boots on his feet and a plaid flannel shirt

on his back. The only thing that had marked him as a
reserve deputy sheriff was a vest and, from what the
other men said, he didn't even always wear that. Of
course, everyone must just know he was the lawman
on duty; it was such a small town.

Marla watched Les step off the café porch and start
walking down the street. He must be making his usual
morning patrol. Fortunately, the sun was starting to
lighten up the day, so he might even be able to see
while he did it.

Les felt the snow crunch beneath his boots as he
moved down the one street in Dry Creek. Usually he
thought it was an advantage to have only one street in
town. Today, though, he would have liked a million
other directions to turn.

He stopped when he got to the church. The Nativity set was still all lit up even though the sun was beginning to rise. The wise men stood to one side with
their hands overflowing with gold baubles. The blond
angel was hanging from a wire attached to the rain
gutters of the church. Les took a minute to look closely
at the rain gutters and note that whoever had written
the note was right. Someone did need to add another
wire or the angel would eventually fall.

Les looked back at the wise men and wondered
why one of them hadn't been taken instead of the lone
shepherd. They certainly looked more exciting than
the missing figure. Everyone he knew, except him-

self, would pick flash over something drab any day. Strangely, it didn't make him feel any easier in his mind about the theft.

When he could delay no longer, Les walked farther down the street and then started up the path to the Gossett house. Until Marla and her children moved to town, the house had been closed up. Old man Gossett had spent some time in prison before he died and no one had taken care of the house. Someone had enough civic pride to paint part of the picket fence that faced the street so the property looked somewhat cared for if an outsider happened to look at it on a casual drive through town. None of the people in Dry Creek liked to see the town buildings look neglected and Les couldn't blame them.

As he walked up the path, Les saw how the weather had started to flake the white paint off the house until there were large sections of exposed gray boards. Even the snowdrifts couldn't disguise the fact that the yard had gone to seed. Only the pine trees in the back of the house had flourished, growing together in thick clumps of muted green.

Les was halfway up the walk when someone turned off the light inside the house. For the first time, Les thought maybe the little girl really had stolen the shepherd. What else but guilt would make someone turn off the lights when a visitor was coming to the door? Usually people turned a light on when someone was walking toward their house.

When Les stepped on the porch, the door opened a crack. It was just enough for Les to see a small portion of a woman's face. There was one brown eye and a hand holding the side of the door. The hand covered up most of what face would have shown in the crack. The room behind the face was in darkness. Les wouldn't have recognized the woman even though he had met her last Friday in the hardware store.

"Mrs. Gossett?"

The woman nodded.

Les wished she would open the door wider. Regardless of what he'd told himself, he was looking forward to seeing more of the woman's face. He hadn't taken a very good look at her the other day in the hardware store and he'd like to see her better. There was no particular reason to ask her to open the door wider, though. Especially because it was cold out and she was probably just keeping her heat inside like any wise Montana housewife would do.

"I brought something to eat," Les said as he held up the white bag. "For the kids. And you, of course."

He had a feeling he could express himself a lot better if the woman didn't keep eyeing him as if she was going to slam the door in his face any minute now.

At his words, her face stiffened even more. "We have enough to eat. You don't need to worry about us."

Les had coaxed frightened kittens out of their hiding places many times and he reminded himself that patience usually won out over fear.

"It's only a few doughnuts," Les forced his voice to be softer. "Linda, at the café, thought the kids might like them."

The woman's face relaxed some. "Well, I guess doughnuts are different."

The woman opened the door and Les gave her the bag. He waited a minute in hopes she was going to ask him inside. It would be easier to talk to her if she was relaxed and not looking at him through the crack in the door. But once she took the bag, she closed the door so it was back in its original position.

"Please tell the woman—Linda—thank you for us. We haven't had a chance to get over to the café yet, but it's a very nice gesture."

Les was afraid the woman was going to think he had just come by to bring her the doughnuts, so he said his piece. "I'm doing a search of houses. We've had some property stolen from the church."

The woman frowned. "We don't go to church."

The woman turned a little as if she heard something inside the house.

"You don't need to go to church to take something."

The woman snapped back to look at him. "Are you accusing me of stealing? From a church?"

"No, ma'am." Les ran his finger around his shirt collar. "It's just that I did think that maybe your daughter—well, do you know where your daughter was last night?"

The woman turned again to look inside the house.

Les figured it was one of the children who had been distracting the woman, so he wasn't surprised when he heard her whisper to someone. "Just be patient. Mommy will be right there."

The woman turned back to look at Les. In all of the turning, the door had opened a little farther. "Becky was here with me last night."

The woman was wearing an old beige robe that was zipped up to her neck and she didn't have any makeup on her face. She had strong bones, Les noticed. And a weariness to her that made him think she'd come through a long patch of hard times. He couldn't let his sudden sympathy for her change what he needed to do, though.

"Was your daughter with you for the entire night?" Les could see into the rest of the large room behind the woman. The windows were all covered so the room was in shadows, but he could make out most of it. Not that there was much to see. Except for a wooden sitting chair, there was nothing there. Maybe the family's furniture was still coming on a moving truck.

"Of course, all night. Where else would she be?" The woman was looking straight at him now. "I don't even know why you're asking me these questions. You came straight to my door. I saw you. You're not asking everybody. Just because we don't have blond hair and blue eyes like everyone else around here, it doesn't mean we stole something."

"No, of course not." Les was bewildered. Did everyone around here have blond hair? He hadn't noticed. Still, he'd come to do a job and he might as well get it done. "I'm talking to people because someone stole one of the Nativity figures from the set in front of the church."

"That has nothing to do with us."

Les nodded. "I just wondered, because whoever took the figure wanted to trade it back to the church for a Suzy bake set."

A little girl's squeal came from behind the door. Les couldn't see the girl, but he could hear her as she said, "A Suzy bake set! The one with the cupcakes?"

"No, dear, I don't think so," the woman said with her face turned to the inside of the room.

Why was it that the line of a woman's neck, when she turned to look over her shoulder, always reminded him of a ballet dancer? Les asked himself. Marla— well, Mrs. Gossett—had a beautiful neck.

The woman turned back to look at Les. She even gave him a small smile, which made the knot in his stomach relax. No one who was guilty would smile. But then, maybe the mother didn't know what the daughter had done.

The woman continued, "I'm sorry. I think every little girl everywhere wants that Suzy bake set in the cupcake edition. It's quite the thing. I don't know if you can even find it in the stores anymore."

Les nodded. Maybe that's why someone had written the demand note. Maybe they thought the church would have extra pull with a store. "Whoever took the shepherd left a note." He held the paper out to her. "I think a girl might have written it."

The woman didn't even look up to read the note. She just shook her head. "If that's where you're headed, you should know my daughter is only four. She can't even write her name."

"Oh." Les had not known the girl was so young. He didn't think a girl that age could even lift the shepherd figure. The thing was plastic, but it was heavy enough. And it was bulky.

"She's going to learn to write her name," the woman continued, as if she was making a point. "We believe in schooling. She'll go to preschool a couple of days a week in Miles City after the holidays. Most kids here probably already know how to write their names, but Becky didn't get a chance to go to preschool in Los Angeles. If she's behind, she'll catch up."

"I'm sure she'll learn to write in no time," Les said just to put the woman at ease, since her daughter's schooling seemed important to her. "Kids learn fast."

Les hoped he was speaking the truth. What did he know about kids? He knew he should forget about the kids and say goodbye, but he found he didn't want to rush off. Not now that, with the sun fully up and spreading its sunshine all over, Les noticed that some of the shadows were gone from the woman's face.

He wondered if she would go out to dinner with

him after all. Now that they were talking about education instead of crime, she seemed a little friendlier.

"I—ah—" Les swallowed. "We have a good school in Miles City. You don't need to worry about that."

The woman smiled. "I'm glad to know that."

Les wasn't prepared for the woman's full smile.

He swallowed again. "Thanks for talking to me. Let me know if you see anything suspicious. It's probably just some kids playing a prank. Wanting to see if I can figure out that XIX clue they left. I wonder if it's part of a math equation."

Les had been ready to turn and walk away when the smile fell from Mrs. Gossett's face and something in her eyes shifted. She'd suddenly gone tense.

"Is there something you want to tell me?" he asked.

She shook her head. The weariness was back on her face. "The XIX. Where was that?"

"At the end of the note."

The woman bit her lip nervously. "Are you going to be in town for a little while?"

Les didn't flatter himself that she wanted to see him again, but he nodded. "I'll be at the café for another half hour or so. If you think of something that might help, let me know."

She nodded.

There wasn't anything more to say, so Les gave her a goodbye nod. "It was a pleasure to talk with you, ma'am. And welcome to Dry Creek."

Les turned and left. He hoped Mrs. Hargrove would

be happy with his little welcome speech at the end. He'd even meant it.

Marla barely waited for the man to step off her porch before she closed the door and locked it. Of course, turning the lock was just habit. She had nothing to fear from the reserve deputy sheriff. Although, if her suspicions were right, she might not want to hear what he had to say to her and her children if she had to take her son over to the café in a few minutes.

"Sammy," she called.

Becky was happily walking around with her bunny slippers and frog pajamas on. But it was almost seven o'clock and Marla hadn't heard from her son yet this morning. Usually he was up by now even though it wasn't a school day. She'd thought earlier that he was sleeping in. Now she knew he was just hiding out.

"Sammy, come out here."

Marla leaned back against the locked door and looked around. For the first time she wondered how she could have fooled herself so completely. She could paint the rooms in her house with gold leaf and the people here wouldn't respect them. Not if Sammy had stolen the Nativity shepherd from the church and tagged that note with the 19th Street gang symbol. Her family would be marked as troublemakers regardless of how their house looked or what their ethnic background was. People were scared of gangs, and rightfully so. If they figured out Sammy had wanted to be in a gang, there would be no new start for them. The whole move up here would have been pointless.

"Sammy!"

Her son stepped into the living room. He was wearing a long white T-shirt and baggy pants. It was typical gang clothes for south central L.A.

"I thought you were going to throw those clothes away," Marla said. They didn't have many clothes, but Sammy did have some jeans that fit better. And why did he need to spike his hair?

"I've got to wear something." Sammy glared at her. "I can't go around naked."

Marla felt that sometimes she didn't recognize her son. "You have those jeans I got for you to wear when you start school here—"

"They don't fit." Sammy shrugged. "I'm saving them for when we paint the house."

Marla forced herself to relax. She supposed that clothes were the least of her worries, although people did form opinions about young people because of the way they were dressed. "I just want to be proud of you."

Sammy grunted. "What's in the bag?"

Marla looked down. Becky was sitting on the floor and had already opened the white bag Les had left with them. She hadn't taken anything out, although she had a grin on her face.

There were so few smiling moments for Becky these days that Marla didn't want to spoil this one by questioning Sammy right now. The sheriff would be in town for another half hour. They had time to eat a bite.

"The woman at the café sent us over doughnuts for breakfast." Marla said. "Wasn't that nice of her?"

Becky nodded and beamed up at her. "Yes, Mommy."

Sammy grunted.

Marla didn't react to Sammy. Gratitude wasn't the big problem of the day, either. "Let's go sit at the table when we eat them. We don't want to get everything sticky."

Sammy had already walked over and looked in the sack Becky held. For the first time this morning he reminded Marla of the little boy he had been. "Hey, there's jelly doughnuts. Cool. I can see the raspberry filling coming out of one of them."

"Let's take them to the table," Marla repeated for Becky's ears.

"I am, Mommy," Becky said as she stood up and then reached down and grabbed the bag.

Marla watched her children walk into the kitchen together. Becky was holding the bag of doughnuts, but Marla could see that Sammy was guarding them as he walked with his sister. What was she to do? Marla asked herself as she leaned back against the door. Sammy's heart was good. Look how careful he was to help Becky without taking the sack from her. An aggressive child would just grab the bag. But not

Sammy. He had always had a warm place in his heart for his little sister.

She was surprised it hadn't all clicked together for her earlier when she was standing there talking to the deputy sheriff. Becky might not have written that note asking for a Suzy bake set, but Sammy had. He knew what Becky wanted for Christmas. Becky had been talking about that bake set for weeks. Marla had even wondered if she might be able to squeeze the money out of her budget for one. She hadn't been sure if she could do it, so she hadn't said anything to either of the children. She'd just let her suggestion of hand-made gifts stand.

Maybe that had been a mistake. Marla realized that if she had told Sammy she was buying a few presents after all, maybe he wouldn't have taken that shepherd. Somewhere in all of this, she was partially at fault.

She couldn't help but think that Jorge would have known what to do for Sammy. Maybe Sammy felt free to misbehave because he knew she wasn't as sure of herself as Jorge had been in disciplining him. She wasn't used to flying solo as a parent and she wasn't sure she could do a good job of it. Sometimes a growing boy needed a father.

Marla listened to the voices of her children in the dining room for a minute, then started forward to join them. She was going to have to do her best to give Sammy what a father would.

Marla was glad the card table and folding chairs

had fit in the luggage carrier on top of the car when she moved up here. Her children were sitting at the table now. It might not be as sturdy as the table she would eventually buy for them, but it was important for them to have a place to sit down and eat together. For all of Sammy's sullen ways, he'd never protested eating dinner with the family.

Sammy had put white paper plates and plastic cups on the table. He'd even brought out the gallon of milk. Marla was pleased that they had waited for her.

Marla let everyone finish their doughnuts before she cleared her throat.

"Becky, will you go to your room and get dressed, please?"

Becky didn't always end up with a matching outfit, but she liked to dress herself and Marla encouraged her to be independent.

After Becky left, Marla turned to Sammy. "Is there something you need to tell me?"

"Nah," Sammy muttered, his face flushing.

Marla counted to three. "Did you take a shepherd from the church's Nativity scene?"

Sammy's face got redder. "It's just a stupid shepherd. They don't even exist anymore. At least, not anywhere except in Mexico. I mean, who needs them? We're through with that life. We're turning white."

Marla kept her voice even. "Just because we moved up here, it doesn't mean that we're not still part Hispanic."

Sammy grunted. "I haven't seen any *amigos* around."

No one would know Sammy was Hispanic by looking at him. She knew he identified himself with his old *amigos,* but maybe it was time for them all to step away from their background a little bit.

"You'll meet some new friends when you go to school."

"Yeah, right."

"We're not ashamed of being Hispanic." Marla tried again. "We're just getting to know people slow and easy. We don't need to be any particular ethnic group for a while."

Sammy grunted.

Marla decided she couldn't talk about their heritage all morning.

"You know it's wrong to take things that don't belong to you. We'll go over to the café and talk to the deputy who was here asking about the shepherd. Then you'll give the shepherd back and we'll talk about what your punishment will be."

Marla was hoping that if Sammy confessed to what he had done and returned the shepherd, no charges would be filed. She didn't know how much the Nativity figure was worth, but she doubted it had a high enough value to make this anything but a misdemeanor. Once they figured that out, she'd talk more with Sammy about his other feelings.

"I could give up Christmas," Sammy offered. "Not that it's going to be anything, anyway."

"I'm hoping to make sweet pork tamales," Marla said.

Sammy looked up. "With the green chilies?"

Marla nodded. "If I can find a nice pork roast to use in the filling."

"Well, maybe I could give up Christmas after the tamales are all gone."

Marla smiled. "We'll talk."

Marla wondered how she could make Sammy feel more at home in Dry Creek. She knew he missed his friends. Even though those friends were not good for him, he was still entitled to miss them. A few days ago he'd gotten a letter from a boy back in Los Angeles. Sammy had protested, but eventually he'd agreed to let her read the note about some baseball, his lucky baseball, that he'd left behind and how the boy was going to get it to him soon.

At least Sammy had one friend there who didn't sound like a gang member. She hoped baseball wasn't gang code for something else. She couldn't forbid Sammy to have contact with everybody, though. A boy needed some friends, and the note sounded fine. Maybe she had been wrong to postpone school for him by the few weeks that she had. Of course, it was too late to change that now. The classes would be on Christmas break next week, anyway.

"Let's see if Becky is ready," Marla said. "We want to go over while the sheriff is at the café."

"He's not a regular lawman, is he?" Sammy asked with a frown. "He doesn't look like the police or anything."

"I suspect he's close enough to the real thing."

"I'm not afraid of him," Sammy announced.

Marla figured her son was lying about not being afraid when he took Becky's hand to hold while they walked down the street to the café. He shrugged off the hand Marla tried to rest on his shoulder, but she was glad he had Becky's hand at least.

They had to pass the church to reach the café and Marla looked over at the Nativity set. Since the church was on the same side of the road as her house, she couldn't see the lighted figures from her windows. It was nice just knowing they were there, though. She'd heard someone say that the whole town of Dry Creek planned to sing carols around the Nativity set on Christmas Eve.

Marla hadn't taken her children to church here yet, and once everyone knew what Sammy had done they might not be welcome, anyway, especially not if they made the gang connection. But she hoped they would at least be able to hear the carols being sung. Listening to Christmas carols took Marla back to her childhood.

During some of their poorest years as a family, the best part of Christmas for her had been sneaking into the back of a church and listening to the singing.

Her life seemed brand-new every Christmas when she heard those songs. After a few carols, she didn't care that her only gift was whatever came in the charity basket from whatever group had been assigned her family. She'd never joined a church or anything, but she somehow knew that the world had been changed forever on that first Christmas night.

She had put that wooden cross up in her bedroom at the new house and, if she wasn't sleeping by the fireplace that night, she would study it before she turned off her light. Her husband had found some peace by looking at the cross, but so far that peace continued to elude her. The only thing she felt when she looked at it was longing. Longing for security. Longing for a better life for her children. Longing for things she could not even name.

Marla could see the sheriff through the café window. He was sitting at a table waiting. She didn't know whether to be relieved or disappointed that he was still there. She knew Sammy needed to acknowledge what he had done, but she hoped the sheriff wouldn't make the connection to the 19th Street gang. Somehow the sheriff had seemed more intimidating to her this morning than he had when she'd first met him in the hardware store.

She wondered if she should tell him about Sammy's feelings for his old friends. Maybe the man had once been the odd one out like Sammy was these days. He was a strange one, that man. He looked so quiet, but something in his eyes said he saw everything. She hadn't noticed it until this morning. Would he see what was behind a boy's vandalism? She could only hope for mercy if he did.

Chapter Four

Les was on his second cup of coffee. He was sitting in the café hoping Mrs. Gossett would come by and tell him what she suspected about the missing shepherd. He'd already answered the questions of everyone waiting for him back in the café and he was getting tired of lingering when he had work to do.

"So she didn't say *anything* about the shepherd?" Charley asked him again.

Charley, Mrs. Hargrove and Elmer were sitting at the table next to him, watching him drink coffee. Les would feel more comfortable if they'd take their focus off him, but he couldn't tell people where to look. He supposed it all went with the job, anyway. They were curious, and he didn't have the gift of chatter. But maybe he should try.

Les shook his head and cleared his throat. "I don't think she knew anything about it before I told her. At least, that's how she acted."

He felt comfortable saying that much. He wouldn't mention the expression that had come over the woman's face when she had time to think about the Suzy bake set for a moment or two. When she thought about it, she had suspected something. He could see it in her eyes; they had turned from annoyed to scared in a heartbeat. He wasn't going to make his suspicions public, however. He knew how fast gossip could spread and he didn't want the family tried and convicted before they even had a chance to talk to anyone about the whole situation. Besides, he could be wrong.

"Another refill?" Linda asked as she walked by his table.

"I better not." Les looked at his watch. He'd been sitting here for almost thirty minutes. He'd give it another five. He still had those cows to feed. Besides, he was beginning to feel foolish waiting for someone who wasn't showing up.

"Here they come," Elmer announced. He'd positioned himself so he could look out the café window and see the road to the left. "A boy, a little girl and the mother. They look serious, too."

Les felt his neck knot up. "Maybe we shouldn't all be sitting here waiting for them."

"Oh." Elmer shuffled his chair around so it wasn't facing the window.

"Let me get my knitting out," Mrs. Hargrove said as she lifted her bag up to the table and started to rummage around in it.

"I could go over to the counter and get me a dough-nut," Charley announced as he stood up.

"Get me one, too?" Elmer asked.

Les wasn't sure what was worse—the sudden staged activity or the stares that would have faced the family otherwise.

"I need to get a fresh pot of coffee," Linda said as she started walking back to the kitchen.

Les deliberately did not turn around in his chair, so that he continued facing away from the door. He didn't even turn when he heard the click of the door opening and felt the rush of cold air on his neck. He believed in giving people some room to move. And he could not be sure that Marla Gossett was here to talk to him. Maybe she had walked over here with her children so they could thank Linda for the doughnuts.

Les could almost feel someone looking at him. He wished now that he'd turned around before the family entered the café.

"Sheriff Wilkerson," the woman finally said.

He turned in his chair, trying, and probably failing, to look natural.

He hadn't expected them to be huddled together. The woman looked frightened.

"You can call me Les."

"Could we talk to you outside?" The woman stood beside the boy.

This was the first time Les had gotten a chance to look at the boy. If he'd seen him before, he would have made the connection earlier that he was the one who had taken the shepherd. The boy had a sullen look on his face that reminded Les of himself at that age. He had on a wrinkled white T-shirt that was too big for him and his hair looked as if it had tried to face down a tornado and failed.

The boy hadn't been out of bed for long and Les wondered if he just hadn't had time to do things like comb his hair. Most likely it wasn't a matter of the time of day. The boy would probably still look that way at noon. Les guessed life was not going the way the boy wanted it to and likely it hadn't been for some time now. He wouldn't be the first kid in that situation to steal something. Les might have turned to petty crime himself if he hadn't found a church at that age instead. A boy needed to belong to something that challenged him, whether it was a sports team or a youth group.

Les stood up. "I'm just on my way out, anyway."

"You and the kids come back in and have breakfast when you've finished with Les here," Mrs. Hargrove offered with a smile for Marla. "My treat."

Mrs. Hargrove had her knitting in her lap and her needles in her hand.

"I'm sorry, but we can't," Marla said. She didn't want to discourage the woman's friendliness. "Maybe some other morning. We have a lot of things to do today."

"At least stop for coffee and orange juice," Linda

added with another smile. She was holding a pot of coffee. "I just made some fresh coffee. That doesn't take much time and it's on the house."

"You've already given us the doughnuts." Marla put a hand on each child's shoulder even though Sammy scowled up at her. "I hope you'll let me pay for them."

"Absolutely not."

Marla nodded. "Well, then, we appreciate them. Don't we, children?"

Marla squeezed each child's shoulder and they each murmured something.

In that instant, Marla had a flashback to the times when her mother had done the same awkward thing to her and she'd had to mumble her gratitude to the latest person who had taken pity on their family. It was still hard for her to say thank-you when someone did something nice for her. It was always worse when she had to say thank-you to a charity person.

Marla wondered if her mother had felt as overwhelmed being a single parent after her father died as she did. Still, next time she'd refuse the doughnuts. The price of charity was too high. Not that there was likely to be a repeat of the gesture, not when people found out that Sammy had taken the church's shepherd.

"Well, thank you again," Marla said as she turned. She was only now getting used to the heat in the café. It was cold outside, but she had no desire to have the conversation with the sheriff where it would be overheard by others. She didn't think there was much chance that the news of Sammy's theft would stay a secret in this small town, but she had to try. She didn't want to see the way people would look at her and the children after they knew what Sammy had done. Still, those looks would be better than what they'd receive if people put the clues together and figured out that Sammy gave his allegiance to a Hispanic street gang.

The deputy sheriff was already standing over by the door.

"Thanks," Marla said as the deputy sheriff opened the door for her and the children.

The winter air was cold, but Marla waited for the man to close the door and turn to face her and the children before she began. "Sammy has something to say to you."

The deputy sheriff squatted down a little so that he was at Sammy's height. "I'm listening."

Marla still had her hand on Sammy's shoulder and she could feel her son tense up. Whether it was because she had her hand on his shoulder or the deputy sheriff made him nervous she didn't know.

"That whole Nativity thing is stupid. Shepherds don't even exist anymore."

"Sammy," Marla said softly. "We don't say things are stupid. Besides, that's not what we came here to say."

The boy's chin jutted out and he was silent.

Marla wondered if she was going to have to confess on her son's behalf.

Instead, the deputy sheriff started to talk. "Well, I know one real shepherd who would disagree with you. I'll introduce you some time. I have some sheep myself. Even a few little lambs."

Sammy looked up at that, but didn't say anything.

The sheriff continued, "I wanted to thank you for calling our attention to that wire. If we hadn't seen it, the angel would have fallen. We'll have someone take care of it."

Sammy glared at the deputy sheriff. "It doesn't matter if an angel falls. It's supposed to be able to fly, anyway, isn't it?"

The man chuckled. "I'm afraid our angel isn't quite up to that yet."

Marla had forgotten that Becky was listening until her daughter spoke. "Maybe that's what the shepherd did. Maybe he flew away."

Marla decided she needed to do something before Les Wilkerson thought they were all crazy. "Sammy."

Sammy looked up at her rebelliously for a moment and then lowered his gaze. "Nothing flew away. I took it."

Everyone was quiet.

"Was there any particular reason?" the deputy sheriff finally asked thoughtfully. "I know the church will work with you if—"

"I just took it, okay?"

The deputy sheriff nodded. "You know it's considered stealing?"

"So arrest me already." Sammy still looked defiant.

"Oh, surely, you won't arrest him?" Marla spoke in a rush. "He's only eleven. I know it's wrong, but—"

The deputy sheriff held up his hand. "Nobody's talking about arresting him."

"He'll bring it back." Marla turned to her son. "Won't you, Sammy?"

Sammy stared straight ahead for a minute before he nodded.

"Well, we appreciate that," the deputy sheriff said. "People have been looking forward to having that Nativity scene outside the church when they sing carols on Christmas Eve. It just wouldn't be the same without the shepherd."

"I said I'd bring it back," Sammy said.

The man nodded. "Then we can talk about what kind of consequences there should be for what you did."

"He'll be punished," Marla said in a rush. Maybe the deputy sheriff wasn't going to tell everyone about the theft. Maybe they had a chance at a new life in this town after all. "You don't need to worry about that. I'm taking away his television privileges. And he'll have extra chores to do."

They didn't have much of a television, but Sammy did like watching sports on it.

"Maybe he should do some chores for the church, too," the man said.

"Of course," Marla agreed. "He could sweep the floors or maybe clean some windows."

She didn't know what she would tell people about why Sammy was doing any of those things, but she would think of something without making it sound as if he was doing any good deeds.

"He could always help Mrs. Hargrove with her Sunday-school class," the deputy sheriff added thoughtfully. "She has a lot of first graders and she's always looking for extra help when they practice for the Christmas program."

Marla saw all the color drain out of Sammy's face. Well, the lawman had finally gotten her son's attention.

"Is that like *babysitting?*" Sammy asked, his horror evident. "Would people see me?"

"Well, people would need to see you," the deputy sheriff said calmly. "You might even need to stand up and sing with the kids when they do their piece in the program. They're the angel choir."

"But I'm too tall," Sammy said quickly. "They'd all be baby angels. And I don't have blond hair."

"I think you'll do all right," the man said. "I'm sure Mrs. Hargrove has a pair of wings that are large enough for you. And there will be all different colors of hair in the angel choir."

"I'd have to wear wings? In front of people?"

The lawman nodded seriously. "With gold glitter on them. The kids make the wings in class, so you'll be able to make yours really sparkle. You probably remember how to cut with those little scissors."

Sammy was starting to turn a little green.

"And a halo," the deputy sheriff continued with a straight face. "I don't know if you'll wear sheets or bathrobes yet, but Mrs. Hargrove will figure that out. You'll need to be in something white."

"I want a halo," Becky said happily as she hung on to Marla's coat.

Marla patted Becky's head without answering.

Her son looked shell-shocked.

"But the first order of business is to bring the shepherd back where he belongs," the man said. "Do you need help in getting him back?"

Sammy shook his head.

"He'll bring the shepherd back right away," Marla said. "And if there's any damage, we'll fix it."

The shepherd was plastic and Marla realized Sammy might have scratched some of its paint off here or there. If he had, they'd paint over the scratches until the shepherd was as good as new.

"Oh, I'm sure the thing's in fine shape," the deputy sheriff said. "Sammy here knows he'll have even more chores to do if something happens to it."

The boy swallowed and then nodded.

"You're sure you don't need any help bringing it

back?" the deputy sheriff asked again. "It's kind of big."

Sammy shook his head. "I'm big, too."

Marla waited for her son to walk off the porch and head back to their house. She wanted to talk to the deputy sheriff for a minute, anyway, without Sammy overhearing her.

"Thank you," Marla said when Sammy was half-way to their house. She looked up at the man. She didn't know why she'd ever thought he wasn't confident enough to be a lawman. He looked completely in control. "I appreciate you talking to my son."

The man nodded. "It's my job."

For the first time, Marla noticed that the man had a tan line on his forehead. The cold air gave the bottom part of his face a red tinge, but his forehead, which had no tan, was even whiter than it had been inside the café. She wondered if it was really his job to have conversations outside in below-freezing temperatures just to save a young boy's pride.

"And I promise I'll talk to Sammy again myself," Marla continued. She looked the man in the eye so he would know she was serious. "He's not a bad kid. He's just trying to get adjusted to a new place. And he misses his old friends."

"I can understand that. It's hard when a kid moves around."

Marla took a deep breath. "This is a final move for us. We want to make this our home."

"I'm glad."

Marla watched the man's face to see if he was being sarcastic. After what he had just found out about Sammy, she would be surprised if any lawman would welcome them into their community. But there was nothing but friendliness in the man's eyes. Of course, he didn't know Sammy's biggest goal was to be in a street gang.

"Thank you," Marla said. She let a few moments pass. "I, ah, I was wondering if you were going to tell anyone about Sammy taking the shepherd?"

"Well, there's no official record of it, if that's what you mean. He won't have a police record or anything."

"Oh." Marla hadn't even thought about that. She'd just been worried about the community gossip. "That's good."

"No one here knows that it was Sammy," the man continued. "I'm hoping we can wrap it up before any more people even know that the shepherd is missing."

Marla nodded. "Thank you. It's just that, with the kids—"

The man held up his hand. "I know how sensitive boys that age can be about everyone talking about them."

Marla stood on the porch and thought how nice it was that the deputy sheriff genuinely did seem to understand. Maybe Sammy would benefit from talking to a man like this one. The only advice anyone had given to her on how to be a solo parent was to suggest she find a man who would relate to her son. They meant someone like an uncle or a grandfather, and she had dismissed the idea because the only relatives she had left were in Mexico and she didn't want to send Sammy down to them. But seeing this man today made her wonder. Maybe someone besides a relative would be willing to help Sammy.

She gave up the thought as soon as it passed through her mind. She could not ask the man standing in front of her to take on Sammy's problems. He was having this conversation with her only because it was his job, anyway. She should just say thank-you and let the man get back to work.

She didn't have a chance to say anything, though, because she heard a rumble start. At first she thought it sounded like some kind of distant thunder. Then there was a loud crack. But that didn't make any sense. There were no clouds in the sky and it was snow weather, not rain weather.

The deputy sheriff didn't wait to figure out what the sound was. He started running toward it.

Marla heard the café door open behind her, but she didn't turn to see who had come out. Instead, she grabbed Becky's hand and followed the deputy sheriff as fast as she could with her daughter beside her. When he turned into her driveway, she knew for certain that the sound was from her house. Or, at least, from near her house.

But what would make a noise like that? She hadn't

hooked up the gas furnace yet, so she knew it wasn't a gas explosion. The roof didn't look as if it had caved in and no windows appeared to be broken. In fact, it had sounded like something falling instead of exploding.

Becky couldn't keep up, so Marla let go of her daughter's hand when she was inside their front fenced yard. She was safe here.

"Follow Mommy," Marla whispered as she started running faster.

She still heard footsteps and, hopefully, one of the people following her would see to Becky. Marla was scared. Whatever had fallen could have hurt Sammy. She should have asked him where he had hid the shepherd instead of just asking him to bring it back. A father would have known to ask that of a young boy.

Marla had just assumed her son had hidden the shepherd in some nice safe place. A father would have suspected otherwise. Maybe some women could be good fathers to their sons, but she was not one of them. She was a failure as a single parent, and Sammy was paying the price.

Chapter Five

Les saw the woodpile as soon as he rounded the corner of the house. Of course, his eyes didn't go to the woodpile as much as they went to the boy standing precariously on the half of the stack that had not tumbled to the ground ten seconds ago.

The cut logs that hadn't fallen were likely to go at any minute. And if they did, Sammy would fall with them.

"Don't move," Les said softly as he forced himself to stop and take a deep breath. Les didn't want to panic the boy any more than he already was. "We'll get you down—just hold yourself steady."

Les heard the sound of footsteps behind him and he held up a hand without turning around. He didn't know what noise would do to the balance of those old cut logs, but the fewer people walking close to the wood the better it would be.

Les took a step toward Sammy. "Do you ever play football?"

"Yeah, sometimes."

Les took a few more steps until he was close enough so that Sammy could see his eyes. "Good. That's good."

Les steadied himself, all the while locking into Sammy's gaze. They would need coordination to make his plan work. And trust. Sammy needed to trust him. "Have you ever tried a flying tackle on someone?"

"Of course," Sammy said. "I'm not a baby."

"No, no, you're not, son," Les said as he took a step closer yet.

"I'm not your son," Sammy said.

Les held out his arms. "I want you to pretend you're taking a flying tackle and aim yourself right at my chest."

If the boy tried to jump straight down, Les was afraid the pressure on the logs would cause another slide, toppling both of them. They might not die, but they'd have some broken bones.

"Now?"

Les kept his eyes on Sammy's. He could see the fear in the boy, but he could see some bravery, as well. It was too bad the boy had lost his father. Even now he could tell how sensitive the boy was to that fact. Most boys would have let the son remark slide. For all the embarrassment his parents had caused him, Les was still glad neither of them had died young, as Sammy's dad had done.

Les nodded. "Now."

Marla bit her lip as she listened to the deputy sheriff and her son. She didn't want to call out and make Sammy fall, but she could barely stand to keep silent. She stood at the corner of the house, careful not to go any closer. She didn't want Sammy to look at her instead of the man. The air was cold on her face. She knew because she'd blinked away a tear and it felt warm sliding down her cheek. She wasn't close enough to see if there were any tears on Sammy's face.

She wished she'd spent more time in this overgrown area behind the house instead of worrying about what people saw in the front of the house. Maybe if she had, she'd have wondered about what would happen if moisture got inside that tall stack of firewood and then someone stood, or even jumped, on top of it. The early snow here had been heavy enough with moisture to make all of those logs slick. She knew that from the log pieces they had brought inside the house to use in the fireplace.

If she'd been paying more attention, maybe she would have either braced the wood up or pulled it down to size. If her husband were still alive, he would have noticed and done something about it.

Her son looked so small. He had his legs braced on top of the woodpile, and Marla could almost see him draw in his breath. She hoped the deputy sheriff knew what he was doing.

Suddenly she noticed those baggy pants Sammy was wearing and wished she had insisted he change into the ones that fit better. All of that loose denim could catch on a log and make him trip instead of jump. That would be disastrous.

Marla felt someone put a hand on her arm and she looked over to see Mrs. Hargrove at her side. The older woman had Becky with her and several others behind her.

"I've been praying," Mrs. Hargrove whispered to Marla as she squeezed her arm. "Your son's in God's hands."

Marla nodded. She wasn't one to deny other people their faith. She had her wooden cross, but she'd never actually prayed to God. She didn't even know much about people who claimed to talk to God.

Of course, there were a lot of things she didn't know much about. Science. Art history. Latin. She always figured she could learn what she needed to know about any of those things when the time came. She should have started learning about prayer after Jorge died, however. She believed Jorge had come to some faith in the end. She should have explored that.

Now she wished she'd gone to a church and tried to at least learn a thing or two about prayer. Fortunately, Mrs. Hargrove seemed to know what she was doing. At least, the older woman seemed confident.

"Thank you," Marla whispered.

Sammy bent his knees slightly and arched himself into space. Just like that.

Marla's heart stopped beating as she saw her son's body sail. *Please, God,* she breathed. Then she saw him hit the deputy sheriff in the chest. The deputy let Sammy knock him to the ground, but as he fell the man folded Sammy into him and rolled them both away from the woodpile.

"Thank you," Marla whispered again as another tear slid down her cheek. She didn't know if she was thanking God or Mrs. Hargrove or the deputy sheriff or all three of them.

The woodpile shook slightly, then the logs that were still in place began to crash down. Marla noticed the deputy sheriff had moved Sammy and himself even farther away from the falling pieces of wood. They were safe.

Mrs. Hargrove let go of Marla's arm. "My word! That was something."

Marla wiped away another tear. "I'm going to give Sammy a talking-to he won't forget."

"I bet it feels like he's taken ten years off your life. Thank God Lester was here to help. That man has a sense of balance like something you've never seen. Used to be quite the football player around here— until he quit playing, that is."

Marla nodded. She appreciated the sound of Mrs. Hargrove's voice. It made everything slow down a little. She'd have to remember to thank the deputy sheriff. She was glad she'd never voiced any of her reservations about his abilities to keep Dry Creek safe. She looked over at where the man stood with Sammy now and wondered what she had been worried about earlier. She was sure the deputy sheriff could protect Dry Creek from anything.

Becky walked around Mrs. Hargrove and hugged Marla's legs. Marla patted her daughter's head.

"It's nice to see that Sammy likes Lester," Mrs. Hargrove said from her place at Marla's side. "Look at them talking away."

Sammy and Les *were* talking. And gesturing. And Marla suddenly remembered why Sammy had been back here, anyway. He'd been going to get that plastic shepherd he'd stolen from the church.

"Well, look at that," a man's voice said behind Mrs. Hargrove. "Over there at the end of the woodpile."

Marla didn't know how many ends a woodpile could have, but it didn't take more than one good look in the general direction of where the wood had been to see what the older man was talking about.

"There's our shepherd," Elmer said triumphantly, and then he paused. "Or what's left of him, anyway."

The shepherd looked as if he had been hit by a rock slide, which, Marla supposed, he almost had been. The plastic staff in his arm had been broken off and a log had dented his face. She couldn't tell from where she stood, but it looked as if some of the brown on his beard had been scraped off. He probably had more damage in the part she couldn't see.

"Well, what's the shepherd doing back here?" Charley asked as he stepped forward until he was even with Mrs. Hargrove.

"I don't think that's important now," Mrs. Hargrove said softly.

"Well, it didn't walk over here," Elmer said as he, too, stepped forward. "I wonder if Les brought it over."

Marla watched as the deputy sheriff and Sammy started walking over to them. Les had his hand on Sammy's shoulder and her son looked okay with it. Except for this morning, Sammy had been shrugging off her hand when she tried to guide him in that manner, even though he used to let his father steer him that way all the time. Marla had thought it was just something Sammy didn't like, since he was a little older. Now she realized it was just her hand he didn't want.

"Well, when would Les have time to do that?" Charley turned around and asked. "He came right over here from the café."

Marla looked away from her son and back to those near her. She could tell the instant Charley understood what it meant that Les had come here after the café. When no one had been surprised at seeing the shepherd away from the rest of the Nativity set, she realized that the deputy sheriff was not the only one in Dry Creek who had known that the plastic figure was missing.

"Well, no harm done," Charley murmured, half to himself.

"But—" Elmer started to ask, and then stopped when he saw the look on Charley's face.

"No harm done," Charley repeated as he stepped back to stand beside Mrs. Hargrove. "Those sheep aren't real, anyway, so they don't need a shepherd."

"Maybe the angel can watch them," Becky said. "They're just babies."

"Yeah," Charley agreed. "They're just babies."

"It's good to take care of the young ones," Elmer added.

Marla knew what the older people were trying to do. And it was nice of them. But she also knew what that kind of pity turned to and she knew that, given some time to think about it, all three of those older people would begin to look down on her family. It was just the way of it. They would think she wasn't raising her children right or that the children were just naturally bad or something.

"Sammy took the shepherd," Marla said. She might as well get that part of it out there. She wouldn't tell them her son was halfway to being a gang member, but she could face them knowing about the shepherd. "He—he—well, it's been a hard year. We'll pay to have it fixed, of course. Or to buy a new one."

Les and Sammy arrived just as Marla spoke again. "Of course, we should buy a new one. Just let me know where to buy it."

"There's no need to do that," Mrs. Hargrove protested. "The church can take care of it."

"Besides, the women sent away for the set," Charley said. "I don't think you can get it without the soup-can labels and I'm not sure how much more soup we can eat around here."

"Sammy's already promised to fix it," Les said. "We've got it all arranged."

"I don't know," Elmer said. "Did you see the hole in the shepherd's head?"

Les nodded. "I think we can fix it."

"We can pay you for your time," Marla offered. She didn't know where she was going to get all this money, but she did not want to be indebted to anyone in this small town.

"Sammy's going to help me with some chores," Les said. "We've got a deal. I help him—he helps me."

Now, why did that make her feel so left out? Marla wondered. She should be grateful a man was taking some interest in Sammy. "Thank you."

"And, of course, he's also helping the church," Les said with a smile for Mrs. Hargrove. "Meet your new Sunday-school helper."

"Oh, my," Mrs. Hargrove said with a smile. "That's wonderful. I need someone to help me get the class ready for the Christmas program."

Marla wished she could tell what people were really thinking. Mrs. Hargrove was acting as if everything was just the way it was supposed to be. Marla couldn't believe, though, that the woman didn't have any feelings about having a young thief assigned to help her with her Sunday-school class. Marla would rather people just showed their horror and got it over with. That way she wouldn't have to wait for the day when they made it clear that, as charitable as they had been to the poor family when they so desperately needed help, they didn't really consider the Gossett family on the same level as everyone else in their town.

Marla knew all about the price one paid for charity. She just hoped she could spare her children that knowledge.

"Sammy isn't used to church," Marla said to Mrs. Hargrove.

"I don't much like glitter," Sammy added. "On my wings. If I have to be an angel."

Maybe it was his near fall, but Marla noticed Sammy didn't look as upset about his wings as he had earlier.

"Well, maybe we'll think of something else to put on your wings," Mrs. Hargrove said as she stepped close to Sammy. "Why don't we go back to the café and talk about it? You and your sister never did get your orange juice."

Marla decided it was too late to hold on to her family's pride and she answered Mrs. Hargrove's look with a nod. "Thank you. I think I'll stay here for a minute, if that's okay."

Mrs. Hargrove nodded. "You don't have to worry about the kids when they're with me."

"Tell Linda I'll pay for their juices when I get there."

"I've never met anyone so determined to pay for everything," Les said.

Marla hadn't noticed that he'd walked closer to her. Maybe that's because all she could see was that Sammy was walking beside Mrs. Hargrove and she had her hand on his shoulder and he was actually smiling up at her. Marla knew Sammy certainly never smiled at *her* when she tried to put her hand on his shoulder. Not the way he did with Les and Mrs. Hargrove.

"My son hates me," Marla said before she remembered that the deputy sheriff was practically a stranger to her. Sure, he'd just helped her with her son, but he was doing that because he was on duty. She forced herself to smile up at him. "I guess all sons have problems with their mothers."

Les grunted. "He doesn't *hate* you. He was scared. Maybe even a little embarrassed."

Marla nodded. She wasn't about to bare her soul to someone she hardly knew. "I never realized the woodpile was such a danger to the kids."

Les relaxed. For a minute there, he'd thought Marla was going to fall apart. Nothing made him more nervous than a woman who looked as if she was going to lose control of her emotions. He'd been mistaken, though. She was just feeling the normal guilt that any parent would feel when they had not foreseen a danger that one of their children faced.

He'd watched her eyes lighten as she talked. Her face was still pale from the cold and her eyes were damp as if she'd cried a bit. It was funny that her tears didn't bother him. The thought of her crying made him want to move closer to her, not flee.

"The wood will be fine now that it's not in that pile," Les said. He couldn't just stand there and stare at her. She'd think he was having a shock reaction to what had happened, and he didn't want to worry her. "I'm surprised old man Gossett didn't have a wood chute on the back porch. Usually people have a rack like that to keep a good supply of logs inside where it's dry. Then there's not so much danger of the woodpile falling."

"We don't have anything like that," Marla said.

Les noticed how her hair curled around the wool scarf she had around her neck.

"I could make you a chute," Les offered.

"Oh, I couldn't ask you to do that."

"It's no problem."

"Well, I'll pay you."

Les shook his head. "Nobody needs to be paying anybody."

He wondered what made this woman so determined to pay for any friendly gesture anyone made toward her. He considered it a small mercy that she didn't keep protesting when he refused her payment this time.

She looked up at him. "I can never repay you, anyway. Not after you saved my son's life."

Ah, here come the tears, Les thought. He was glad it was just the two of them. He wouldn't want to be seen comforting Marla in the middle of the street in Dry Creek. He would have a dozen people watching and speculating on when he'd be proposing to her. But back here, behind the house—well, he wouldn't mind if she needed a shoulder to cry on.

"I suppose it's just all in a day's work for you, though," Marla said as she blinked away the tears in her eyes.

"What?" Les snapped back to reality. Gone was the warm, golden picture of Marla turning to him for comfort. She didn't even see him as anything more than a public servant out to do his duty.

"Well, I suppose it's not every day that you rescue someone from a woodpile," Marla continued with a bright smile. "I'd guess it's mostly drug problems, isn't it?"

"Whatever gave you that idea?"

"Your morning foot patrol. I figure you're out looking for drug dealers."

Les shook his head. "It's more a stray-cat patrol than anything at that hour."

"Oh. Well, that's good, then. What kind of crime *do* you have in Dry Creek?"

Les had never thought he'd be sitting on an old log behind a girl's house at his age. And if he had pictured himself doing something like that, he'd certainly never expected to be spending the time telling her about the crime life in Dry Creek. And even if he'd seen all those other things coming, he would never, ever have expected to be enjoying it so much. He liked watching her eyes while he told her stories.

Chapter Six

Marla didn't know why the deputy sheriff didn't just put handcuffs on Sammy and escort him into church. Or brand his forehead with a *T* for thief. She had expected Les to check to be sure that Sammy showed up in Mrs. Hargrove's Sunday-school class, but she hadn't expected him to wait for them in front of the church.

Les wasn't even standing on the porch or near the Nativity set like the other church people. There was no mistaking his interest for being social rather than business. He was pacing back and forth on the edge of the street, clearly waiting for them. He looked so official everyone must notice it. Especially because, Marla saw as she got closer to him, he was wearing his khaki sheriff's uniform.

She'd never even seen Les in a uniform until now. He never wore a uniform when he walked around Dry Creek. That alone should tell people he was working. It certainly made a statement to her.

Marla kept her back straight. She didn't want people to think she was bothered at being on the business end of a sheriff's concern. After all, Sammy was making amends. They had nothing to be ashamed of.

"He's not in a suit," Sammy muttered. He was walking on one side of Marla and Becky was on the other. "And he's the sheriff."

"He's got his uniform on. And he's the temporary sheriff," Marla said. She didn't know why that made a difference to her, but it did. It meant that someday when Les Wilkerson passed her on the streets of Dry Creek he wouldn't be obliged to greet her just because he had her son in some kind of casual probation situation. He wouldn't need to be an official keeper of her son's schedule. He'd be able to choose whether or not he wanted to be their friend. He might even change out of his uniform when he planned to meet her.

"He's wearing boots. Why can't I get boots?" Sammy continued.

Marla took note of Sammy's comment with hope. His amigos didn't wear cowboy boots. Of course, they didn't wear suits, either, and that was Sammy's biggest complaint this morning.

Not that she blamed him about the suit. She could blame him for other things, but not for that. She'd bought both of their suits at a discount store in the garment district of downtown Los Angeles so they'd have something appropriate to wear for Jorge's funeral. And she hated the black suit she had on even more than Sammy disliked his suit.

After Jorge's funeral she'd vowed never to wear her suit again. The thing made her look like a crow. She'd noticed that fact when she looked in the mirror after the funeral. It was the worst day of her life, and all she could do was think of the crows in the cemetery where they had buried Jorge. She'd been struck at the time how much her black suit made her look like them, all squawky and ugly and sitting on lone branches in those trees, each one spread out so they were all by themselves looking fierce and protective of their aloneness.

The suit didn't just make her look like a crow, it made her feel like one, too.

She had almost given the suit to the Salvation Army before she moved up to Dry Creek, and now she wished she had. The only other thing resembling a dress she even had in her closet was a south-of-the-border senorita skirt-and-blouse set. She couldn't wear that to church here, though, so if she hadn't had the black suit, she could truthfully have told herself she had nothing to wear and maybe she could have justified staying home. Instead, she was left with trying to make that suit look better with a coffee-colored tank top and a black pearl necklace. She'd even found a gold circle brooch to wear on the lapel.

She wasn't sure any of it softened the suit enough, and she had finally given up. Maybe if she went for the grim look, people would stare at her instead of spending so much time studying Sammy, anyway.

"You're here," Les said when Marla and her children came within speaking distance.

Marla nodded with a quick look at the assortment of people gathered at the steps leading into the church. "We said we'd be here. It's our agreement."

Not for the first time, she wished Sammy hadn't stolen something from a church. Of course, she wished mostly that he had never stolen anything from anywhere, but if he had to steal, why a church? She'd rather have to volunteer for a school function or even put in some hours at the local hardware store. But a church? She didn't know anything about churches. The truth was they scared her a little bit.

She'd certainly never expected to have a sheriff's escort when she entered the church in Dry Creek for the first time.

Everyone was watching her and the kids as they walked up to the steps leading into the building. She wondered if she had "visitor" stamped on her forehead. If she did, it probably said "official visitor—sentence being served."

"Welcome," a man said, dipping his hat to her as she walked past.

"Good to see you here," another added with a smile.

Fortunately, Les reached Marla's side about then and he ushered her through the rest of the people standing on the church steps. Marla didn't know what she would say to any of them if they asked her if she knew what had happened to the missing shepherd. Of course, they might not even need to ask the question if they thought about Les escorting them into the church in full uniform.

Marla didn't know how a man could be so self-contained. Les didn't look as if he was doing his duty this morning, but he didn't look relaxed, either. He nodded to various people, but he had his hand on her elbow and he was guiding her up the stairs.

Marla would have paid good money to know what was going on in that head of his. He'd cut his hair since she'd seen him earlier in the week. And he was wearing some cologne that smelled good. He gave everyone a smooth smile, but his eyes looked a little anxious. She hoped he wasn't worried that Sammy would back out of his agreement. Sammy had his problems, it was true, but he didn't go back on his word. At least, she didn't think he did.

Marla sighed. She needed to face the fact that she didn't know her son very well anymore.

Les wondered for the first time if it was such a good thing to have suggested some service to the church as a way for Sammy to make amends for taking the shepherd. Marla and the kids all looked as if they were facing a judge. Or an executioner. He'd liked the way Marla looked in the bathrobe better than he did in this suit of hers. Maybe the suit material was scratchy and that's why she held herself so stiffly. She might have been annoyed with him when she answered her door in her bathrobe the other morning, but she'd looked happier then than she did now.

"Mrs. Hargrove will tell you how to do everything," Les said to Sammy as he motioned for the boy to continue up the walk ahead of him. "You might even surprise yourself and have fun."

"He's not supposed to have fun," Marla said as she stepped closer so only Les could hear her words. "He's supposed to learn a lesson."

"Well, it doesn't need to be painful. Mrs. Hargrove likes to keep things happy in her class. There's lots of singing and stories."

"So I could take my suit jacket off?" Sammy asked as he looked up at Les. "I don't want to scare any little kids."

"You'll wear the suit jacket," Marla said.

Les lifted his hands in surrender. "Your mom's the one with the say here."

"Nobody wears a suit," Sammy mumbled. "It's lame."

Les shrugged. "They say it makes you look older."

Sammy looked up at him skeptically. "Old enough to be *dead* maybe."

"I'm just repeating what the girls say."

"Then why don't you have a suit on?"

Les wondered suddenly if he should have a suit on. Marla was wearing a suit. Her son was wearing a suit.

Maybe she expected everyone to be wearing suits. That's probably the way it was in Los Angeles. Suddenly he was unsure of himself. He'd put on his uniform because it was the most dressy thing he owned. But maybe it had been a mistake.

"Don't talk that way to the sheriff," Marla scolded Sammy quietly. "It's none of our business how he's dressed."

Les looked down at his khaki slacks. They were clean. And pressed. He even wore his regulation dark tie with his uniform shirt. He looked at the other men who stood around the Nativity set. No one there was wearing a suit or a uniform. Of course, Pastor Matthew would wear a suit. But he would probably be the only man in the church building wearing one. Unless anyone counted Sammy. Les had a spurt of empathy for the boy.

"Hey, what happened to the shepherd?" one of the ranch hands from the Elkton place called over to Les when he was at the top of the stairs. "He was the only figure in the whole Nativity set that I can relate to and he isn't here."

Several ranch hands were standing around the Nativity set admiring it. Les could see where one of them had brought in a bale of straw to scatter around the manger. Mary was surrounded by the stuff.

"The shepherd got a bit damaged," Les said. He was speaking, but people were looking at the space where the shepherd had been. He was grateful to have the attention off himself. "Don't worry, though. We're fixing him up. He'll be better than new before you know it."

"That angel needs to be rehung," another ranch hand said. "She's going to fall if we don't do something."

Les nodded. Sammy had called it right. "Maybe we can get a ladder from the hardware store after church and restring her."

Marla had been holding her breath when Les was talking to the men. She was surprised the other men didn't ask more questions about how the shepherd had been damaged. But they seemed to trust that Les was taking care of whatever was wrong. She hoped the rest of the people in the church were as easily satisfied about the shepherd.

Someone rang a bell and suddenly everyone was walking up the steps into the church. Marla was grateful that Les hung back and walked with her and the children instead of going ahead with the other men.

Marla relaxed as soon as she walked into the church. There, at the front, was a large wooden cross. It reminded her of the one she had at home. It was made of the same hard polished wood. She wondered if the people here knew what Jorge had discovered by looking at his cross in his dying days.

The air smelled of pine—someone had placed a big Christmas tree in front of the church, off to the left side. There was a piano on the right side and a young blond woman sat at it playing a Christmas hymn. The notes sounded full and smooth.

"The adults have a class up here," Les said. He seemed to be nodding a greeting to a dozen people while he talked to her. "Mrs. Hargrove will take Sammy and Becky down to her class."

"But shouldn't I be with them?"

"Ma," Sammy protested. "You don't need to come."

"They'll be fine with Mrs. Hargrove. And don't worry about Becky. Mrs. Hargrove already suggested she might like her class better than the one for the younger kids, especially if Sammy is there. Here comes Mrs. Hargrove now."

Marla knew the children would be okay with the older woman. She was just so used to having them with her. She wondered if she would be okay without them.

Mrs. Hargrove greeted everyone and pointed the children in the direction of a doorway before Marla finished wondering what she should do. She relaxed when even Becky seemed unconcerned that Marla wasn't going with them. Her children were growing up.

"The kids' classes are in the basement," Les said as he nodded to the nearest row of pews. "The adults sit up here in comfort."

The pews were the same smooth wood as the cross, but Marla wasn't sure she would be comfortable even if the pews had deep cushions. As a child, church people had given her family charity baskets, but they had never invited them to come to their churches. If Marla had to be in a church at all, she would like to be in the back row so she could duck out if she discovered she wasn't welcome.

Unfortunately, Les wasn't gesturing toward the back row. And so Marla reluctantly walked with him to the front pew.

"I'm not used to churches," Marla said quietly as Les waited for her to enter the aisle space before him. "They make me a little nervous that I'll do something out of place."

"Don't worry. You can't make any mistakes," Les said as she sat on the pew and he joined her.

"I brought something for the offering plate. It's not much, but—"

"You don't need to put anything in the plate."

"I can afford to give something to the church."

Marla wondered how everyone could be so relaxed and friendly to everyone else. She'd already been given more welcoming smiles than she'd ever seen in Los Angeles. In ways the small town of Dry Creek reminded her of the town in Mexico where her mother had grown up. Marla had spent a couple of weeks with one of her aunts there when she was a teenager. People had the same unconscious interest in a stranger there as they did in Dry Creek. In Los

Angeles, no one looked at strangers. Here, everyone looked her in the eye and greeted her.

"Surely some of them know about Sammy and the shepherd," Marla said, her voice low so only Les could hear.

"I doubt it. Mrs. Hargrove can keep a secret, and she'll see that Charley and Elmer watch their tongues, too."

Marla relaxed. Maybe things would work out for them in Dry Creek, after all. Maybe she was worrying too much. Maybe people were more tolerant here than she expected.

The pastor stood up then and walked to the front of the pews, opening his Bible on the way.

Marla had never heard the story of the young Mary before. Oh, she knew all about the baby Jesus being born in a manger and the angel proclaiming the good news to the shepherds. Anyone who received Christmas cards knew that much. But she had never heard anyone talk about how Mary must have felt when she was pregnant and had to ride that donkey off into a new land just to satisfy some bureaucrat someplace.

Marla had never expected to feel kinship with someone in the Bible. She thought all those people had lived golden lives where they floated on clouds and lived the special sweat-free lives of saints. She had never imagined Mary would possibly have had morning sickness. Or felt fat, just as Marla had felt during both her pregnancies.

As the pastor spoke, Marla got a vivid picture of how awkward everything must have been for Mary. There was no hot water in the manger. Not even a bed to lie down on. Marla knew firsthand how it felt to not even have basic furniture. And to be a woman in a strange land. She knew about that, too.

Marla might not be pregnant right now, but she, like Mary, knew the uncertainty that children brought to a woman's life. She didn't know for sure what to do with Sammy. He didn't seem to want her sympathy and support. Marla really identified with Mary, though, when she realized that Mary had also needed to trust a man with her deepest secret.

Marla looked over at Les when the pastor talked about how vulnerable Mary must have felt, knowing Joseph could judge her harshly. He not only knew her secret; he also controlled her future.

Les wouldn't be a bad person to trust, Marla supposed. Although she couldn't help but notice he was scowling at the man who had sat down on the other side of her. This was the same man who had greeted her outside at the Nativity set, and he seemed harmless enough. There, the man smiled at her again. She could see Les's scowl out of the corner of her eye. She wondered if Joseph had spent the trip to Bethlehem scowling, too. No wonder Mary always seemed so quiet in those pageants.

The adults' class ended with a prayer for peace in Dry Creek and throughout the rest of the world.

Marla looked around to see if anyone focused on the cross at the front of the church when they prayed, but it seemed as if everyone just closed their eyes. Someday when she knew everyone better she was going to have to ask someone about the purpose of the cross in prayer. The cross looked too important to be a decoration, but she hadn't seen anyone do anything with it. Of course, she didn't want to ask any questions now that would reveal her ignorance.

After the prayer, Les suggested that they have some coffee in the kitchen area. He looked as if he had something to say, but somehow no words ever came out, so Marla just followed him. She counted herself lucky that she didn't have to ride a donkey along the way.

Les wondered how he could have forgotten the ranch hands. He should have known they would all be at church when word got out that a new single female was going to be there. Most of them came, anyway, during the Christmas season, so an eligible woman was just an added bonus.

"That man has worked at the Elkton place for almost ten years now," Les finally said as he nodded toward Byron and then led Marla back to the table where the coffee was being served. He didn't want to criticize Byron, but he hoped Marla would realize a man who only worked on a ranch wasn't as ambitious as a man who actually owned his own ranch.

"That must be nice," Marla said.

Les looked at her. How could it be nice?

"To work in the same place for that long."

"Yeah, well." He barely restrained himself from mentioning that he had worked in the same place for almost twice as long and it was his own place.

Les noticed that Byron was walking back to the coffee table just as they were. The ranch hand didn't have a suit on, but Les could plainly see that the man's shirt and pants went together as if they belonged in a magazine ad somewhere. Of course, Les's shirt and pants matched, as well, but khaki and khaki didn't exactly make a man stand out from the pack.

Les felt a frown settling on his face. Byron was dressed like a man who charmed women, and Les knew the ranch hand could do it. Byron had even talked himself out of eating soup during the drive for labels and the women he'd charmed to do that were safely married, so they didn't even have anything to gain by giving in to his smiles. Les calculated every man in Dry Creek had had to eat ten extra cans of soup to make up for Byron's share.

Les knew that women didn't judge men by the same scales other men used, however. Marla probably liked a man like Byron, Les thought as his frown deepened.

Les had just decided to stop thinking about the man when Byron planted himself squarely in their path. Les still had his hand on Marla's arm and he felt his grip tighten slightly. She was, technically, his guest and he wasn't giving her up to Byron. Still, he supposed he needed to be civil. "Do you mind if we pass? We're going for coffee."

Byron turned with a grin. "Thanks. Don't mind if I do join you. I heard Mrs. Hargrove made cowboy coffee this morning."

Les knew he had lost the battle before Byron even turned his attention to Marla.

"I don't think I've had the pleasure of meeting you," Byron said to Marla with that smile of his.

Les saw Marla turn a little pink. He could tell by the slight sparkle in her eyes that Byron's smile was not wasted on her. Of course, how could she know that Byron had perfected that smile in front of a mirror? At least, that was the rumor when Les had known him in high school.

"This is Marla Gossett," Les said. What else could he do? "Marla, meet Byron Stead."

Marla nodded as she looked at Byron. "What's cowboy coffee?"

"Good enough for a cowboy and strong enough for his horse, too."

Les almost shook his head. How did the man make it sound as if he'd invented something wonderful? Mrs. Hargrove had made the same coffee she made every Sunday and it had nothing to do with cowboys or horses. Byron had a way with words, all right. Les was just waiting for him to make some reference to the poet Lord Byron. The man had been named after the poet, but Les knew full well that it didn't mean Byron had any real writing talent. In fact, if his high school record still held, he couldn't even spell.

Of course, Les supposed it wasn't spelling that put those sparkles in women's eyes. Still, any self-respecting ranch hand would change his name to Brian, no matter what nonsense his mother had been thinking when he was born.

"There's cinnamon-orange tea this morning, too," Les said to Marla as the three of them reached the coffee table. "They always have it out around Christmas."

"I'll get you a cup of the tea unless—" Byron started.

"I can get it," Les interrupted. He was the host.

Byron looked at him in surprise, and Les supposed he couldn't blame him. Les had never competed with the ranch hands for a woman's attention before. Les had always thought a woman who was taken in by the likes of someone like Byron wasn't the woman for him, anyway. Unfortunately, that included most women. He wasn't going to risk that it included Marla.

"I was going to say—unless you want to try the coffee," Byron continued with a smile for Marla.

Les watched Byron move his shoulder slightly to make it seem as though Marla was with him and not with Les. Before Les could step forward to block Byron, Marla stepped forward herself.

"Shouldn't I be checking on the children?" she said with a look at Les.

Les nodded, even though no one ever needed to check on their children in Sunday school here. "It wouldn't hurt."

Les had never been prouder than when he was walking Marla to the steps that led to the downstairs classrooms. He knew he was a quiet man; he liked it that way. But it did feel good to have a woman choose to walk off with him in that quietness instead of drinking tea with Byron.

"Does Sammy have to put in a certain number of hours?" Marla asked as she started down the stairs.

Les felt his pride leave him. He'd forgotten there for a minute that Marla was walking with him because he was the deputy sheriff and she was worried about her son. "No, there's no set hours."

Marla nodded. "I'm sure the time he spends with Mrs. Hargrove will only help him." Then she looked up. "And with you, too. I can't thank you enough for helping him."

"It's no problem."

Les's only consolation was that Marla had already agreed to bring Sammy out to his ranch tomorrow so they could begin work on repairing the shepherd. Once he had her out there, he wouldn't need to worry about any other single ranch hands. Mr. Morales was supposed to drop by tomorrow morning, but he was old enough to be Marla's father.

Les could see the part in Marla's hair as he followed her down the stairs. Her hair fell straight on both sides of the part and he liked the way it swayed as she walked. He thought with a start that it looked like Mrs. Hargrove's coffee when it was being poured into one of the larger church mugs. Which, now that he thought about it, wasn't a half-bad piece of poetic nonsense for a rancher to come up with.

He silently thought the words. *Your hair is like coffee, pouring straight...to—straight to—*

Well, Les told himself, he'd finish the words later. It was the thought that counted. Women liked poems about their hair. Byron, the poet, would never have found the words to an image like that, Les told himself with satisfaction. Maybe he'd put some sparkles in Marla's eyes yet.

Chapter Seven

Marla drove her car down the long gravel road, wondering if the metal sign she'd seen earlier indicating that this was the Wilkerson ranch was accurate. If it was, Les's place was huge. A fence ran along one side of the road, and on the other side, hills covered with dead brown grass stretched all the way to the distant mountains. Snow lay here and there, especially in the ravines, and the ground still glistened from last night's frost.

Fortunately, the road was clear. Two tire ruts showed the way. She had driven over a cattle guard in the road as she entered the ranch, but she had not seen any animals yet. They must be tucked away in some of those snowy ravines.

Marla looked over and saw Sammy staring out the side window. Becky was in the backseat.

"Big, isn't it?" Marla asked. The only other time she had visited a ranch like this was in Mexico, where one of her uncles worked. He'd driven her around and told her about things like cattle guards and ravines and drought.

Sammy grunted. "I don't see those sheep he was talking about."

"The babies?" Becky asked from the backseat.

"If they're young, they probably need to be near the barn."

That was Marla's best guess. Her uncle had never taken her to the ranch's buildings, and she'd never had pets to care for. But the young ones probably always needed special care no matter what species they were. And a barn was an awful lot like the stable where Mary had stayed when she had the baby Jesus, so Marla figured the babies would always be there.

"Maybe we'll see the little lambs," Becky said.

"Maybe."

It was Monday and Marla was bringing Sammy out to the sheriff's place so that they could start fixing the Nativity shepherd. Correction, she told herself. They were going to Les's place. He had asked her to call him Les, and she'd done pretty well at church yesterday until she'd thought of him in his law enforcement role. Somehow it didn't seem right to call him by his first name when his duty required him to discipline her son. Still, she would try to honor the man's request when she saw him today.

She wondered if Les had unloaded the plastic shepherd. He had put it into the back of his pickup last week and he'd driven a late-model car to church, so she hadn't seen the pickup since. She supposed he wouldn't have been able to leave the plastic figure in his pickup if he had to use the vehicle for chores, but she had hoped Sammy would be there to help him carry the figure inside to where they were going to work on it.

She wanted Sammy to see every ounce of effort that was going into righting his wrong.

They should be reaching Les's house soon, Marla thought as she started up a slight incline. She looked at the clock on her dashboard and saw that she was right on schedule. He'd suggested they come for a nine-o'clock breakfast, and it was ten minutes to the hour. It would take her a few minutes to get the car parked and the kids' jackets zipped up again before leaving the car and then going to Les's door.

Marla hadn't told the children that a real shepherd might be there this morning, as well. From the man's name, Mr. Morales, Marla suspected he was Hispanic. She almost hoped so. She didn't want to hide her Hispanic background any longer, and with another Hispanic there, it would be natural to mention that she and the children were of the same heritage.

Les had seemed pretty easygoing so far. She'd just have to trust him to accept their Hispanic roots without letting his mind wander to any thoughts of big-city gangs. Up here, she doubted anyone had even heard of the 19th Street gang. Maybe she was worrying for nothing. She knew Sammy had used the gang symbol on his note, but no one seemed to be asking what it all meant. Of course, she knew why he'd written it. He had been missing his *amigos* in Los Angeles. But missing his old friends wasn't a crime no matter how unsuitable those friends were.

Les looked out the kitchen window for the hundredth time that morning. He could see the road coming up to his house through this window, so it was the only window worth looking out when he was expecting someone.

The house and barn had already been here when he'd bought the ranch land, or he would have built them on one of the higher pieces of ground. Fortunately, it never flooded this far from Big Dry Creek, so the lower elevation wasn't a problem. And the dip in the land did help with the wind. Being stuck down in this bowl made it hard to know when company was coming, though, and Les liked to be prepared when people drove up to his place.

Not that he could stand preparing any more than he had this morning.

He had been up since five o'clock trying to get everything ready for Marla and the kids, and he hadn't done anything for the past hour except pace from the kitchen window to the living room. Back and forth. He went over his mental checklist.

He'd scoured down the kitchen and swept out the

barn yesterday after church. He usually kept Sunday as a day of rest, but he figured the Lord knew how he felt about company coming. At first it was going to be only a little bit of cleaning. The barn was a big old building, and Les was proud of the restoring he'd done to it. He'd replaced most of the stalls and added a workshop space with an electric heater. He hadn't had a chance to work on the old hayloft, though, and he'd have to remember to caution everyone not to go up there. All in all, he was proud of the barn, and it always looked good when it had been swept clean of hay.

After he'd finished in the barn, he'd brought the plants in from the porch and set them here and there around the living room. He'd place a plant on the bookcase and then notice that the coffee table looked a little beat-up, so he'd move the plant there until he noticed that the windowsill looked naked with nothing on it. That's what he'd been doing earlier this morning.

Finally Les had faced the fact that there was nothing else he could do. Marla and the kids would either like his home or they wouldn't. Somehow, the starkness of that realization wasn't as comforting as he'd thought it would be. He looked around for something more to do. He was beginning to see why women in the old days had doilies to arrange on their furniture. It gave them something to do before company was coming.

When Les had finished positioning the plants for the third time that morning, he'd decided he better start to make the scones. He'd gotten the recipe from a website on his computer the day he'd brought the damaged shepherd figure back here. Even then he knew he'd want to give Marla and the kids something to eat when they came out, and the scones looked simple enough to make.

Les's mother used to make scones when she had women friends come over, so he decided they were the thing to make for Marla.

Les believed a man could do anything with a computer behind him. He'd used his computer to design a bridge over the creek that flowed through his north pasture. He'd calculated the amount of feed he needed to raise a calf to be a yearling. He had absolute faith that a computer could help him make scones.

Last night Les had left the scone directions on the kitchen counter next to a bowl. Any kind of baked goods tasted best if they were fresh from the oven, so he didn't want to bake them Sunday evening.

Not all men would know that fact, Les told himself. A smart woman would recognize the benefits of marrying a man who had done his own cooking for years. Not that it was time to be talking about marriage with Marla. He'd be happy if he could get her to go out on a date with him. And kiss him. A kiss would be a good thing. Maybe if he worked in the poem about her hair, she'd start thinking of him as someone she'd like to kiss.

The scones were barely in the oven when Les

started to worry that he'd forgotten to latch the gate on the lamb pen. He knew he never forgot to close any gates completely, but he kept trying to remember if he'd heard the click of that particular gate. If it didn't click, a lamb could nudge it open if he tried hard enough.

Finally Les decided he should go check. It wouldn't look good if Marla came over the hill and the lambs were running all over the place. She would think he couldn't take care of things. No woman wanted to kiss a man who couldn't take care of things.

Les put on his winter coat and stomped back out to the barn.

The gate was latched, but one of the lambs was standing just inside it looking rather forlorn, so Les took a minute to give him some help back to his mother. By the time Les got back into the house, the scones had burned a little. The burn was more of a dark brown than a black and, ordinarily, Les would have pronounced them good enough to eat.

But he didn't want to serve burned scones to Marla, so he made a batch of biscuits. Fortunately, he could make biscuits in his sleep. He had a jar of homemade rhubarb jam that Mrs. Hargrove had given him for Christmas last year. He'd been saving it for special company, and today was about as special as it was likely to get.

Les felt as if he'd thrown hay bales all day by the time he saw the car coming up his driveway.

Then he remembered he wanted to have classical music playing when Marla drove up, so he quickly went to the stereo in his living room and turned it on. He wanted her to know that a rancher could be cultured. He wasn't putting his complete faith in his biscuits, even though Mrs. Hargrove had once pronounced them the lightest ones she'd ever eaten.

Unfortunately, Les had forgotten about the plant he'd just placed on top of the shelf above the stereo. The one that hadn't looked quite right on the coffee table. He'd been so sure the philodendron would balance out the room with its vine of leaves that trailed down to the stereo itself. Les had to lean forward to find the CD he wanted to play. He heard footsteps on the porch at the same instant he saw the pot above him begin to tip.

Marla heard a faint crash. She had her hand all ready to knock on the kitchen door, but when she heard the crash, she froze.

"Something fell," Sammy said.

"I'm sure Deputy Wilker—I mean, Les—has it all under control."

It hadn't sounded like a person falling, so Marla figured Les was all right.

"Maybe he dropped the shepherd again," Becky said.

"Sammy, don't—" Marla started, but it was too late.

Sammy was already leaning over and looking in the window at the side of the kitchen door.

"Ah, he's all right," Sammy said as he straightened.

Les opened the door.

Marla started to smile. The man had a leaf in his ear. And a trail of dirt on his shirt.

"I hope you like Beethoven," Les said as he stood there looking a little uncertain.

Marla nodded, and then she heard music fill the house. There must be speakers in every room. "It's lovely."

Les relaxed. "I can do Bach instead, if you'd rather."

"I like them both."

Marla was surprised to remember how much she liked classical music. Jorge hadn't liked it, calling it funeral music, so she'd turned the car radio away from the classical station years ago. She hadn't turned it back, but she promised herself she would. She had no one to please anymore but herself, and it felt good.

"Come in and have a seat at the table while I go change."

Marla tried not to be too envious as she looked around the kitchen. Les had gone into another room and, for once, her children were quietly sitting, waiting for him to come back and serve them the biscuits he'd promised. She would have to remember that the smell of baked biscuits was enough to make her children behave.

Their silence left Marla time to look around. What

a kitchen this was. She wished her mother was alive to see it.

When had a kitchen like this become an impossible dream for her? It wasn't even the appliances that she envied, although they were all better than the ones she'd ever had. It was the space. Her mother always said she wanted a kitchen big enough for dancing, and Marla had understood why when she had seen one of her uncles dance with his wife in their kitchen one day in Mexico. A kitchen big enough to dance in would hold a table sturdy enough for children's games. A kitchen like that was meant for family life.

Her mother had never had a kitchen like that in her whole life.

The kitchen in Marla's house was cramped. It wasn't much bigger than the one in her old apartment, and that had been a galley kitchen with barely enough room for one person to move up and down the aisle from refrigerator to sink to stove.

When Les came back wearing a clean shirt, Marla flushed. She shouldn't be sitting here wishing she had this man's kitchen. "Can I help with anything?"

"Thanks, but it'll only take me a minute."

There were already place mats and plates on the table. Les got the biscuits and some butter before he sat down. Then he reached for the jar in the center of the table and popped its seal. Marla saw the homemade jam and forgot all about the appliances.

"Is that rhubarb? Don't tell me you made that?"

Les shook his head. "It's from Mrs. Hargrove."

"Good. I was going to start feeling intimidated if you knew how to make jam. I'm afraid my cooking is pretty plain."

"You make good tamales," Sammy said. "Remember, you said if you got a pork roast, you'd make the sweet ones for Christmas."

Marla caught her breath. She hadn't intended to tell Les about her heritage this soon in the day. She looked at him and didn't see anything new on his face. She turned to Sammy. "I don't have the pork roast yet. I've got it on my wish list, though. We'll have to see if they have a small one at the store."

"Now tamales, that's something I don't think I could ever make," Les said as he walked back to the refrigerator. "I make quesadillas once in a while, but that's as far as I go."

"Do you like Mexican food?" Marla asked. She supposed it didn't really matter one way or the other, but she was hoping to have at least one friend in Dry Creek and, she had to admit, it would be nice to have a friend who enjoyed her family's food and traditions. The deputy sheriff's acceptance of her and the kids mattered to her.

"Love it," Les said as he brought back a bowl of cut orange sections. "Just don't know how to make it."

"Oh." Marla smiled. She could take care of that part of it.

Les sat down and looked at Marla. "Do you mind if we say grace?"

"Of course not."

"Want to join hands?" Les held out his hands, one to Sammy and the other to Marla.

Marla wondered why she'd never thought to say grace with her children. Maybe if she'd spent some time talking to Sammy about God, her son would not have felt the need to idolize a bunch of criminals. Of course, to do that, she would have had to learn something about God herself. After her time in church yesterday, she thought she could do it, too. A God who had time for women like Mary might have time for her, too.

She was already learning more about prayer. For starters, there was something powerful about holding a man's hand in prayer. Marla let the feelings of security and abundance fill her. Everything seemed good when she bowed her head and held on to Les's hand as he prayed.

A few seconds later she was wondering how long people were supposed to hold hands. Les had finished praying and he'd let go of Sammy's hand, but he still held hers. Not that she was complaining exactly. It was just odd. She'd opened her eyes when he said "Amen," and he'd looked over at her. She couldn't help but notice that his eyes were the color of moss. A friendly sort of moss with flecks in them. And his smile. He had a nice smile.

"I have a cross," she said to Les.

"Huh?"

He was still smiling. Only now he was rubbing the knuckle of her little finger.

"On my wall. The cross I have." She took a breath. "I know it's not like saying prayers and all of that. But…"

Marla supposed she should expect someone like Les to think she was a heathen. "It's just I've never known a man who prayed before—well, my uncles do, but I don't see them much."

"That's because they live in Mexico," Sammy said calmly. "Can I have a biscuit now?"

"It's not polite to ask," Marla said automatically.

Les flushed and let go of her hand. "Sure. Biscuits coming up for everyone."

"I can butter my own," Becky said as she lifted her knife to demonstrate.

"Just don't let her at the jam," Sammy said as he took a biscuit off the plate Les passed to him. "She'll get all sticky."

"I'll put the jam on for her," Marla said.

Marla had watched Les and she was beginning to wonder if the man was slow. Sammy had all but announced their heritage and Les hadn't reacted at all. Usually people at least had a question or two when someone told them about their roots. In fact, now that she thought about it for a moment, it was only polite to make some comment.

"My uncles live close to Puerto Vallarta," Marla said as she took the biscuit plate from Sammy. "My mother came from around there."

Les nodded as he split his biscuit and started to butter it. "My mother moved here from Boston. She had a hard time getting used to the casual way things are done around here. Not enough *sirs* and *ma'ams* to please her."

"But, at least the temperature would be about the same, wouldn't it?" Marla said politely. "Or is it colder here?"

Les grunted. "It's colder here than anywhere."

Marla was beginning to wonder if her coming from Mexico was the same to Les as his mother coming from Boston. She hoped it was. Since he hadn't made any comment, she would have to assume it was.

"It's warm in the state of Jalisco."

Les looked up.

"That's the area around Puerto Vallarta where my mother was born. There's lots of marine life. Tropical vegetation. Some shopping."

"Sounds great. I'd like to see it sometime."

"The police carry guns there," Sammy offered. "You should go and find out how they do it."

Les smiled. "Reserve deputy sheriffs don't need to carry guns."

"But you have one, right? If you needed it, you could get it?"

Her son looked a little anxious.

"Sammy!" Marla said. Why did young boys always want to know about guns? She wished Sammy never even thought about who carried a gun and who didn't. Fortunately, Sammy had never carried one, not even with his fascination with the 19th Street gang. She'd asked him that question directly and he'd told her no.

"That's all right," Les said to Marla, then he looked at Sammy. "No one should carry a gun just because they can. I have a rifle I keep in my pickup so I have it with me when I go up to the mountains. But that's the only time I might need it."

Sammy didn't seem particularly satisfied with Les's answer, but Marla shot him a warning glance. She didn't want Les to think that Sammy was overly interested in violence. Which he wasn't, of course. She still hadn't been able to ask herself if Sammy might have lied to her about whether or not he had handled a gun. But this kind of conversation could give Sammy a reputation as a troublemaker, whether he had ever done anything or not.

"That's the pickup you take when you come into Dry Creek?" Sammy pressed. "The one with the red stripe down the side."

"It's the only pickup I have."

Sammy nodded.

"I'm sure you keep your pickup locked," Marla said. She didn't want Sammy's curiosity to lead him into trouble.

"No one locks their pickups around here, but I keep

the bullets with me, so the rifle isn't loaded, if that's what worries you."

Sammy didn't seem to react to that added piece of news, so Marla relaxed. Maybe she was being paranoid about Sammy's past. After all, that was behind them. He was in a new place now and none of his old friends could reach him here. There hadn't even been any more letters after that first one about the baseball he left behind. Her son was fine.

Before long breakfast was over and Les announced that it was time to go to the workshop in the barn. He assured them that Mr. Morales would come in around ten o'clock and help them with the shepherd's face.

"Is Mr. Morales Hispanic?" Marla asked.

Les shrugged. "I think so. I'm not sure where he comes from, though. He's never mentioned any family."

"Will he bring his sheep with him?" Becky asked.

"I'm afraid not." Les smiled at Becky. "But I have some lambs that have been wanting to meet a little girl."

"Like me?" Becky squealed.

Les nodded. "Just like you."

Les had extra scarves for the children to wrap around their necks and he helped Becky put her mittens on.

Marla noticed that the rancher was patient with her children. Those mittens weren't easy. He'd already shown that he would risk injury to himself to save her son from a bad situation. And he was helping Sammy make amends for breaking the shepherd, when many men would have just scolded him instead. Most men, she had noticed, would rather talk to a child than actually do something like put on a mitten or help a boy learn to repair something he'd broken.

If she was keeping score, Marla would have to admit that Les ranked high on the could-be-a-dad list. She was beginning to wonder why he was still single. He looked like the kind of guy women would marry in a heartbeat. He didn't have a handsome face. It was too weathered for that. But he had regular features and the nicest eyes. All of which probably meant he was single by choice.

Marla frowned as Les opened the door for all of them so they could go outside. Maybe he was single because he was so committed to the church. She wondered if Les was that kind of a religious man. That would certainly explain why he was kind to children and took such good care of his lambs and only kept a gun in his pickup instead of on his hip like most lawmen would do.

Marla's frown deepened. She never would have thought of Les as some type of kind, priestly uncle, but now that she was adding it all up, it made sense. She knew he didn't swagger around like some men, but he was strong enough for that if he had wanted to. Not many men could resist that temptation, especially when they'd just been a hero as Les had been the other day.

There was no getting around the fact that Les was unusual.

Well, she was glad she'd realized this early. She wasn't going to make the mistake of thinking he was interested in her in any romantic sense. She had a bad enough record just figuring out normal men like her late husband. She didn't need to start guessing about whether or not some saint loved her.

Chapter Eight

The barn was nicer than Marla had expected. It was cold outside, but she felt the heat the minute she stepped inside. There were hay bales lining one side and glass windows on the other. Several cows stood switching their tails in the sunshine that came in through the tall windows. Everything was neat and cozy. It made her feel good that Les kept such a warm, clean place for his animals, especially because in the spring most of the animals would probably be mothers and little babies.

Les pointed Marla and the kids toward the workshop room that he had made in one section of the barn.

"But what's up there?" Sammy asked before they reached the workshop.

Les looked up. "The hayloft. No one goes up there, though. It's not safe."

Marla could see where boards above her were sloping down. There were even a couple of places where a board had broken off and there was a hole in the ceiling of the lower part of the barn. There were thick beams holding the boards in place so they wouldn't be able to fall, though, so people were safe walking around below the loft. And Les had strung a rope across the wooden stairs at the side of the barn leading up to the hayloft to warn people not to climb the stairs.

Sammy shrugged as he stared up at the loft. "It looks okay. I've been in worse buildings."

There were some deserted buildings in Los Angeles and Marla was appalled to think that Sammy had actually been inside any of them. "That's why we came up here. You need to stay out of places like that."

"I should have fixed the hayloft last year."

"Oh, I didn't mean your place. You don't have to fix anything for us."

"I just didn't think I'd have company out here in the barn."

"We're not exactly company. You're doing us a favor by helping with the shepherd."

"I'm happy to do it. It's not a favor."

"Well, it's certainly a kindness."

Les opened his mouth, then closed it again. "Well, thank you."

Marla nodded. She was glad to have that settled.

Marla noticed that both Sammy and Becky had been watching her and Les.

"You don't have to worry about me. I won't go up

there," Becky announced a little primly. "I just want to see the lambs."

"You're a good girl," Les muttered.

Sammy grunted. "That's because she still thinks Santa is watching."

Marla flushed. She didn't want to discuss their lack of Christmas presents in front of Les. He was so nice he would probably think it was a hint for charity, and that was the last thing she wanted. She wanted Les to be real with them. That couldn't happen if he saw them as people needing charity. In her experience, no one ever gave charity without looking down on the person they gave it to.

"Santa still needs to do his shopping," Marla said. She vowed she was going to go home and put in an order from the J. C. Penney catalog. She knew by heart the page number that had the Suzy bake set advertised. She'd already decided to get it. And while she was ordering she'd get Sammy a football at the same time. Maybe if Sammy had a football, Les could throw him a few passes now and then when he came into Dry Creek. That was assuming Les would want to be around any of them once that shepherd was fixed.

Marla looked over at the man. He certainly looked as if he wanted to be around them now.

Les turned on the light in the workshop when he led everyone inside. He was glad he'd spent so much time finishing up this workshop, because he was pleased to be able to share it with Marla and the kids.

"Up there's the tool cabinet and over there's the refrigerator."

"Cool," Sammy said as he looked at the refrigerator. "Do you keep stuff to drink in there?"

Les smiled. "There are usually a few sodas and maybe some canned fruit. But the reason it's there is to hold any medicine I need for the animals."

Sammy was still looking around. "And it's got its own heat. A guy could go camping in here."

"There's even a fold-up cot and a sleeping bag in that closet. Sometimes I sleep out here during calving season."

Les had to admit it felt good to have Sammy share his enthusiasm for the workshop. He supposed that's what a father must feel like a hundred times a day when his son enjoyed something the man had built.

Marla and Becky stayed in the workshop while Sammy went with Les to bring in the damaged shepherd figure.

"You're doing a good job," Les said as Sammy shouldered his full share of the weight of the shepherd. The Nativity figure was plastic, but it was also heavy. Les had parked his pickup next to the barn door and he and Sammy were carrying the shepherd over to the workshop.

"It's slippery," Sammy said.

"We'll need to let it warm up before we start working on it. It's probably brittle from the cold. It's the melting frost that makes it feel damp."

"You sure know a lot about snow."

Les shrugged as best he could given the fact that he was carrying the shepherd's head. "You'll learn all about it, too, after a while. Everyone in Dry Creek becomes an expert on snow."

"I like the sun," Sammy said. "There's nothing to do in the snow."

Les nudged the door to the workshop open with his foot. "Nothing to do? Have you ever heard of a sled?"

Les heard a pickup drive into his place. "That'll be Mr. Morales."

They set the shepherd down on the long table that ran along one side of the workshop.

"I'll go get Mr. Morales. The rest of you stay in here where it's warm."

Les walked outside to greet his friend. The ravine where Mr. Morales had his cabin shared a fence with Les's largest pasture. Mr. Morales usually went to Miles City instead of Dry Creek, but Les meant to invite him to the Christmas Eve sing that the church was doing this year.

The conversation about the Christmas Eve service was still going on when Les and Mr. Morales reached the workshop.

"I need to get to the Dry Creek church more often," Mr. Morales said as he followed Les inside.

"I can't imagine my life without the church," Les

agreed as he turned to introduce Mr. Morales to Marla and her kids.

Marla listened to the introductions and made the appropriate responses. But she was thinking about Les's words about the church. She'd never thought the church had anything to offer someone like her, but after listening to what the pastor had said yesterday about Mary, she wasn't so sure. She hadn't realized God cared about humble people. For some reason, she always thought he wanted the rich, popular people to fill his churches. There had never seemed to be any room for her there.

Marla waited until Mr. Morales took the children out to see the lambs before saying something to Les.

"Remember that man Byron in church yesterday?"

Les looked up from the toolbox he was lifting and grunted an acknowledgment.

"I was wondering if he meant it when he said he was available for questions about the church?"

"He's an usher. He passes those cards out to everyone. He's not supposed to be the one answering the questions. He only collects the cards."

"Oh."

"Anyone could answer your questions," Les said, then cleared his throat. "I could probably answer some."

"Oh, I wouldn't want to bother you. You're working on the shepherd today."

"I've got time. Besides, I'm a deacon in the church.

Byron is only an usher." Les frowned. "Of course, he's a good usher. If you want to find a place to sit, he's your man."

Marla nodded. She didn't even know what a deacon was, and she didn't want to show her ignorance by asking. She did know what an usher was, though. Maybe she should start off small and talk to him first. "Well, we don't need to do anything today."

"We could make an appointment," Les offered.

Marla nodded. "That would be nice."

"Mrs. Hargrove might be willing to watch the kids so we can talk."

"Oh, I don't know—"

"We could have dinner together. At the café."

There, Les told himself. He had done it. He had asked Marla out on a date. The whole town of Dry Creek would be talking when he showed up in the café to have dinner with her.

"I would pay, of course," Les added when Marla didn't say anything.

Les hated to admit it, but his respect for Byron was growing. It wasn't easy to charm a woman and Les had a sinking feeling that he was failing at it.

"You could have anything on the menu." Les wondered if he should have offered to take her to Miles City. The Dry Creek café had good food, but it never pretended to be an elegant place. Come to think of it, he would have to drive her to Billings to find an elegant place.

"That's very nice," Marla said. "But I would insist on paying for my share. I mean, I'm the one with the questions."

"Oh." Now that Les had gone to the hard work of asking Marla out, he found he definitely wanted it to be a date and not just two people eating dinner together. "I could ask you some questions, too."

The words were out of Les's mouth before he even thought of them. He was sure they were something Byron would say.

"About what?" Marla was frowning now.

"Ah—well, maybe the kids." Les figured that was a safe topic. Women always liked to talk about their children. He'd heard Byron ask mothers at church about their children and it always seemed to go well.

"They're good kids."

Marla was looking at him the way she had the other morning when she was peeking out the crack in the door and he was asking about Becky.

"I know," Les said softly. Then he did what he'd wanted to do that morning when he'd first seen her almost closing the door in his face. Her reached out a hand and touched her cheek. "They're great kids."

Marla blushed.

"How about tomorrow night for dinner?"

Marla nodded.

Les decided that the one thing he needed to add to his workshop was a stereo system. He'd like a little music about now.

When Mr. Morales brought the children back they joined in working on the shepherd. They used putty Marla had mixed up to fill in some of the breaks in the shepherd's back. Les was making a brace for the putty so that it would stay in the places they wanted it to and dry right. Sammy helped Mr. Morales mix the right color of paint to match the shepherd's robes.

Marla decided that she hadn't had such a happy time since her husband had died. She had her children with her. They were having a good time. Mr. Morales reminded her of her uncles, and he'd already promised to come visit them when he came into Dry Creek. And then there was Les.

It was four o'clock before they finished for the day. The putty needed to dry overnight and they planned to paint it tomorrow.

"The shepherd's going to look just fine," Les said as he wiped a little extra putty off the worktable.

Les had eventually covered the worktable with a canvas tarp so that the putty didn't get over everything.

"Would you mind folding the tarp?" Les asked Sammy. "That way I can load some feed up for Mr. Morales to take with him."

Marla held her breath. She knew Les was trusting Sammy with the Nativity figure by leaving him alone with it. She forced herself to add to the trust.

"I'll take Becky inside and get her washed up," Marla said.

Sammy nodded.

Marla noticed her son stood a little taller. Or at least, it looked to her as if he did. A boy needed to be trusted if he was going to turn into a solid young man. She was grateful Les seemed to realize that. Maybe Les really did want to have dinner with her so he could talk about the children. Somehow that thought wasn't as welcome as it had been earlier. Children weren't exactly good date conversation. Oh, well, she'd have several hours tomorrow to talk to him about the children while they all finished up the shepherd. Maybe he'd get his questions answered then and they would have time to talk about other things at dinner.

Chapter Nine

Les sat down at his breakfast table the next morning with several articles spread out in front of him. He'd done a search on his computer and pulled the articles from the digital archives of the *Los Angeles Times*. Any other time, if he had found the information he wanted so quickly, he would be telling himself that he could do anything with his computer beside him. Now, though, he didn't feel like congratulating himself.

Yesterday evening, after he'd finished his chores, Les had gone back into the workshop to be sure that the putty was drying in the cracks of the shepherd's back. He kept a high-wattage bulb in the overhead light in the workshop, so he had no trouble seeing the marks in the corner of his worktable. Someone had taken one of the small paintbrushes and painted "XIX" on the wooden table.

Les had forgotten about the numbers that had been on the note. He'd found out who took the shepherd so fast, he hadn't bothered with any follow-up. It hadn't taken him long with his computer to find out that those numbers were the symbol for the 19th Street gang. The articles in front of him told the rest of the story. Murders, robberies, lots of drugs. The 19th Street gang wasn't a social club.

He wondered how long Sammy had been a member. It said in one of the articles that the gang recruited boys as young as nine. Sammy could be hard core by now.

Les rubbed a hand over his face. No one was who they seemed anymore. He had thought Sammy was some young mischief maker who just needed a little attention. That might be like saying the latest serial killer was just a choirboy who needed a little more applause. If Les had learned anything in his reserve deputy training it was that a lawman couldn't go by stereotypes. He'd made a rookie's mistake. But who would look at an eleven-year-old boy and ask if he was a member of one of the most vicious big-city gangs around?

And who would look at the boy's mother and ask if she was capable of withholding that kind of information from the local reserve deputy sheriff? Marla had clearly known what that gang symbol meant and she'd kept silent.

Les got up to get another cup of coffee. It was going to be a long day. He might even call in an emergency request to the church's prayer chain. Mrs. Hargrove headed up the prayer chain and he could give her some generalities without saying what was going on. She was good about that. And he could definitely use the help of other believers on this one.

He'd be sure to move that hunting knife he kept in the workshop to another place. Marla and the kids would be back here in a couple of hours. Les wondered if Marla planned to ever tell him about her son. She certainly hadn't made any effort to tell him yesterday while they sat together filling the cracks on the shepherd's back. They had worked away for a good hour while Mr. Morales showed the kids how to feed the lambs. She'd told him this and that about her life in Los Angeles and he'd told her more than he usually told anyone about his childhood. None of what she'd said hinted at something like this, though.

It was too bad, Les told himself as he sat at the table. Trust—and truth—were such vital parts of any relationship. Suddenly, restoring that shepherd didn't seem so important. He supposed he should go out and paint over the gang symbol before everyone got here. That would at least send a signal to Sammy that Les had noticed something.

Not that it would probably mean anything to the boy. He probably didn't know Les had a computer and could find out what the symbol meant. Kids that age never realized what other people knew. It was probably just a gesture of arrogance that made him paint that "XIX" again. Either that or the kid was planning something.

Well, Les told himself, he would be on his guard today. The romantic nonsense had certainly been wiped out of his eyes. He'd be watching the boy. And the mother, too. Little Becky was probably the only one of the family who had been honest with him. Her only goal was to get that Suzy bake set in the deluxe edition.

For the first time that morning Lester smiled. It was a bitter smile, but he felt it inside. He knew how it felt to want something so badly everything else faded away. He and Becky had that in common, at least. Maybe he should just go ahead and order that Suzy bake set online. If he did the rush delivery, it would be here before Christmas. Then at least one of them would get what they wanted. His growing dream of having a family would have to wait.

Marla had brought tortillas and cheese so she could make everyone quesadillas for lunch. She even had a jar of a special salsa she'd brought with her from Los Angeles. She knew Les liked quesadillas and yesterday Mr. Morales had said he liked them, too. She had no idea why no one was eating them now with any enjoyment.

Yesterday had been magical, and today was—well, not.

It was because of Les. She had forgotten how a

man who was in a bad mood could influence everyone around him. Not that Les was in a bad mood exactly. He was certainly polite to everyone. And he wasn't snapping at people for doing this or that. It had taken her a minute to figure it all out this morning. Les was never very talkative. He was a quiet man. But he had been a quiet man who seemed to relax into other people. She'd felt more herself around him yesterday than she had felt anywhere in a long time.

Today there was no relaxing. All his walls were up. He was more official than he had been when he was knocking at her door investigating the theft of the shepherd. He'd at least smiled at her then.

Marla looked at him more closely. He was sitting at the table opposite Sammy. No one had said anything for the past minute. Even Becky was quiet.

"More quesadillas?" Marla finally asked.

"Yes, *gracias,*" Mr. Morales said as he held his plate out. "They are good."

Marla used a fork to serve the older man another quesadilla. "I'm glad you like them."

At least Mr. Morales was still friendly to her. She liked being around him. His speech and mannerisms reminded her so much of her uncles, and she hadn't seen them in years. She wrote to them, of course, but her Spanish wasn't very good. Besides, it wasn't the same as seeing their faces. She had listened as Mr. Morales told her children about the life of a shepherd while they'd worked on the Nativity figure together this morning.

After everyone had finished eating, there was no reason to linger in the house.

It was late afternoon before they finished with the shepherd. The cracks in the figure had all been filled with putty and painted to match the color of either the shepherd's skin or his garments. Mr. Morales had fashioned a covering from thick paper to repair the hole in the side of the shepherd's head. Several coats of varnish had weatherproofed the paper so it would be able to tolerate the snow.

"You won't be able to tell he was ever broken," Les said as they started to clean up their putty knives and brushes.

"Good," Sammy muttered.

"He'll be dried tomorrow if you want to help me set him back up," Les said to the boy. He felt an urge to help Sammy unscrew the lid on the old jar that held the used paintbrushes. The lid was encrusted with dry paint and didn't open smoothly. But Les wasn't sure the boy would welcome his help.

"I guess," Sammy said.

Les knew the boy was probably disappointed because no one felt the same camaraderie they'd felt yesterday. But yesterday they were all different people.

"Well, we'll put the shepherd back to work," Marla said a little too cheerfully.

"He has to take care of the lambs," Becky added wistfully. "They don't have anyone to take care of them."

Les swallowed. "I've been keeping an eye on them."

"You'll come by our house?" Sammy looked up from the jar.

Les nodded. He supposed he would have to go by and pick the boy up if they were going to set up the shepherd together. "And I'll see you tonight, when I come to pick up your mother for dinner."

"Oh," Marla said. "I thought we'd just meet at the café."

"No, I can come by and pick you up."

Les wondered if the woman didn't want him in her house. It hadn't looked as if she'd had much in the house when he glanced in the other day. But drugs didn't take much room to hide. It might even be normal for drug houses not to have much furniture. Now that he was thinking about it, Marla had shown a definite interest in how much drug use there was in Dry Creek.

Les felt his gut tighten. He hadn't considered until now that she might be a member of that 19th Street gang herself. She could have gotten involved in the gang with that dead husband of hers. One of the articles he'd read said that happened more often than people knew. Come to think of it, she'd never said how her husband had died. She'd never said how she made a living, either.

He thought back to when he'd sat with her on that

old log behind her house. He'd told her everything she needed to know about crime in Dry Creek. She had played him for a fool. He should have just given her the keys to the city and been done with it.

He wondered if she had agreed to have dinner with him so she could find out more about criminal prospects in Dry Creek. It would be useful if she meant to set up a drug business behind the law's back. He knew most people in Dry Creek would say no to drugs, but there were bound to be some kids who would say yes. It was his job to protect those kids.

Les wondered how it was possible to dread a dinner so much and still have the thought of it bring out every longing he had. The only good thing was that he didn't have any more town secrets left to tell her and she probably wasn't interested in his personal secrets.

"I'll see you at six, then," Marla finally said. She didn't look any happier about dinner than he did, Les thought. But it didn't matter; they were going to go on a date.

There was a little more silence as they all just looked at the shepherd figure.

"He doesn't look very strong," Sammy finally said.

"Oh, he's strong," Mr. Morales said. "All shepherds are strong. They have to be. They protect the lambs from wolves and other things."

"Oh," Becky said, and then gave an anxious look to Les.

"Don't worry," he said. "There aren't any wolves

around Dry Creek. They don't like to come into towns. You're safe. The lambs by the church are safe."

"Even if wolves got to Dry Creek, you would shoot them with your rifle, wouldn't you?" Sammy asked.

Les looked into the boy's eyes at that comment. Either the boy was a very good actor or he was scared of something. Somehow, Les doubted it was the wolves. "Usually we try to trap wolves instead of shooting them, but—yes—if there is no other way, and someone is in danger, we will shoot them."

Sammy relaxed. "Those sheep by the church are plastic, anyway."

Les nodded. "They certainly have no worries."

"You'll have to bring your pickup with you tonight, won't you?" Sammy asked.

Les nodded. "I guess."

He usually used his pickup when he went into Dry Creek in the winter. In the summer months he didn't have to worry about traction on the road, so he used his car more often. Roads, even his gravel road, tended to get slippery in the winter after the sun went down.

Les looked at Sammy again. The boy was rubbing his hands along the hem of the shepherd's cloak. There had been no damage there and there were no cracks to be filled.

"Is there something wrong?" Les finally asked.

Sammy looked up and shook his head.

Well, Les told himself, he had tried to reach the

boy. If he was a seasoned gang member, a little bit of concern wouldn't stop him from his plans, anyway.

For the first time all week Les wished the regular sheriff were back. Les had been prepared to arrest someone when the sheriff was gone; he hadn't been prepared to have it mean anything to him, though. He hadn't realized until now that the regular sheriff had such a tough job. No wonder the sheriff had wanted to go to Maui.

Chapter Ten

Marla looked inside her closet and hoped something new would be there. Unfortunately, all she saw were the same T-shirts and blouses she always saw when she opened her closet. For the first time ever, she wished she'd had jobs in her life that required a woman to wear a dress. Maybe then she would have something suitable to wear to dinner with the deputy sheriff.

It suddenly hit her. She was going for a date for the first time in almost sixteen years. Not that it was a real date. There wouldn't be any hand-holding or kissing. Would there be? Oh, dear, she hadn't kissed a man except for her husband in the past sixteen years, either.

Marla looked around. She needed to relax. If the sheriff was anything like the way he had been this afternoon, there wouldn't even be any friendly conversation to worry about.

The only thing in her closet to wear that wasn't

jeans was that black suit. Oh, and her fiesta blouse and skirt, but she wasn't going to wear that, especially not on a cold winter night. She'd look totally out of place. And it would look as if she expected a party, which she didn't. It was only dinner.

Finally Marla decided to wear her newest pair of jeans and a chocolate-brown sweater. It looked casual and—well, casual was probably the best thing she could say about it. She stood in front of the mirror in the bathroom and added a thin gold necklace that her husband had given her one year for Christmas.

She lifted her hair and twisted it back, but then decided to leave it hanging straight. She had never been a woman who dressed elegantly and there was no hope of starting now. It was just that having a touch of glamour about her might make her feel more confident.

Her eyes were clear, though, and she had on a light lipstick. She put a dab of perfume behind one ear and a tissue in her pocket. She was ready. And she had twenty minutes to wait before Les would be there.

Marla left the bathroom and walked into the dining room. Sammy and Becky were sitting together at the folding table playing a card game called Birds.

Marla felt her nervousness leave her. Now, this was what was important in her life. She needed reminders like this that Sammy cared about his sister. He was a good boy. Moving to Dry Creek had been the best decision she had made in a long time. "You can take the game with you when you go over to Mrs. Hargrove's, if you want. It'll keep you busy."

"I don't know why we have to go to a babysitter's," Sammy muttered as he looked up at her.

"Becky's only four. She needs someone to watch her," Marla said as she walked over to where they sat. "You're going along so Becky doesn't feel alone. And to help Mrs. Hargrove with Becky."

Sammy rolled his eyes. "I don't think that lady needs any help. You should see her with those Sunday-school kids. They don't even want to get into trouble."

Marla put her hand on Sammy's shoulder. "I'm proud of you for helping in that Sunday-school class."

Sammy didn't shrug off her hand. Instead, he looked up at her. "Is this something you're going to be doing a lot? This going out with the deputy sheriff?"

"Oh, I wouldn't say we're going out," Marla protested. "We're just getting together to have dinner. And it's only this one time."

Marla remembered now that this had all started because she had some questions she wanted to ask about the Dry Creek church. She should have put a stop to this dinner before it went this far. She could have just gone over to Mrs. Hargrove's house with the kids and asked the older woman her questions. She'd rather talk to Mrs. Hargrove than Les any day. That is, if Les was going to be all stiff around her as he had been today. She had liked talking to him on Monday; he'd been friendly then.

"The sheriff's not so bad," Sammy said as he looked back down at the Bird cards he held in his hands. "At least, he knows how to do lots of stuff."

"Is he going to be our new daddy?" Becky looked up as she asked.

Marla flushed. She supposed her children weren't any more comfortable with her going on a date than she was. "We're just going to dinner. It's barely a date. People don't get married after just one date."

"How many dates did you have with Dad?" Sammy asked. "Before you got married?"

"I don't remember."

"More than ten?"

Marla nodded. "Many more than ten. So you don't need to worry about the sheriff."

"I wasn't worried."

"Well, good, because you don't need to be."

There was a minute of silence.

"He walks you home, though, doesn't he?" Sammy asked suddenly. He glanced up at Marla and then back at his cards.

"Oh, I don't know. I don't think it particularly matters."

"You don't want to come home alone when the house is all dark," Sammy said emphatically. "It could be creepy then. You need to ask him to walk you home."

"Well, if we do anything, we'll probably just walk

over to Mrs. Hargrove's and then walk back from there," Marla said. "It's not far."

"Then he could walk us all home," Sammy said with satisfaction. "We should leave some lights on in the house, too. So when we get home, it's not dark."

Marla looked at her son. She still had her hand resting on his shoulder and she gave him a squeeze. Something was going on. Maybe it was the move itself that was making him feel so vulnerable. He'd never given this much thought to darkness in his whole life. "Are you worried about something?"

Sammy shook his head.

Marla looked at him some more. "They don't have many streetlights in Dry Creek, do they? Not like they have in Los Angeles."

Marla had never seen darkness as deep as the nights she'd spent in Montana. She liked it because she could see the stars, but she could understand how a child might not find the night comforting.

"I'm not afraid of the dark," Sammy muttered as he stared at his cards.

"Well, we'll talk about it later if you want."

"Isn't it time for us to go over to Mrs. Hargrove's?" Sammy asked as he folded his hand of cards.

Marla supposed that whatever Sammy's problems were, they could wait until the morning. The best time to talk to Sammy was at breakfast. Maybe she'd make them pancakes tomorrow and spend some extra time just sitting with him. Sammy was never one to confide his problems easily. In the meantime, he was right. It was time to get everyone ready to go over to Mrs. Hargrove's house.

Les had known his dinner date would cause a little gossip in Dry Creek. Any date seemed to be prime news, and he hadn't asked a woman out in over a year. He'd expected Mrs. Hargrove to tell Linda, and maybe Charley, that she was babysitting the children so he and Marla could have dinner together.

But even knowing all that, Les was surprised at how much work Linda had done. Usually, if Linda suspected a couple was on a date, she put a candle on their table. When he and Marla stepped into the café, however, they stepped into a Christmas fantasyland. There were twinkling Christmas lights everywhere. Since Elmer had worried about the electricity the church was using, Les hoped the older man didn't see this.

"Oh," Marla said with pleasure in her voice. "I like Christmas lights."

Les liked Christmas lights, too. He just wasn't sure he wanted a thousand of them shining down on him while he ate his steak.

Linda had draped strands of blinking white lights from the pipe that hung down in the middle of the room and they spread out to hit every corner. They were hooked to every side of the room, too. And a dozen places in between.

"It's beautiful," Marla said.

Les nodded. The lights throbbed. He wondered how much wattage was in the room. Fortunately, the lights were all white, so at least the glare was even.

Les took another step into the café so the door could swing closed behind them. "It's warm."

It was cold outside and Les felt the air inside the café take away the slight chill that had come from walking the children over to Mrs. Hargrove's place and then walking Marla back to the café. He had parked his pickup at Marla's. It seemed pointless to drive when everything was so close.

"Does she do this every Christmas?" Marla whispered as she slowly twirled around to see all the lights.

"No, she doesn't."

Marla had a look of such childish wonder on her face that in an instant Les forgave everyone for meddling in his date. It was almost impossible to look at Marla's face and reconcile her with the picture of a drug-dealing female gang member that had been bothering him all day.

"Linda did it for us," Les said softly as he motioned Marla forward.

There was only one choice for a table. Sitting in the middle of the café, there was a table draped in a white tablecloth, with a vase holding a long-stemmed red rose in the center. The table was sitting under the pipe that came down from the ceiling, so all the lights gathered to that one point. It was like sitting in the middle of a huge circus tent.

"I've never had anyone do something like this for me," Marla said as she stepped toward the table.

Les swallowed. Marla was the kind of woman men should have slain dragons for. What kind of man had her husband been that she had never felt special like this before? Even if he was into drugs and crime, couldn't the man have put some effort into letting his wife know that she was beautiful?

"You look nice tonight," Les said as he held out a chair for Marla.

Les had barely sat down himself when he heard the music start. At first he assumed it was a CD playing on the stereo system Linda had in the kitchen. On other special occasions in the past, she had turned up the volume and cranked out everything from romantic waltz music to Christmas carols. There was a roughness to the quality of the music, though, that made him wonder.

When Les turned around, he was shocked. There was Elmer, wearing a suit and playing a harp. Les recognized the suit; Elmer wore it to funerals. He didn't usually wear a tie, though, and tonight the older man was cinched tight with a black tie.

The harp looked like the secondhand instrument Mrs. Hargrove had asked the church to buy for a past Christmas program. No one had played the thing in the program. Elmer was making a valiant attempt to play it now. He gave Les a smile and a brief thumbs-up sign between strums.

When Linda came out wearing her chef's hat, Les wasn't even surprised. Nothing was normal tonight.

"I didn't know we still had that harp," Les said when Linda handed him a menu.

"Oh, yes," Linda said as she handed another menu to Marla.

Les thought Linda might elaborate, but she didn't. The café owner just stood there with a proud smile on her face as though she had single-handedly wrought a miracle.

"New menu?" Les guessed.

"I thought you might like the Asian pork loin."

Les nodded. No one got away with ordering a hamburger when they were having a date at Linda's café. "Sounds good to me."

"I have a gallon of spiced apple cider chilling in the back, too. Just in case you'd like to make a toast."

Les looked at Marla. She was pink with pleasure. "How about it? Do you want to try the cider? Linda gets it in specially from Washington."

"Yes, please. It all sounds wonderful."

Linda smiled. "I want this to be a night you both remember."

Les figured he, for one, wasn't likely to forget it.

"I just wanted some information about the church," Marla said.

Linda smiled even wider. "Mrs. Hargrove will know all that. She does the flower arrangements when we have them in front of the altar."

Les was starting to think things weren't adding up right.

"I'm surprised you don't do the flowers," Marla said. "You've decorated your café beautifully. It looks like we're sitting here under a chandelier."

"Or a diamond," Linda agreed as she started to turn to walk back to the kitchen. Before she made her full turn, though, she stopped for a second and winked at Les.

It suddenly all came together in Les's mind. He'd given Mrs. Hargrove that cryptic prayer request this morning. He hadn't said much except he had an important decision to make today and it could have life-altering consequences, so he wanted to be sure he was on solid ground before he took any steps.

He wanted the people of Dry Creek to pray about whether or not he should get a search warrant for Marla's house to see if she was hiding any drugs. Instead, they had put it together with his date tonight and thought he was going to propose here and now. The toast. The harp. Elmer's suit. It all added up. No wonder Elmer was sitting over there grinning at him.

"The church is made up of God's people," Les said to Marla as he moved the candle so he could lean closer. "Sometimes that's a good thing. Sometimes it's a real pain. But if you want to know about the church, all you have to do is ask."

Then he reached over and took her hand in his.

All the butterflies in Marla's stomach relaxed when

Les took her hand. She was worried that the people here tonight were trying to make more of the dinner she and Les were having than Les was comfortable with. But when he took her hand, she knew he was okay with it all. However it had happened, they were on a date that wasn't just a dinner. And the man in question was fine with it.

"I don't know much about church," Marla began, then took a deep breath. "But my husband had this cross. When he was sick, he used to look at it."

Marla told Les everything. She hadn't planned to tell him it all. She thought she'd just ask about why her husband had been able to wring meaning from that wooden cross and she hadn't been able to get so much as a warm feeling from it.

Instead, one question led to another, and she told him about her husband's confession to her before he died. She told him about the anger she felt because she'd had no time to even ask her husband any questions about his confession. She didn't know why he'd been unfaithful. She stopped short of asking him if he thought there was something wrong with her as a woman. Maybe her anguish showed in her eyes, though.

"Your husband was a fool," Les said. They'd both received their plates some time ago and the food was growing cold. Les didn't seem to care. "He didn't deserve a woman like you."

Marla blinked back a tear. "Thank you."

Les felt a tear in his own eye. He knew God was merciful. Somehow, no matter what this woman in front of him had done, she had a sweetness that a man could put his faith in. She still hadn't told him anything about why her family was involved with this gang, but he was sure there was a good reason.

The café had remained empty except for the two of them. Les knew Linda was turning away customers, because several times the door had opened and she had stepped over to have muted conversations with whoever it was. Finally Elmer had given up on playing the harp and moved out to the porch to stall any hungry people.

Les should have cared about how much inconvenience he was causing his neighbors. But he knew Linda was giving people take-out containers from the back door, so at least no one was starving. And for tonight, he liked having the privacy. Marla had shown him her grief. He'd answered with emotions he hadn't even known he had.

He knew he should ask her about the gang symbols her son was leaving everywhere. He probably should even ask her if she did drugs herself. But tonight he didn't want to be Les Wilkerson, Reserve Deputy Sheriff. He didn't even want to be Les Wilkerson, upright citizen. He just wanted to be a man telling a woman she was beautiful in his eyes.

"You should eat," Marla finally said to him. "Your dinner's getting cold."

Les smiled. "Linda buys to-go containers by the boxful. But you should eat."

Neither one of them seemed ready to take up a fork, so Les reached over and took Marla's hand again.

Linda had either unplugged some of the Christmas lights or half the strands had burned out. Whatever the reason, he and Marla no longer sat under a spotlight. In fact, the twinkling lights overhead were quite romantic.

"You know, I wrote a poem," Les said. "About your hair."

Marla reached up with her free hand and touched her hair. "I don't have enough highlights."

"Your hair is beautiful."

Marla smiled.

Les breathed deeply. All was well with the world.

Then he heard some loud muttering out on the porch. It had been going on for the past minute or two, but Les had figured it was just one of the ranch hands who wanted to come inside to eat and didn't want to go around back for a takeout.

It couldn't be that, though. He frowned, then turned to face the door. He recognized Mrs. Hargrove's voice.

"It's Sammy," Mrs. Hargrove said as she finally opened the door. The older woman and Becky walked into the café and Mrs. Hargrove didn't even turn around to close the door. A cold wind blew inside. In the time Les and Marla had been sitting there, the sky had turned to deep night. It must be almost eight o'clock.

Marla stood up. "What?"

"I can't find him," Mrs. Hargrove said. The scarf was off her head and she looked distraught. "I've looked everywhere."

"Well, he has to be around here," Marla said. She stepped away from the table and walked toward the café door. "Did you look at our house?"

Les stood and followed Marla.

Mrs. Hargrove nodded. "It's all dark there."

"But we left the lights on," Marla protested. "Surely he's not sitting by himself in the dark."

Les walked over to the coatrack and got Marla's coat. He picked up his own while he was there.

"Wherever he's gone to, we'll find him," Les said as he held Marla's coat for her to put on. There were not many places to hide in Dry Creek, not even for an eleven-year-old boy.

Linda came out of the kitchen wiping her hands on a towel. "Maybe he's visiting with those friends of his. The two guys that stopped to give him back his baseball."

"His baseball!" Marla said, and Les saw her face go white.

In that word, Marla had gone from worried to terrified. Les wished for the first time tonight that he hadn't let Marla's eyes distract him from what he needed to do. He had to ask her about her past.

"Are they from the 19th Street gang?"

Marla stared at him. "You know?"

Any hope Les had that Marla had no connection with the gang died. He nodded. "I know."

"We have to find Sammy," Marla said as she turned to the door. "I don't know if that's where they're from or not."

Elmer came inside and looked at Les. "What's wrong?"

"Mrs. Hargrove. You and Becky stay here." Les turned to Elmer. "Get everyone inside and lock the doors. And turn out those Christmas tree lights. People are in a fishbowl in here if someone looks in the windows."

Elmer nodded.

"And pray," Les asked. He looked at Mrs. Hargrove, Elmer, Linda and Becky all huddled together by now in the middle of the room. "Pray and pray."

"I'll go with you," Marla said as Les walked to the door.

Les hesitated. "Do you know these guys?"

"They're with my son," Marla said. "I have to go."

Les nodded. He didn't know if it was better to have her with him or not. The only thing he knew for sure was that he could watch her better if he had her with him. He had no idea what the guys really brought to Dry Creek. If the "baseball" was code for a drug shipment, he might have to confront Marla before the night was out. It was highly unlikely two guys would be bringing a drug shipment to an eleven-year-old boy unless the boy's parent was also part of the deal.

Chapter Eleven

It took them an hour to work their way through Dry Creek. Les knocked at the door of each house and asked if anyone had seen any strangers. At each place, the people inside said no. Les cautioned everyone to lock their doors and stay inside tonight. Then he searched the church and the hardware store.

"He's got to be here. Someone's lying," Marla finally said.

They had come back to the middle of the street in front of the café. The ground was frozen, but there was no new snow, so it was impossible to tell if any unknown vehicles had come through town.

There had been no other conversation between them since they had started looking. Once, when he saw that Marla's fingers were getting cold, Les had taken off his gloves and given them to her, but neither one of them had spoken.

"My neighbors don't lie," Les said. *Unlike some*

people I know, he almost added, but didn't. He knew the less said the better. He needed to keep his mind focused and forget about his heart. If she was part of some drug-delivery scheme, he might need to arrest her before the night was over. He didn't think he could do it if he allowed his feelings to show.

The one streetlight in Dry Creek shone above them. Les could see how the cold had made Marla's cheeks turn rosy. Her lips were chapped and it looked as if she might have been crying at some point tonight.

"Would Sammy run away with these guys?" Les asked.

"No!"

Les looked at Marla. The one thing he knew for sure about her was that she cared for her children.

"I'll get my pickup and drive down the road a bit."

"I'm coming with you."

Les nodded. It did seem that, whether they wanted to be or not, they were tied together for tonight. Les heard his boots crunch on the frozen ground. Marla's footsteps were more muffled, though. He looked down and saw that she was wearing some kind of thin dress shoes. Her feet must feel like blocks of ice.

"We've got time to stop at your place so you can change shoes."

"I'm fine," Marla said. "You don't need to stop for me."

Les didn't argue. He just walked past his pickup, which was parked in her driveway, and kept going until he reached Marla's front door. "I can wait here while you get your shoes."

It wasn't politeness that made Les wait. He knew if he went inside Marla's house again he would be looking for places where she could hide illegal substances. Of course, he would be limited in that. He'd rather just wait until he had a search warrant.

Marla nodded and took a key out of her pocket to open the door. The lights were on in every room. They had already looked into the rooms of the house earlier and had left the lights on. It was the first place they had gone after they left the café.

Les watched Marla enter the living room and then he realized the guys could have circled back. "Wait. I'm coming."

Les cleared each room before he let Marla enter it. He'd have to protect her if he arrested her, anyway. He might as well start now. He watched as Marla reached into her closet and pulled out a pair of tennis shoes.

He frowned. "Do you have some heavy socks to go with those?"

Marla shook her head. "But my regular socks do fine."

Les shook his head. He never understood why people would move to Montana and not buy some thick socks. Those socks she was holding were meant for the summer.

"Here. Sit on the bed," Les said. He didn't want to have someone trailing along behind him with a case of frostbite developing. He'd probably have to see to that, too, if he arrested her.

Les took off Marla's shoes and pulled off the thin socks she was wearing. Then he put his hands around her right foot. He kept his hands there until her skin had warmed and then he began to rub her feet gently, just enough to get the circulation going.

He tried not to wonder why Marla was holding herself so stiff.

Marla knew why women sometimes ran off with an unlikely man. He rubbed their feet. Ahhhh, that felt good even with the shooting tingle. She held herself steady, though. She didn't want Les to know how she was feeling. His hands were warm and he cradled the one foot while he started rubbing the other one. It wasn't right that a man who didn't trust a woman could rub her feet.

"We should be going," Marla said.

"We're almost done."

In another minute, Les put her socks on and then he put her tennis shoes on and tied them. He even held her steady for the first couple of minutes while she stood in place. After that, it was quick work walking back through the house.

"You should turn your furnace on before we go," Les said as they walked through the living room. "It'll be cold as ice in here by the time you get back."

Marla flushed. She didn't want to admit that they had no gas in the tank for the furnace. She'd been using the fireplace. "We'll be fine. You don't need to worry about us."

Les grunted as he opened the door, but he didn't say anything else.

Marla wasn't sure that Les was as worried about Sammy as she was. The way Les had questioned everyone in the houses around, it was clear he was looking for those two strangers more than he was looking for Sammy. How did he know that Sammy was even with those guys? Maybe he'd seen them and gone into hiding?

Marla stepped onto the porch and turned to lock her door. She supposed locking it now was only habit. The only things of value in her house were her two children, and neither one was home.

Something was not right about Sammy's departure, though. Just because two guys from his old gang had shown up, it didn't mean that Sammy would choose to go off with them. She thought he'd learned a lot since they had come to Dry Creek. He'd even gone to Sunday school.

Marla followed Les to his pickup.

Why would a boy Sammy's age go off with a couple of… Marla hesitated. She didn't really know what to call the two young men. Linda had said they were both Hispanic and wore bandannas around their heads. They seemed to be around sixteen or seventeen years old and Linda had thought she saw a couple of big motorcycles on the other side of the street.

Sammy loved motorcycles, she remembered with a sinking heart. And he'd been forced to go to Sunday school, so anything he learned there he probably considered meaningless. And he missed his amigos. Still, he knew better than to go off with two strangers, anyway, didn't he?

Les walked to the passenger side of the pickup and opened the door for Marla.

Marla was not used to anyone opening doors for her. "Thank you."

Les grunted.

Even being in the cab of the pickup was warmer than being outside. Marla was glad they were driving for the next part of the search. She assumed the truck had a heater that worked and that Les was not hesitant to use it.

She wondered if Sammy was cold, wherever he was. She wondered if those two strangers would think to keep him warm. Then she wondered if the two strangers weren't really strangers after all. Maybe Sammy considered them his best amigos. Maybe Sammy had even invited them to come here before he left Los Angeles.

Maybe Les was right about her son after all, Marla thought. She looked over when she heard the latch on the other door click.

Les opened the door on the driver side and started to step up into the cab. He was halfway in when he stopped and stared at something behind Marla's head.

"My rifle's gone."

Marla had never been in Les's pickup before, but she'd seen where men around here put their rifles. They had a gun rack on the inside of the rear window. She turned and looked, and he was right. There was no rifle.

"Maybe you forgot it at home."

Les shook his head. "The only time the rifle leaves its place there is when I've pulled it out to clean it or use it."

Marla drew in her breath. She knew what he was thinking. "Sammy wouldn't have taken it."

"He sure has asked about it often enough."

"But that's just natural young-boy curiosity. You know how young boys are."

Les turned to look at her. She thought he might even feel sorry for her. "He took the rifle, Marla. That's not some prank like the shepherd, even. That's theft of a firearm. I'll have to call it in to the county sheriff."

"But you are the sheriff."

"I can't just ignore this, if that's what you're thinking."

"No, I know," Marla said softly. "But maybe it's not the way you think. Maybe the other guys took the rifle."

Les snorted. "They wouldn't have even known it was there. I doubt they happened to just be looking in old pickups."

"They could have been," Marla insisted stubbornly.

Les didn't say anything for a minute.

"You said it wasn't loaded, anyway," Marla added. "I'm surprised they didn't just leave it here."

Les nodded. "They must have thought they knew where they could get the bullets for it."

"It's the middle of the night. Even if they went into Miles City, there wouldn't be a store that would be open."

Les shook his head. "They're not heading for a store. They're heading for my place."

Marla's protest died on her lips. Could Les be right?

"Sammy already knows the way. He's been there twice." Les hesitated. "Besides, he put his mark on my place."

Marla looked up.

"The XIX sign. He painted it on my worktable out in the barn. I saw it last night after you'd left. Maybe he already had my place picked out."

Marla bowed her head. She had no protests left. Les believed her son was guilty.

"He could be hurt," Marla finally said. "He's not very big for his age. I think that's why…"

She didn't bother to finish. What did it matter why Sammy had gotten involved with the 19th Street gang?

"I just hope—" Marla continued, then stopped.

"Mothers are supposed to hope," Les finally said gruffly. "And with God, all things are possible, so I'm not one to deny anyone the right to hope."

Marla nodded. She wondered if Mrs. Hargrove

would pray for Sammy tonight as she had when he was on top of that woodpile. Of course, when the older woman prayed the first time, she had not known Sammy was suspected of any wrongdoing. Marla doubted very many church women would pray for a gang member who was loose in the community around them.

"I'll go to the café and call it in for backup," Les said. "Then I'll decide what to do."

"Please don't hurt Sammy."

"I never hurt anyone if I can help it."

Marla sat quiet. She had to know. "You're going to get another gun to take, aren't you?"

Les was silent for a moment. "I need to assume they're armed and dangerous. I will need a gun if I hope to control the situation."

Marla felt colder inside than she had felt all evening, even when she was outside. She thought she'd been worried when it looked as if Sammy was guilty. But it was nothing to the worry she felt now that he might be shot.

This was exactly why she had moved to Dry Creek. This little town was supposed to protect her son. What had she done wrong?

Les drove over to the café. The lights in the window were still off, and he had to knock loudly on the door and identify himself before anyone came to let them in.

Linda opened the door. A stream of light came from

the kitchen doorway. Marla noticed that the plates were still on the table from when she and Les had started to have dinner. Only a few bites had been taken from each meal. The Christmas lights were dark and now the black wires connecting them all to the center looked like spider legs. The evening had gone from a fantasy to a nightmare in just over an hour.

"We're all back in the kitchen," Linda said as she shut and locked the door behind them.

"Becky?" Marla asked as she let Les walk ahead of them.

"She's taking a nap on Elmer's coat." Linda smiled at her.

"Thank you." Marla reminded herself that everyone didn't know what was going on. She was sure Linda wouldn't still be smiling at her when she discovered Les thought Sammy had stolen a gun.

Marla heard Les on the telephone when she followed Linda into the kitchen. He was trying to muffle his words some, but the kitchen wasn't that big and everyone could hear what he was saying. Marla was hesitant to look anyone in the eye, but she had to.

She turned to Mrs. Hargrove. "Would it be okay for Becky to spend the night with you? I can't leave her alone in the house and—"

"Of course," Mrs. Hargrove said as she stood up from the small table where she'd been sitting. She put her hand on Marla's arm. "My daughter's old room is always ready for a guest. It will be my pleasure."

"Sammy's in trouble," Marla blurted out as she looked up into the older woman's eyes. "I don't know how to pray, but…"

"We'll pray together," Mrs. Hargrove said as she opened her arms.

Marla went into the hug.

"Our Father who art in heaven," Mrs. Hargrove began to murmur into Marla's ear. Each word calmed Marla's fears more. She didn't even notice when Les finished his phone call and came over to stand beside her.

Marla wondered if Mrs. Hargrove had a wooden cross hanging somewhere. The older woman seemed to expect more of God than anyone Marla had ever known.

"Thank you," Marla said when the prayer was finished and she had stepped away from the hug.

Mrs. Hargrove nodded. "Don't you worry about Becky. I'll take good care of her."

"I know."

There was a moment's silence.

Then Linda spoke. She was looking at the floor and her voice was muted. "I feel so bad. It's all my fault. I should have had sense enough to realize those two guys were bad news. I just didn't want to interrupt and—"

"It's all right." Les put his hand on the young woman's arm. "We've all made mistakes tonight. We can't go around putting the blame on anyone."

Except for me, Marla thought. She knew Les blamed her. It didn't help any that she blamed herself, too. She must have missed some clue that Sammy was corresponding with his old amigos. She remembered the letter about the baseball, but Sammy had said it was nothing. He hadn't even answered it. She doubted he had a stamp to mail a letter, and there was no place to buy a stamp in Dry Creek. She hadn't even had any stamps most of the time since they'd been here. The few times she'd had a letter she'd waited until she needed to drive to Miles City and then mailed it at the post office there.

Marla mentally shook herself. She couldn't be worried about a stamp. Not when Les was quietly talking to Elmer in the other room and she thought she heard the word *tonight.*

Chapter Twelve

"They'll back us up," Les said to Elmer. The two men were leaning on the side counter in the café. Neither had bothered to turn the main light on. They were content with the soft rectangle of light spilling out from the kitchen. "There's just no way for them to get in close enough without being seen."

For the first time ever, Les was grateful that his home was built in a dip in the landscape. His backup from the sheriff's department in Miles City should be able to come within a mile of his place before they had to shut off their car lights. It was that last mile or so, though, that was making it difficult to come up with a plan.

"No one can see to drive down that road at night, not if they turn their headlights off. There's too many ruts. And it's too far to walk in the dark," Les continued. There was some moonlight tonight, but the moon wasn't full. If it hadn't been for the streetlight, he and

Marla would have had a hard time walking around Dry Creek in the darkness.

Elmer nodded. The older man had ranched in the area all his life and Les respected his opinion on how to get around at any time of year, but particularly in the winter months.

"I'd say it'll snow before long out there," Elmer added. "And even without snow, that slope leading into your place is slippery in the middle of the night. Don't know of many men who could do it without even a flashlight to help them."

Les was almost sure Sammy had taken the two strangers to his place. It was the only place Sammy knew how to find, and he also knew Les wasn't going to be home in the early part of the evening. It made an ideal hiding place.

Les felt he had let the people of Dry Creek down. He should have questioned Sammy earlier today about his relationship with the 19th Street gang. He should have asked him if anyone was coming who would pose a threat to the people of this town. Although Sammy could easily have lied, so maybe it wouldn't have made any difference.

"I don't think they'll stay long at my place. They're probably just interested in finding some bullets for that rifle."

Elmer nodded. "But they'll stay the night. They probably think no one checks their barns at night. The boy doesn't know any other place to take them, anyway. Not in the dark."

"His name's Sammy." Les didn't like the thought of Sammy being reduced to first "the boy" and then just a number in some juvenile center.

"Huh?" Elmer flushed.

"Never mind," Les muttered. It wasn't his choice, or Elmer's, either, that would put Sammy in detention. Sammy had made his own choices; if he lost his name, that was his doing.

Besides, he had more people to think about than Sammy. He knew that the black of night would probably stop the trio from exploring too much until the sun rose. But tomorrow would be a different story. All they would have to do would be to find a gravel road and follow it a mile or two until they reached someone's home.

"Someone's got to stop them tonight," Elmer said, as if he wasn't sure Les agreed. "Tomorrow they'll be able to head over to the Redfern place. You know Chrissy Redfern is alone in the house with her new baby these days. I heard Reno is driving that truck route for his sister. Their place isn't far from yours. It wouldn't take them guys long to find it if they just head out from your place tomorrow and make that left turn. I don't see them driving up to the Elkton ranch because of its size. But if they go the other direction, there's Mrs. Nolan alone on that place of hers. Now that her son's gone, she'd be an easy target."

Les held up his hand. He'd already thought of each of his neighbors. "Believe me, I know."

The theft of his rifle had changed everything.

The sheriff in Miles City had agreed with him that something had to be done tonight. They were both responsible for the well-being of the people in this part of the state and there was no limit to the damage two—or maybe three—armed gang members could do if they went around to the smaller ranches. A lot of people still didn't even lock their doors during the day.

"There's no question that we're going," Les said. They had to. "We just need to figure out what the best way is to get a few men into my place tonight without them being seen."

"Horseback," Elmer said without hesitation. "A horse is the only animal that can walk down that slope of yours without needing even a flashlight."

Les nodded. It was certainly worth considering. "We could come in from the Redfern side. That fence between our two places runs fairly close to the draw leading down to my place. I don't know how many horses they have that would make the ride, though."

Elmer shrugged. "We could always call over to the Elkton place. The boys there would be happy to join us."

The Elkton ranch was the only one of the ranches that had a large crew of workers still. The other places might hire summer help, but the men at the Elkton were seasoned year-round ranch hands. They were

Montana men to the core. Les knew he could count on them if he found himself in a tight situation.

"I'm going to call them now," Les said as he headed back toward the kitchen.

Marla stepped out of the kitchen before Les reached the doorway.

"You need to take me with you," she said.

There wasn't enough light to see her eyes, but Les felt the despair in them, anyway. He would stake his life on the fact that she was worried about her son. What he didn't know was whether she was worried about him because he was innocent or because he was guilty.

Les shook his head. "It's too dangerous."

"I'll sign a waiver saying you're not responsible if I'm hurt."

Les looked at her. "You think I'm worried about a *lawsuit?*"

Marla lifted her chin. "If you're taking guns with you, I'm going."

Les wondered when his life had become so complicated. Elmer was standing behind him, not even bothering to pretend he wasn't listening. Mrs. Hargrove was eyeing him through the doorway of the kitchen. Les supposed if his friends hadn't given him any privacy when they thought he was proposing marriage, he couldn't expect them to give him any now.

"It's because of the guns that you can't go." Les

held up his hand. "And not just the guns we have. It's the gun we know they have, too."

"They don't even have bullets."

"I keep bullets in one of the drawers in the workshop," Les said. "I have them on the top shelf in my closet, too. It won't take them long to find bullets."

Les didn't add that Sammy might already have found the bullets when he was working in the workshop on that shepherd figure.

Marla might have come to the same realization, because she bit her lip. "All the more reason for me to go."

Les shook his head.

"If you don't take me with you, I'll go, anyway. I know the way to your place. I've already driven there two times."

"I can't let you do that."

Marla stepped back, but her voice was still strong. "You can't stop me. Not unless you're going to arrest me or something. Is that what you're going to do? If you are, you might as well do it now."

Marla put her hands out as if she was ready for handcuffs.

Les didn't even carry handcuffs. "You know I don't have enough to arrest you on."

Les heard an indignant gasp, and this one wasn't from Marla.

"Lester Wilkerson, I can't believe you would seriously consider arresting Marla," Mrs. Hargrove said as she stepped out of the kitchen. "Not when you're planning to propose to her."

"Oh."

"Oh."

There was a chorus of surprised female reactions and one startled grunt from Elmer.

"I'm sorry. I shouldn't have said—" Mrs. Hargrove began.

"But he hasn't asked yet, has he?" Linda interrupted. "No one's drunk the cider."

Les just looked at the two women. "When someone makes an unspoken prayer request, that doesn't mean people can speak out what they think it might mean in some fantasy. Unspoken is unspoken. I wasn't talking about proposing to anyone."

"Oh." That one came from Marla.

She was holding herself too still. Les felt her tension. Whoever she was and whatever her relationship was to that gang, she was so close to tears she could barely keep them in. Les could see her struggle.

"Not that whoever gets your promise to marry him won't be one very fortunate man," Les said softly.

Now that Mrs. Hargrove and Linda had done their damage, they slid back into the kitchen like cowards, dragging Elmer with them.

"I'm still going with you," Marla whispered. Her eyes were black pools of determination. "You can't keep me away."

Les nodded. What she asked for was probably

against a hundred regulations and the regular sheriff would have Les's badge when he heard about it, but Les was still going to do it. He had no doubt Marla would head out to his place on her own. If she wasn't in league with those two strangers, she could end up getting shot. If she was working with them, they'd know he was coming and he could be shot.

"You'll stay with me, though," Les said. "And when I say duck, you duck. You'll be quiet when I say for you to be quiet. There will be others along with us and I'll not have you jeopardize their safety in any way. Promise?"

"I promise," Marla said. "And thank you."

Les grunted. They said a fool was born every day; he knew of at least one who had been born on his birthday. If Sheriff Carl Wall ever got back from that fancy honeymoon trip of his, Les was going to ask him how a lawman handled stubborn women.

His only hope was that once Marla got a good look at the horses they would have to ride she would change her mind about going with him.

Marla reminded herself that Mary had been forced to ride a donkey to get where she needed to go. Then Marla looked at the defiant glint in the eye of the horse looking at her from across the barn and she wondered if a donkey wouldn't be easier to handle.

Marla was with Les and Elmer at the Redfern barn and Chrissy was showing them the two horses that could make a ride tonight. It was a little before midnight, but Chrissy had been expecting them because of Les's call. She looked too young to be the mother of two children, one a three-year-old son. She had on an old sweatshirt and sweatpants, and her blond hair was pulled back and tied with a scarf.

The Redferns' barn was smaller than the one Les had, and Marla thought it looked more like what she imagined that manger scene with Mary and Joseph would be like. For one thing, there were more kinds of animals around. But that might be only because there were chickens nesting on a tall shelf in one of the horse stalls, and once they had been woken up, they kept squawking until it seemed as if there were a lot of animals besides the cows and horses in the poorly lit barn.

"You can borrow my boots," Chrissy suggested to Marla. "If they're too big, I have lots of thick socks."

"Thank you." Marla wondered why Montana people had such a fascination with their socks.

Chrissy was still looking at her critically. "And I have a wraparound scarf, too. That will keep your face warm."

Marla looked over at where Les and Elmer were talking. They were stroking the heads of the two horses while they whispered together about something.

"I don't want to hold them up." Marla jerked her head at the men. "I'll do fine with what I have on."

"It'll only take me a minute to get them," Chrissy

said as she started walking to the barn door. "Besides, they have to wait for the guys to get here from the Elkton ranch, anyway."

Marla nodded. Of course they needed to wait. There were only two horses at the Redfern place and with Les, Elmer and her, they would need three horses. Marla looked at the two disgruntled horses standing beside the men now. She hoped she was the one who got the other horse that would be coming. She would guess that Mary's donkey had been grateful for the privilege of carrying her around on its back; those two horses looked as if they'd just as soon stay in their warm stalls for the night and not be bothered with doing anything for anyone.

Marla changed her mind about the horses when the Elkton men called to them from outside the barn. She went to the door and looked out. Some of those horses looked fierce. One was stomping his feet impatiently and another was blowing into the air. They looked as if they were ready to go into battle. She wondered why no one rode donkeys anymore.

"Is that all?" Les asked from where he stood just outside the barn door. "Don't you have another horse?"

Marla was glad Les recognized that none of the horses she'd seen tonight were suitable for her. She'd never been on a horse before; she needed a gentle ride.

There was a yard light that illuminated the area by the barn, and eight men with horses stood there waiting. The men all had heavy coats on their backs and boots on their feet. They all had Stetson hats on their heads, too, and when Marla looked more closely, she saw that they had knit scarves under their hats. It looked as if the hats held the scarves in place.

When the men heard Les's question, they looked at each other.

"Didn't Byron say he'd do that?" one of the men finally muttered.

Marla looked again. She did recognize Byron, the man from church on Sunday.

"Weren't you supposed to bring the other horse?" another man finally said directly to Byron.

Marla saw Byron shrug. "I figured she'd rather ride with someone, since I doubt she even knows how to ride. I thought I'd let her ride with me."

Les looked at Marla suspiciously. "You never said anything about not being able to ride a horse."

"Maybe I can ride," Marla said.

"I should have known." Les shook his head. "Well, that settles it—you have to stay here. We don't have a horse for you, anyway."

"I can ride with someone."

"She's welcome to ride with me," Byron said as he walked his horse closer to the barn door. He smiled down at Marla. "I always have room for a lady to ride with me."

Les groaned. "She's riding with me. Let's get going."

Marla thought it might be safer to ride with Byron.

Les was looking even more disgruntled than the horses did. "I don't mind riding with Byron."

Les glared at her. "You're riding with me."

Marla followed Les over to the horse he had for the night. Chrissy had already said that one was named Stubby for *stubborn*. She reached out her hand and lightly touched the horse's side.

"You don't need to be frightened," Les said softly as he came up beside her.

"I've never touched a horse before."

Les smiled briefly. "I figured that."

Les put one of his feet in the stirrup and swung himself into the saddle.

Then he reached down for Marla's hand and moved his foot out of the stirrup. "Put your left foot there and swing up when I say."

Marla took his arm and put her foot in the stirrup.

"Now."

"Oh." Just like that, Marla was on the back of a horse.

"You okay?"

"I think so." Marla squirmed a little. She had not thought the horse's back would be quite so wide.

"Good. Move in as close as you can and hold on to me."

Marla didn't want to get too close, so she settled in with a couple of inches between her back and Les's. And then the horse took a step forward and she plastered herself to his back. How did anyone ever stay seated on these things? Weren't they supposed to be as comfortable as rocking chairs?

Les had taken the horse outside the barn to join the other riders. It wasn't until everyone stood in the security light in the yard that Marla noticed every saddle except the one on Les's horse also had a long leather pocket. Out of that pocket stood a rifle.

Marla shivered, and it had nothing to do with the cold night air or the fact that she was riding on an animal that could, at any minute, rid himself of her. What chance did the night have with so many rifles around?

"God bless you," Chrissy called softly as the horsemen all started to file past the barn.

Marla smiled at Chrissy and waved. She would have felt better if Mrs. Hargrove had been here to pray for everyone. She could only hope that wherever the older woman was, she was praying.

The night had a scattering of distant stars and she could see the subtle shift in the sky from black to deep gray that signaled there were clouds above them.

"Here," Les said, and Marla felt him reach back toward her with something. She took it in her hand. It was a soft wool scarf like the ones the other men had around their necks. "Put it on. It's going to be snowing any minute now."

Marla wrapped the scarf around her head and rested her cheek against Les's back. He was wearing a heavy wool jacket, and if she leaned her cheek against the black jacket for a couple of minutes, the wool became warm. With the scarf wrapped around her and her face pressed to the warm space on Les's back, she was almost cozy in all this darkness.

She saw her first snowflake. It settled on Les's jacket near her face, glistening for a moment before her breath made it melt. The air felt moist and smelled damp. She could feel the pull of Les's arm muscles through his jacket as he used the reins to guide the horse.

Les was at the head of the line of horsemen. No one spoke. The only sounds were the horse hooves scraping the ground. They rode down a ravine until they reached a barbed-wire fence.

"Go ahead and cut it," Les said to another man who had stepped down from his horse. "I don't have cattle in this pasture right now, anyway."

The horsemen bunched up together as they waited for the fence to be cut.

"You doing okay?" a man leaned in and asked Marla.

With his hat pulled over his face, it took Marla a second to recognize Byron. She smiled at him. "Yes. Thanks for asking."

"If you need any help, let me know."

"She's fine," Les interrupted with a look over his shoulder at the other man.

When the fence was cut, the horses started to move again. Marla felt the cold on her legs above the line of the boots she had borrowed from Chrissy and on the back of her head where the wool scarf did not reach.

Les shifted in the saddle and Marla shifted with him. She wondered if Mary had ever ridden behind Joseph's back on that donkey. She hoped for the young girl's sake that she had. Despite the problems Marla knew would face them all when they reached the barn, she felt safe riding behind Les.

Chapter Thirteen

Les put his hand up and everyone pulled their horses to a stop. They had ridden up to the edge of the ravine surrounding the buildings on his ranch. The sheriff's department from Miles City should have had time to get themselves in place by now. Not that they would be close enough to do much if everything fell apart. The only place for them to wait, and not be seen, was well back of the last rise before the dip that led down to his buildings.

The night was still dark, but the light layer of snow that had been falling would make them all stand out more as they approached the house and barn. They would need to be especially quiet.

Les leaned back a little so he could feel Marla's warmth against him. He was going to have to find her a place to stay where she would be out of any trouble that might start. Probably the best thing would be to have her stay with the horses.

Les scanned the buildings. There was a subdued light coming from the window in the back of his barn. It was from the section that was now the workshop. He never kept a light burning when he left the workshop. Sometimes he used a night-light in the barn during calving season, but at this time of year there was no need for a light.

"Someone's there, all right," Elmer whispered as he rode up beside Les.

Les nodded. He had already noted that as they rode around the edge of the rise to the place that dipped down behind his buildings, he could see the front windows to the barn and no light was showing through them. Since there was a light in the back window, that meant whoever was inside had covered the windows in front. The road into his place looked squarely at those front windows. Which could only mean that whoever was inside his barn was trying to hide the fact that they were in his workshop. They would not expect anyone to see the window in the back.

Les wondered briefly if they were planning to catch him unaware or if they were hoping he just wouldn't check the barn when he got back home tonight.

"We'll leave the horses behind the house," Les whispered to the other men as he touched the flank of his horse to urge him to keep going down the slight hill. The snow made the ground slippery and the horses had to pick their way down.

Someone listening closely could have heard the

sounds of hooves sliding across small rocks. The person would have to be outside, though, and Les was betting that none of the young men in his barn would want to linger outside on a night as cold as this one. And they had no reason to be outside. They were no doubt inside waiting for the sound of his pickup and the glare of his headlights coming from the opposite direction.

It took twenty minutes to ride from the top of the rise to the flat area in back of Les's house.

Les was relieved they had made it to the house without anyone inside the barn looking out that back window. He hadn't expected them to look and wasn't sure that they would see anything, anyway, since their eyes would not be accustomed to the dark. All they might have seen was a shadowy shape. An old mountain man would know to investigate something like that. Young men from the city wouldn't give it a second thought.

Les dismounted, then lifted his arms up to Marla. She practically fell into his arms, and he held her steady for a minute when her feet touched the ground.

"Cold?" he asked.

Marla nodded. "Sore, too."

"Maybe you should sit here and rest." Les had been trying to figure out how to convince Marla she needed to stay somewhere safe, and had concluded that his best plan would be to not tell her it was for her safety. "We need someone to stay with the horses."

"Stay with the horses! I don't know anything about horses."

Marla's voice had gotten a little high.

"Hush," Les said in a soft whisper. "We don't want anyone to hear us."

No sooner had the words left his mouth than Les wondered if Marla would like the young men inside the barn to hear them. He probably should have gagged her at some point tonight before they got this close.

He wasn't sure he could have done it even if he had thought of it, though. Les told himself that when the regular sheriff got back to Dry Creek, he was going to turn in his reserve deputy sheriff badge. He'd let someone else go around putting gags on people.

"You're not going to make lots of noise and warn them, are you?" Les asked.

The night had gotten even darker than when they'd started out and Les could not see Marla's face clearly. Of course, with the scarf wrapped around it, he wouldn't have been able to see much of it even if it had been a full sunny day. He still had his hands on her arms to steady her, though, and he could feel her muscles tighten in indignation.

"All I want is for everyone to be safe," she said.

Les nodded. "That's why we don't want to give them a chance to use that rifle. Which means no noise."

"I understand that."

"Good."

Les looked around. He wished he hadn't kept the area around his house so tidy. There was nothing to tie the horses to. He'd even taken out the old clothesline when the posts started to rot. Since he didn't need the line, he'd never replaced it. He had an old lawn chair where he sat in the summer and looked at the wildflowers that grew all the way up the rise, but that wasn't enough to keep a horse from straying.

"You'll have to hold the reins," Les finally said as he turned to Marla. He couldn't spend all night looking for somewhere to anchor the reins.

"For all the horses?"

Les nodded, then looked at the men in front of him. "Elmer, maybe you could?"

"I'll stay with her," the older man said. "But if I hear trouble, I'm going to let these horses fend for themselves and come help."

Les nodded. "Thanks."

"Where shall we go in?" one of the Elkton ranch hands asked as he unsnapped the scabbard holding his rifle. He drew the long Winchester out and cradled it next to his shoulder.

"I figure we'll circle the barn. A man at each window. Don't worry about breaking the windows. Just don't do it until they know we're there." Les took the rifle Elmer handed to him.

"Everybody loaded?" Les asked as he cracked the rifle he'd just been given and made sure there were bullets in it. He knew the Elkton ranch hands took their rifles when they went into the far pastures on horseback, just in case they ran into wolves or maybe even a mountain lion if they were high enough in the hills.

Les saw a series of Stetsons nod.

"Well, then," he said, his voice still low, "I'll go around by the entrance and see if I can make sense of what's happening inside. Remember, we want to avoid any gunplay."

Les saw Marla wince.

"We plan to do this quietly," Les added for good measure. "Everyone take their station by a window, but wait until we figure out what's happening inside. Those boys might just be hanging out and happy to give up the rifle and come out peacefully."

"Maybe they didn't even take the rifle," Marla whispered.

Les nodded. "That's possible, too."

He supposed it was *possible,* Les told himself. In the realm of what was possible, maybe Mrs. Hargrove had stolen it. Or Linda, at the café. Or Santa Claus. Still, he couldn't say no to the hope that sprang up in Marla's mind.

When Les had talked to the sheriff in Miles City, they had gone over strategies. They had decided not to use a bullhorn and call out to the young men inside until Les could figure out where Sammy stood on all of this. Les didn't want to risk anyone making

Sammy their hostage just in case he hadn't gone with the other men willingly.

It was a small chance that Sammy was innocent, but Les wanted to give him every benefit of the doubt even if it made his own job tonight more dangerous.

"It wouldn't hurt to say a prayer before we head out," Les added.

To a man, the ranch hands bowed their heads.

After they prayed, they each gave their reins to Elmer and followed Les over to the barn.

Marla watched as the men walked away. She could see dark shadows as they moved toward the barn. A snowflake fell on her eyelash and she blinked it away so she could see better. The men looked so powerful walking in the dark with their rifles resting against their shoulders and pointing to the sky. Each man walked differently. All of them were wearing tall leather boots, though, and she could hear the muffled sounds of their boot heels hitting rocks here and there.

"They should have bulletproof vests," Marla whispered.

Elmer grunted in response. "Don't worry about that boy of yours. Les will take care of him."

Marla didn't say that she'd meant Les was the one who should have the bulletproof vest. She supposed it was expecting too much for the Dry Creek people to forgive her and Sammy this time around. It was one thing for Sammy to steal the church's shepherd; it was another for him to help steal the sheriff's rifle. She looked over at Elmer. The older man had changed out of the suit he had worn earlier this evening. If he had been willing to play the harp because he thought Les was going to propose to someone, Elmer would probably take Les's point of view on anything.

Which was as it should be, Marla thought to herself. Les belonged here; it was good that his friends stood beside him. She might wish that they were her friends, too, but one look at Elmer's face and she knew it wasn't true. He didn't trust her, either.

When this night was over, Marla thought to herself, she would have to start packing again. She had to believe Sammy was innocent in all that was happening tonight, but even if he was innocent, their days of being welcome in Dry Creek were likely over. Her neighbor from Los Angeles had been right. People in small towns didn't like having gang members show up in their towns. Not that she could blame them, Marla thought. She didn't like the gang showing up in her family, either.

Les put his hand against the front of the barn. The old boards were dry from many years of sun and wind, but he kept them painted, and a few years ago he'd had the boards all sanded down. He had taken off his gloves to give them to Marla and now the wet snow on the barn chilled his fingers. He looked up and could see a couple of the Elkton men ahead of him, each stationed at one of the windows in the front of the barn.

The windows had been an extravagance a decade ago when Les had them installed. He liked to have the extra sunlight for the calves. He'd never thought he would be using them to help disarm some big-city gang members.

Les inched toward the smallest door that led into the barn. He had a huge cattle door on one end of the barn that he could open if he needed to, but there was a smaller door he could use, as well. He knew there was some risk in opening even the small door, but there was no other way, outside of looking through a window, to see what was happening inside the barn. He didn't want to use a window because that made a man too vulnerable. If the gang members inside were watching anything, they would be watching the windows, waiting to see headlights as a pickup came down the same drive they had used.

Les stopped close to the door. He could see the single tracks of what looked like two motorcycles. They must have driven them inside his barn for the night. If he hadn't seen the light from the back window, he wouldn't have a clue that someone was in his barn tonight.

It was just too bad there wasn't a way to see everything better. Suddenly Les realized that there was a way. Permanently braced against the barn was a ladder that led up to the hayloft. If he could get up there, he could look through some of those cracks in the floor of the loft and look right down into the barn and the

workshop both. The last place anyone would be looking would be at the ceiling.

Les walked by several Elkton men and whispered
his plan to go up to the hayloft.

The ladder was sturdy and, with his rifle strapped
over his shoulder, Les was able to make the climb to
the loft quietly. The hayloft was open all year round
and Les only had to swing himself onto the floor when
he reached that opening. There were old straw bales
lying around and straw dust everywhere. The wind
had blown some snow in tonight and the bales were
wet to the touch when Les leaned on several of them.
It was darker inside the loft than it had been outside
and he waited for his eyes to adjust.

Les carefully walked on the floorboards. He knew
if he stayed close to the stacks of bales, his extra
weight would not be enough to make the boards creak.
When he got to a good-size crack, he knelt and put
his eye to the space.

The two strangers were there, all right. One of
them was sitting on the worktable and the other had
pulled in a wooden stool Les kept near the stalls. They
weren't doing anything. The drawers in his workshop
had all been pulled out and the contents dumped on the
worktable already, so they must have finished searching for things. They had the rifle. It was lying on the
floor by the man sitting on the stool. An opened box
of bullets was next to it, so Les assumed they had
loaded the gun earlier.

As Les looked more closely, he revised his opinion that these were men. Linda had said she estimated the two strangers at being around seventeen, but Les had figured they were probably a year or two older. Seeing them now, though, he wondered if they were a year or two younger. They were really teenagers instead of men.

The one sitting on the worktable had tattoos covering his arms and he was holding a hammer in one hand, swinging it softly. Les looked at the other teenager, too. Neither one was wearing a coat. They looked cold.

Maybe they'd be glad to give up their adventure.

Les had to move to his left and look through another crack before he saw Sammy. His heart was glad when he saw that Sammy was bound, both hands and feet, and lying in a corner of the workshop. Maybe Marla wasn't the only one who had kept hoping that her son was a victim instead of participant in all of this. Sammy had a bruise on his face, but other than that he looked all right.

Les moved his hand to prepare to stand and felt some small pieces of straw move with him. His hand was wet and that's what had made the straw stick. Unfortunately, the straw that didn't stick was also lifted and it was now slipping through the crack he'd been looking through.

Les held his breath as he watched the straw float down to where the boys were. He'd have to wait for their attention to move to something else before he dared to lift himself up from the floor.

Sammy was the only one to look up. He gave a half grunt of surprise and then closed his mouth.

"What'ja doing now?" the guy with the hammer demanded of Sammy. "Didn't I just tell you to shut up?"

"Maybe he wants you to hit that shepherd of his again," the guy sitting on the stool said with a sneer. "Teach him to keep quiet. We're hiding out here. We don't need any little kid whining."

"Ah, ain't nobody coming out here tonight," the guy with the hammer answered. "It's snowing out there. The cops will all be someplace drinking coffee."

"Still, he should be quiet."

"Well, if it makes you feel better, here." The guy swung the hammer and hit the shepherd.

Les winced. No amount of putty was going to fix that Nativity figure now.

"You're going to be sorry you did that," Sammy growled as he struggled with the ties around his feet. "When I get my hands free, I'm going to—"

Both of the guys laughed.

"Yeah, you and who else are going to come get us? You got any amigos around here that'll help you whip us?"

Sammy was quiet for a moment. Then he started to talk, low and fierce. "Yeah, I do. That shepherd belongs to God. You mess with His shepherd and He'll take your guts and grind them up until you'll wish you were dead. And then He'll have the buzzards come and drop you in the fire pit. And then—"

"Whoa—hey, man," the guy with the hammer said. Les thought he looked a little nervous. "I get your point."

"No disrespect to your God," the other one said.

"Well…" Sammy hesitated. "He's not my God, but I know a woman, Mrs. Hargrove, and—"

"Your amigo is a *woman?* So is she sexy?"

"Mrs. Hargrove? No way. She's old."

"Your amigo is an *old woman.* And she's going to help you whip us?"

Both of the guys laughed a little.

Sammy nodded emphatically. "God does what she asks Him to do. He'll come and get you if she says she wants you to be gotten."

"You mean she puts out a curse? My grandmother used to know about curses. I don't want any curses around me. They can shrivel a guy up. Some guy my cousin knew died from a curse like that."

Les figured, with all the talking going on down there, it was a good time to make his move back to the ladder. He only hoped Sammy didn't scare the other two guys too much. He'd rather have them half-asleep than all wide-awake and spooked.

Les climbed down and walked along the side of the barn again. Now that he knew where everyone was located in the workshop, he knew he could open the large cattle door without anyone seeing it. He oiled the hinges on that door every fall and he knew it wouldn't make a sound as it slid open tonight. The guys inside the workshop might feel a sudden drop in temperature when the cold air came into the barn, but they wouldn't hear anything to make them suspicious.

After stopping to tell the men from the Elkton ranch what his plan was, Les walked over to the cattle door and swung it open. The door opened to the wide aisle that ran down the center of his barn. The workshop and the horse stalls were on one side of the aisle. The cattle stalls were on the other.

The horse inside the barn was the first animal to notice the cold air, and he gave a loud whinny of protest. A couple of chickens squawked as Les slipped into the barn and inched his way along the side of the workshop. He moved to the workshop window that faced the front of the barn. He'd already noticed it was closed. No one inside would be able to hear him.

When he reached the workshop door, Les pushed on it gently. Sammy was the only one facing the door and Les hoped that the boy wouldn't give anything away. Once he had the door open a crack, he could hear them talking inside. They were still on the subject of curses.

"What was that?" one of the gang members said. Les thought it sounded like the guy sitting on the stool. He was the one with the rifle lying on the floor beside him. "Did you hear that?"

"Ah, you're just spooked," the other guy said. "It was the horse out there making noise."

"No, it was after that."

"Then it was the chickens. Relax."

Les knew he hadn't made any noise. The two of them were just jumpy after all the talk about curses.

"There it is again," the nervous one said. "And it ain't no chickens. I'll bet it's the cops."

"We haven't even seen any headlights," the other one said.

"No, but they're here…"

Les was wondering if the guy somehow saw the backup team from Miles City up on the rise. He supposed if someone up there had turned on a flashlight or something they would be seen. Suddenly a rifle shot shattered the window of the workshop.

Les decided it was now or never.

"Put your hands up. You're surrounded," Les yelled. He didn't stand where they could see him, but they could sure hear him.

Les heard the sound of windows breaking all over the barn.

"We've got a hostage!" one of the boys screamed out. He was so young his voice ended in a high squeak.

"What you've got is trouble," Les yelled back. "Put the rifle down and come on out here with your hands in the air."

That's when Les heard the thunder coming. The first horse to come galloping into the barn was Stubby

from the Redfern place. Then there were a couple of
the Elkton horses. Then there was—

Marla! She was chasing the horses. Or rather, trying to catch them. She had a rope outstretched and
was looking at the animals in panicked frustration.

"Get back!" Les yelled, but he wasn't sure she could
hear him over the sounds of horse hooves.

The men from the Elkton ranch sure didn't hear
him. They all had a fondness for their horses, and
they were sliding into the barn to calm them down.

"Who's there?" the youngster with the rifle shouted
from the broken window. He swung the rifle around
as if he didn't know who to shoot first.

Les heard eight rifles cock at the same minute.

"What the—" The teenager with the rifle saw all
the rifles pointing at him.

In one motion, the men from the Elkton ranch had
swung onto the backs of their horses while keeping
their rifles trained on the boy in the window.

"It's time to give it up," Les said smoothly as he
walked toward the teenager. There were too many
guns ready to fire for his comfort. "No need to make
this harder than it is."

Les saw the gang member looking at the Elkton
men. The ranch hands had their Stetsons pulled low
and the collars of their sheepskin coats pulled high
around their necks. They had one hand on their horses
and the other steadying their long-barreled rifles, all

aimed at the teenager standing in the broken window of the workshop.

"You don't want to get hurt," Les continued softly as he took a few more steps closer. "Give me the rifle."

"Who are you guys? Some kind of a posse?"

The teenager dropped his rifle through the workshop window and it fell to the floor in the barn.

"We have a right to be arrested by the cops." The other teenager spoke up from inside the workshop. "We have our rights. Nobody is going to string us up."

"Drop the hammer and come out here," Les said.

The boy dropped the hammer as if it was on fire. "I'm not armed. No one can shoot me. I demand police protection."

Les heard several cars coming to a stop outside his barn.

"I think that's your protection now," Les said as several deputy sheriffs came inside the barn.

The two youngsters saw the uniforms and would have run to the deputies if the horses hadn't been in their way.

Les decided he needed to make the aisle in his barn wider. Between the horses and the deputies and the chickens that had been spooked and were flapping around, there wasn't enough room for Marla to get through to the workshop where Sammy was.

"He's all right," he turned and yelled just in case she could hear him.

Les stepped inside the workshop and saw Sammy where he had been earlier.

"You are all right, aren't you?" he asked as he walked over and squatted beside Sammy.

"God got them, didn't He?"

Les nodded as he started to unknot the rope around Sammy's hands. "He sure did."

"I'm going to be a cowboy when I grow up," Sammy announced. "And get me a hat and a rifle."

"Oh, no, you don't," Marla said as she stepped into the workshop. "You won't have any kind of gun."

"Les?" Sammy looked up in appeal.

"Listen to your mother," Les said as he moved to the knot on Sammy's feet. "She knows what she's talking about."

Sammy wasn't the only one who should have listened to Marla, Les thought to himself. He should have listened and believed a little more in the innocence of her son. He was going to apologize, but before he could get any words out, Marla had hurried Sammy up and rushed him out of the workshop. Les thought it seemed a little bit as though she couldn't stand to be in the same room with him.

Chapter Fourteen

Marla wrapped the blanket tighter around Sammy. After talking to Les, the deputy sheriff from Miles City had asked her and Sammy if they'd like to ride home in one of their cars. She was sitting with Sammy in one car and the two teenagers were sitting in the other car. The men were all standing outside talking and remounting their horses. The dome light was on inside the car, so Marla didn't have any trouble picking out the various men, even though the men who had been riding horseback were all wearing hats. She knew Les because of his coat.

Marla thought she should be content. She had her son sitting next to her and he wasn't hurt or even pulling away from her. He was safe and, hopefully, he had learned his lesson. She should concentrate on that and not wonder what could have been between her and Les if he'd been able to trust her. Trust was very important.

Maybe he still didn't trust her. He certainly hadn't seemed to want her to ride back with him on his horse.

Marla turned her attention to Sammy.

"Hopefully, you learned not to give out your address to people who shouldn't have it," she said. "Those guys shouldn't have even known how to find you up here."

"I didn't give them our address. They got it from our old landlord."

"Ah," Marla said. "Well, I'll have to call him."

"They told him they needed to send me back my baseball."

"Well, he shouldn't have believed that." She would think he would have been less gullible. Maybe he was and they'd paid him for the address.

"But they did have my baseball with my name on it and everything. More than one. Every time I got a baseball, they took it from me."

Marla blinked. How many times had this gone on? "But why didn't you tell me?"

"You were busy with Dad."

"Ah," Marla said. She probably wouldn't have paid any attention to a missing baseball in those days, anyway. She put her arm around Sammy's shoulder. "I'm sorry I wasn't paying enough attention back then."

Sammy shrugged. "It's okay. Dad wasn't there to play catch with me, anyway."

Marla pulled Sammy closer. "You still miss your dad, don't you?"

Sammy nodded.

"Well, we're going to spend more time together. You, me and Becky."

Sammy looked up. "I wouldn't mind if we had other people around, too."

Marla held her breath.

"Like Mr. Morales," Sammy added. "He's a good guy. And Les isn't too bad. And I like Mrs. Hargrove. And the woman at the café who gave us those doughnuts."

Marla nodded. "There's lots of good people in Dry Creek."

Marla told herself she needed to postpone moving. She knew small towns could be unforgiving, and she and her children had probably made the worst first impression they possibly could have. She did not expect the people of Dry Creek to want them to stay even when it became clear to them that Sammy hadn't taken the sheriff's rifle. They would still say he'd brought the wrong kind of people to their town, and they would be right. But not even the people of Dry Creek could get all that talking done overnight.

She'd have to give the kids a hint, but she could wait until after Christmas to start packing up their boxes. Maybe by then, Sammy and Becky would feel better about moving. She could even just move into Miles City, which wouldn't be far away—and they would be going to school there even if they lived in Dry Creek, so it might not make too much difference to them.

Yes, Miles City would be a good place to go. It would be a fresh start. Of course, she'd have to rent a place for them to live in Miles City. She wondered if someone would be willing to buy the house in Dry Creek.

Her mind was still trying to figure out how she'd pull off a move when the deputy sheriff came back to the car.

"Well, we've got it all wrapped up," he said as he slid into the driver's seat "Ready to head home?"

"Thank you, Deputy—?"

"Sutter, ma'am. Deputy Sutter," he said as he started the car.

"And you're from Miles City?"

"I sure am," he said with a grin in the rearview mirror. "I've lived there my whole life."

"Well, then, you can tell us about it," Marla said.

Marla saw Sammy listen intently to the deputy talk about how the kids in town played softball in Bender Park and every year went to the rodeo called the Bucking Horse Sale.

"Can I ride in the rodeo?" Sammy demanded.

"Maybe someday," the deputy said. "But you have to grow taller first."

Sammy nodded. "I grow pretty fast."

Marla relaxed back into the seat as the deputy's car climbed up the slight hill leaving Les's place. Sammy would make the move to Miles City just fine. It made sense to move, anyway. There weren't very many other children for him to play with in Dry Creek. Miles City was a much bigger town. She was determined her children would have a fresh start and not have a negative reputation dogging their footsteps through their childhood.

When they got to the top of the rise, Marla looked back. All the lights were still on in Les's barn. She could even see the horses outlined in the light. She wondered if she'd ever see that barn or house again.

Les was standing by his barn, watching the taillights of the deputy's car as it drove away.

"Humph, so the great Lester Wilkerson is finally bitten," said a voice to his left.

Les didn't need to turn around to know who it was. "You should talk, Byron. You wine and dine them all."

Byron chuckled. "Maybe so. But you don't see me standing there looking like the dog someone left behind. All alone at home."

Les turned and looked at the man. "No, we don't see that, do we? Makes me wonder which one of us is the sorriest, though."

"Hey, don't take it out on me," Byron said as he raised his hands in surrender. "I'm on your side in all of this."

That fact made Les feel even worse. How had he ended up on the same side as Byron?

"Everybody's leaving," Les finally said. The truth was that the other riders had already gotten a couple of yards' head start on Byron. Les had promised them all a free piece of pie at the café the next time they were in town; he'd call Linda tomorrow and give her a deposit.

Byron took the hint and saddled up. "Remember, if you get lonesome, we've always got the coffeepot on in the bunkhouse in the winter."

"Thanks," Les said. There was a time when he'd enjoyed hanging out in the Elkton ranch bunkhouse. Maybe that time would come again. At the moment, though, all he wanted to do was go inside his house and sit.

The next day the Suzy bake set deluxe edition came in the mail for Les. He'd forgotten that the other night he'd ordered it online and checked the rush delivery box. Les had one of the ranches that were far enough outside Dry Creek to have actual mail delivery. Places that were close in were expected to pick up their mail at the hardware-store counter. Les had never been as grateful for the privacy of individual mail delivery as he was when he saw that box. He didn't want anyone to know he'd just gotten a Suzy bake set. Especially because he was suddenly unsure of what to do with it.

Oh, he knew he was going to give it to Becky. But should he just knock on the door to the Gossett house and hand it to her? He wasn't even sure he was still welcome there. And if he handed something to Becky, he had to have something for Sammy. It had occurred to Les sometime in the night that Sammy might have been leaving him those gang symbols as a warning.

If Sammy hadn't left them, Les wouldn't even have known what he was up against. He owed the boy for that. So he definitely needed to get a present for Sammy. And, of course, if he gave something to the kids, shouldn't he give something to Marla?

It was a good thing, Les told himself, that he had his chores all done before the mail came, because he sure wasn't getting anything done after it was delivered. Finally he decided that if he was going to waste the day, anyway, he might as well drive into Miles City for supplies. If he happened to find a present for Sammy while he was there, so much the better.

The fact that he would have to drive through Dry Creek to go to Miles City was not important. Of course, as reserve deputy sheriff, he should check that the lights were still on in the Gossett place. He might even ask Linda at the café if anyone had seen the family today. After all, it was his duty to be sure that all the citizens of Dry Creek were safe.

Marla saw Les's pickup go by her house. She'd expected him to do his usual walk through Dry Creek this morning, but he hadn't. He'd stopped at the café, but then he just got back into his pickup and drove out of town. She had been waiting for him, too, because she'd realized last night when she got home that she still had the gloves he'd lent her. She wanted to return them.

She also realized she hadn't thanked him for untying Sammy last night. Her hands had been so cold she wouldn't have been able to do it. Of course, the fact that her hands were frozen was partially his fault. He'd left her to hold those horses' reins, and she hadn't been able to keep them straight with the gloves on, so she'd taken the gloves off.

She hoped she never had to see a horse again as long as she lived.

And she could have told Les all of that if he'd walked down the street so she could go out and talk to him.

Marla looked down the street. Maybe Linda knew when he was coming back. Maybe he was just going to do his walk a little later in the day because last night had been so, well, exciting.

It took Marla fifteen minutes to get a coat and mittens on Becky. Sammy had them both beaten. The children were anxious to go to the café—Marla had told them they could have a cup of cocoa. She decided they all needed to go out some. She hoped Linda would still treat them the same after all that had happened last night.

The cocoa was made with real milk. Marla couldn't remember the last time she'd had cocoa with real milk. She looked up at Linda. "This is great. Usually it's just from those packets."

"Growing kids need their milk," Linda said.

Marla tried to detect some difference in the way the café owner was treating them today. So far, she couldn't find any, but she had figured it would take the gossip and nervousness time to grow in Dry Creek, anyway. People hadn't had time to cluster together yet and decide they didn't want anyone in their town who might bring in gang people.

"I noticed the deputy sheriff didn't do his usual walk this morning," Marla finally said between sips. She kept looking at her cup so it would look as if she was only making an observation that anyone could make.

"He's going into Miles City to do some Christmas shopping," Linda said. "At least, that's what I'm assuming. He kept asking me what kind of present a young woman would want."

"Oh." Marla knew it was nothing to her if Les bought Linda a present. The two of them had known each other forever, in any event.

"I told him he had to listen for himself. Most women will say they want this or they want that. All a man has to do is pick one."

"Well, that's good advice." Marla sipped her cocoa. Linda was really a very nice young woman. If Les was looking in that direction, she would have to congratulate him on his good taste.

Not that he would have a quick courtship. Linda had been too supportive of Les when she thought he was going to propose to Marla to make anyone imagine the café owner was romantically inclined toward Les.

"I want a Suzy bake set," Becky announced as she set her empty cup down on the table.

"I have a cupcake pan at home I can give you," Marla said. "We can make cupcakes in that."

"I have a jar of Christmas sprinkles in the back," Linda offered. "You could make some pretty Christmas cupcakes."

Marla noticed the disappointment in Becky's eyes.

"They'll be grown-up cupcakes, then. Won't that be fun?" Marla said.

"Yes, Mommy."

"I'd like to see your cupcakes when you have them all made," Linda said softly. "I bet they'll be beautiful."

Becky nodded.

Linda went into the kitchen and Marla set four dollars down on the table. She knew from the menu that a cup of cocoa was a dollar. She left the fourth dollar as a tip.

Linda gave Becky the bottle of sprinkles, then looked at the dollar bills. She gave three of them back to Marla. "There's a junior special on cocoa."

Marla frowned. "It doesn't say anything about that in your menu."

Linda waved her hand. "We never put our children's specials in the menu. We just tell people that come in with children. We don't want to make our regular customers feel bad."

"I see," Marla said. "But I'm not a child."

"Don't worry. I gave you all the junior special. It's my reward for you bringing in new business."

Marla looked at her.

Linda nodded cheerfully. "Children like yours will grow up to be my future customers."

"We'll come back," Sammy assured her as he set his empty cup on the table. "Even if we're moved to Miles City. We'll come back for cocoa."

"What?"

Marla blushed. "It's just that the children will be going to school in Miles City, anyway. And it'd be more convenient if we were there."

"And I broke the shepherd here," Sammy said as he wiped the cocoa off his face. "He's broken so bad even Les can't fix him."

"Well, yes, but it's only a plastic figure," Linda protested. "Surely you wouldn't move because of that."

"We're not doing anything before Christmas," Marla assured the woman as she stood. That would give the nervous ones in Dry Creek time to voice all the reasons why it would be just as well if the Gossett family did move someplace else. "And Sammy's right. We will still come back and say hello."

"Thanks for my sprinkles," Becky called as they walked toward the door.

"Yes, thanks for everything," Marla added as she opened the door.

The air outside was warmer than it had been yesterday and Marla kept a steady pace with the children as they crossed the street.

"There's where the shepherd should be." Sammy pointed to the Nativity set as they walked past the church. "Right there by those sheep of his."

"Les is taking care of the sheep," Becky said with a worried look on her face. She looked up at her mother. "Isn't he?"

"I'm sure he is, sweetheart."

Marla wondered how long her children would continue to think that Les could fix all the problems in the world.

Chapter Fifteen

Les looked at the presents on his table and wondered if he'd made a mistake. He'd wrapped Becky's Suzy bake set in red paper and the junior-size Stetson he'd gotten for Sammy in green paper. All the wrapping paper only made the pork-loin roast for Marla look worse than it had when he'd started his wrapping, though.

Not that the roast looked bad. He'd talked to the butcher himself and gotten a prime piece of fresh meat.

It's just that he was starting to wonder if Linda's advice had been so good. She'd told him to buy something the woman in question had said she wanted, and the only thing he could remember Marla saying she wanted was a pork roast to use in her tamales. Looking at the roast, though, he was beginning to think he should have bought her a gold brooch instead. His mother had always liked a gold brooch for Christmas.

Of course, he hadn't noticed that Marla wore any

jewelry, so she might not like any kind of a brooch, either. And jewelry meant a bigger thank-you than a roast. Les didn't want to make Marla feel uncomfortable with his presents.

He'd already caused her to have to sit through that circus at the café the other night when people thought he was going to propose. Les wanted to save her further scenes. He wanted her to know he intended to court her in a quiet, respectful manner. He didn't want her to think he was pushing her to make a decision.

After all, Les told himself, he couldn't expect her to have the same certainty that he felt about them getting together. He'd always been someone who knew right away what he wanted. It could be because he'd seen his parents bend and sway so much over the years. Whatever it was, he knew he wanted to have Marla at his side in his life. So the first Christmas present was important.

Maybe it was too soon to even give a present, though.

In fact, Les told himself as he unwrapped Sammy's hat, he should just let the items sit in the big box they were in and not even make them into presents. He'd just leave the box on the steps of the house tonight, without his name on it. That way, no one needed to worry about whether the present was too little or too big. And no one would need to thank anyone.

Les was relieved he'd finally figured out what to

do. It was cold enough that he wouldn't need to worry about refrigerating the roast. If he got up and drove into Dry Creek before he did his morning chores, the box would be on Marla's doorstep when she woke up.

And he'd have the joy of giving a merry Christmas to her and her kids without anyone feeling awkward, including himself. Les looked at the box again. It looked a little drab. Maybe he should stuff some of the wrapping paper in the corners of the box. Sort of fluff the whole thing out.

He could just picture Marla getting the box in the morning. She'd be pleased. Just picturing her face was reward enough for him. He didn't need some big thank-you.

Marla was furious. She'd just opened the door this morning, and what did she see? A charity box. Her family had received enough of those when she was a child that she recognized all the characteristics. The toys for the children weren't wrapped, but there was wrapping paper placed in the box so the parents could do it. As though that made the presents actually come from the parents. And of course, there was the ever-present large food item. At least someone in the church had had some cultural sensitivity and had given her pork for her tamales instead of a turkey.

Marla almost sat down and cried. She had lived all those years in Los Angeles and never been reduced

to being the target of a charity box. At least in Los
Angeles they asked a family if they wanted a box. A
family had to sign up on a list or wait in some line.
Here in Dry Creek, everyone just assumed her family was the poorest family around.

She resisted the urge to go out onto the street and
see if there were boxes on any other porches. She knew
there wouldn't be.

And the worst part was, Marla thought, she was
going to accept the box. It was only three days until
Christmas. The refund check hadn't come yet. How
else would she get a Suzy bake set for Becky and a
cowboy hat for Sammy? She couldn't deny them those
presents, not even if it cost her all her pride to keep
them. She just wished there was something she could
do to show people that she wasn't the desperate charity case everyone apparently assumed she was.

Marla fretted for an hour before the idea came to
her. If it was more blessed to give than to receive, then
she just needed to out-give the church people to regain
some of her pride. Of course, she didn't have money
to give anyone. But now that she had the pork roast,
she could have lots and lots of tamales.

Maybe—and this thought brought a smile to her
face—she would give a tamale to anyone in Dry Creek
who wanted one. She didn't quite know how to go
about presenting her gift, but Mrs. Hargrove would
know.

* * *

The next morning Les sat in the café drinking his second cup of coffee and scowling at the frost on the windows.

"Calf sick?" Linda asked as she quietly refilled his coffee cup.

"No, why?"

Linda shrugged. "I've just never seen you this worried before. I figured it must be something wrong at your place."

Les sighed. "No, my place is fine."

Linda set her coffeepot on the table and sat in the chair opposite Les.

"Then what's wrong? Anything I can help with?"

Les snorted. "You've already helped enough."

"Me? What did I do?"

Les caught himself. "Sorry. I should have just thanked you for your advice and let it be. No one forced me to take the advice."

"This is about that present?"

Les nodded. "I got her what she said she wanted, but now I'm wondering if it's the right thing."

Linda smiled. "I've never seen you this worked up over a present before. Anyone I know?"

"It's none of your business." Les did his best to glare at Linda. He didn't need gossip going around about him and some present. His heart wasn't really in the glare, though. He had other problems to trouble him.

"Well, if you don't think that what this mystery

woman said she wanted is what she really wants, then at least get her something that she needs," Linda said. "You can't go too far off base when you get someone what they need."

Les set down his coffee cup and grinned at her. "I should have thought of that before."

"Good. I'm glad that's solved." Linda stood up. "Do you want me to keep your coffee hot for when you finish your walk around town?"

Les shook his head. "I don't have time to walk this morning. I've got to go back into Miles City."

He needed to buy someone a pair of thick socks. Marla was probably the only one in Dry Creek who didn't own any winter socks. She'd probably like that better than that pork roast, anyway. And she needed them.

His problems were solved.

Marla knew Les was having his cup of coffee in the café. She had seen his pickup parked outside and she'd put on her jacket so that when he walked down the street past her house, she could go out and thank him for what he'd done for Sammy. She owed him her thanks and she meant to say as much to him.

She was trying not to be obvious about looking out her front window, but she did notice when he stepped outside the café and stood on the porch. He wore his bulky black jacket and Marla remembered, just for a moment, how the wool had felt against her cheek in the cold. She wasn't sure anymore if it was the wool or the solid weight of Les himself that she'd found so comforting that night. She should thank him for letting her go with him then, though, as well as for what he'd done for Sammy.

Les took a long look down the street in both directions and then walked right back to his pickup. He opened the door, got inside, then drove through town just as he had yesterday.

In all the time Marla had been in Dry Creek, the one thing that had happened every day, rain or shine, was that Reserve Deputy Sheriff Wilkerson did a morning patrol down the street. She'd never seen him find any problems on his morning walk, but he faithfully made it nonetheless.

Until now. Marla felt herself grow cold, and she had a fire already going in the fireplace. It suddenly hit her that the only reason Les would stop making his morning patrol was that he was avoiding someone. And that someone could only be her and her family. Who else had given Les Wilkerson any trouble lately?

Marla walked over and sat on a folding chair. She put her elbows on the table and just sat there. She had thought Les was becoming attached to her and her family, but it wouldn't be the first time she hadn't been able to read a man's heart right. If she hadn't known her own husband was being unfaithful, how could she expect to know the intentions of a man she'd met for the first time a little over a week ago?

At least she hadn't made a fool of herself over him.

She had her dignity, at least. And she and the children would be moving after Christmas, anyway. Oh—the children. What would she tell the children about Les? Sammy had asked about the man yesterday, and Marla had said he was probably busy. She wasn't sure how long that answer would satisfy her son.

Les was the first man Sammy had attached himself to since his father had died. Maybe Sammy would be content to see Les in church. She was sure the man would attend the Christmas Eve service, and that was only two days away. He would have to be friendly to Sammy in church. There had to be rules in the Bible about that.

Thoughts of the Christmas Eve service reminded Marla that she had a lot to do before then. She'd talked to Mrs. Hargrove yesterday and the older woman had been delighted with Marla's idea of serving up sweet pork tamales after the Christmas carols were sung around the Nativity scene.

Which meant, Marla told herself, that she would need to get busy. She would show the town of Dry Creek that she and her children weren't charity cases if it was the last thing she did before leaving town.

Thinking of leaving town reminded Marla that she needed to ask Linda if the café had some empty boxes they were planning to throw away. Marla had already burned all the boxes she had packed for their trip up here. She hadn't planned that they would ever move again, and the boxes made good starter material for the fireplace. She'd used the last piece of cardboard for the fire this morning.

She'd miss the fireplace, too. Last night she and the children had roasted hot dogs for dinner. Maybe in their new place in Miles City, they would have a fireplace.

Les sat at his kitchen table again. He'd finished his evening chores and he was looking at the presents he'd bought today in Miles City. What had looked so practical in the bright afternoon sun in Miles City was now looking a little disorganized in the unforgiving glare of his overhead light. He looked around his kitchen as though there would be a solution to his problem, but there wasn't.

He'd just have to make the best of it. Les had found some thick wool socks for Marla at one store in Miles City, then he'd remembered Sammy and Becky. They would need thick socks this winter, too. So instead of the neat pair of socks he'd first envisioned, he had a jumble of socks. He had, of course, realized that one pair of socks wouldn't be enough for any of them. So he'd gotten ten pairs for each of them.

And now he didn't know if he should just put them all in a box together or if he should divide them so it was obvious there were three types of socks. He supposed the socks he'd gotten for Becky would be easy enough to identify. He confessed he'd gotten a little carried away with Becky's socks. He hadn't even known they had socks for little girls that had ballerinas on them. And the princess socks. Of course, they weren't thick, but how could he not buy those? He could have passed on the mermaid socks, but they were blue and the T-shirt Becky had worn the other day was blue.

Fortunately, Sammy's socks were easy to buy. White, extra-thick athletic socks were what he needed, especially for gym class at school.

Les had been a little uncomfortable buying Marla's socks. He'd had no idea that women's socks were so much softer than the ones men bought. He'd been rubbing his fingers over a pair of socks when the saleslady had come over and asked if he needed help. He'd quickly bought ten pairs of socks, in various pastel colors, just because he didn't want the woman to think he had a sock problem or anything.

Marla woke up the day before Christmas Eve and looked at the wooden cross that hung on the wall opposite where she rolled out her sleeping bag each night. The one thing she needed to do before she moved to Miles City was talk to Mrs. Hargrove about that cross. Maybe the older woman would be able to tell her what her husband had gained from it.

The sun was just beginning to rise as Marla walked through the house for the first time that day. She didn't even bother to look out her window to see if Les was going to make his patrol. In fact, she was going to leave the blankets on the windows until it was past the time when he usually made a patrol. That should let him know she wasn't waiting around to see if he would walk down the street. And even if she had been watching in the past couple of days, it was only because she still had Les's gloves and she needed to return them to him.

Marla was making tamales today, with the help of Sammy and Becky, and she was too busy to watch the street traffic, anyway. She was looking forward to sharing her tamales with the people of Dry Creek tomorrow night at the Christmas Eve service.

Les got the word from Elmer who had talked to Mrs. Hargrove who had talked to Linda. He couldn't believe it, though. Marla and the kids were moving! Because Sammy had taken the Nativity shepherd.

"I thought all that about the shepherd had been settled," Les said to Linda as he marched into the café. "That's no reason for anyone to leave town. The first time Sammy damaged the shepherd it was an accident and the second time it wasn't even him doing it."

"Don't tell me about it. I agree with you," Linda said as she finished setting silverware on one of the tables.

It was midafternoon and no one else was in the café.

"You're sure that's what Marla said?" Les asked.

"Ask her yourself if you don't trust me. She even came in here asking for boxes."

"But she's making her tamales for everyone for tomorrow night."

Les knew the tamales were important to Marla and that's why he hadn't gone over there and bothered her. He figured tomorrow night was soon enough to wish her a Merry Christmas.

"I think they're her goodbye present to us all."

"Well, I won't eat one, then. I'm not saying goodbye."

Linda looked at him. "Have you told her how you feel? Maybe that would make a difference."

"It's too soon to say how I feel," Les said. He sat down at a table. He was one miserable person. "She'll think it's all just a come-on if I start babbling about how much I'd miss her and how I think her hair is beautiful and that she's the perfect woman for me."

"I could vouch for you. I could tell her you've never said anything like that to another woman."

Les looked at her. "How do you know?"

Linda smiled. "You're a legend of sorts around here, Lester Wilkerson. You and Byron. Him for saying everything to everyone and you for not saying anything to anyone. Ever. We women talk, you know."

"Well, I'm a quiet man," Les admitted.

"Tell me something I don't know."

There was a moment's silence. "I did write a poem

about how her hair reminded me of Mrs. Hargrove's coffee. I could recite that to her."

Linda looked at him dubiously. "Maybe you could sing her a song instead. You've got a good singing voice and there's got to be a thousand love songs around."

"But would she listen to me sing her a song? She wasn't very happy with me when we had to go after Sammy."

"Well, I..." Linda's voice started off confidently and then trailed off. "You haven't talked to her since that night?"

Les shook his head. "I know I should have trusted her to know her own son. Instead, I got all carried away thinking she might be dealing drugs or something herself."

"Marla? Oh, she's not the type."

Les nodded miserably. "And if you could see that, do you think she'll forgive me for not seeing it?"

Linda hesitated and put her hand on his arm. "I hope so."

"Maybe if I could fix that old shepherd up, she wouldn't feel like she and the kids had to move."

"Mrs. Hargrove said something about replacing that shepherd, too. I think she's working on some idea."

"I'll eat more soup. Just sign me up."

"You know, maybe I could make a shepherd, too," Linda said.

Les stood up. He had work to do if he expected to get that shepherd in a kneeling position again.

Chapter Sixteen

Christmas Eve turned out to be a clear night. When Marla looked straight up, she could see stars. She wished one of them was as bright as the one the wise men had followed, but she was happy to see the lesser stars sprinkled across the dark sky, anyway. Not every star could be the brightest one. She knew that in her own life.

Marla had packed a hundred foil-wrapped tamales and Sammy was pulling them along in an old play wagon that had been behind their house when they moved there. Marla thought her husband's uncle had probably used it to pull wood in for the fireplace. The wagon was a little lopsided, but she and the children were walking slowly and the wagon kept up.

Marla wondered if anyone in the church would be struck by the irony that she had packed the tamales in the same box that had been left on her doorstep with the children's presents and the pork roast. She certainly hoped so, because she'd gotten another charity box this morning. This one had no name, either, and it was filled with socks. Usually charity boxes had socks and mittens, but this one had just socks. Not that she was complaining. The socks were wonderful, soft and pretty. If whatever group who left the sock box had also left a card saying who the box was from, she might have been able to convince herself it was a present. But if a gift like that was anonymous, it was a charity box.

She couldn't live in a town that pitied her. She felt a little sad walking down the street toward the church with her children at her side. This evening would probably be their last celebration in the little town.

It was best that they moved to Miles City. She owed Sammy and Becky a hometown that would respect them.

Marla could already hear the people talking. The porch light was on at the church and people were gathered around the Nativity set at the foot of the outside stairs. The only figure in the Nativity that she could see was the angel. It hung from the rain gutters of the church proclaiming good news for everyone.

Marla looked down to be sure Becky was keeping up.

She smiled at her daughter. No matter where they lived, all was well.

Marla had had a long discussion with Mrs. Hargrove yesterday about the wooden cross, and she knew a lot more now about religious symbols. Her husband had not really been getting any answers from that cross; he was probably just remembering what he knew of the Bible when he looked up at it. Mrs. Hargrove told her she could have the same insights. She planned to meet with Mrs. Hargrove next week again to talk about it.

"Look," Sammy said as he stopped the wagon.

Marla looked up. "Oh."

The people had parted so that the three of them could see the full Nativity scene.

"They've got shepherds," Sammy shouted.

Marla didn't even tell him that one shouldn't shout in church. She couldn't believe what she saw, either. Right there, where the shepherd should be but wasn't, there were four other shepherd figures. Even though none of them lit up like the original shepherd, there were so many shepherds that the sheep were outnumbered.

Sammy left the wagon where it was and ran to the Nativity set. She saw Les bend down to talk to him.

This was a picture Marla knew she would never forget.

And then she saw Sammy walk behind one of the shepherds, and the whole thing lit up with white Christmas lights. Someone had made a luminary in the shape of a shepherd. Or, rather, it was a hundred luminaries grouped together to make a shepherd.

The luminaries were as much a Hispanic tradition as the tamales were, even if these luminaries were made from aluminum cans instead of paper bags. There were Christmas lights in the cans in place of candles and the light reflected on the metal of the cans until the shepherd glowed more than the angel above him.

With luminaries and tamales, Marla felt as if she was having one of her childhood Christmases.

The light from the luminary shepherd also made it possible to see the other shepherds. One shepherd was made from what looked like an old scarecrow. The scarecrow's hat had been replaced by a simple robe and the figure had a cane in its hand. Another shepherd was simple cardboard cut to the shape of a shepherd. And then the last shepherd was standing so still it took Marla a minute to realize who it was. Mr. Morales was standing there. He even had a real lamb in his arms.

Mrs. Hargrove walked over to stand beside Marla. "Do you like them?"

"They're beautiful."

The older woman nodded. "We wanted to make Sammy feel good."

Marla looked over at her son. He was looking from

the shepherds to Les and then back again. "I think you've done that."

"Good."

Someone with a microphone climbed the church steps and led everyone in singing "Silent Night." Marla pulled the wagon to the table that had been set up for serving the cocoa. Linda helped her lift the box onto the table, then they both moved closer to the Nativity figures. Marla glanced over to where Les stood with her son. Les had to be the one who had made the tin-can shepherd. She'd seen all the cans he had in his re-cycle bin in the barn. Who else would have that many cans all the same size?

Les told himself that this was peace. For the first time he had to agree that the Nativity project was worth all the soup everyone had eaten for months. People gathered around the figures as though they were expecting them to spring to life right in front of them then and there. Maybe it was because Mr. Mo-rales was standing with the plastic figures and he had let the lamb down so it could wander around. There was life mixed in with all of the lit-up plastic.

Sammy was standing beside him and Les let his hand rest on the boy's shoulder. The two teenagers who'd been arrested the other night had confessed to the deputy in Miles City that they had been harass-ing Sammy. He had never been a full member of the

19th Street gang. Les was glad of that. Not because he wouldn't stand beside Sammy if he had to pay the consequences for anything he had done in his young life. Les just didn't want Sammy to have seen the hard things that those two teenagers had seen.

He figured the teenagers would do some time in a juvenile facility and then face some additional probation time.

There was always a price to be paid for mistakes, Les told himself. But there was a world of mercy, too. He had to remind himself of that when he looked over at Marla.

Marla had moved closer to the Nativity figures, along with Linda. Both women looked as if they were enjoying the singing, although Linda kept edging away from the Nativity as though she had something else to do.

Before long, Linda had made her way to Les's side.

"I'll look after Sammy and Mrs. Hargrove has Becky," Linda said. "Here's your chance."

"Now?" Les had pictured a nice quiet conversation with Marla. Someplace where all his neighbors weren't gathered.

"She's planning to move after Christmas."

"So soon?"

Linda nodded.

Well, Les hadn't worked with animals in his life without learning that sometimes it was all about the timing of things. If now was the only time he had to take his chance, he meant to take it.

Marla was only vaguely aware of how the singing voices were changing around her. Linda's soprano voice had faded and a deep bass voice was growing nearer. She wasn't paying too much attention, though. The words of the Christmas carols were all she heard. They made her believe it was truly possible to have peace on earth and goodwill to men.

"Hi," someone whispered near her ear.

Marla didn't have to look to know it was Les. She frowned. The goodwill-to-men sentiment was becoming a little more difficult to maintain. Still, she hadn't had a chance to thank Les. Or to give him back those gloves of his. She pulled the gloves off her hands.

"Here." Marla gave them to him. "I've wanted to return these."

Les frowned. "But you'll need them. You don't have any gloves."

Marla curled her hands into balls and stuck them into her pockets. "They're your gloves, and I'll do just fine. Thank you."

Les was still looking at her. "What's the point of keeping your toes warm in those socks if you freeze your fingers off in the meantime?"

Marla became very still. Her hands weren't the only part of her that was turning cold. "You know about the socks?"

"Of course."

He said it as if it was such an easy thing and no betrayal at all, Marla thought. "Who else knows?"

"Well, I suppose Linda knows. Or at least, it was her idea. And if Linda knows, then…"

Marla spun around. Two of the people who she thought were closest to being her friends were the ones who had started the charity-box business. What did they do, anyway? Sit around and talk about all the things she and her children didn't have? It was humiliating.

She was going home.

Marla took only one step before she remembered the children. This was Sammy's moment. He was standing beside Linda looking at those shepherds as if they'd been made just for him. And they had. She turned in the other direction and saw Becky snuggled up beside Mrs. Hargrove. The older woman was wearing a long coat and Becky was standing inside the folds of it with just her face poking out.

She might be stomping off to go home, but her children had already found a home. Was her pride worth taking the children away from all that? Marla knew she had bad memories of charity boxes and things like that from her childhood. But, maybe, sometimes charity was just a community helping their own. Her mother had made receiving charity seem like such a shameful thing. Was it possible for her to accept charity and not make Sammy and Becky feel bad about it?

She looked around her. She had to stay in Dry Creek. This was their home. She might have to swallow her pride every day she lived here, but she would do it for her children.

Everyone was singing "Hark the Herald Angels Sing" and Les was over talking to Linda and then they were both walking toward her. Great. This was just what she needed. Marla did a couple of quick blinks so neither one of them would see that her eyes had started to tear up. There would be enough time to cry when she got back to her home. It might be a humble home and they might not have all the things other people in Dry Creek had, but they were here to stay and—

"Here," Les said as he pushed Linda forward. "She'll tell you I mean what I say. That I'm an honest guy."

Marla noticed that the singing had stopped and everyone had turned and looked at them. Of course, Les and Linda couldn't see everyone watching, because they had their backs to them.

Linda looked a little startled, but she nodded. "Les is one hundred percent solid."

"I work hard and I own my place free and clear. Tell her."

"Les, Linda—there's—" Marla tried to tell the two

that everyone was listening, but they were intent on speaking.

Linda nodded again. "He takes his duties very seriously. There's even some talk of him running for sheriff if—"

"I'll never do that." Les interrupted the other woman with a frown. "Don't make promises I can't keep. You've already messed up with the socks."

"What socks?"

Linda stood there looking bewildered and Marla felt some of the tension ease within her.

"There's people—" Marla tried again.

"What do you mean, 'what socks?'" Les's voice was rising. "That was your suggestion. Something she needed."

"He got you *socks?*" Linda asked, turning to Marla. "That was his big romantic present to show you how he felt about you?"

Marla thought surely Linda would see everyone listening to them. Maybe she did. Les still hadn't.

"Well, I didn't think the roast was enough," Les muttered, then let his voice get louder. "And you said I couldn't go wrong if I got her something she needed."

"But socks?" Linda shook her head.

Marla was starting to smile and she felt the warmth of it right down to her toes. "They were nice socks. Ten pairs and some for each of the kids, too."

"They needed socks," Les repeated as he started smiling along with Marla.

"But where's the romance in that?" Linda protested.

"He wants her to be warm?" suggested one of the people watching.

Linda shrugged. "Well, maybe that works."

Les looked up at their audience, and the thought crossed his mind that his parents had never once had a public argument about socks.

"Very, very warm," Les added as he put his arm around Marla and realized he didn't even mind all the onlookers. He was beginning to think that if the only way two people could communicate was to yell everything out in a crowd as his parents had done, it was still best to communicate. Otherwise, a man ended up giving a woman socks when she really wanted—

"I still don't know what you want for Christmas," Les whispered.

"I haven't got anything for you, either," Marla whispered back.

Then someone in the crowd yelled out, "Have they kissed and made up yet? I can't hear what they're saying."

Sometimes, Les thought, an audience could even have the right idea.

Marla saw the affection in Les's eyes as he dipped his head and gave her a kiss. She wasn't sure when someone started singing again, but she wondered if the song was something about stars. Or were the stars what she was seeing? All she could remember were the stars she'd seen that night when she snuggled up against Les's back when they were riding the horse together.

"Merry Christmas," Les lifted his head to whisper.

He didn't even give her a chance to repeat the greeting to him before he kissed her again.

Epilogue

Everyone in Dry Creek, except Marla, knew Les was going to propose. Of course, he hadn't told anyone he was going to ask Marla to marry him. The citizens of Dry Creek had known Les since he was a boy, however, and they had never seen him carry a dozen red roses down the street in Dry Creek before—and certainly not in the middle of a snow flurry. They had also never heard him stand by a woman's front door and try to serenade her with an old love song from the forties. Fortunately, it hadn't been snowing that time, but it was windy enough that shutters were slamming this way and that all over town and half the dogs were howling.

It was clear that Les hadn't wanted to be seen or heard, and that only added to the gossip. There was so much talk about Les's unusual behavior that the old men who sat around the woodstove in the hardware store started to make predictions on when Les would give up trying to impress Marla and just pop the age-old question.

Charley thought the younger man wouldn't make it through January. Charley had been a farmer all his life and he knew Les had already started his calving season. A farmer didn't get his full quota of sleep during calving season and his resistance would be down. An impatient man would just say what was on his mind and forget about dressing it up with frills.

On the other hand, Mr. Morales, who came to sit with the old men at times, said Les would most likely wait to propose on Valentine's Day, because women liked the grand romance of that kind of timing.

Once Mr. Morales had spoken, they all agreed that it must be what Les was planning. It only made sense. Les had always been practical. He lived an orderly life and he would pay attention to things like the calendar. Besides, Les himself must know he wasn't a romantic kind of a man. He could use the help of Valentine's Day to back up his proposal. What man couldn't?

The old men all nodded to each other and decided Valentine's Day would be it. Pastor Matthew, who clerked part-time at the hardware store, even bought a couple of bottles of sparkling cider to keep in the small refrigerator behind the counter so that they could all celebrate when they heard the good news.

The men kept watch out the hardware-store window all day on Valentine's Day, but they didn't see anything unusual. Eventually Les did show up to take

Marla to dinner at the café, but the two kids were with them when they left Marla's house and none of the men thought Les would be so unromantic as to propose in front of the children.

When Valentine's Day came and went without a proposal, the men were disappointed and more than a little concerned. Les might not be as flamboyant as other men when it came to courting a woman, but the men had all figured he would eventually gather enough courage to ask the big question. It was the sort of thing a man had to do if he expected to gain a wife.

There was some discussion about what they could do to help Les. Eventually, they decided it wouldn't do Les's confidence any good for him to know how worried they were. Still, they had to do something, so they went to see Mrs. Hargrove.

"He's just giving her space," Mrs. Hargrove said. She was standing beside her open door because the men had asked their question as they stood on her porch. "Young people are big on this space stuff."

"If he gives her enough space, she'll plumb leave town," Charley grumbled.

"Women didn't need space when we were young," Elmer muttered.

"Well, times are different now," Mrs. Hargrove said firmly. "Besides, Marla just became a Christian. Maybe Lester is being considerate and giving her time to adjust to the changes in her life."

The men were all silent for a moment as they looked

at their boots. They wondered if Les wasn't being too considerate, but they didn't have nerve enough to say that to Mrs. Hargrove.

"That cider the pastor bought isn't going to keep forever," Charley finally muttered, and they turned to leave.

The men decided there was nothing they could do, but they did, unconsciously or not, feel a little bit of sorrow every time they talked to Les. If their conversation happened to turn a time or two in the direction of how a man needed courage in his life, they meant well by their words.

If Les understood what they were trying to tell him, he never indicated it.

By the end of March, the men in the hardware store had run out of predictions. Les had not only missed Valentine's Day, he'd also missed Lincoln's Birthday and St. Patrick's Day. The men reluctantly agreed that Les simply wasn't going to ask Marla to marry him.

When they heard Les had finally given in to Mrs. Hargrove's pleas and agreed to sing a solo in church on Palm Sunday, they decided he was turning his thoughts to other things besides romance. And they would be there to show their support. After all, not all men were called to be married. They decided they would give him some of that space Mrs. Hargrove talked about.

Les's voice rang out clearly that Sunday morning as he sang about the palms that had been laid before

Jesus as He made His triumphant entry into Jerusalem. If Les smiled a little more than usual, everyone just figured it was because he was imagining what it would have been like to see Christ on that first Palm Sunday.

It wasn't until just before the closing prayer that Pastor Matthew announced that Les had an announcement to make.

Even when Les turned and held out his hand to Marla, it took a few seconds for the old men to realize what was happening.

The pleased, pink smile on Marla's face told the whole story, though.

"I'll be," Elmer muttered. "He did it without us."

"I guess she had enough of that space," Charley whispered to Mrs. Hargrove.

Les didn't even get all his words out before the congregation was clapping away.

"You could get married right now," someone called out.

Les shook his head. "We've got it all planned."

"It'll be soon," Marla added with a smile. "And you're all invited."

The wedding was in May. Several women from the church helped Marla prepare enough sweet pork tamales to feed everyone for the reception. Marla knew her Hispanic roots were completely accepted in this small town when everyone ate their tamales with such enjoyment. She wished her aunts and uncles from Mexico could be with her, but they had sent a beautiful veil made of Mexican lace for her to wear. And Mr. Morales had become as dear to her as her own uncles. The shepherd walked her down the aisle and was the first one to shout "Hallelujah" when Les kissed her for the first time after they became husband and wife.

* * * * *

Dear Reader,

The Christmas season never ceases to move me and I like nothing better than to read, or write, a Christmas book. That's probably why my first Dry Creek novel, *An Angel for Dry Creek,* was set around the small town's Christmas pageant. I had great fun focusing on the angel in the Nativity story. Angels dazzle, after all. They sizzle. They have loud voices and great news to impart. What's not to love about an angel?

For some reason, though, shepherds aren't so readily embraced. They have no special powers. No flashing lights. No halos. They are simple working men doing the best they can for their sheep. They're usually not handsome or debonair. What they are is dependable. While their sheep are sleeping, the shepherds are guarding them. Shepherds protect their flocks; they fight off any wolves that come around. They are the quiet heroes of everyday life.

In *Shepherds Abiding in Dry Creek* I deliberately chose a hero, Les Wilkerson, who is like a shepherd. He has no swagger to him, no poetry. But you can rely on him to keep his promises and to be there when you need him. He will keep you safe. I've known men like Les and I'm sure you have, too. It's easy to take such men for granted. If you have a shepherd hero in your life, Christmas is a good time to say a special thanks to him for his steadfastness.

Thanks for reading *Shepherds Abiding in Dry Creek*.
May it add to the richness of your Christmas season.

Sincerely yours,

Janet Tronstad

QUESTIONS FOR DISCUSSION

1. Marla's husband asks for forgiveness and then dies before there is time for Marla to talk to him. Have you ever forgiven someone when there was no way you could talk to them directly about what had happened? Did you use any special techniques? How did it feel for you to forgive this person?

2. Part of the reason it was so difficult for Marla to forgive her husband was that she wondered if he thought she was inadequate as a wife. What types of things make a woman feel inadequate as a wife?

3. What are some thoughts from the Bible that define what a good wife is?

4. What are some things we can do to remind ourselves of how God sees us in all our roles?

5. Marla moved to Dry Creek so her children would have a better/safer life. She was particularly worried that her son might be getting involved in a gang. Do you think she did the best thing by moving away? Should she have stayed and helped her son battle the temptation toward gang life? What would you do?

6. How do you think a community should respond to things like the stolen shepherd? Did the community of Dry Creek handle it in the best way? What else could they have done?

7. Part of the reason Sammy got into so much trouble was that he was keeping secrets from his mother. How should communities encourage children to seek help from adults when they are in trouble?

8. Part of Sammy's punishment was to help Mrs. Hargrove with her Sunday-school class. Is this a punishment for someone like Sammy? Why or why not?

9. Marla worried that her Hispanic heritage would not be accepted in a place like Dry Creek. Think of times when you have been the different one in the group. What did you learn from that experience? What did Marla do to share her heritage?

10. Les learned not to let his fears of becoming like his parents limit his life. What fears hold you back in your life?

Linda Goodnight

brings you a tale of a cowboy you can trust.

Rancher Austin Blackwell sees Annalisa Keller as a wounded person with too many secrets. This town is the perfect place for her to start over—just as it was for him. Trying to keep his own past hidden, Austin finds himself falling for Annalisa, whose warmth and love of life works its way into his heart…and promises never to leave.

Rancher's Refuge

Where every prayer is answered....

Available December 2012, wherever books are sold.

REQUEST YOUR FREE BOOKS!

2 FREE INSPIRATIONAL NOVELS
PLUS 2
FREE
MYSTERY GIFTS

YES! Please send me 2 FREE Love Inspired® novels and my 2 FREE mystery gifts (gifts are worth about $10). After receiving them, if I don't wish to receive any more books, I can return the shipping statement marked "cancel." If I don't cancel, I will receive 6 brand-new novels every month and be billed just $4.49 per book in the U.S. or $4.99 per book in Canada. That's a saving of at least 22% off the cover price. It's quite a bargain! Shipping and handling is just 50¢ per book in the U.S. and 75¢ per book in Canada.* I understand that accepting the 2 free books and gifts places me under no obligation to buy anything. I can always return a shipment and cancel at any time. Even if I never buy another book, the two free books and gifts are mine to keep forever.

105/305 IDN FEGR

Name _____ (PLEASE PRINT)

Address _____ Apt. #

City _____ State/Prov. _____ Zip/Postal Code

Signature (if under 18, a parent or guardian must sign)

Mail to the **Reader Service:**
IN U.S.A.: P.O. Box 1867, Buffalo, NY 14240-1867
IN CANADA: P.O. Box 609, Fort Erie, Ontario L2A 5X3

Not valid for current subscribers to Love Inspired books.

**Are you a subscriber to Love Inspired books
and want to receive the larger-print edition?
Call 1-800-873-8635 or visit www.ReaderService.com.**

* Terms and prices subject to change without notice. Prices do not include applicable taxes. Sales tax applicable in N.Y. Canadian residents will be charged applicable taxes. Offer not valid in Quebec. This offer is limited to one order per household. All orders subject to credit approval. Credit or debit balances in a customer's account(s) may be offset by any other outstanding balance owed by or to the customer. Please allow 4 to 6 weeks for delivery. Offer available while quantities last.

Your Privacy—The Reader Service is committed to protecting your privacy. Our Privacy Policy is available online at www.ReaderService.com or upon request from the Reader Service.

We make a portion of our mailing list available to reputable third parties that offer products we believe may interest you. If you prefer that we not exchange your name with third parties, or if you wish to clarify or modify your communication preferences, please visit us at www.ReaderService.com/consumerschoice or write to us at Reader Service Preference Service, P.O. Box 9062, Buffalo, NY 14269. Include your complete name and address.

LIREG11B

Love Inspired® SUSPENSE

RIVETING INSPIRATIONAL ROMANCE

Police detective Austin Black assures desperate single mother
Eva Billows that he'll find her son, who went missing from
his bedroom in the middle of the night. With his search-and-
rescue bloodhound, Justice, Austin searches every inch of
Sagebrush, Texas. And when Eva insists on helping, Austin
can't turn her away. Eva trusts no one, especially police, but
this time, Austin–and Justice–won't let her down.

TEXAS K-9 UNIT

TRACKING JUSTICE

by

SHIRLEE MCCOY

Available January 2013 wherever books are sold.

www.LoveInspiredBooks.com

LIS44520

Brave police officers tackle crime with the help of their canine partners in TEXAS K-9 UNIT, *an exciting new series from Love Inspired® Suspense.*

Read on for a preview of the first book, TRACKING JUSTICE *by Shirlee McCoy.*

Police detective Austin Black glanced at his dashboard clock as he raced up Oak Drive. Two in the morning. Not a good time to get a call about a missing child.

Then again, there was never a good time for that; never a good time to look in the worried eyes of a parent or to follow a scent trail and know that it might lead to a joyful reunion or a sorrowful goodbye.

If it led anywhere.

Sometimes trails went cold, scents were lost and the missing were never found. Austin wanted to bring them all home safe. Hopefully, this time, he would.

He pulled into the driveway of a small house.

Justice whined. A three-year-old bloodhound, he was trained in search and rescue and knew when it was time to work.

Austin jumped out of the vehicle when a woman darted out the front door. "You called about a missing child?"

"Yes. My son. I heard Brady call for me, and when I walked into his room, he was gone." She ran back up the porch stairs.

Austin jogged in after her. She waved from a doorway. "This is my son's room."

Austin followed her into the room. "How old is your son, Ms….?"

"Billows. Eva. He's seven."

"Did you argue?"

"We didn't argue about anything, Officer…"

"Detective Austin Black. I'm with Sagebrush Police Department's Special Operation K-9 Unit."

"You have a search dog with you?" Her face brightened. "I can give you something of his. A shirt or—"

"Hold on. I need to get a little more information first."

"How about you start out there?" She gestured to the window.

"Was it open when you came in the room?"

"Yes. It looks like someone carried Brady out the window. But I don't know how anyone could have gotten into his room when all the doors and windows were locked."

"You're sure?"

"Of course." She frowned. "I always double-check. I have ever since…"

"What?"

"Nothing that matters. I just need to find my son."

Hiding something?

"Everything matters when a child is missing, Eva."

To see Justice the bloodhound in action, pick up
TRACKING JUSTICE by Shirlee McCoy.
Available January 2013 from Love Inspired® Suspense.

SUSPENSE

RIVETING INSPIRATIONAL ROMANCE

TEXAS K-9 UNIT

Lawmen that solve the toughest cases with the help of their brave canine partners.

Follow Lone Star State police officers and their canine partners in action each month as they get closer to not only uncovering a mastermind criminal but also finding love.

TRACKING JUSTICE by Shirlee McCoy
January 2013

DETECTION MISSION by Margaret Daley
February 2013

GUARD DUTY by Sharon Dunn
March 2013

EXPLOSIVE SECRETS by Valerie Hansen
April 2013

SCENT OF DANGER by Terri Reed
May 2013

LONE STAR PROTECTOR by Lenora Worth
June 2013

LISCONT13

Romance blooms in the midst of a Rocky Mountain winter

Winter of Dreams
by CHERYL ST.JOHN

If Violet Kristofferson had known that her new employer was the town undertaker, she might never have come to Carson Springs as his cook. Yet she needs a fresh start away from scandal. And Ben Charles's unflinching faith could be her path to something truly precious—a new family.

The Rancher's Sweetheart
by DEBRA ULLRICK

The cowboys on her uncle's ranch show Sunny Weston no respect—except for foreman Jed Cooper. A riding and roping contest is Sunny's chance to prove herself. But now that she's falling for Jed, will she find courage to take the biggest risk of all, and trust her heart?

Colorado Courtship
Available January 2013

Love Inspired® SUSPENSE

RIVETING INSPIRATIONAL ROMANCE

TRUSTING THE WRONG PERSON CAN BE DEADLY...

Lillie Beaumont's dark past has just turned up on her porch–
fatally wounded. The dying words of the man imprisoned
for killing Lillie's mother suggest hidden secrets. Criminal
Investigations Division special agent Dawson Timmons agrees
to help Lillie face these painful secrets. But Dawson fears that
a murderer is waiting to strike again. And this time, Lillie is
right in the line of fire....

MILITARY INVESTIGATIONS

Serving their country and solving crimes

Don't miss the action in

THE GENERAL'S SECRETARY

by

DEBBY GIUSTI

LIS44521